Phoebe Salomon bolted upright in bed and found herself panting breathlessly in the middle of a dimly lit room. She could not discern her surroundings and at first thought she was in her cell at the Presidio Asylum for Incurables. Leaning back against the pillows, she tried to focus her thoughts. Slowly it all came back to her—the escape from the asylum, the altercation on the pier, the rescue by a Chinese man and his servant, the ride to his home somewhere in Chinatown, the sickness and dizziness she had been feeling ever since her arrival. The last thing she could remember was waking up and being given some sort of medicine, then falling back asleep. Everything else was blackness.

As Phoebe explored the unfamiliar surroundings, the room began to spin, and her heart raced faster and louder, an incessant drumming that was pounding her into unconsciousness. She reached up toward a lamp on the dresser and caught a glimpse of dark-clad figures pushing through the doorway and crowding over her. She rolled over and fell onto her back, but she never felt herself hit the floor. And as she hurtled into the blackness, she wondered if somehow she had tumbled through the window and was sailing down into the courtyard—or if this was merely that dark, familiar abyss.

SAN FRANCISCO

THE DECEIT

PAUL BLOCK

Created by the producers of
**Wagons West, Stagecoach,
Badge,** and **White Indian.**

Book Creations Inc., Canaan, NY · Lyle Kenyon Engel, Founder

LYNX BOOKS
New York

THE DECEIT

ISBN: 1-55802-188-4

First Printing/March 1989

Produced by Book Creations, Inc.
Founder: Lyle Kenyon Engel

This is a work of fiction. Names, characters, places, and incidents are either the product of the author's imagination or are used fictitiously. Any resemblance to actual events, locales, or persons, living or dead, is entirely coincidental.

This book is published by Lynx Books, a division of Lynx Communications, Inc., 41 Madison Avenue, New York, New York, 10010. The name ''Lynx'' together with the logotype consisting of a stylized head of a lynx is a trademark of Lynx Communications, Inc.

Printed in the United States of America

0 9 8 7 6 5 4 3 2 1

*To the men and women of San Francisco
who with courage, faith, and dignity
are triumphing over this nation's
greatest health crisis.*

---

*And to Connie Orcutt,
whose sensitivity and spirit
are a constant source of inspiration.*

San Francisco 1896

ONLY SELECTED STREETS ARE SHOWN

- ☐ BUILT-UP AREAS
- ▨ PARKS, SQUARES, RESERVATIONS, CEMETERIES
- ▦ UNDEVELOPED LAND
- ⊞ CITY STREETS
- ⊪ RAILROADS
- ⟋ OTHER ROADS, PATHS

0   ¼   ½   1 MILE

FORT

PRESIDIO RESERVATION

PRESIDIO BARRACKS

MOUNTAIN LAKE

PUBLIC SQUARE

LAKE

CITY CEMETERY †

GOV'T RES.

CALIFORNIA

CLEMENT

FERRIES & CLIFF HOUSE

R.R.

SUTRO

SUTRO BATHS & AQUARIUM

POINT LOBOS

HEIGHTS

CLIFF HOUSE

A ST.

GOLDEN GATE RACE COURSE

B ST.

C ST.

D ST.

GOLDEN GATE PARK

H ST.

PARK & OCEAN R.R.

I ST.

J ST.

K ST.

SEAL ROCKS

Pacific Ocean

OCEAN BOULEVARD

N

3ᴿᴰ AVE.

2ᴺᴰ AVE.

4ᵀᴴ AVE.

FIRST AVE.

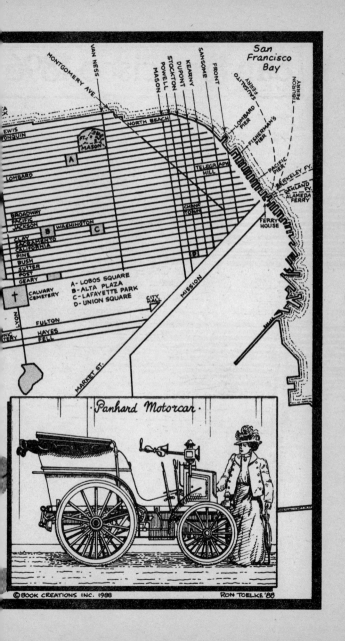

San Francisco Bay

MONTGOMERY AVE.
VAN NESS

POWELL
MASON
STOCKTON
DUPONT
KEARNY
SANSOME
FRONT

SAUSALITO FERRY
TIBURON FERRY

NORTH BEACH

FT. GEO. MASON

LEWIS
LONGUIN

LOMBARD

BROADWAY
PACIFIC
JACKSON
WASHINGTON
CLAY
SACRAMENTO
CALIFORNIA
PINE
BUSH
SUTTER
POST
GEARY

TELEGRAPH HILL

CHINATOWN

LOMBARD PIER
FISHERMAN'S PIER
PACIFIC PIER
BERKELEY FY.
OAKLAND FY.
ALAMEDA FERRY

FERRY HOUSE

CALVARY CEMETERY

A - LOBOS SQUARE
B - ALTA PLAZA
C - LAFAYETTE PARK
D - UNION SQUARE

CITY HALL

MISSION

NIC
TERY

FULTON
HAYES
FELL

MARKET ST.

·Panhard Motorcar·

© BOOK CREATIONS INC. 1988   RON TOELKE '88

SAN FRANCISCO

THE DECEIT

Prologue:
June 22, 1896

"THANKS FOR OPENIN' THE DOOR," HAROLD MUTTERED sarcastically when no one answered his knock. He shouldered his way into the front office of the Presidio Asylum for Incurables, one hand clutching the neck of a bottle wrapped in brown grocer's paper, the other gripping a lantern he had removed from a peg in the entryway. Harold was a short man, not much older than twenty, with a round baby face and incredibly small hands and feet. He wore the gray wool jacket of a night orderly, with a blue and gold asylum insignia on the breast pocket.

"Murray?" Harold called, raising the lantern and looking around the small, dingy room. "I got the whiskey."

Seeing he was alone, Harold placed the lantern on the desk amid the papers and folders that once had been stacked in neat piles but over time had merged into a precariously balanced mass. The dust that swirled up around the lantern chimney—as well as the bottle clenched in Harold's fingers—gave clear evidence to the degree of professionalism of the asylum staff.

1

Despite their obvious shortcomings, the workers at the Presidio Asylum prided themselves on efficiently running the largest such establishment in San Francisco. They viewed their operation as a warehouse of sorts—a place where society could place its aberrations and be confident they would not have to deal with them again. Incoming patients—or loons, as they were called, the term patient giving the false sense that treatment was being provided—were given numbers and herded into private or group cells, depending on the funds provided for them. Outgoing patients usually did so in a recycled pine box, unless they were fortunate enough to be transferred by their families to facilities offering some sort of evaluation and treatment.

At the Presidio Asylum, treatment consisted of a monthly visit by Dr. Trevor Danin, a general practitioner of uncertain repute and the brother-in-law of the asylum owner. His monthly visit involved nothing more than a brisk walk down the corridors and an occasional glance into the cells inhabited by the unfortunates warehoused at the Presidio.

Like their fellow members of society, Harold and his co-workers wanted as little contact as possible with the loons, so he found it surprising that Murray was off in the wards somewhere and not dozing at the office desk. He glanced up at the wall and noted that Murray's cudgel and ring of keys were missing from his peg on the wall, confirming he had made a visit to the cells.

Removing his coat and tossing it onto a wooden chair against one wall, Harold flopped down onto the padded desk chair. Swiveling left and right and tapping his foot, he began whistling as he tore the paper from the bottle and unstoppered it. He snatched a glass from amid the mounds of paper, ran a finger around the inside to remove the heaviest grime, and poured a shot of the amber liquid. Smiling and leaning back in the chair, he tossed down the whiskey, gave a slight gasp of pleasure, and poured a second shot.

He was on his fourth round when he saw the note stuck on the nail on the back of the door, where orderlies left messages for one another. Putting down his glass, he stood and crossed to the door. Bringing the note closer to the lantern, he saw the words *Eight o'clock Monday night* scrawled across the top and read that Murray had gone to transfer the woman in cell number seven on the first-floor northeast corridor to one of the second-floor general wards.

Scratching his chin, Harold wondered what was taking Murray so long. He tried to conjure up an image of the woman in cell seven, but the faces of the loons were a blur of hollow expressions. Unless, however, the woman was that pretty blonde they had admitted only a few weeks before. She had been little more than a vegetable then, unable to move or speak. But she had recovered her faculties—at least as much as any of the Presidio loons ever did—and had exhibited unusual spunk and intelligence, despite her right arm's being next to useless. Harold would have thought her normal had his experience at the asylum not taught him that diseases of the mind take many curious forms.

He grinned as he poured and quickly downed another drink. Yes, if that was the new loon's cell, Murray might be taking a bit more time than usual, having his own little party while leaving Harold to celebrate with a bottle.

But the senior night attendant had been absent from his appropriate post long enough, Harold decided. He put down the glass, stoppered the bottle, and tucked it under his arm. Taking the cudgel and key ring from his own wall peg, he picked up the lantern and headed out into the front corridor and over to the locked gate that separated the lobby from the patient wards.

It took a few awkward moments of fumbling with the cudgel, lantern, bottle of whiskey, and ring of keys before Harold was able to insert the proper key in the lock and swing open the gate. Kicking the gate shut behind him, he turned down the narrow, dimly lit northeast corridor and made his way past the padlocked doors, ignoring the occasional whine or shriek that came from the occupants behind them.

Stopping in front of a door on the left, he opened the small, eye-level viewing window, which bore a faded numeral seven, and glanced inside. "Murray, you in there?" he called. There was no response, nor was there any light in the cell, so he could not see if it was occupied.

Closing the window, Harold juggled the items in his hands and managed to find the key that fit the cell door. Unlocking the padlock and removing it from the clasp, he dropped the keys into his jacket pocket, then shifted the lantern to his left hand. The whiskey bottle was still tucked under his left arm, leaving his right hand free to wield the cudgel.

"Here I come," he announced with a grin as he yanked the heavy door open a few inches with his right hand. Inserting the cudgel into the opening, he swung the door wide and stepped into the cell.

The lantern light danced along the dirt-smeared walls as Harold turned in place, surveying the tiny room. He saw at once that no one was on the bed, which was no more than a thin straw mattress on a wooden frame against the right-hand wall. Nor was anyone seated at the small table and chair along the far wall.

He was turning to leave when his foot struck something. Holding the lantern out, he squinted, trying to make out the object at his feet. Suddenly he jumped as he realized it was a body lying facedown on the floor with shards of glass spread all around it.

"Murray!" he gasped as he recognized the senior night attendant, his jacket missing, his cudgel lying at his side. For a moment Harold thought the portly man had gotten drunk and passed out there, but then he remembered that the cell had been locked, with Murray on the inside.

Stepping closer to the body, Harold grunted as he pushed at it with his foot to roll it over. He knew that something was terribly wrong—that somehow the woman in this cell had attacked the night attendant and escaped—but he was not ready for the sight that awaited him when he finally managed to roll Murray onto his back. His face was all but destroyed, the sightless, bulging eyes fixed at the ceiling, the left cheek sliced open from the eye to the chin, the nose a crushed, pulpy mass. There was something dark and bulbous at the forehead, and Harold leaned closer and squinted again, partly to focus, partly in disbelief at what he was seeing. Murray's skull had been horribly smashed open, the bone torn away.

With a shriek, Harold backed away from the body. The whiskey bottle slipped from under his arm and shattered at his feet, causing him to jump back even farther. His left shoulder bumped into the doorjamb, and he screamed again and spun around, as if someone had tapped him from behind. This time his wrist struck the jamb, and the lantern shattered against the frame, spraying his legs and the wall with kerosene as it fell to the floor.

Harold's eyes widened with shock, and he cried out again, but the sound was drowned out by a horrifying *whoosh* as the burning wick ignited the pool of kerosene at his feet, the flames racing up his trouser legs and setting the front of his jacket on fire. He started to jump and spin in circles in an attempt to put it out, but the movement only fanned the flames, and soon the whole front of his jacket was on fire.

Screaming hideously, Harold struggled to remove the bulky jacket. The lapels ripped and the buttons popped off as he tore it from his shoulders and threw it against the wall. But still his pants were on fire, and he could feel the heat searing his legs and stomach. No longer screaming, he staggered over to the bed, groped for the thin blanket crumpled in the corner, and began to beat at the flames. But the threadbare material ignited almost immediately and spread the fire.

In agony, Harold looked toward the door and commanded his legs to run, but he felt them giving way and slipped down onto one knee. Across the room the flames engulfed the doorway, which had been doused by kerosene, and licked at the walls, lighting the entire cell.

Pain spread across Harold's back, and when he smelled the sickening stench of burning flesh, he knew his clothing was fully aflame. With a final effort of will, he rose to his feet, reached toward the body on the floor, and moaned,

"Murray . . ." as if his dead friend would somehow rescue him. He stumbled backward, struck the frame of the wooden bed with the back of his knees, and fell backward onto the straw mattress.

The last sound Harold recalled was the crackling of the bug-infested straw going up in flames. Then everything turned a brilliant orange, which slowly faded to black. The searing heat softened into a comforting warmth that poured all around him, lifting him off the blazing mattress and carrying him upward into the cool night air.

One

At the northeastern edge of Golden Gate Park, a little more than a mile from the Presidio Asylum for Incurables, Aidan McAuliffe paid the driver of a hansom cab and asked him to wait for a few minutes. Offering his arm to the young woman beside him, he led the way up the walk to the Hotel Willard, an imposing two-story house, fronted by a portico with four massive gold columns.

Entering the hotel, the interior of which looked like a cross between a mansion and a bordello, the couple was greeted by a colorful woman whose unconventional though respectable establishment catered to San Francisco's bohemian community of singers, artists, and writers. After exchanging pleasantries, she quickly took her leave so Aidan and the lady could be alone in the parlor.

A few minutes later they were in each other's arms, and Aidan knew Rachel Salomon would not be returning to her family's mansion on Nob Hill that night.

"Do I have to leave?" she murmured, staring into his pale-blue eyes. She reached up and felt the firm line of his clean-

7

shaven jaw, then ran her fingers through his thick, dark-brown hair.

Aidan answered with a long, passionate kiss as he lifted her off her feet and carried her past the sofa, pausing only to blow out the flame in the lantern chimney. Rachel clutched him tightly around the neck, whispering in his ear as he brought her through the parlor and up the long, winding staircase that led to his room.

At the top of the stairs Aidan stopped long enough for Rachel to turn down the wall lamp, and then he continued on to his room. He had left it unlocked, so he turned the knob and backed through, shouldering the door shut behind him. It was only then that he lowered Rachel to her feet. They stood in the dark room, their lips touching and parting, their tongues searching, tentatively at first, then with growing passion.

Aidan's gray pinstriped suit jacket was draped over his shoulders, and Rachel lifted it and let it drop to the floor, then undid her own black wool coat and let it fall to her feet. As she leaned back in his arms, her hands caressed his neck and moved down to his shoulders. When she squeezed his arms, she felt him wince and remembered that his left shoulder had been wounded slightly only a few hours before. It had been a terrifying evening, with a deranged gunman shooting at them as they dined at an elegant little Italian restaurant called Il Calderone.

"Does it hurt?" she asked, gently touching the bandage that covered his bare upper arm where the shirt sleeve had been cut away.

"I'm fine," he assured her, cupping her chin and smiling as he gazed into her emerald eyes, which looked soft gray in the thin light that filtered through the window.

Aidan led Rachel to the window so he could better see her features as the light shimmered across her high cheekbones and full, sensual lips. He lightly kissed her lower lip as he stroked her long copper hair, which was pulled up in a sweep and held in place with an Oriental lacquer comb. Gently he pulled the comb free, and as her hair cascaded around her shoulders, he drew her closer and kissed her neck, breathing in the delicate aromas of her perfume and hair.

"I love you," he whispered into her ear, and he felt her body quiver as she gripped the hair at the back of his head and whispered that she loved him, as well.

Aidan turned to kiss her full on the lips, but Rachel pulled back and placed her hands on his chest. "We should send away the cab," she said softly, but already her fingers were undoing his silk tie and tossing it aside. She removed his stiff white collar, then began opening the buttons of his shirt.

"He can wait," Aidan replied as he reached around and felt for the hooks at the back of her green silk gown.

"Yes, but I can't," she breathed, spreading open his shirt lapels and running a hand across his chest. She felt his grip tighten, and she closed her eyes and leaned back.

Clasping her firmly around the waist, Aidan reached up with his other hand and again caressed her hair, which took on an even brighter copper hue as the city lights played through the window. Her features were aglow from the dancing light.

Rachel's lips parted, and she opened her eyes and pulled Aidan to her. The light intensified, suffusing her face and hair with a bright, orange glow.

With a gasp, Aidan pulled away from her and spun toward the window.

"What . . . ?" Rachel started to ask, but then she, too, saw that the light was not some supernatural aura but was from a very real—and horrifying—source. To the north, perhaps a mile away, the dark night sky was turning a brilliant orange, like a sunset playing not upon clouds but upon billows of thick, black smoke.

"My God!" Aidan exclaimed. "The city's on fire!"

Rachel slowly shook her head. "I don't think so. . . . That's to the north—the Presidio—not downtown. But something very big is on fire."

9

As they stood looking, the first flames could be seen in the distance above the intervening rooftops.

"People may be injured. I have to get over there," Aidan pronounced as he buttoned his shirt. It was light enough to see clearly now as he crossed the room and snatched up the black medical bag he had purchased in San Francisco to replace the one he had left in London.

"I'm coming with you," Rachel said as she picked up his gray jacket and held it open.

Putting down the medical bag, Aidan eased his injured left arm into the sleeve, then pulled the jacket on and buttoned it. "I think it would be wiser if you took the cab back to—"

"I'm coming with you," she repeated firmly.

Aidan saw her determined look and nodded. He helped her into her coat, then picked up the medical bag and ushered her from the room. Making their way downstairs, they headed outside and were glad to see the hansom cab still parked across the street.

The cabbie was standing in the raised driver's seat at the rear, gazing toward the orange glow in the sky. "Looks like quite a fire," he commented almost matter-of-factly as they came across the street.

Aidan yanked open the cab door and helped Rachel inside. "Will you take us there?" he asked the cabbie.

"The fire?" the man muttered, sitting down and scratching his head in surprise. When Aidan nodded, he added, "You sure about that?"

"I'm a physician. They may need my assistance."

"All right," the cabbie said, taking hold of the reins.

A moment later the cab was off at a trot, heading west along Fulton Street. At the next corner, where Fulton became D Street, the driver turned right onto First Avenue a bit too quickly, and the vehicle lurched precipitously to the left. But then it righted itself, and the man slapped the reins and urged the gray mare to greater speed.

With the driver's seat at the upper rear, the passenger compartment offered an unobstructed view through the front window. Looking to the left, Aidan could just make out the grandstand that sided the Golden Gate Race Course, an oval track that ran from just below C Street to the far side of A Street, with straightaways along Second and Fourth avenues.

As the hansom cab crossed A Street, Aidan glanced to the right and saw the eerie shadows cast by the firelight among the headstones of the Odd Fellows' Cemetery. This section of the city was dominated by four large cemeteries: Laurel Hill, Calvary, Masonic, and Odd Fellows'. Watching the headstones race by, Aidan found himself wondering how long San Francisco would be able to bury its dead within the city before running out of available land. His concern was already being raised by city officials, and five years later, on August 1, 1901, an order would be issued to halt all further burials within San Francisco. Thirteen years after that, the cemeteries would be closed and the remains moved beyond the city limits.

Leaving the cemetery behind, the cab continued north, finally reaching Pacific Avenue, which bordered the Presidio Military Reservation. Over fifteen hundred acres of rolling, wooded hills, the peninsula's northernmost tip, called the Presidio, had been a military base since the days of the Spanish.

The flames could clearly be seen once the cab had made a right turn onto Pacific Avenue. As it approached Central Avenue, a block from the Presidio's eastern edge, Rachel and Aidan were able to discern the source of the fire—a huge brick building, set back on a broad expanse of lawn, the left wing of which was almost fully engulfed in flames.

Rachel grabbed Aidan's arm. "It's the asylum."

"Asylum?" he repeated as the cab came to a halt in front of the open gate at the center of the wrought-iron fence that surrounded the grounds of the forbidding edifice.

"The Presidio Asylum for Incurables." She almost had to shout to be heard above the roar of the fire.

"An insane asylum?" he asked, and she nodded.

Taking up his bag, Aidan pushed open the door and stepped

out. He almost lost his balance as the cab lurched, the horse stamping in fear as flames shot from the windows of the building. When he steadied himself and turned, he immediately felt a blast of heat against his face and had to shield his eyes.

The driver, who was fighting the reins to steady the horse, leaned over the side of the cab and shouted, "I gotta get 'er away from here!"

Aidan was already helping Rachel out, and he turned to the cabbie and shouted back, "Go for help! Get the fire—"

"They're already here!" the man cut in, waving a hand toward the burning building. Indeed, several horse-drawn steam pumpers were on the grounds, and people could be seen racing in and out of the right side of the structure, which was not yet on fire.

"What do I owe you?" Aidan called up to the driver as he closed the door.

"No charge!" the man yelled in reply. With a nod, he slapped the reins, and the horse took off down Pacific Avenue, racing away from the inferno.

Aidan wrapped an arm around Rachel's shoulder, and they turned toward the blazing building. For the first time they realized the intensity of the fire, which had all but consumed the interior of the left side of the two-story structure, leaving only the brick shell standing. Apparently the firemen considered the entire building a loss, for they were making no effort to fight the fire and were using their hoses instead to protect an entrance at the right end of the building, where survivors were being dragged and carried from inside.

Aidan and Rachel started through the gate, heading toward the entrance where the firemen were working. They had to hold their coats tight against the blast of wind that battered them from behind as the air was sucked toward the building to feed the flames. The sound of the fire was a deafening, unearthly roar, accompanied by hisses and crackles and punctuated by an occasional thunderclap as a window exploded or a section of wall or ceiling collapsed.

As they circled the area where the flames were at their greatest intensity and approached the right side of the building, they heard other sounds, as well—equally unearthly but more horrendous, for they were the shrieks and screams of the patients still trapped inside.

Aidan felt Rachel clutch his arm more tightly, and he held her closer and looked into her eyes. Tears were running down her cheeks, but he could not tell whether it was from anguish or in reaction to the smoke.

"I'm all right," she said; he was forced to read her lips, for he could hear little above the fiery din.

As they approached one of the pumpers, they saw a fireman racing through the open door where the others were working. He wore a knee-length coat of heavy india-rubber cloth, and his face was hidden behind a curious-looking mask with glass covering the eyeholes and a canvas skirt hanging down over his nose and mouth and tied around his neck. He was dragging along a pair of choking, gagging men dressed in the striped muslin pajamas worn by the male patients; the women wore plain muslin skirts and blouses.

The fireman waved for assistance, and a man working the pumper ran over. Together they led the patients away from the building and out across the lawn, where they were turned over to a pair of policemen. As the firemen returned to the building, the officers dragged the patients to a nearby tree and handcuffed them to the trunk, facing inward. The patients seemed unaware of what was happening and fell to their knees, their bodies racked with coughs.

Now Aidan and Rachel noticed numerous other patients on the lawn, where they were being guarded by a phalanx of armed police officers. Most patients were cuffed around trees or tied to the iron fence, with a few trussed up like hogs and left squirming on the ground. The ones who had suffered the worst injuries and were not at risk of running off were lying unattended around the yard.

"Come on!" Aidan called as he led Rachel across the lawn toward the tree where the two men had just been cuffed.

13

"Stop, there!" a voice shouted as he knelt beside one of the patients and eased the man's head back.

Aidan glanced up at the approaching officer and called out, "I'm a physician."

This seemed to mollify the policeman, who turned his attention to Rachel.

"She's my nurse," Aidan quickly added, figuring Rachel would be left alone if they thought she was working with him. He signaled for her to open his medical bag, then looked back at the officer and said in a disapproving tone, "Why are these men cuffed this way?"

"They're crazy," the man replied, looking at Aidan as if the reason was obvious. "We've got orders to make sure they don't escape. Some already did before we got here. It'll probably take us all night to round them up."

The man Aidan was holding began to wheeze and gasp, as if struggling for air. Aidan tried to calm him down, but he jerked back and forth in distress, his wrists being chafed by the cuffs. The man to whom he was cuffed was thrown back and forth by the movement but seemed oblivious to what was happening.

"Uncuff these men," Aidan demanded. When the policeman made no move to comply, he repeated the command more forcefully.

"I can't," the officer insisted. "We've got orders—"

"I don't care what your orders are," Aidan cut him off. "If you don't release this man, he'll die!"

The policeman looked around awkwardly, then shrugged and reached into his pocket for the key. Aidan had to hold the patient's wrist securely so the officer could fit the key into the lock and remove the cuff.

"The other cuff, too," Aidan commanded, and the officer scurried to the other side of the tree.

As soon as the man's hands were free, his body stiffened, and he fell backward against Aidan, nearly knocking him over. With Rachel's assistance, Aidan eased the man onto his stomach, then turned his head to one side and forced open the jaw. He began pressing firmly on the man's back, helping him work up the phlegm from his lungs.

The other patient was on his knees, leaning listlessly against the tree, his arms hanging loosely at his sides with the handcuffs still suspended from his wrists. The policeman stooped down and grabbed hold of the cuffs to fasten them together around the tree. But as he started to pull them around the trunk, the man yanked back his arms, wrenching the cuffs from the officer's hands. His eyes opened wide, and with an unnerving grin, the patient jumped to his feet and staggered back away from the tree.

The policeman scrambled to his feet, as well, but the man had backed away several feet and was swinging his arms, as if the handcuff attached to each wrist were a medieval morning star—the spiked iron ball, suspended from a chain, wielded by crusaders.

"Stop!" the policeman demanded, approaching cautiously. But the man kept swinging his cuffs and grinning wickedly as he backed away from the tree and headed toward the open gate and the darkness beyond.

Aidan looked up from the patient he was working on and saw what was happening. "Put them down," he said to the man calmly, nodding toward his wrists. "No one is going to hurt you. Just put them—"

"Stop!" the officer shouted again.

The man looked at Aidan, then over at the policeman, who was coming toward him. He shook his head, turned, and started to run.

"Don't!" Rachel screamed as she lunged toward the policeman, who had drawn his revolver.

It was too late. He squeezed the trigger, and the gun bucked in his hand. The patient staggered, tried to raise his hands to his back, then stumbled and fell facedown on the ground.

Rachel ran across the lawn and threw herself down beside the mortally wounded man. Aidan raced up beside her and placed his hand on the man's back, which jerked spasmodically and then was still, the breath going out of it in a long, fading hiss.

Glancing bitterly at the policeman, Aidan muttered, "Bastard." Beside him, Rachel was sobbing uncontrollably, and he pulled her close and comforted her.

"Why? Wh-why?" she mumbled as he held her close and patted her back.

Rising, Aidan lifted Rachel to her feet and stood holding her until she was calm. Then he led her back to where he had left the other patient. Another policeman was on hand, and the two officers had turned the patient toward the tree and were cuffing his hands around the trunk. The man lay there on his stomach, his arms stretched out in front of him as he coughed and wheezed painfully.

Aidan stooped down, closed his medical bag, and picked it up. "You didn't have to kill him," he said disdainfully as the two officers finished their task.

"He was crazy," the officer replied. "I couldn't let him escape." He turned to Rachel. "Sorry, ma'am. But I've got my orders." He shrugged and walked away.

"Come," Aidan said, putting his arm around Rachel. "There's nothing to be done here."

Aidan led her across the lawn, and together they examined the other patients. Most were suffering from smoke inhalation, though some had suffered burns or other injuries. After making sure the police had contacted area hospitals and summoned ambulances, Aidan began treating the worst of the burn victims, using cloth from the patients' own clothing to wrap wounds that were at risk of infection. He had but a scant supply of morphine in his bag, and he used it only on those who were the most severely burned. One woman had suffered a fractured leg when a ceiling beam fell on top of her, and with Rachel assisting, Aidan set it, using a broken iron fence rail as a splint.

Soon ambulances from local hospitals started arriving, and Aidan found himself working alongside four other physicians and surgeons. Rachel was joined by half a dozen nurses, each of whom assumed she was a fellow nurse. Since Aidan had been on the scene first, he organized the medical efforts and saw to it that the tied-up and handcuffed patients were released and transferred by ambulance or wagon to hospitals in the area.

The fire was continuing to rage, advancing toward the right wing of the asylum. Sections of the roof had caved in on top of the trapped patients, and increasingly the victims being brought out were dead or seriously injured, suffering from severe burns and multiple fractures. Aidan quickly examined each one to determine whether he or she could be immediately transferred to a hospital or would first require treatment.

There was no rest for the medical workers. The surgeons frantically set bones and treated the worst of the burns, while the nurses bandaged burns and administered morphine and other painkillers. At least medical supplies had arrived with the ambulances, and wounds could be properly cleaned and dressed.

Seeing how desperate the patients were and how few nurses were on hand, Rachel did not have the heart to admit she was not one of them. She did her best to imitate the way the others were binding wounds, though she was careful to avoid being called upon to give an injection. When she was uncertain what to do, she consulted with Aidan, who would patiently explain the proper procedure while continuing with whatever case he was handling at that moment.

An hour later the flames had raged through the eastern and central part of the structure and were spreading into the remaining west wing. The fire fighters had brought out the last of the patients from the northwest and southwest wards and could now do little more than take preventive measures to protect neighboring buildings. Fortunately no houses stood directly adjacent to the asylum, so the fire was able to be contained to that one structure.

Rachel was on hand as a particularly distraught young woman was being loaded into one of the last remaining ambulances. The woman, who had just regained consciousness, had been overcome by smoke in her cell, which was in an area the flames had not yet reached.

As Rachel knelt inside the ambulance and tried to make her comfortable, the woman's babblings grew increasingly hysterical. Despite Rachel's attempts to calm her, the patient kept jerking her head from side to side, alternately muttering and yelling. Had she not been strapped to the stretcher, she would have thrown herself off.

"She's been like that ever since they brought her out," a nurse said as she came up to the back of the ambulance and looked in at Rachel and the woman.

"Isn't there something we can do?" Rachel asked.

"We're low on sedatives. But now that we're about done, I'll see if one of the doctors can give her something." The nurse turned and walked off.

"It's going to be all right," Rachel soothed as she placed a comforting hand on the patient's forehead.

The woman jerked her head right and left, as if trying to escape Rachel's touch. As the woman continued to babble, Rachel thought she heard the words "my baby" repeated several times.

"Baby?" Rachel asked, leaning closer to the woman. "What about your baby?"

The jerking movements eased slightly, and her eyes briefly fluttered open. Then she repeated the phrase "my baby, my baby," though in a far calmer tone.

Rachel assumed the woman was having some sort of hallucination, but to keep her quiet, she asked, "Do you have a baby?"

"Yes," the woman said in a surprisingly clear voice. Her eyes opened wide, and she looked up at Rachel. "My baby. I want my baby."

Rachel felt something tugging at her dress, and she looked down to see that the woman had managed to grab hold of the skirt, despite her arm's being strapped in place.

"Where is your baby?" Rachel probed.

The woman struggled to fight back her tears. It took a

moment for her to compose herself enough to speak, and then she blurted, "Inside." She tried to raise her head and look out the rear of the ambulance toward the still-burning building. "In there."

"There's a baby in there?" Rachel said incredulously, and the woman broke down sobbing and nodded. "But that's crazy."

"No!" the woman shrieked. "Not crazy! My baby is in there . . . was born in there. Don't let her die!" She became hysterical again, her body jerking wildly beneath the restraining straps.

Just then the nurse returned with one of the doctors—a kindly-looking man in his fifties, with graying hair and a bushy mustache. He climbed into the ambulance and approached Rachel. Opening his medical bag, he took out a syringe and a small vial of liquid.

"We'll have her calm in a moment," he said with a noticeable Eastern European accent.

"Doctor," Rachel began cautiously. "This woman claims her baby is still inside."

"Probably her imagination," he commented with a nod.

"Did anyone check her cell?"

The doctor looked up at Rachel in surprise, then smiled. "My dear," he said in a somewhat patronizing tone. "There are no babies in an asylum. The woman is obviously deluded." Inserting the needle into the vial, he tilted it up and pulled back the plunger to fill the syringe.

"But perhaps she gave birth while she was there, and—"

"Half these women have lost babies or husbands or whatever. And many of them are confused enough to think their loved ones are still alive." He shook his head sadly. "We can pity her, but we simply cannot risk the lives of our fire fighters over some patient's delusion."

The woman on the stretcher gave a startling shriek and tried to bolt upright against the straps, then called repeatedly for her baby. Rachel held her firmly but compassionately, and soon the woman grew quiet again. Her eyes fluttered open and closed as she drifted in and out of consciousness.

"What if she's telling the truth?" Rachel asked as the doctor put away the vial and cleared the syringe of air.

"This woman was pulled out of the upper southwest corridor." When Rachel looked at him questioningly, he turned to the rear of the ambulance and waved his arm toward the section of building where the fire was most intense. "It's over there on the right—at the rear. They were able to get everyone out before it caught fire. There was no baby."

The doctor started toward the woman. Just then Aidan McAuliffe walked past the rear of the ambulance, and Rachel called him over.

"This woman claims a baby was left behind in her cell," Rachel told him. "And I believe her."

The older doctor stopped what he was doing and looked back and forth at the two women, then turned to Aidan and shook his head. "The woman is deluded," he pronounced, not clarifying which woman he was referring to.

"But if she isn't . . ." Rachel pressed.

"Where did they find her?" Aidan asked as he climbed into the ambulance and came over to the stretcher.

"On the second floor—the southwest wing."

Aidan leaned close to the woman and gently turned her face toward him. Her eyes were open now, and she looked up expectantly at him. "My baby," she muttered, and began to sob softly.

"How old is your child?" he asked.

"Two—three weeks," she stammered. "I'm not sure."

"What is your name?"

"Me?" She looked up at Aidan uncertainly, then seemed to gain strength from his deliberate, trusting tone. "Norma," she whispered.

"You are very pretty, Norma," he told her as he stroked her matted brown hair. "Why were you in there?"

"I . . . I drink too much. Sometimes I forget where I am . . . what I'm doing. I get these spells and—" Her eyes widened in fright as she looked between the two doctors. "But I'm telling the truth about my baby. They wouldn't have let me keep it—would've taken it away. So I didn't let them know. I kept her hidden . . . under my bed." Her eyes filled with tears again. "My baby! Don't let her die!"

"I won't, Norma. But you have to calm down. Do you understand?"

The woman looked up at him and choked back her tears, then nodded.

"That's better." Aidan smiled. "Now tell me the number on your cell."

"My cell?" Her forehead furrowed as she tried to remember. Then she replied, "Two thirteen."

"Two hundred thirteen?" he asked, and she nodded. Turning to the other doctor, Aidan waved a hand at the syringe and said, "Don't give her that unless it becomes absolutely necessary."

Agreeing, the doctor asked, "What are you going to do?"

"Check on that baby."

As Aidan started from the ambulance, Rachel grabbed his arm. "You can't go in there yourself. Get one of the fire fighters."

"Don't worry." He patted her hand and smiled. "I'll be happy to leave the heroics to them."

Climbing down from the ambulance, Aidan hurried over to a group of fire fighters congregated around one of the steam pumpers. Calling over one of the older men, who seemed to have been in charge during the rescue operations, he said, "We have to send someone in there to check cell two hundred thirteen. It's in the upper southwest wing."

The fireman looked at Aidan skeptically. "What for?"

"There might be a baby in there."

"A baby?"

"One of the patients claims she gave birth recently and kept the infant hidden under her bed."

The fireman stared at him incredulously, then broke into a wide grin. "You're kidding, right?" When Aidan's expression grew more serious, the man added, "They're crazy. They say anything that comes into their heads."

"I think she's telling the truth."

"Look, mister, I don't care if she said the pope himself just gave birth to a little baby boy. No one's going back in that building. It's too unstable. Most of the second floor has collapsed, and what's left could go at any minute."

"But if there's a baby—"

"I'm not getting my men killed over some crazy woman's fantasy." He abruptly turned and walked back to his men.

Stubborn prig, Aidan thought, shaking his head in frustration. He considered returning to the ambulance and performing an internal examination to prove the woman had recently given birth, but just then there was a series of small explosions that caused him to spin around and look in the direction of the southwest wing. The intense heat of the advancing flames had caused a number of windows to blow out, and he could see that in a matter of minutes the wing would be fully involved.

"Damn!" he muttered. Realizing he was wasting precious time, Aidan strode to the back of the pumper, where the fire fighters kept their equipment. Pulling off his suit jacket, he grabbed one of the heavy india-rubber coats, slipped into it, and fastened the metal buckles.

He found one of the curious-looking antismoke masks in a box marked *Eye and Lung Protectors* and examined it a moment to figure out how it worked. Donning the contraption, Aidan tightened the band until the india-rubber mask fit snugly over his face and drew the cord in the bottom of the porous canvas skirt around his neck. He was just tying it when he noticed a number of sponges in the box. Recalling that he had seen the firemen soaking them with water and inserting them into the skirt portion of the mask, he held one under some water dripping from a hose at the back of the pumper. He slipped it up under the skirt and positioned it so he would be breathing through it, then tightened the strings at the back of his neck.

Donning a pair of rubber gloves and a helmet made of leather treated with flame-retardant chemicals, Aidan walked briskly toward the door at the right side of the building. The other firemen, who had not seen him putting on the outfit, paid little attention as he approached the doorway. It was not until he passed through and disappeared into the smoky interior that one of them commented to the chief that a fireman had reentered the building against orders.

Aidan was unaware of the commotion taking place outside as the chief mustered his men and determined it was not one of them who had disobeyed his orders but the doctor, whose jacket at the back of the pumper betrayed his actions. Aidan's full attention was focused on getting his bearings and trying to make his way through the thick smoke that all but obliterated his vision. His progress was further hindered by not having been in the building before, as well as by the amount of smoldering debris that choked the hallway. Crumbled ceiling plaster lay under charred wooden beams that had given way above, and he had to climb over some piles and circle others that were still burning. Occasionally the smoke cleared enough for him to see through huge gaps in the ceiling above, where the second floor had collapsed.

He had gone halfway down the northwest corridor toward the center lobby when he came upon a staircase, which led up to the second floor. Most of the stairs were still intact, though the railing was charred and burning in places. He cautiously placed his foot onto the first step, testing to see if it would hold his weight. It seemed to support him, so he stepped up and tried the second one. As he shifted his full weight onto it, the step gave way with a shuddering crash, and Aidan's foot went through to the floor, his knee banging against and collapsing the third step.

Regaining his footing, he kicked at the fourth step, and it, too, gave way. Moving back, he looked upward at the flimsy staircase and realized he could not get to the second floor that way. He noticed that a hallway alongside the stairs headed toward the rear of the asylum, where Norma's southwestern wing was located, so he started down it, relieved to discover that the walls and ceilings were largely unscathed by the fire. Apparently the narrowness of the passageway and its north-south direction had served as a firebreak of sorts against the flames, which had traveled along the main corridors from east to west.

The smoke was thick in this hallway, but Aidan found it surprisingly easy to breathe through the eye and lung protector. The porous canvas and sponge filtered out most of the smoke particles, while the moisture cooled the hot air. Still, some of the smoke worked its way around the tight-fitting mask, causing his eyes to burn and tear.

Aidan could hear beams crashing in the distance, and he quickened his pace, at last reaching the archway that opened onto the southwestern corridor. This end was a mirror image of the other, with a matching staircase leading to the second floor.

As Aidan stepped into the corridor, he was forced back by a sheet of flames moving along the walls and ceiling. Already sections of the second floor had collapsed to his left, and he had little doubt that in a matter of minutes the rest of the wing would lie in smoldering ruins.

Looking at the stairway beside the connecting hallway, he wondered if it would hold his weight. It seemed sound enough, so he decided to take his chances and proceed. This time he did not place his foot on the middle of the step but rather against the very edge, where it connected to the wall and would be the strongest. Doing similarly with his other foot, he started up the stairs, gingerly at first, then with increasing speed. Halfway up, he rounded the landing and continued to the second floor.

He was almost forced back by the blast of heat and flames at the top of the stairs, but ducking his head, he ran into the corridor and turned blindly to the right. The fire was all around him, working its way up the walls and burning along the ceiling.

Some twenty feet from the stairway, the fire diminished

somewhat, and he was able to stop and get his bearings. The flames were rapidly advancing on him from behind, and he could not pause for long. As he continued down the hall, he frantically searched the heavy wooden cell doors for a number. Some of the doors were smoking from the heat and were on the verge of combusting. He could see remnants of painted numbers on them at eye level, but most had peeled and melted, and he could make out only portions of the numerals.

Near the end of the corridor, he saw what looked like a numeral three on one of the open doors. Praying his luck would hold and that it was cell two hundred thirteen, he dashed through the doorway. Turning to his right, he saw the dark form of the bed through the smoky haze and thought he heard what sounded like a baby whining. His heart raced as he dropped to his knees and reached under the narrow wooden frame. When he waved his arm left and right and felt nothing, he bent lower and looked underneath. There was nothing there. As the whining grew louder, he realized it was only the hissing sound of air being sucked by the fire through cracks in the outer wall.

Aidan stood and shook his head in dismay. There was no time left; he would have to get out of the building before it collapsed around him. He stepped out into the hall and started back toward the staircase but could make it only halfway before the intense heat drove him back. Peering through the sheet of flames, he saw that the archway leading to the stairs was fully engulfed.

Suddenly there was a terrifying rumble, and then the roof in front of him came crashing down into the corridor. The floor heaved as if from an earthquake, and as Aidan fell to his knees, the eastern end of the corridor gave way and collapsed, taking the staircase with it and shooting a blast of fiery wind down what remained of the southwestern wing. Aidan felt as if his body would explode, but then the sensation passed, and he realized he was still alive and the corridor behind him was intact. Some twenty feet from where he was kneeling, however, the building was completely gone.

He struggled to his feet. The flames were still advancing down the corridor, and he knew there was little time left before the rest of the structure gave way.

What in God's name am I doing? he thought, suddenly realizing the gravity of his situation. *The woman's probably deluded,* he told himself as he looked around for a way to make his escape. *Why the hell didn't I examine her or at least confirm she was lactating?*

He was about to retreat down the hallway when he glanced back at an open cell door that had just caught fire. He noticed that as it was charred by the flames, the wood did not blacken as quickly where the numerals had been. As he stared at the door, the number two hundred thirteen became visible for a brief moment, then slowly turned black.

Aidan shook his head to clear his smoke- and tear-blurred vision as he looked through the flaming doorway. He could not tell if the inside of the cell was on fire, but he knew he could not come this far without seeing it through to the finish. Drawing in a calming breath, he ran through the doorway, bursting through the flames.

Aidan turned in place in the center of the tiny cell. All around him, flames were streaming through what remained of the walls. Near the window a section of roof had collapsed, taking part of the outer wall with it. Stepping over several heavy beams, he found the bed and saw that the mattress had begun to smolder. He grabbed hold of it, yanked it off the wooden frame, and threw it across the room just as it burst into flames.

Dropping to his knees, he reached under the bed and felt a bundle. Pulling it out, he discovered the tiny baby wrapped in the thin woolen blanket issued each of the patients. He almost screamed with joy, but then he saw that the infant was not moving and might well be dead. There was no time to examine or treat it; he could only pray it had survived by being placed on the floor where the smoke was the thinnest.

He quickly unbuckled his protective coat and placed the bundle inside. Holding the baby tight against his chest, he dashed back through the flaming doorway and staggered down the hall. He was choking now, since the moisture in the sponge had evaporated and more of the smoke was getting through. But he disregarded the burning in his throat and hurried as quickly as he could.

At the end of the hall Aidan discovered a window large enough for him to climb through. But it was covered on the outside with a locked iron grate. The glass had already blown out, so he took hold of the grate with his free hand and tried to push it away. It would not budge.

Cursing, Aidan raised his right foot and kicked at the grate. It bent slightly but would not give. Again and again he smashed the unyielding metal, doing little but denting it. Turning around, he saw that the flames were advancing rapidly. He knew there was no other way out, so he raised his foot and gave a final, furious kick. To his joy and surprise, the top half pulled away from the brick wall. He kicked at it several more times, and finally it broke free and went falling down to the ground.

As he leaned out of the window, Aidan saw that a crowd had gathered below. They were pointing up at him and shouting, and he thought he saw Rachel among them. He could hardly breathe now, the smoke having clogged the pores of the canvas, and his lungs burned. Reaching up with one hand, he yanked off the mask and dropped it to the floor, then leaned back through the window and breathed in the smoky air. His eyes were watering so badly that he could hardly see, but he thought he heard voices shouting for him to jump. It might have been his imagination, but he knew he had no other choice, so he climbed through the window and sat on the ledge.

He was wondering if he should drop the baby down to the crowd before jumping. But as he tried to gauge how high he was, he saw something white below him. Suddenly he realized that the firemen had opened a round, canvas jumping sheet, which they were holding chest-high about six feet from the building. They continued to shout for him to jump, and as the heat behind him grew unbearable, he clutched the tiny infant to his chest and pushed away from the building, sailing through the air on his back.

The wind went out of him as Aidan struck the canvas sheet and it collapsed inward, dropping him gently to the ground. He felt everything spinning, and it was all he could do to pull open his coat and hand the bundle up into a sea of waiting arms before the blackness overcame him.

When Aidan regained consciousness, he was lying inside an ambulance with Rachel kneeling at his side.

"You're going to be fine," she whispered as she smiled down at him and wiped his forehead with a cool, moist cloth.

"The . . . the b-baby?" he stammered.

"Over there." She moved to one side so that he could look across the ambulance to where the woman named Norma was holding the baby in her arms, which had been unstrapped. "She's going to be fine," Rachel told him. "The doctor said she was quite blue, but she came out of it almost as soon as she started breathing the fresh air."

The ambulance shifted as someone climbed into the back. It was the older physician, who came over to Aidan's stretcher and remarked in his thick accent, "That was quite a performance you gave." He grinned down at Aidan. "You had to prove me wrong, I see."

"I'm sorry," Aidan said weakly. "I didn't mean—"

"Don't apologize," the doctor said, shaking his head. "I like a man with the courage of his convictions." He paused a moment, then added, "And now I would appreciate it if you would be my guest at Pacific Hospital, at least until we determine that you have not suffered any undue effects from your adventure." Moving to the front of the ambulance, he tapped on the wall, then turned to Rachel and said, "If you will hold on, please."

The wagon bed lurched as the driver started up the horses and drove the ambulance away from the crumbling ruins of the Presidio Asylum for Incurables.

Two

AT ABOUT THE SAME TIME THAT THE FIRE WAS TAKING HOLD at the Presidio Asylum for Incurables, Damien Picard was pulling a buggy into the stable at the rear of the Salomon family mansion on Nob Hill. When the butler, Cameron, came out into the courtyard to see if he could be of assistance, Damien remained hidden in the shadows of the buggy seat and waited while Nina Salomon walked out of the stable and sent the man away, saying she wanted to be left alone and would see to the horse herself. Cameron looked surprised that the madam of the house would consider unhitching the animal, but he kept silent and obligingly retreated.

Damien knew full well that Nina had no intention of dealing with the animal. Her concern was that no one know she had brought home a young gentleman who, to the older woman's obvious pleasure, had agreed to spend the night.

As soon as the butler was gone, Damien climbed out of the shadowed driver's seat and unhitched the mare. Nina pointed to the appropriate stall, and Damien led the animal inside and removed its harness. Then he retrieved his brown derby and silver-knobbed cane from the buggy seat and joined Nina in the courtyard.

"Are you certain my staying overnight won't be an imposition?" he asked innocently, well aware of what her answer would be. Leaning nonchalantly on the cane, he fixed her with a warm smile as he admired her tall, youthful figure and smooth, elegant features. Nothing about her betrayed her forty-five years, from her expressive brown eyes to her long brunette hair, which held no trace of gray.

"I wouldn't have invited you if it were an imposition," she replied. "As I said before, I . . . I would rather not be alone just yet."

Nodding, Damien gently took her hand and patted it comfortingly. He knew Nina's visit to the asylum had greatly upset her. After all, she was struggling with the secret demon of knowing she had committed her youngest daughter to an institution where the only hope was that she would not suffer unduly. It was true that Nina had felt justified in committing Phoebe, who had suffered a breakdown that left her catatonic. But what Nina did not know was that when Damien had visited Phoebe in her cell earlier that evening while Nina waited in the buggy, the young woman had seemed remarkably recovered. It was a secret Damien intended to keep from Nina, enabling him to wring as much money as possible out of her for Phoebe's care, which he had arranged to be reduced drastically.

Damien's grin held a note of smugness that would have faded rapidly had he known that Phoebe, only a short time after his visit, had killed the night attendant who had come to transfer her to the general ward—or that subsequently the asylum had caught fire and was at that very moment going up in flames. Instead, he lifted Nina's hand to his lips and kissed it softly. "For as long as you need me, I'll be here," he breathed, his faint French accent betraying his New Orleans Creole heritage.

Nina seemed a bit disconcerted as she looked up at the

handsome blond-haired man, who was the friend of her youngest son, Maurice, and was twenty years her junior.

Sensing her discomfort, Damien whispered, "You're so young and radiant, you simply cannot be Maurice's mother."

"I . . . I was quite young when I married."

"Little more than a child, no doubt. Your husband truly robbed the cradle."

"Charles was quite a bit older, it's true."

"Let's not speak of your late husband," Damien said, leading her toward the back door. "He's gone now, and you must make a new life for yourself. Tonight you must promise to begin putting the past behind you. It's time to stop grieving and start living again."

Nina opened the door and ushered Damien inside. Signaling him to remain quiet, she led the way to a rear staircase that brought them upstairs. Reaching the second-floor landing, she took hold of his arm and started down the hall.

"My children's rooms are on the third floor, though I don't expect anyone home tonight. Jacob has his own town house nearby, and Maurice and his new wife are staying there. Rachel and I . . . had words. I expect she'll take a room at a hotel. And, of course, Phoebe . . ."

"Yes, I understand," Damien replied soothingly. But what he actually understood was that Nina was informing him that they would be left alone to pursue whatever mutual interests they might have. Feeling her hand quivering against his arm, he had no doubt that she would like to uncover those interests in bed.

He could not help but smile. A mature woman, especially an attractive one like Nina who had never been properly attended by her husband, was far easier to seduce than the young fillies he usually favored—and as Benjamin Franklin once wrote, so much more grateful afterward. It was Damien's intention that such gratitude would take the form of a liberal income for the foreseeable future.

"This was Charles's room," Nina announced, stopping

before one of the doors and pushing it open. "I've turned it into a guest room."

Entering, she reached for a switch on the wall and turned on the brass electrolier, which was suspended in the center of the room. Damien was both surprised and impressed at seeing the pair of incandescent carbon bulbs light up inside the gilt-finished glass shades. Though electric lighting was growing in popularity, it was still a rarity in private homes. Glancing around the large, well-furnished room, he noted that the table lamps were the more common gas type.

"It's a lovely room," he said, concealing his awe at the richness of the furnishings as he placed his hat and cane on the plush chair of the Louis Quatorze desk that dominated the wall to the left of the door.

"I hope you'll be comfortable," Nina replied somewhat awkwardly as she turned to face him.

Taking hold of her hands, Damien grinned mischievously and said, "As comfortable as a man can be when forced to sleep in his clothes."

Nina looked at him curiously, then suddenly declared, "Oh, dear me, I'd forgotten that your things are at your hotel. How foolish of me. But we can solve that."

Slipping her hands free, she crossed the room and opened a large mahogany wardrobe. She looked through the contents, glancing back at Damien a couple of times, then settled on a blue silk dressing robe, which she removed from its hanger and brought over to him.

"I recently bought this for my husband, but he never had the chance to wear it." She held it against Damien's brown suit and nodded. "It should fit you perfectly."

"I'm sure it will be fine." He tossed the robe onto the four-poster and again took her hands in his. "You've been through so much. If there is any way I can help . . ."

Nina stared into Damien's piercing blue eyes. As if a wellspring of thoughts and emotions were coursing through her mind, her eyes filled with tears, and she gripped his hands more tightly to keep from falling.

Realizing her response had as much to do with feelings of guilt as with his own effect upon her, Damien decided to draw out those feelings, so that her gratitude would be that much greater when he helped her overcome them. "You're thinking of Phoebe again, aren't you?"

"I . . . How can I not?" Her eyelids fluttered, and the first tear ran down her cheek.

"You mustn't blame yourself. You didn't make her get pregnant, did you?"

. "But I forced her to have that abortion, which left her so hopelessly . . . hopelessly . . ."

"Insane," Damien concluded. "You didn't make her insane, Nina," he insisted, squeezing her hands. "It was the shame of her pregnancy and her suicide attempt—it was everything she went through. Phoebe doesn't have your strength. There are few people who do. Few mothers would have had the strength to—"

"To commit their own daughter," she interjected, lowering and shaking her head.

Damien cupped her chin and lifted her face toward his. "You had the strength to do what was right for Phoebe . . . and for the rest of your family."

"You mean by not telling them she's alive?"

"There's nothing left to do for Phoebe but see that she has the best of care. But it was in your power to protect your other children—your family name—from the scandal that would erupt if the truth ever came out. How would the customers of Salomon's Emporium feel knowing that one of the Salomons got herself in trouble, tried to commit suicide, and ended up in an asylum for incurables? What would that do to business—to the future prospects of Phoebe's brothers and sister?"

"And her son," Nina muttered, looking down again.

"Yes . . . her son, as well." He left unsaid what Nina had trouble admitting aloud—that Phoebe's baby, which had survived the botched abortion attempt, had been secretly turned over to a foundling home, where it was later discovered by

Aidan and Rachel and then adopted by Maurice and his new wife, Merribelle. It was that action that had caused such a violent rift between Nina and her children.

"Is that what Phoebe would want?" Damien pressed. "Would she want to be the cause of suffering to her own siblings? To her own son? Isn't it better that they continue to think she has died . . . that they remember her the way she was before her illness?"

Nina gave a slight nod but kept her eyes lowered.

Raising her head again, Damien wiped the tears from her cheeks. "There, now. No more regrets. I promised you I'd see to it that Phoebe always gets the best of care, and I won't let you down. It's time to forget the past—to look forward to what the future has to offer."

As Nina looked up at him, Damien concentrated all his attention on her, focusing it through his eyes as if he were speaking with them. It was a trick he had learned as a child growing up in his mother's New Orleans bordello, when he and his younger half-sister held staring contests that quickly became contests of will. He prided himself on never having lost such an encounter, though in time his sister was able to battle him to a draw.

Though Nina exhibited an inner strength Damien found admirable, he could sense her insecurities and knew she could never defeat him—in a contest of eyes or of will. Already her gaze was faltering, and she covered her discomfort by saying, "I hope I haven't imposed on your kindness, Damien."

He gave a short laugh. "And now it's you who's worried about creating an imposition." He raised her right hand to his lips, but this time he turned it over and delicately kissed the palm. Leaving her hand resting against his cheek, he whispered, "Between friends, there are no impositions. And when strangers meet, nothing is as imposing—and enticing— as becoming friends."

Damien felt Nina being drawn to him, and he parted his lips slightly, as if preparing for a kiss. He prolonged the moment, savoring the feeling of holding this wealthy, sophisticated woman under his control. But Damien had already decided he would not make love to Nina tonight. Better to draw her in slowly—to let her dream of what it would be like in his arms—so that when the moment finally came, he would utterly dominate her and she would be ready to do whatever he desired, both in bed and out.

Damien was about to end the temptation and suspense by pulling away and professing how tired he was. But to his surprise, Nina acted first, averting her eyes and backing away from him.

"I'm sorry," she said in a tremulous voice. "It's quite late. . . . I should be going." She glanced up at him, the uncertainty clearly written in her eyes. Then she turned abruptly and headed out into the hall.

"Are you all right?" Damien asked as he walked over to the door.

"Yes . . . yes, I am," she replied hesitantly, her back to him as she stood partway down the hall. "But I'm very tired." Crossing her arms in front of her chest as if she had a chill, she looked back at him and smiled politely.

"Yes. It's been a long day for you." He gave a shallow smile in return. "Will I see you in the morning?"

"But of course." Her chest heaved as she caught her breath, and she looked very awkward and self-conscious. "I really must be getting to bed," she muttered. Turning away, she headed down the hall and stopped at one of the doors on the right. She paused a moment, glancing back down the hall at him. Then she opened the door and disappeared inside.

Damien stared down the hallway, shaking his head and smiling ruefully as he wondered whether to be pleased at her reaction or not. Either his effect on her was so powerful that she was frightened of its consequences and hence would fall all the harder when the moment came, or else this Nina Salomon had a stronger will than Damien had suspected and might not succumb so easily to his charms.

"A worthy challenge," he mused, his smile growing more genuine as he backed into the guest room and closed the door. Glancing around at the costly furnishings, he breathed, "And a worthier prize."

It was a couple of hours before dawn when Phoebe Salomon woke up among some bushes near the waterfront at the northeastern corner of the Presidio. She had sought shelter there during the night after escaping from the Presidio Asylum for Incurables and making her way down the steep trails that led through the wooded military reservation.

Phoebe felt strangely dizzy and thickheaded as she pulled herself to her feet and started walking toward nearby Lewis Street, which bordered San Francisco's northern shore. The morning was not overly chill, yet she was exceedingly cold, and she pulled her gray wool jacket tight about her.

Shivering, she came to a halt and looked out across the moonlit water, the shoreline dotted with dinghies, single-masted barques, and the small lateen-sail feluccas favored by the Italian fishermen who plied their trade in the waters off San Francisco Bay.

Where am I? she thought, trying to get her bearings as she ran her left hand through the matted blond ringlets framing her face. It was quite dark, but the mix of moonlight and distant city lights was bright enough for her to make out her surroundings. Yet nothing looked familiar, as if she had been plucked from wherever she was before and had been deposited in a strange, alien land.

She looked down at the jacket she was wearing and wondered where she had gotten it. Seeing the insignia on the right breast, she read upside down the words *Presidio Asylum for Incurables.* The memories came over her in waves: her confinement in the tiny cell, the visit by a stranger named Damien, the night attendant coming to move her to the general ward. She closed her eyes but could not stop the rush of horrifying images: the fat little man trying to drag her from the cell, her striking out with the man's cudgel, his body lying there in a pool of blood, her running desperately into the night.

THE DECEIT

She had not wanted to kill the man—only to stop him from hurting her. As she saw herself clubbing him again and again, her right hand began to clench into a fist, and she felt a searing pain shoot up her arm. She tried to raise her arm, but it hung loosely at her side. It had been left crippled and virtually useless after she had thrown herself in front of the cable car, yet she had been able to use it when she was forced to protect herself in the cell. With an effort of will, she raised her right hand slightly and again tried to clench her fist. The pain was not as severe this time, but the action seemed to drain her of what little strength she had.

Realizing she was at the foot of the Presidio—and not far from the asylum—Phoebe forced herself to start walking down Lewis Street, heading toward the waterfront district. She could hardly feel her feet touching the rough pavement as she made her way on unsteady legs past the dark stone buildings of Fort Mason, rounded the corner of Larkin Street, and continued east on North Beach Street. There were more buildings here, most of them ramshackle affairs, some of them disreputable-looking taverns with lights still shining inside as middle-of-the-night revelers enjoyed a final whiskey before stumbling off to bed.

She continued walking, though she had no idea of her destination. Though her body was still shivering, she began to feel extremely hot, her forehead beading with sweat that ran into her eyes. With her good left hand, she wiped away the moisture and staggered onward, her head swimming, her body heavy yet feeling as if it were floating along the street.

Somewhere deep within her, a faint voice told Phoebe she was feverish and should seek help. But another voice warned her to speak to no one, lest she be captured and sent back to that horrible, rat-infested cell. And overshadowing both voices was the feeling that all of this was nothing but a dream—that when she awoke, she would find herself in her comfortable bedroom on Nob Hill.

Phoebe shook her head. *No, I cannot go home,* she told herself. It was her own mother who had committed her to the

Presidio Asylum. Nina would undoubtedly send her back were she to return home. And after what Phoebe had done to that fat little man, if those guards got hold of her . . . She shuddered at the thought.

Suddenly a shadowy figure loomed in front of her, causing her to jump with surprise. It was a man, and he said something that might have been lewd or perhaps was merely an offer of assistance to a young woman alone in the night. Shaking her head fretfully, she shoved her hands deep in the pockets of her jacket and hurried past him.

Phoebe almost ran into an older couple who were embracing near the doorway of a noisy tavern, and she muttered an apology, then stumbled away. Blindly she followed the bend in the road as North Beach Street became East Street, the wide thoroughfare that was lit by gas lamps and hugged the eastern shore. In the distance she could see the long piers, with names like Lombard Pier and Fishermen's Pier, where great clippers and steamships sat pointed into the bay, waiting to catch the tide. And beyond them, ready for the morning traffic, were the steam ferries to Sausalito, Tiburon, Berkeley, Oakland, and Alameda. They spoke of freedom— of escape.

Yes, I will escape, she told herself, feeling as trapped here on the waterfront as she had been in her cell.

Just as she was wondering how to achieve that goal, she realized her left hand was clutching some paper inside the jacket pocket. Pulling it out, she was surprised to discover a pair of ten-dollar bills, apparently left there by the night attendant. At last she felt a glimmer of hope. With the money, she could purchase a ferry ticket, then catch one of the trains in Oakland. No one would know where she had gone; she would be free. Perhaps in time she could return home, when she was certain it was safe and Nina would not try to send her back.

Phoebe felt increasingly light-headed as she hurried down East Street and approached the first of the long piers, located at the foot of Lombard Street. Several large ships were docked there, taking on goods bound for ports all over the world.

Perhaps one of those, she thought as she stepped out onto the wooden pier and came to a halt, wondering to what distant port her twenty dollars would take her. But even in her fevered imaginings, she knew it was hardly enough money to get her down the coast to Monterey.

Now that she had stopped moving, the light-headedness intensified, and she felt herself swaying in place, as if on the verge of falling or floating away. And she was so very hot that she unbuttoned the jacket and pulled it open, revealing the coarse muslin skirt and blouse issued the women at the asylum.

"What'sa matter, ma'am?" a lilting voice called, and Phoebe tried to turn toward it but was unable to move.

"You don't look too well," a second, deeper voice put in from her other side. She managed to tilt her head in that direction and saw a burly, bearded man wearing a black wool seaman's cap.

"You all right?" the first voice asked, and now a tall, gaunt sailor stepped into her view. He was smoking a cigar, but he dropped it to the pier and stamped it out.

"She looks sick," the burly one said.

"I . . . I'm fine," Phoebe tried to answer, but the sounds that escaped her throat were twisted around and garbled into nonsense.

"She *is* sick," the thin man pronounced, grabbing hold of her right arm as if to steady her.

A stab of pain shot up through her elbow, and she tried to jerk free. She cried out, but her words were distorted and unintelligible.

"It's all right, lady," the big one told her as he took her other arm. "No one wants to hurt you."

"She looks bad," his friend said, his voice growing more agitated. "Maybe we better get a doctor."

"What's your name?" the other sailor asked. "Where you from?"

Phoebe twisted in place, her head swinging wildly as she tried to free herself from their grip.

"What kinda dress is that?" the thin man said to his partner, nodding at the drab muslin outfit underneath her jacket. "And this ain't no jacket for a lady."

"Look here," the big fellow exclaimed, grabbing hold of Phoebe's jacket lapel and pulling it toward him to read the insignia on the breast pocket. "She's from that asylum up at the Presidio—the one that burned down last night. She must be one of them that escaped."

The thin man leaned toward her, examining Phoebe's face closely. "You crazy? You one of them crazy folks?"

"No-o-o-o!" Phoebe yelled, but her cry got caught in her throat and became little more than a wailing moan.

"Yeah, she's one of them loonies," the burly man declared, chuckling deeply. "We got us a loon!"

"Maybe we better get the police," the other sailor suggested nervously, almost as if he were afraid he might catch whatever ailed the woman. "I hear they got search parties out for the ones that sneaked away."

"Not so quick," his partner replied, pushing the thin man aside and grabbing both of Phoebe's arms. "First I wanna see the pretty lady dance." He began to spin Phoebe around him in a circle, her feet dragging on the wooden planks of the pier as pain shot through her right arm.

"Come on, stop that," the other man feebly implored. "She's crying."

"Aw, don't be frightened, little lady." He kept spinning her in a circle. "We just wanna see you dance."

The two sailors were startled by the sound of a door slamming, and then a deep, rasping voice called out in a thick Chinese accent, "Stop that this instant."

Turning to the voice, the big man stopped in place, propping Phoebe up as she sagged in his arms. His partner jerked his head around and saw that an ornate landau coach with matched white horses had pulled up at the foot of the pier. The man who had emerged and slammed shut the door was not tall but imposing in size, with a huge head and hands, a massive girth, and an eerily pasty complexion that was enhanced by his embroidered, deep-purple robe. His scalp was completely shaven, save for the black, braided queue at the back of his head. Even in the flickering light of the streetlamp, the sailors could see that his thick lips were curled in a frown.

"You two," the Chinese man called. "You sail aboard the *Jade Reef,* is that not so?" Though his words were heavily accented, he spoke flawless English.

The thin man took a cautious step forward and nodded.

"And you know that I am the owner of the *Jade Reef?*"

"Yes, we do, Mr. Chien," he replied in a respectful tone.

With a slight grimace at hearing his name misused, the man in the embroidered robe said, "You will call me by my full name, Sung Chien." He had come to expect such ignorance from Occidentals, so he did not bother explaining that in his culture the surname precedes the forename, just the opposite of English.

"Yes, Mr. Sung Chien," the sailor replied, backing away as Sung Chien approached the bigger man, who was still holding the young blond woman.

"What is the meaning of this?" Sung Chien asked as he came up to where they were standing.

The big man looked beyond Sung Chien and saw that three other Chinese men had climbed out of the coach. They were far younger than the middle-aged shipowner and were dressed in plain black jackets and trousers, with matching black slippers that made a padding sound as they approached. They came to a halt several feet behind Sung Chien and stood at attention, waiting to do his bidding. Their features remained impassive, and though they were not overly big, each was quite muscular and obviously knew how to handle himself in a fight.

"This lady's not well," the burly seaman explained, turning away from Sung Chien's phalanx of bodyguards.

Phoebe was crying softly but was no longer making an effort to free herself from the sailor's grip.

"Let her go," Sung Chien commanded with a flick of his wrist.

The big man shrugged and released his grip. Phoebe dropped to her hands and knees and continued to sob.

Signaling his men to stay back, Sung Chien approached the young woman and knelt beside her. Touching her arm ever so gently, he said, "Are you all right?"

Looking up, Phoebe saw the Chinese man for the first time. She was startled, but he smiled so compassionately that she felt a flood of relief. "I . . . I'm f-fine," she managed to stammer, her voice weak but understandable.

"Did they hurt you?" he asked.

She looked back and forth between the Chinese man and the sailors, then lowered her gaze and remained silent.

"They will not bother you again," he promised as he stood and helped her to her feet. She was so unsteady that Sung Chien had to grip her arm to keep her from falling. He signaled to one of his men, who came over and took hold of her. Seeing the look of fear in her eyes, Sung Chien told her, "He is with me. He will help you."

Phoebe seemed to accept what he said and grew calmer.

"What is your name?" Sung Chien asked, but again Phoebe lowered her gaze and did not answer. "Then I will call you Liu—the Stranger. You will come with me to my house, and I will see that you are given food and a place to rest."

"But . . . but I . . ." Her words trailed off as she looked nervously at the men surrounding her.

"Please do not worry, Liu. No one will hurt you. But you cannot be wandering the streets in this . . . this state." He waved his hand to indicate her clothing. "Certainly we can find something more appropriate for you."

Sung Chien snapped his fingers, and the bodyguard holding Phoebe led her back to the landau. As she was being helped inside, Sung Chien turned back to the sailors, his frown returning. "You treated that woman like a cur dog."

"But she's just one of them folks escaped from that asylum last night," the big man protested.

"She is a woman, and you showed her no kindness."

The thin man began to shake his head. "I told him to leave her alone—to get the police."

"Yes, I heard you." Sung Chien's expression softened ever so slightly. "Now, you will leave your friend here and return to the *Jade Reef,* and you will say nothing of this woman to anyone. Do you understand?"

The sailor nodded, then looked nervously at his mate. "But what about—?"

"You will return at once," Sung Chien repeated more firmly, "or else you will be put off the ship and your wages forfeited."

"Yes, sir," the man replied meekly. He gave his friend a helpless shrug, then turned and scurried away. A moment later, he was heading up the gangplank onto a large steamer docked alongside the pier. He glanced back once at his friend, then disappeared onto the ship.

Back on the pier, Sung Chien's two remaining bodyguards had taken positions a few feet on either side of the burly seaman. They remained impassive as their master asked the man, "What is your name?"

"McManus," the man grumbled.

"And you like working on the *Jade Reef,* Mr. McManus?" The sailor eyed him suspiciously. "Why?"

"I ask you this question because it will be up to you whether or not you continue to sail aboard my ship—aboard any of my ships." He paused for effect, then smiled and added, "Or aboard any ship that sails from this harbor."

"Now look, Mr. Sung Chien, we was just having a bit of fun. We wasn't—"

"Yes . . . fun." The heavyset Chinese man smirked. "And so shall we." He gave one of the bodyguards a slight nod, then turned back to the sailor. "Will you accept your punishment, Mr. McManus? Or will you seek some other line of work? For make no mistake about it . . . I can see to it you never work in this harbor again.''

McManus stared into Sung Chien's eyes, gauging the threat. He glanced at the two bodyguards, then nodded brusquely at the shipowner.

''A wise decision, Mr. McManus.'' He spoke in soft, rapid Chinese to his two men, then smiled again at the sailor. ''After punishment has been administered, my friends will escort you onto the *Jade Reef*. You will stay aboard until the vessel sails in three days. Then you may resume your duties. Is that understood?''

''Get on with it,'' McManus grunted.

Sung Chien spoke again in Chinese, after which he turned and walked back to the landau. The bodyguard who had escorted Phoebe into the coach emerged from inside and held the door for his master. Without looking back, Sung Chien climbed the hanging iron steps and disappeared inside. The bodyguard closed the door, then joined his partners on the pier.

McManus made no effort to resist as the three men dragged him over to a dark corner of the pier and pulled his shirt off his shoulders. Instead he kept his eyes locked on the landau, even as two of the bodyguards grabbed his arms in a viselike grip and forced him to bend forward.

The coach interior was not lit, and McManus was unable to tell if Sung Chien was watching from the shadows. But then the rotund Chinese man leaned through the window and, with a wave of his hand, signaled his men to proceed.

As Sung Chien disappeared back inside, the landau started forward. It was already halfway down the street when McManus heard a sharp snap and felt a searing pain across his shoulders that made him bolt upright. He gritted his teeth as the men in front of him tightened their grip, pulling him back down. Again there was the snap of leather, and his body jerked against the lash of the quirt being brought down on his back.

THE DECEIT

It was not until the fifth stroke that McManus allowed himself to scream, followed by a string of long, bitter oaths directed at the bodyguards, the wealthy shipowner, and everyone ever born the son of a Chinese woman. It seemed to work, because the young men released his arms and let him drop to his hands and knees. They muttered to one another in their own language, and then two of the men grabbed hold of his arms and proceeded to drag him along the pier.

"Sons-a-bitch coolie bastards!" he cursed as they hauled him up the gangplank. "Goddamn rice-belly canaries!"

If the young men knew what he was shouting, they gave no sign, for they bowed politely as they left him kneeling on the deck and padded back down to the pier.

McManus grabbed the railing, pulled himself up, and shook a fist as they strode away along the pier. "Your mothers were a bunch of flat-backing, nestle-cock hurry-whores!" he called after them, but they had already disappeared into the streets. "Canaries! Goddamn chandoo-smoking canaries!"

Three

THE LOBBY OF PACIFIC HOSPITAL WAS LIT BY FOUR BARE electric bulbs hung at even intervals along the ceiling. But already the light of dawn was filtering through the glass front door and the windows at either end of the room, giving the white walls a soft orange cast.

Rachel Salomon sat alone on a wooden bench near the front reception desk, which had been unattended for most of the past few hours. She knew the staff was busy handling the extra workload created by the fire at the Presidio Asylum for Incurables, yet she wished someone would tell her how Aidan McAuliffe was doing. He had looked so battered when they put him in the ambulance and was so weak from the effects of the smoke that she could not help but worry about his condition, despite being assured earlier that he would be fine.

"Ah, Nurse, I've been looking for you," a voice called in a thick Eastern European accent.

Rachel turned toward the corridor beside the reception desk and saw the physician with the graying hair and bushy mustache who had accompanied Aidan and her to the hospital. As he came out into the lobby, she stood to meet him. "I'm not a nurse," she corrected him.

"But I assumed . . ."

"I was with Dr. McAuliffe when we came upon the fire, so naturally I tried to help."

"But you acted so professionally. You have no training at all?"

"None whatsoever." Rachel grinned. "But recently I've had more than one opportunity to see a surgeon in action."

"Might you be referring to the injury your friend received?" Without waiting for her reply, he continued, "During my examination, I noticed he'd been treated recently for a gunshot wound, and he explained about the shooting."

"How is he doing?" she asked anxiously.

"Wonderfully. In fact, he's already up and about. He's dressing now, and then you can go in and see him."

Rachel gave an audible sigh. "I was so worried. He looked so bruised and weak."

"You had every reason to be concerned. But the injuries all proved to be superficial. Now that he's cleaned up and has rested a bit, he looks like a new man."

"Thank you so much."

The physician raised one eyebrow slightly as he looked at Rachel more closely. Suddenly he realized he was staring, and with a look of embarrassment he said, "I'm sorry, but now that I think about it, you look familiar. Have we met before?"

"I don't believe so, Dr. . . . ?"

"We haven't been formally introduced, have we?" He smiled and held out his hand. "I am the chief surgeon here at Pacific Hospital—Dr. Tadeusz Obloy."

"Ta-*day*-oosh," Rachel carefully repeated, shaking his hand. "An unusual name. Polish?"

He nodded. "I was born in Krakow. And you pronounced it beautifully. Most of my American friends give up and call me Thaddeus."

"Tadeusz is much nicer."

"I was named for my countryman, Tadeusz Kosciuszko" —he slowly pronounced the surname as Kosh-*choosh*-ko— "who fought so valiantly in the American Revolution and had the dubious distinction of having both his names mangled by the American public."

"Yes, I learned about him in school. But I'm afraid I was taught to pronounce it Kos-kee-*oos*-ko."

The doctor grinned and threw up his hands in frustration. "Do you see what I mean? At least no one has trouble with a name as simple as Obloy."

"Well, Dr. Obloy, I'm pleased to meet you. My own name is quite simple: Rachel Salomon."

"Salomon," he repeated slowly, letting the name roll around in his mouth for a moment. "Yes, that's it! I've seen your picture before. You're one of the Salomons of Salomon's Emporium, are you not?"

"My father was Charles Salomon. And my mother is—"

"Nina Salomon, of course," he exclaimed, clasping his hands together. "Why, anyone who reads the society pages has heard of her." Suddenly he gave a sheepish look and shrugged his shoulders. "Not that I read those pages, at least not that often . . . but my wife often speaks about the good works your family has done."

"Thank you," Rachel replied, looking a bit uncomfortable herself. To change the subject, she asked, "Will Aidan—uh, Dr. McAuliffe—be able to leave soon?"

"I'm ready to release him right now, but I'm afraid he refuses to go. Perhaps you can talk some sense into him." He turned and motioned her down the hall toward Aidan's room.

"I don't understand," she said, following beside him as they started down the corridor. "It doesn't sound like Aidan to want to stay cooped up in bed."

"That's precisely the problem. I want him to go back to his hotel and get some more rest, but he insists on staying and helping with the patients we brought in last night. Perhaps you can convince him otherwise.''

Rachel smiled but did not bother to say that doing so would be a pointless exercise.

Obloy turned down a hallway to the left, then stopped in front of a door on the right and rapped lightly. ''Dr. McAuliffe? Are you ready for visitors?''

There were footsteps. Then the door opened, and Aidan stepped out, dressed in a crisp white shirt, black trousers, and a white hospital jacket, all of which had been provided him by Dr. Obloy. There were a few scratches on his face and a small bandage just above his left eyebrow, but he looked remarkably fit and relaxed. He immediately took Rachel's hands in his own, and from the look in his eyes, it was apparent he would have taken her in his arms if not for the older physician's presence.

''It's good to see you up and about.'' Rachel gently squeezed his hands. ''You look so much better.''

''And I feel better, thanks to Dr. Obloy and his staff.''

''I'd feel a lot better if you'd take my advice and go back to your hotel,'' Obloy put in.

''But I really do feel fine,'' he assured the physician. ''I want to check on the patients I treated last night. And you can't deny that you're understaffed today; I heard some of the nurses talking about it.''

''Yes, but we'll manage—''

''Then you can use another pair of hands. Unless, that is, you're uncomfortable allowing an unfamiliar doctor—''

''Of course not,'' Obloy declared. ''Remember, I had an opportunity to watch you in action last night, and I must say I was impressed.''

''Thank you.''

''I'll tell you what. . . .'' Obloy looked back and forth between Aidan and Rachel, his head bobbing affirmatively. ''I'll agree to let you spend as much time as you want working on the wards, but on two conditions.''

''Which are?''

"First, you must agree to rest another half hour or so over a good breakfast. We have a small dining room for the staff, and I'll arrange for a hot meal to be prepared."

"Agreed," Aidan said enthusiastically.

"And the second?" Rachel asked a bit skeptically.

"Ah, this condition is the more serious one," Obloy proclaimed with import. "You mentioned, Dr. McAuliffe, that you recently arrived in San Francisco and may be taking up permanent residence here."

Aidan shot Rachel an awkward glance and saw she was masking a look of pleasant surprise at learning he was considering making San Francisco his home. "Yes, I've been thinking about it," he admitted.

"Excellent. You'll find this city most hospitable to foreigners like us. Which brings me to the point. I was impressed with the way you handled those patients last night—especially given the shoulder wound you sustained yesterday. And a little while ago, I took the opportunity to ring up the hospital where you were treated, and I received a full account of the emergency operation you performed in the middle of a restaurant to save the life of a man wounded in the gunfire. Believe me when I say that skilled and resourceful surgeons like you don't come along every day. As the chief surgeon here at Pacific Hospital, I'd like you to consider joining our staff."

Surprised and touched by the offer, Aidan turned to Rachel, who looked equally pleased.

"Don't rush into a decision," Obloy insisted. "But promise that you'll give it careful thought." He swept his hand in an arc, taking in the surroundings. "Pacific Hospital is not a large institution, but I truly believe we're doing some excellent work here and are at the forefront of surgical techniques. When you've had a chance to look around and acquaint yourself with our operation, I think you'll be impressed with our facilities and with some of the innovative equipment we've installed."

"I'll certainly consider your offer," Aidan said, shaking Obloy's hand.

"Excellent." The older physician turned to Rachel now. "And make sure you take Dr. McAuliffe outside and show him the grounds. I think you'll both find that our Pacific Heights location affords one of the most breathtaking views of the city and the bay." He paused, then added, "Now, let's see to that breakfast I promised you."

Dr. Obloy turned and motioned them down the hall, then led the way through the corridors to a fairly large dining room that held four round tables. The kitchen could be seen through an open door on the right-hand wall, and a large window on the far wall afforded a spectacular view of the sun rising over the bay.

As they entered the dining room, a portly middle-aged woman appeared in the kitchen doorway. "Good mornin', Dr. Obloy," she sang out cheerfully, curtsying politely to the chief surgeon and his guests.

"Hannah," he replied with a broad grin. "I know we're early, but if you and your sisters have that stove fired up, perhaps you can prepare some breakfast for these guests of mine. They're simply famished, and there's nothing more satisfying than your famous sourdough pancakes."

"We'd be delighted," she said, coming forward and pointing Aidan and Rachel to one of the tables. "Won't you be havin' some yourself, Dr. Obloy?" she asked.

"Not just yet. But make sure you keep a batch of that batter ready for when I get back."

Hannah nodded and disappeared into the kitchen, closing the door behind her.

"Hannah will take good care of you," Obloy promised as he pulled out a chair and held it for Rachel. When she and Aidan were seated, he added, "Enjoy your breakfast, and remember what you promised." Cocking his head slightly, he gave a wink, then turned on his heels and departed.

"Were you serious?" Rachel asked Aidan as soon as they were alone.

"About considering his offer?" he asked.

"Not exactly. . . ." She hesitated, then continued, "I mean about staying here permanently."

"Where else would I go?"

"You could return to your practice in London . . . or go home to Edinburgh."

Aidan shook his head. The thought of returning to London brought to mind the condition of his leaving that city, as an escaped convict, fleeing for his life after being framed for murder and sentenced to the gallows. A young woman, bleeding from a poorly done, back-alley abortion, had been brought to his office late one night, and despite his attempt to save her, she had died. When her family, the wealthy Mayhews, learned of Aidan's involvement, they had assumed he was the abortionist and had done everything in their power, legal and otherwise, to have him convicted of murder.

"I'm finished with London," he stated with resolve. "Or maybe I should say it's finished with me."

"But when your murder conviction is overturned . . ."

"Remember, I only have Jeremy Mayhew's promise that he'll have my name cleared."

"But it was his family who had you framed after his sister died. And now that you've saved his life and he knows you're innocent, surely the courts will—"

"There's no saying what the English courts will do. They may overturn the murder conviction but still charge me with unlawful flight."

"But you had to do that—or else you would have been hung." She reached over and took his hand. "I have faith that when the truth comes out, your name will be cleared and you'll be able to return to England if you want to."

"Is that what you'd like?" he asked.

Rachel looked down and shifted uncomfortably on the chair. "You know I wouldn't."

"Then why suggest it?"

"I want you to do what you'd like—what you think best. I

don't want you staying in San Francisco only because you have nowhere else to go.''

''Is that why you think I'd be staying?''

''Didn't you just say, 'Where else would I go?' '' She looked up at him expectantly.

''I said that because I . . . I didn't want you to feel any obligation toward me.''

''Obligation? Surely you know my feelings are more real than that.''

It was Aidan who shifted uncomfortably now. ''Yes, I know—and so are my feelings toward you. But I don't have much else to offer just now. I have no money of my own and have been forced to live on the kindness of friends. And I have no idea what the courts will do. I may have to return to England and face additional charges.''

''At least you *do* have friends . . . and the offer of a job. That's a beginning.''

''Yes, it is,'' he replied, patting her hand. ''And it's all thanks to you. If you hadn't helped me escape from England, I don't know what would have become of me.''

''Then let's assume things will keep getting better. They simply have to.''

''Why is that?''

''Because I insist they do,'' she answered with a grin. ''And I *always* get my way.''

''Always?'' he said skeptically, raising one eyebrow. ''What if you hadn't wanted pancakes for breakfast?''

''You're right. What I'd really like are sausages and eggs.''

Just then the kitchen door opened, and Hannah emerged, bearing two large platters of food. One held a heaping stack of pancakes, the other several links of sausage and a steaming mound of scrambled eggs.

''The doctor said you were famished,'' Hannah explained as Aidan stared openmouthed at the platters. ''I'll bring out the coffee directly,'' she added, turning and retreating into the kitchen.

"See?" Rachel said smugly, nodding toward the sausage and eggs.

"How did you do that?" Aidan asked incredulously.

"I said I always get my way." She paused, then started to chuckle. "Of course, it helps to be able to smell the sausage cooking."

"But the eggs . . . how did you—?"

"A woman has to keep a few secrets," Rachel declared, laying a forefinger alongside her nose and winking.

Damien Picard was enjoying the feel of silk sheets against his naked body as he lay back in the big four-poster bed of the guest room that had once been Charles Salomon's bedroom. It was growing brighter as the sun rose over the bay, and he knew he should rise and get dressed. He wondered if Nina had slept as peacefully as he had, and he secretly hoped she had been at least a little restless.

He was just debating whether or not Nina would try to sneak him out of the mansion without the staff's knowing he had been there, when suddenly the door opened and a young woman entered, bearing a footed breakfast tray.

"Your breakfast, ma'am," the woman said, approaching the bed. Suddenly she saw that it was a man under the blanket, and she came to an abrupt, startled halt. "Ex-excuse me, sir. I didn't know you were here."

Damien looked the young woman up and down. Her face was pleasant but ordinary, her mousy brown hair pulled back in a tight, unbecoming bun. But her body was far from ordinary. She was of average height, with a supple, rounded figure and full breasts that seemed constricted by the tight white apron over her black servant's dress.

Sitting up against the pillows and letting the blanket and top sheet slip down from his bare chest, Damien smiled and said in a slightly exaggerated French accent, "I am sorry if I frightened you. My name is Damien Picard. And who might you be?"

"Lydia, sir." She gave a half-curtsy. "I am on the household staff and was just bringing the madam her tray."

"But this is the guest room," Damien responded.

"I know, sir. But Mrs. Salomon was not in her room, and since her husband's death, she sometimes comes in here."

"Yes, I understand." He raised his hands at his sides and shrugged, the movement causing the blanket and sheet to slide the rest of the way to his lap. "But as you can see, I'm all alone. I haven't seen Mrs. Salomon since yesterday evening."

"They didn't tell me you were here," she told him, backing toward the door. "I'm so sorry—"

"Don't apologize. And there's no need to hurry off."

"But you're just waking up. I'll have another tray prepared and bring it up when you're—"

"Don't leave just yet," Damien pressed, giving a slight pout. "Unless I frighten you."

"No, sir. Not at all."

"If I do, it is I who should leave. I have a room at the Baldwin Hotel, and I can return there if you'd prefer. But of course I'd rather remain here, in the guest room, with a pleasant and attractive woman like you."

Lydia looked at him curiously, saw the way he was running one hand across his muscular chest and fixing her with his cool blue eyes. She fidgeted uncomfortably, then found herself returning his smile.

Just then she heard distant footsteps and said in a nervous hush, "Someone's coming; I must leave now."

"The Baldwin Hotel," Damien called softly as she turned toward the door. "Room two forty-two."

Lydia was about to step out into the hall when Nina Salomon appeared in the doorway, wearing a floor-length dressing gown. The equally stunned women halted abruptly, with Lydia almost dropping the breakfast tray.

"What are you doing here?" Nina asked, looking beyond

the young servant to the bed. Damien was lying on his side under the blanket, apparently asleep. "What's going on?" she demanded, this time in a hushed whisper.

"I . . . uh, well, I . . ." Lydia stammered. She glanced over her shoulder and saw that the man named Damien was pretending to be asleep. Taking a deep breath, she said, "I was bringing your tray, but you weren't in your room, so I came to see if you were in the guest room."

"Why would I be in the guest room?" Nina said petulantly, still restraining her anger. Glancing again at Damien asleep in bed, she explained, "I was upstairs seeing if Maurice came home during the night. The gentleman you almost woke up is a friend of his, and I offered him our hospitality for the night."

"Yes, ma'am," Lydia replied quietly, lowering her eyes. "Shall I bring this tray to your room now?"

Nina thought for a moment, then whispered, "No. Please put it over there for our guest." She pointed to a table beside the bed. "And be quiet with you."

Lydia did as told, placing the tray on the table and hurrying back toward the door. As she stepped into the hall, she turned back to Nina and asked, "Shall I bring up another tray for you, ma'am?"

"No . . . I'm not hungry this morning." As the servant started to walk away, Nina called, "Just a moment." She narrowed one eye and looked at the young woman sternly. Then her features softened into what passed for a smile, and in an unusually familiar tone, she said, "I'd appreciate it, Lydia, if you wouldn't tell anyone this gentleman spent the night. His visit is meant to be a surprise for Maurice, and I don't want to risk having my son find out. You'll do as I ask?"

"Of course, ma'am." She curtsied and started to turn.

"Not even Cameron or the rest of the staff, mind you."

"Of course not, ma'am."

"Very good, Lydia. You may go now."

Lydia curtsied again, then rushed down the hall toward the big marble staircase that led to the main floor.

Nina waited until she was sure the young woman was gone. Then she entered the guest room, closing the door behind her. As she approached the bed, Damien cautiously opened one eye, then looked up at her and grinned.

"You were awake?" Nina blurted in surprise. "The whole time?"

"When she came into the room, I didn't know what to do, so I pretended to be asleep," he lied. "Thank you for rescuing me."

"I didn't rescue you," she replied, a bit unnerved. "She was on her way out."

His smile widening, he sat up in bed, again letting the blanket slip from his chest. "Perhaps she was just going to shut the door. You never can tell what effect finding a handsome young man in bed will have on a woman."

Nina seemed unsure of whether or not he was serious, but his smile was so genuine that she found herself grinning along with him. "You're teasing me," she declared, coming closer to the bed.

"Me?" he said innocently. "Make sport of a beautiful woman? Never."

They gazed at each other for an awkward moment. Finally Nina forced herself to turn away. Glancing at the tray on the side table, she said, "There's your breakfast. I'd better be going so you can get dressed."

"Won't you stay a bit longer?"

Looking back at him, Nina shivered slightly. "I . . . I don't think I should."

"Are you afraid of me?"

Nina looked away. "I really should be going. There's a sitting room just down the hall—next to my bedroom. I'll be there when you're finished."

Damien breathed a disappointed sigh. "All right, then. I'll just lie here by myself and enjoy breakfast and the morning paper." Leaning over, he removed from the tray a copy of the *San Francisco Call* for that Tuesday morning, June 23, 1896, and opened it in front of him.

Halting at the closed door, Nina turned to look back at him. He peered up at her over the top of the paper, feigning an expression of indifference, then looked back down at the paper and pretended to be reading.

"I'll see you in a little while," she said softly, turning the knob to open the door.

"If that's what you prefer," he said nonchalantly. He closed the paper and dropped it on his lap. Nina was just passing through the doorway when he gasped and called, "Just a minute! Look at this!"

Nina looked back at him uncertainly, wondering if he were up to some ruse.

"Here . . . the headline!" He appeared quite shaken as he waved her closer and turned the newspaper for her to see the banner two-line headline that proclaimed: *Asylum Blaze Kills More Than Fifty; Police Seek Patients Still At Large*.

"My God!" Nina cried, grabbing the paper and gaping at the headline. "It's the Presidio Asylum . . . it's . . . Phoebe's there. Oh, my God, Phoebe!"

Damien pulled his dressing robe from the bedpost and slipped it on as he rose from the bed. Cinching the belt around his waist, he stepped up behind Nina and gripped her shoulders. "It's going to be all right," he said in as soothing a tone as he could muster.

"But Phoebe . . . my Phoebe!" Nina's eyes welled up with tears.

"Don't lose hope. It says that most of the patients escaped without injury."

Nina shook her head numbly, the tears coursing down her cheeks. "She . . . she's d-dead," she stammered. "And I killed her!" She finally began to sob.

"Don't say that." Damien squeezed her shoulders. "You didn't start that fire, and—"

"But I . . . I p-put her there."

"You didn't make her sick. You only did what was best for her—for your whole family."

"She's dead!" Nina wailed, crying more deeply now.

Turning her toward him, Damien took Nina in his arms and held her close. "You have to stop saying that. You don't even know if it's true."

Suddenly Nina drew in a sharp, gasping breath, and her body went rigid. Looking up at him with eyes open wide, she whispered, "They'll all find out now. . . . They'll discover what I did to her!"

"No one will know," he assured her. "She was admitted under a false name. Even if the worst is true and she died, it will be a different name they give out."

Far from being reassured, Nina started shaking her head and crying even more deeply at the image of her daughter perishing in the flames.

"There now," Damien soothed, holding her closer. "Everything will be fine—you'll see."

Nina choked back her tears. "But what . . . what if she's out there somewhere . . . lost . . . wandering about?"

Damien felt his own body stiffen at the thought of Phoebe's returning home and Nina's discovering he had betrayed her trust by arranging for her daughter to be transferred from her private cell to the general ward. Masking his concern, he whispered, "She's fine—I'm sure of it. I'll go there today and make certain, if you'd like."

"But it's gone. It's burned down."

"I'll find someone who knows, if I have to check every hospital where they took the survivors."

"You'll do that?" she asked, looking at him hopefully.

"For you, Nina, yes."

"Today?"

"Right now," he promised. "As soon as I get dressed."

"Yes, right now," she muttered, pulling herself away from him and wiping her tears. She forced a smile. "You've been so kind, Damien."

"It is my pleasure to serve you."

59

"Thank you, Damien."

"Now, if you'll excuse me, I'll get dressed and start out at once."

Nina took his hand and raised it to her lips, kissing it as a gentleman would a lady's. "If there's any way I can help," she told him.

He started to shake his head, then said, "Come to think of it, there is one small thing."

"What is it?"

Damien shook his head again and waved off the thought. "It's too much to ask."

"No, please, tell me," she pressed.

"Well, you see, I arrived in town just yesterday and took a room at the Baldwin Hotel. I was planning to go to one of the local banks today and arrange for additional funds to be transferred from my account in New Orleans, but I may be tied up with . . . with this other business. And I'm afraid that until those funds are wired to me . . ."

"You're short on cash?" she asked as if relieved it was nothing more serious.

He shrugged and smiled sheepishly.

"I have plenty of cash in my room, and I'll make you out a bank draft to carry you over until your funds arrive."

"You're really too kind."

"No, you're the kind one, helping the mother of a friend with her troubles."

"I'm sorry, but I simply cannot think of you as Maurice's mother—as anyone's mother. I'm helping because I like you very much . . . because of who *you* are."

"Thank you." She looked down and blushed. The moment passed, and she grew more agitated again as she thought of her youngest daughter and what might have become of her. "I'd better go to my room and prepare that draft," she said, backing toward the door.

"I'll come down as soon as I'm dressed," he told her. As she reached the door, he raised his hand and said, "One other thing, Nina. Is it possible to leave without being seen?

What with my visit to the asylum last night and the fire, it might be best if we weren't seen together . . . at least until we're sure of your daughter's fate.''

She nodded. ''There's a balcony outside my room and a stairway that leads to the rear garden. No one will see you go.''

''Good.''

''What about Maurice?'' she asked, remembering that Damien had come looking for him.

''I think it would be better if he didn't know I was in town yet. Let's give this thing a chance to blow over.''

''Yes, that would probably be best.''

''For now it would be wise if we take care that no one sees us together.'' When Nina looked at him with concern, he added, ''If you need me, just call the Baldwin Hotel, and we can arrange a time to meet. I'm in room two forty-two.''

''Two forty-two,'' she repeated, nodding.

''Don't hesitate to call.''

''I won't.''

''And I'll ring you up as soon as I have word about Phoebe.''

''Thank you, Damien.'' She pushed open the door.

''Everything will be fine,'' he promised. ''Trust me.''

''I do, Damien.'' She smiled again, then slipped out into the hall and closed the door behind her.

Damien listened as her footsteps receded down the hall. Then he picked up the newspaper that lay crumpled on the bed and crushed it in his fist. ''Damn,'' he muttered, shaking his head. ''Just when I had everything worked out, the damn place had to go up in flames . . . probably burned to death my little ticket to riches, as well.''

He tossed the paper onto the bed and walked over to the wardrobe where his brown suit was hanging. As he removed the trousers from the hanger, he considered the possibility that Phoebe might still be alive—either wandering the streets or recovering in a hospital.

If she talks, he thought grimly, *if they realize she's no lunatic, I may have to get out of this town before I had planned.*

"Never," he said aloud. He would not let Phoebe come between him and the Salomon fortune. There was simply too much to gain here to let it be ruined by some half-crazed woman whose own mother had shunted away rather than see the family name besmirched. Damien would have to complete the job left unfinished by the fire if that proved to be the only way to keep Phoebe Salomon from reappearing and interfering with his plans.

Looking down at his hands, Damien realized he was clutching the trousers so tightly that he was creasing the material. He eased up on his grip and forced the anger from his body. "Save it for something that matters," he told himself with a rueful smile. "Save it for Phoebe."

"How is she doing?" Sung Chien asked in his native tongue as he entered the lavishly appointed bedroom on the upper floor of his Chinatown home.

Looking up from her chair beside the bed on which the American woman was lying, the young servant saw her master entering the room. She quickly rose and bowed. "There has been no change," she responded in Chinese.

"She just lies there?" he asked, and the woman nodded.

Sung Chien stared down at the woman who lay seemingly asleep on the large, black-lacquer bed. Her coarse muslin clothing had been replaced with an Oriental blue silk robe, which was largely obscured by a heavy embroidered coverlet, and she had been given a sponge bath. With her long blond hair washed and combed, she looked far prettier than she had at the pier, yet her pale, mottled complexion and the sweat that continued to bead on her brow indicated she was still quite ill.

"Liu," Sung Chien called gently, using the name he gave her at the pier. "Little stranger," he added, continuing in English, "are you feeling better now?" He repeated the Chinese name again, but the sleeping woman did not react.

THE DECEIT

"She does not stir," the servant said in Chinese. "But at least she has had no more fits."

"I never saw anything like that," Sung Chien commented, also in Chinese, as he stared at the woman on the bed. "We bring her into the house shivering with fever, and suddenly she collapses to the floor, body rigid, mouth drooling, eyes gone white. Have you seen this before, *niu yung*?" he asked, using the appropriate title for a female servant.

"In Soochow there was an old woman who had such fits."

"Were they able to cure her of this evil?"

The servant bowed her head but did not respond, indicating that the answer was in the negative.

"If it can be cured, the *tai fu* will know how," Sung Chien declared. "He will be here shortly." Turning on his heels, he swept from the room and disappeared down the hall.

Before resuming her seat, the young servant reached into a porcelain bowl on a wooden stand beside the bed. She drew a long piece of cloth from the murky-looking liquid inside the bowl and wrung it out. Folding it several times, she leaned over the bed and touched it to the woman's lips, squeezing some of the liquid into her mouth.

As she was returning to her seat, Sung Chien reappeared in the doorway. Beside him was an older and far shorter man, whom the servant immediately recognized as Hsiao Ch'u, the well-known proprietor of a medicinal-herb shop at the corner of Dupont and Jackson streets. Despite being little more than four feet tall, Hsiao Ch'u was a commanding presence with his flashing black eyes and long white hair, which was tied in a pigtail that reached to his knees. It was a presence enhanced by his reputation as the foremost practitioner of the Oriental healing arts in San Francisco.

Having been in the herb shop several times on errands for her master, the servant smiled as Hsiao Ch'u entered the room and approached.

"Good day, *niu yung*," Hsiao Ch'u said in high-pitched Chinese, bowing to the young woman, who was quite petite but still almost half a foot taller than he.

"Good day, *tai fu*," she replied, using the respectful form of address for a Chinese doctor. She bowed in return.

"I will leave you to your examination," Sung Chien said from his position in the doorway. With a bow, he headed off down the hall.

Hsiao Ch'u came over to the bed and looked down at the blond woman, who appeared to be sleeping. Leaning close to her, he said in English, "Are you awake? Can you hear me?" He questioned her several more times in English, but there was no reply.

"Has she been like this all night?" he asked the servant in Chinese, and she nodded.

Turning back to his patient, Hsiao Ch'u pulled down the coverlet and took hold of her right arm. Raising the sleeve to bare the forearm, he carefully positioned his hand so that he could feel her pulse. He did so in a manner far more delicate and exacting than any employed by practitioners of Western medicine, for by detecting subtle changes in the circulation, he was gauging the movement of *chi*, or energy, through pathways in the body.

When Hsiao Ch'u finished, he began to squeeze various points along the woman's body, as if checking for swelling. He started with the wrists, moved up along each arm to the shoulders, then around the neck and face, and finally the abdomen and down along the legs to the ankles.

Glancing at the side table, he saw the porcelain bowl and bent close to it to smell the contents, then dipped his forefinger into the liquid and touched it to his lips. Apparently approving of the herbs the servant had used, he turned to her and nodded. She lowered her eyes and blushed.

"Who taught you to prepare the Powder of the Three Miraculous?" he asked.

"My teacher in Soochow," she explained. "He said it has a calming effect and can reduce fever."

"And so it does." He smiled at her. "But only when there is an excess of damp *chi*. Did you know this woman is suffering from an accumulation of damp *chi*?"

THE DECEIT

The servant hesitated, then replied, "My teacher said to use this mixture when there was fever and sweating."

"You showed great wisdom in employing this."

"Thank you, *tai fu*." Again she looked down.

"What is your name?" he asked, approaching the chair beside which she was standing.

The servant looked somewhat uncomfortable at the request. "You may call me *niu yung*," she said politely.

"I am impressed with the care you have given this woman. You may call me Hsiao Ch'u. Will you not tell me your given name?"

Touched by the honor he was bestowing on her, she bowed her head and replied, "I was raised in the orphanage at Soochow. I did not have a given name, so my teacher named me Kuei Mei."

"Kuei Mei . . . a most unusual name. Did you know it comes from the *I Ching*?"

"My teacher cast my fate on the yarrow stalks the very day I was abandoned at the orphanage. He named me for the hexagram I received."

"*Kuei Mei*," Hsiao Ch'u repeated, saying the name of the hexagram and then translating it into English: "The Marrying Maiden." He nodded and smiled. "A most auspicious name," he proclaimed, returning to his native tongue.

Walking to the trunk that sat at the foot of the bed, Hsiao Ch'u picked up a muslin blouse from a pile of clothes. "Do these belong to the woman?" he asked, and Kuei Mei nodded. He examined it a moment, then looked at the jacket with the insignia of the Presidio Asylum for Incurables. Nodding thoughtfully, he put the clothes in a neat pile and walked toward the door.

"Will you be able to help her?" Kuei Mei asked.

"She suffers from wind and damp *chi* obstruction with wind predominating. You should add some gentian to the Powder of the Three Miraculous to help remove the dampness. I will prepare some other medicines to reduce the wind *chi*. If she does not improve, we will try moxabustion heat to drive out any excess cold *chi*.'' Bowing to the young servant, he added, ''I will arrange with your master for you to pick up the medicines at my shop this afternoon.''

They bowed to each other, and Hsiao Ch'u left the room. He was met partway down the hall by Sung Chien, who was returning to learn the results of the examination.

''Will she be better?'' Sung Chien asked in Chinese.

''You must send the *niu yung* to my shop this afternoon.'' He pointedly used Kuei Mei's title, not her name. ''I will prepare some medicines to remove the fever and clear the *chi* obstructions.''

''But her fits . . . will it cure them?''

''I thought you said there was only one.''

''Yes, just the one this morning, shortly after we brought her here.''

''The seizure may have been caused by the *chi* obstructions. First we must unblock her energy pathways. Then if the seizures return, we will treat them.''

''Good. Very good,'' Sung Chien declared with noticeable relief as he led Hsiao Ch'u down the stairs.

The old doctor remained silent as he followed Sung Chien from the third floor down to the first. But as they approached the front door and prepared to bid each other good-bye, he asked, ''Why did you bring this American woman into your house, Sung Chien?''

The rotund shipowner stopped in place and looked at Hsiao Ch'u curiously. ''This need not be your concern,'' he finally replied.

''I saw her jacket. She was one of the unfortunates in the hospital that burned down last night.''

''She was alone and ill, and I have given her the hospitality of my house,'' Sung Chien said flatly.

''The city authorities are searching for such unfortunates who may still be wandering the streets.''

''But she is no longer wandering, is that not so?'' the bigger man noted with a smug grin.

''The authorities should be informed.''

Sung Chien's smile faded. "You will not concern yourself with these matters. It is for me and my guest to decide when it is appropriate for her to leave."

"You assume a great responsibility here—one that should rightfully—"

"The responsibility is mine, and you will not trouble yourself with this matter again. You, too, are a guest in my home. You have come here as a hireling, and you will conduct yourself in accordance. Many who have chosen to do otherwise have later discovered they have much to regret."

Hsiao Ch'u fell silent as he looked up at his angry host. Though he was unafraid of Sung Chien's veiled threat, he did not want to endanger the ill woman upstairs, so he bowed politely, saying, "I am sorry if I spoke out of turn."

His smile returning, Sung Chien bowed and replied, "There is no need for apologies between respected friends. I thank you again for your service and will send the *niu yung* for the medications you have prescribed."

Sung Chien nodded at a man who was standing off to the side. Stepping forward, the man opened the front door and waited until Hsiao Ch'u had departed. Then he closed the door and retreated into the shadows.

Sung Chien stood staring at the back of the door for a moment, his smile fading again. With furrowed brow, he turned and headed back up the stairs.

Four

AFTER AN UNPRODUCTIVE MORNING VISIT TO THE RUINS OF
the Presidio Asylum for Incurables, Damien Picard visited
the local police station and, pretending to be the cousin of
one of the patients, obtained a list of the hospitals to which
victims of the fire had been transferred. He spent a good
portion of the day visiting the places on the list, as well as
two other asylums, one across the bay in Oakland, where the
uninjured patients were being housed until permanent arrangements were made. So far he had turned up no record of
a woman named Mary King—the alias under which Phoebe
Salomon had been committed to the asylum.

As Damien left a hospital in downtown San Francisco and
approached the cab he had hired for the day, he read the final
entry on the list, a small hospital near the destroyed asylum.
Stepping to the curb, he called up to the driver, "Take me to
Pacific Hospital. It's on—"

"Yes, sir, I know the place," the man called back, tipping
his hat.

Damien climbed into the coach and settled back in the

seat, removing his hat and placing it beside him as the cab pulled away and headed west toward the Pacific Heights district near the Presidio. He passed the time considering his options should no evidence of Phoebe turn up. He would have to lie low until it was certain she was not going to make a surprise reappearance. Once she was confirmed among the dead, he could proceed with his plan.

And what will that plan be? he asked himself as the cab clattered up Jackson Street. When he had discovered that Nina committed Phoebe but told the rest of the family she died, he had seen the perfect opportunity for personal gain. Playing on Nina's guilt and fear, he had offered to see to all the details of Phoebe's confinement and had even pretended she was being moved to a larger, costlier private room. In truth, he had arranged with the night attendant to have her transferred to the least-expensive general ward, where the most destitute patients were kept in bleak, deplorable conditions. Damien had planned to collect the higher fee from Nina and pocket the substantial difference between the cost of the two wards.

Now he saw only two options. First, he could say that Phoebe was still alive, even if she had perished in the flames. He would prepare some phony invoices and have Nina provide him with the money to pay them. True, he would have to keep Nina away from whatever asylum he claimed Phoebe had been transferred to, but it should prove to be a feasible plan. The second option was simply to tell Nina the truth about Phoebe's death and figure some other scam to bilk her of her money. And now that he was beginning to insinuate himself in her life, he sensed there were other schemes that would net him considerably more profit than simply siphoning a few hundred dollars a month in bogus medical bills.

Damien was brought out of his musings by the cab's arrival at Pacific Hospital, a small brick building situated on Pacific Heights with a commanding view of the city. Directing the cabbie to wait for him, he grasped his silver-knobbed cane and headed up the walk.

He was just shifting the cane to his left hand and reaching

for the knob of the glass front door when he stopped short and stared with surprise into the lobby. He quickly stepped to the side of the door and peered in at the woman standing near the reception desk, speaking with the nurse on duty.

For a moment he doubted his eyes, but there was no mistaking that he was looking at Phoebe's older sister, Rachel Salomon. Damien would not easily forget the tall, attractive woman with the copper hair and devastatingly green eyes. She looked as stunning now in her green evening dress as she had in New York City, where they had been introduced by Maurice.

Her presence at the hospital could well mean that Phoebe was a patient there and that somehow the authorities had discovered her true identity and had contacted Rachel. If that were the case, Damien would have to take extra care not to be seen by Rachel.

With a bittersweet smile, he remembered the night of drunken, drug-induced debauchery he had spent with her brother, during which Damien had summoned the unsuspecting Rachel to Maurice's room and had violently forced himself on her. His smile faded as he realized she would certainly take steps to bring the law down on him should she learn of his presence in San Francisco—and that a man matching his description had visited Phoebe in the asylum and had arranged for her transfer to the general ward.

Damien moved away from the door and was about to make his retreat when he saw Rachel disappear down the corridor beside the reception desk. He hesitated a moment, telling himself he should get away while he could. But his curiosity impelled him to risk going inside and seeing what he could find out. Unable to fight the impulse, he stepped up to the door, opened it, and walked briskly inside. Glancing down the corridor to make sure Rachel was not returning, he approached the front desk and positioned himself where he could see anyone coming down the hall.

"May I help you?" the nurse at the desk inquired, looking up at him expressionlessly.

THE DECEIT

"Good afternoon." Damien politely tipped the knob of his cane toward her. "That woman who was just here . . . wasn't that Miss Rachel Salomon?"

"Why, yes, it was."

He grinned broadly and nodded. "I thought as much." Adopting a look of concern, he said in a hushed tone, "I trust none of her family has taken ill or been injured in some way."

"Are you a friend of the family?" the nurse inquired. "Would you like me to summon her?"

"That won't be necessary," he quickly put in. "Miss Salomon and I have not been introduced. But at school I did make the acquaintance of her younger brother—a delightful young man named Maurice. Nothing has happened to him, I hope—or to his mother."

Damien's worried look was so convincing that the nurse's own features softened, and she told him, "No, nothing like that. Miss Salomon is here as a friend of one of the surgeons who is treating those poor victims of last night's fire."

"Ah," Damien sighed, smiling with genuine relief. "Yes, that fire was quite a tragedy. In fact, that's why I've come." He leaned forward slightly, investing the words with great import as he asked, "May I speak confidentially?"

"Why, yes, of course," she replied, a bit flustered.

"My poor cousin, Mary, was a resident at that dreadful place. Her illness has been a great tragedy to her family, especially my dear old aunt. But they've been reluctant to make official inquiries about her condition, because . . . well . . ." He shifted on his feet, the picture of discomfort. "You see, their friends have been told nothing of Mary's illness, and my aunt would be mortified if word got out. I'm not sure her heart could stand it."

"Yes, I understand," the nurse responded sympathetically. "These situations are most delicate."

"I knew you'd understand." Damien adopted his most genial expression. "I'm afraid I've been appointed to visit the various hospitals and make discreet inquiries. By chance was a Mary King admitted last night?''

''I do have a list,'' the woman told him, checking the papers on the desk and coming up with one. ''Identifications were completed this morning. Let me see. . . .'' She scanned the list, then checked it a second time before shaking her head. ''I'm sorry. There's no one by that name.''

''I see,'' Damien said, glancing down the hall to make sure Rachel was not returning. ''Ah, well, it may be for the best.''

''Don't give up hope. She may be at another hospital.''

''We'll know soon enough.'' He tipped his cane at her again. ''Thank you for your assistance.''

Turning away, Damien strode across the lobby and headed outside. Without looking back, he made his way down the walk and opened the door of the waiting cab, calling up to the driver, ''Take me back to the site of last night's fire.''

As the cab pulled away from the hospital, Damien settled in his seat, remembering that night in New York when he had taken by force what Rachel would not offer freely. It was true that he and her brother had been drinking heavily, as well as smoking opium. But he had known what he was doing—and that what he was doing was wrong. Now as he remembered the incident, he wished he had not acted so rashly. Not that he held any great regret at having put Rachel through such a nightmare. Rather, he had not thought far enough ahead, thus complicating his current situation. From this moment on, he would have to use far more foresight and caution.

Just then the cab pulled onto the grounds of the Presidio Asylum for Incurables. One crumbling section of the building still remained standing on the left side, with a lone chimney all the way to the right that still eerily gave off smoke. The rest lay in twisted, charred heaps. Scattered throughout the rubble were workers picking through the debris, searching for additional victims.

Curiously, the section that remained standing was the corridor where the fire had begun, as if the blaze had been less intense at its source and had grown increasingly furious as it progressed through the building.

Damien walked toward the shell of the remaining wing and tried to gauge where Phoebe's cell had been located. Guessing the approximate spot, he headed over to a man working on a collapsed section near there.

"Excuse me," Damien called, gaining the attention of the man, who stood and leaned upon the shovel he was using. "Did you work here before it burned down?"

The fellow shook his head, then pointed toward another man who was working nearby.

"Thanks," Damien called back. He approached the second worker. "You used to work here?" he asked as he stepped a few feet into the rubble, keeping his balance with his cane.

"Yep," the man grunted. "Name's Vincent. Worked the day shift."

"I'm interested in a woman—a new patient who had a cell here on the northeastern corridor, name of Mary King."

Vincent scratched his head and walked a few feet closer. "New, you say?"

"She'd only been here a few weeks. Kind of pretty, with blond hair. And her right arm was crippled."

"Yep, I know the one," the man said with a nod. "Found her over there."

"There?" Damien asked, looking in the direction the man was pointing.

"Down that hall, right where her cell would've been."

"Are you certain it was her?"

"Now, how sure can you be after a fire like this? But there was two bodies in the cell, both of 'em burned so bad you couldn't even tell if they was man or woman."

"Two, you say?"

"Yep. They think one was the night attendant, probably checking on her when the fire started. The other was smaller, about that lady's size."

"And you think it was Mary King?"

"That's what we put down on the list when we carted off what was left of the bodies. Now, if you'll excuse me, I'd best get back to work."

"Yes, of course. Thank you."

Damien stared into what remained of the northeast corridor, then backed away from the ruins.

Dead, he thought, allowing himself a smile.

He turned and walked purposefully to the cab. "Take me back to my hotel . . . the Baldwin," he declared, then climbed inside.

When he got to his hotel, he would have an early dinner, he told himself. Then he would make a telephone call to Nina to inform her of her daughter's tragic death. Afterward, there would be plenty of time to plot the most advantageous move for him to make next.

Nina Salomon sat in front of her dressing-table mirror, idly brushing her long brunette hair, which hung down over her left shoulder. She wore an ebony evening dress, hooked tight at the bodice and cut to display her trim, youthful figure. She had favored this dress during her recent period of mourning for her husband, and though it was appropriately black, there were those who would consider it too daring in its cut to be properly respectful.

Nina looked at herself in the mirror and tried to smile. Though she was forty-five and recently a grandmother, her hair was still lustrous and her skin was as smooth and tight as on the day of her marriage, when she was but seventeen. Still, she was troubled by the circles under her brown eyes that made her normally dark complexion seem a pale gray.

If only I could sleep, she thought wistfully as she placed the silver-handled brush on the table and closed her eyes. It had been so long since she had slept through the night. Of late her mind seemed to wind up during the day and race through the night, with sleep coming only in fitful snatches, haunted by nightmares.

"Phoebe," she whispered aloud. No matter how she tried

to fill herself with other thoughts, the image of her youngest, most delicate child sitting mindless in an asylum cell always reinsinuated itself in her mind. She had not been able to look at Phoebe in the doctor's office following that botched abortion, which had been performed far later in the pregnancy than Nina or the doctor realized. It had caused Phoebe to undergo some sort of seizure that left her catatonic and totally unconnected to reality. It also had left behind a healthy baby boy, whom Nina had secretly arranged to be placed in an orphanage.

"Charlie," she grimly intoned, looking back into the mirror as she voiced for the first time the name the infant now bore. She bitterly recalled the anger and shame she had felt upon learning that Rachel had tracked down the baby at the orphanage. Her rage had increased a thousandfold upon being informed that Maurice had eloped and that he and his new wife, Merribelle, had adopted the bastard child, naming it after Nina's recently deceased husband.

"They're all gone . . . all dead," she muttered as she thought of Phoebe, most likely killed in that awful fire, and her other children—particularly Maurice and Rachel—whom she had thrown out of her house and out of her life.

"Madam," a voice called softly behind her, and she jerked upright and looked into the mirror to see the portly, middle-aged butler standing in the doorway.

"Yes, Cameron?" she asked.

"Your son Jacob is here to see you. I showed him into the parlor."

Nina felt her heart race slightly. Maybe it was not too late, she told herself. Her eldest son had come to call, perhaps to bring an apology from the other children.

Not allowing herself to smile, she said, "Did he inform you why he's come?"

"No, madam. Just that it is imperative he see you."

"Tell him I'll be down presently."

The butler nodded and withdrew into the hall.

Picking up a tortoiseshell comb, Nina deftly worked her

hair into a tight chignon at the nape of the neck and held it in place with a silver-inlaid pin her husband had purchased for her when they were in Madrid. Standing, she angled the oval mirror at the back of the dresser so that she could see her full figure. She adjusted the skirt slightly, brushed off the bodice, and left the room.

Allowing the train of the dress to trail on the wide marble stairs, Nina glided downstairs, suddenly feeling alert and optimistic. She and her children would be reconciled, and perhaps Phoebe would be found alive, with the shock of the asylum fire having somehow restored her sanity. Of course Nina would have to explain why she let the family believe Phoebe was dead, but eventually they would realize that Nina had acted in everyone's best interest and that the care she had provided for Phoebe had ultimately returned her to health. Friends and acquaintances would be told that the story of Phoebe's death had been issued after she had contracted a usually fatal malady and had gone away for treatment, but that she had made an unexpected and miraculous recovery. A few might guess the truth, but polite society would never raise such a delicate issue, and everyone would agree the situation had been handled with the greatest propriety.

Smiling warmly, Nina swept into the parlor and saw her eldest son standing near the fireplace at the far end of the room. Jacob had come from his office at Salomon's Emporium and made a commanding presence in his gray, vested cutaway suit. He had a stocky physique, and though he would not be considered fat, he had begun to regain the weight he had lost during a recent ocean voyage to the Orient. His dark-brown hair had thinned considerably but was balanced by his trim beard. He had firm, pleasant features, highlighted by his bright and expressive gray eyes.

"Nina," he said perfunctorily, using her given name, as all her children did. He crossed the room, stopping at some distance from where she was standing. His relationship with Nina had long been cool, especially since his father had taken ill and Jacob had assumed leadership at Salomon's, so it came as no surprise to Nina that he maintained his distance and made no effort to embrace her.

"Good afternoon, Jacob," she said pleasantly. "What brings you from the office?"

"I thought we should speak." He waved a hand toward one of the green-velvet sofas. "Shall we sit?"

With a nod, Nina crossed to the sofa and sat down. Jacob chose a facing chair.

There was an awkward silence, and then Jacob began, "I'm concerned about the way things stand between you and Maurice."

"Did he send you?"

"He has no idea I've come. I made an excuse when I left him at the store."

"Maurice? At Salomon's? Whatever for?"

"He's decided to go to work there full-time."

"But he always hated the family business."

"I think you'll find that Maurice has changed quite a bit. And it's all thanks to—"

"That woman," she put in with a frown.

Jacob cringed inwardly at Nina's uncompromising attitude toward anyone of whom she did not fully approve. "Merribelle is a delightful woman—precisely what Maurice needs. You often said you wished he'd settle down and take life more seriously. And Belle is the ideal person for him to settle down with. Why, when she first arrived in town, you were quite keen on her." When Nina started to shake her head in protest, he added, "Don't try to deny it. I remember your reaction when you learned her family was quite prominent in Kentucky and raised Thoroughbreds."

"Well, she did seem a sight better than some of the young trollops he's brought home in the past."

"There, you agree."

"That doesn't mean he should have rushed out and gotten married in such haste. Why, such a thing just isn't done. If he'd given me enough time, we could have had a proper wedding—one to be remembered. Instead he's made our family the object of ridicule.''

''It's not that bad, Nina.''

''Yes, it is. To rush into marriage and then show up the next day with a baby . . . You know what people will say.''

''What *will* they say?'' he challenged, again irked by her attitude.

''That he got that woman pregnant and, after she had the baby, brought her home and married her.''

''That's ridiculous. The child is adopted. There are papers to prove—''

''I don't want to talk about that baby,'' she said abruptly, raising her palm.

''Nina, you've got to accept that Maurice and Belle are married and will be raising little Charlie.''

''Don't ever mention that name in this house!'' she said curtly. ''That was blasphemy, what they did.''

''Naming Phoebe's son after Father? It wasn't blasphemy. It was an honor to his memory.''

''Your father was a saint!'' Nina shot back, her face screwed up with rage.

Jacob just looked at her incredulously. He would have laughed were it not so pathetic. After all, Nina had treated Charles like anything but a saint. In fact, Jacob was convinced it was her continual beratement of Charles that had caused him to lose the will to live, leading inevitably to his heart attacks and fatal stroke.

''A saint, I tell you,'' she continued, shaking a fist. ''And to have his name pinned on that little bastard—''

''Shut up!'' Jacob shouted, stunning her into silence. He rose from his seat and looked down at her. ''You won't refer to my nephew—to Phoebe's child—by that word. Is that clear? He's your own grandchild, for God's sake!''

Nina stared up at him, her teeth clenched with anger.

Jacob paced across the floor. Banging a fist atop the marble fireplace mantel, he shook his head and turned to look back at her. "Sometimes you can be unspeakably cruel. You weren't always so bitter. What's happened to you?"

"Is that why you came?" she asked. "To goad me?"

"I came to see if you'd speak to Maurice . . . if you'd apologize—"

"Apologize?" she blurted, rising from the sofa. "Me? Why, you've got some nerve expecting *me* to apologize. And for what?"

"For trying to get rid of Phoebe's baby, for starters."

"I did that for the family—and for the sake of Phoebe's good name. That's all that was left of her."

"No, Nina, you're wrong. There's something else left of Phoebe: her son. And when she died, you should have brought her child here instead of spiriting him off to some foundling home."

"You can't be serious! You expected me to play nursemaid to that . . . that . . . ?" She forced herself to leave the word unsaid. "And how would I have explained it? What would people have thought of your poor sister if they'd have found out she got herself pregnant? What would that have done to the family name?"

"That's all you seem to care about," he grunted, turning away from her in disgust.

"Someone has to," she shot back. "I won't see everything I've struggled to build get torn down by some stupid indiscretion on the part of your sister."

"She's dead," he said in anguish, spinning toward her. "For pity's sake, show some respect."

"Why should I? Phoebe certainly didn't. If she *had* shown some self-respect, none of this would've happened."

Raising his hand, Jacob started from the room. "I won't argue about this anymore. I came here to try to smooth things over, but obviously you have no intention—"

"Don't go!" Nina called after him, her voice edged with fear. "I . . . I don't want to argue either. It's just that when you started accusing . . ." She lowered her eyes and stood rubbing her hands together.

"I didn't mean to accuse you, Nina. But you've got to start taking responsibility for your actions." He paused and was about to continue speaking when the butler came through the foyer and stopped just inside the entrance to the parlor. He nodded to indicate he had a message.

"Yes, Cameron?"

"There is a call for you on the telephone, madam."

"Who is it?" she asked cautiously.

"The gentleman said only that you were expecting his call." Seeing Nina's confused expression, Cameron added, "Shall I take a message?"

"No—that won't be necessary," she said abruptly. "Tell him I'll be right there." As the butler nodded and withdrew, Nina turned to her son. "Will you stay a bit longer?" she asked expectantly.

"Perhaps it would be best if I—"

"Please don't go just yet."

Seeing her anxious, almost frightened look, he felt a small measure of compassion. He nodded and sat back down.

"I'll only be a moment," she assured him, bustling from the room and disappearing through the foyer.

Nina's heart raced as she hurried through the kitchen and into the pantry, where the single telephone in the house hung on the wall. Taking hold of the dangling earpiece, she adjusted the mouthpiece to her height and said, "Hello? This is Nina Salomon."

"Nina?" the voice on the other end asked in an unmistakable French-Creole accent.

"What is it? What did you find out?"

There was a moment of silence, and then Damien Picard said simply, "I'm sorry."

"You . . . you mean . . . ?"

"I'm afraid Phoebe did not survive the fire."

Nina lowered the earpiece and stared numbly at the phone. For a long moment she just stood in silence, and then her head began to bob, and she broke into tears.

"Nina," Damien's voice called faintly in the distance. "Nina . . . are you all right?"

For a long while she did not respond but sobbed quietly, one hand clutching the earpiece, the other pressed over the mouthpiece.

"Are you all right, ma'am?" a voice called from behind her, and Nina spun around to see the young servant named Lydia, who had come up to the pantry door to see what was the matter. Lydia was dressed to go out in a black wool coat and a wide-brimmed straw hat.

Nina stared at the woman a moment, as if wondering who she was and what she was doing there. Though Nina was no longer sobbing, tears still ran down her cheeks.

"Is there something I can do, ma'am?" Lydia asked in concern.

"What do you want?" Nina barked, rubbing her cheeks with the back of the hand that held the telephone earpiece.

"You seem upset. Shall I get someone—?"

"It's none of your concern," she cut her off. Noticing Lydia's attire, she glowered at her and said, "What are you doing, anyway? Where are you going?"

"Why, home, ma'am."

"But it can't be past three o'clock."

"It is four, ma'am."

"What about dinner?" she snapped, focusing all her attention on this insignificant bit of domestic business as if using it to avoid the pain—and guilt—of Phoebe's death.

"I'm not working dinner, ma'am. I've been here since six, and Cameron said it would be all right—"

"Go ahead. Go on home." Nina impatiently waved the woman away.

"If you're certain there's nothing I can do . . ."

"I said I was fine. Now be off with you."

"Yes, ma'am," Lydia replied as Nina turned away.

Nina could hear Damien calling to her, and as soon as the servant was gone, she picked up the earpiece and said into the mouthpiece, "Excuse me, Damien. I . . . I was interrupted."

"Are you all right?"

"Yes, I'm all right," she replied a bit testily.

"I'm really sorry, Nina," he soothed. "But perhaps it's for the best."

"Yes . . . I suppose so. Still, that doesn't make it any . . ." Her voice trailed off.

"I know. But in time you'll see that Phoebe's better off now than she was . . . in that place."

"Yes. I suppose you're right." She sniffled back a tear. "I should be going now. My son is in the parlor."

"Maurice?"

"No, Jacob."

"There isn't any trouble, is there?"

"No. He just came to visit. Don't worry—I'm fine."

"You call me here at the Baldwin if you need to talk," Damien told her. "Any time of day or night; I'll be here for you."

"Yes, I know you will. And I appreciate it—everything you've done."

"We'll speak again soon, Nina. Until then, try not to be too depressed or worried."

"I won't."

"Good afternoon, Nina."

"Good afternoon," she whispered.

Slowly she hung the receiver on the cradle. Turning in place, she leaned against the wall and forced herself to breathe calmly. *Phoebe's dead,* she thought, as if trying to convince herself. *That day in the doctor's office . . . she died that day.*

Closing her eyes, she drew in a deep breath and held it for a long moment, then let it out slowly. Finally she pushed away from the wall and walked from the pantry.

As Nina crossed through the foyer and entered the parlor, Jacob stood and asked politely, "Was it the gentleman you expected?"

Nina stared at him in surprise, thinking that he knew about

Damien Picard. But then she recalled Cameron's comment that the person on the telephone was a man Nina expected would call. She smiled and nodded. "It was just a supplier I had contacted in regard to the extravaganza." She crossed the room and stood by the sofa.

"Really?" Jacob said, looking confused. "But I thought we'd decided not to hold an extravaganza this year."

"Why, y-yes, we did," she stammered, suddenly recalling that due to Charles's death the family had agreed to cancel the fashion show held each summer at Salomon's Emporium. "But I realized it might be good for me—for all of us. It might take our minds off everything that's happened."

"Are you sure you want to take all that on just now? You know how much work it can entail."

"I haven't fully decided. I was just making some calls to see if it's too late to get the supplies we'd need."

"It's already June twenty-third. You'd only have a few weeks to make all the arrangements," he pointed out.

Nina felt backed into a corner, and she rubbed her hands together and walked a few feet toward the foyer. "I'll make a decision in a few days, and then we can talk about it." She turned toward her son. "I feel a bit tired. If you wouldn't mind . . ."

"Of course not," he replied. Crossing the room, he took his derby from a small table near the foyer entrance. "I hope you'll give some thought to what we were discussing earlier."

"About Maurice?" She followed him into the foyer.

"Yes. And his wife, Belle, not to mention Rachel and myself."

"Just what is it you want from me, Jacob?" she asked, coming to a halt by the front door.

"If you'll recall, you threw us out of here and told us never to come back. By rights I shouldn't even be here now."

"You didn't take me seriously, did you?"

"I'm afraid this time Maurice did. He has a new family, and he was hurt when you rejected them."

"I . . . I can't talk about it now." She shook her head and looked away distractedly.

"Just promise you'll consider making amends with Maurice." When she nodded, he added, "You'll do it?"

"I'll think about it," she clarified.

"Good enough." He opened the door. "Good-bye, Nina."

"Good-bye, Jacob," she replied, standing in the doorway as he made his way down the walk to the carriage waiting in the circular driveway.

She stood there in her ebony evening dress, watching as the carriage pulled away from the mansion and headed down the street. "Good-bye," she whispered again, this time to her daughter, Phoebe, as her eyes filled again with tears.

It was dark when Aidan McAuliffe and Rachel Salomon returned to the Hotel Willard. Aidan had spent the entire day at Pacific Hospital, tending to the victims of the asylum fire. Rachel had spent much of the time there, as well, but had returned briefly to the Willard to arrange for a room for herself, since Nina had made it clear that she was no longer welcome at home. Rachel also had telephoned the butler, Cameron, and arranged for him to send some of her clothes to the hotel.

Rachel and Aidan followed the proprietor, Josephine Jeffries, up to their rooms. Josephine was a well-rounded, middle-aged woman with a rich, husky voice that bespoke her years on the operatic stage. She knew only how to look on the bright side of things and wore a perpetual smile that reached all the way to her flashing brown eyes.

"A gentleman brought your bags about an hour ago," Josephine told Rachel as she unlocked one of the doors along the hall and motioned for them to enter.

"That was our butler, Cameron," Rachel explained as she walked into the room.

"I figured as much, since he took the liberty of unpacking your things and setting them out."

"Cameron is quite efficient," Rachel commented.

"Ah, to have a man like that around at one's beck and call," Josephine mused. "And so handsome, too."

"Are you sure it was Cameron?" Aidan teased, following the two women into the room.

"He had a pleasant smile and lively eyes," Josephine declared. "That's the hallmark of a handsome man." She gave a playful frown and poked a finger at Aidan. "Not every gentleman need be as young, slim, and attractive as you, Mr. McAuliffe, to be considered handsome. There are many of us who appreciate a man with a few pounds more flesh and a bit less hair." She turned to Rachel. "You tell Cameron I said so. And invite him back anytime he'd like."

"I will, Miss Jeffries."

Josephine circled the small, well-appointed room, equipped with a canopied double bed, a mahogany dressing table, a Queen Anne's dresser, and a pair of wardrobes. She showed them the door that led to the private bath, then crossed to a door on the other side of the room. Halting in front of it, she turned and swept her hand in an arc, taking in the furnishings. "I hope the accommodations are adequate. At least they should prove convenient," she added, unlocking the door beside her. She looked back at Aidan and grinned. "You'll find your room right through this doorway, Mr. McAuliffe."

Ignoring their blushing expressions, Josephine walked to the open door to the hall. "If you should need anything, my room is downstairs behind the parlor." She started into the hall, then turned and said, "Good night." Without awaiting their reply, she closed the door and headed down the hall.

Aidan and Rachel stared awkwardly at each other, uncertain of what to do or say. Only the night before he had carried her up to his room, each of them eager to make love. And now they were back at the hotel again, this time alone in Rachel's adjoining room.

He walked to her and started to speak, but Rachel touched a finger to his lips and shook her head. Reaching around his neck, she kissed him gently.

Taking her in his arms, Aidan returned her kiss, deeply

and passionately. But when she started to unbutton the white hospital jacket he was still wearing, he pulled back slightly and covered her hands with his own to stop her. "Not just yet," he whispered, stepping back slightly.

Rachel stared in wonderment as he gripped her hands and lowered himself to one knee. "I love you," he whispered, kissing each of her hands. "I know my future is still uncertain, but once my name has been cleared, will you become my wife?"

Rachel's eyes welled up, and Aidan stood and took her face in his hands, delicately kissing the tears as they began to stream down her cheeks.

"I'm sorry," he whispered. "If I've upset you . . ."

Shaking her head, she pulled him close and kissed his neck. "I love you, too, Aidan McAuliffe," she breathed. "And I would be honored to be your wife." Pulling her head back slightly, she saw that his eyes had also filled with tears, and she began to grin. "You look dreadful," she teased. "Your eyes are all puffed up, and there are dark circles under them. This talk of marriage must really disagree with you."

"Never," he asserted.

"Then you must be asleep on your feet. And no wonder, after last night. Perhaps once you've had a good night's sleep, you'll change your mind about marrying—"

Aidan cut her off with a kiss, full on the lips.

After a few minutes, Rachel pulled away and led him over to her bed. "Wait here," she whispered as she walked across the room to the bathroom door. She was already undoing the clasps at the back of her dress as she smiled back at him and disappeared inside.

Aidan circled the room and put out all the lamps but one, which he turned down low. Returning to the bed, he removed his jacket and folded it over the back of a nearby chair. Then he sat down on the bed and began to remove his shoes.

Ten minutes later, Rachel opened the door and stood framed in the light of the bathroom. She was wearing a white silk nightgown, cut low with lace around the bosom. The material clung to her body, highlighting her firm, well-developed figure.

As she doused the bathroom light and started across the room, she saw Aidan lying on the bed, waiting for her. She whispered his name as she approached, her eyes slowly adjusting to the thin light from the lamp on the dressing table. As she came up beside the bed, she noticed he had not turned down the covers, nor had he removed any clothing but his jacket and shoes.

"Aidan?" she asked, but he did not reply. She was about to reach down and touch him when she realized he had fallen asleep.

Standing next to the bed, she debated whether or not to wake him. Finally she shook her head and smiled. Walking over to the dressing table, she blew out the lantern, came around the bed, pulled down the covers beside Aidan, and crawled underneath. She curled up close to him, placing an arm over his chest and nuzzling her head against his shoulder.

"Mrs. Aidan McAuliffe," she murmured with a smile as she closed her eyes and dreamed of the moment they would become husband and wife.

Five

NINA SALOMON HAD DISMISSED THE STAFF FOR THE NIGHT and was wandering through the downstairs of the mansion, lowering the wicks of the table lamps and turning off the electroliers in the mammoth formal living room. She was dressed in an ermine-trimmed, white satin robe, which trailed along the floor as she started from the room. She had not yet removed her rouge and eye makeup, and as she passed the floor-to-ceiling mirror that dominated one wall of the living room, she noted with displeasure that the more liberal amount she had been applying lately was insufficient to cover the lines she had begun to notice on her face.

Nina forced herself to turn away from the mirror. She would not allow herself such thoughts; she was still a young woman, and any lines—any imperfections—were but the temporary aftereffects of her recent emotional upheavals.

As she entered the parlor and began to turn off the lights, the front bell sounded. Not expecting a visitor so late, she assumed it was one of her children returning home, most likely Rachel, since Maurice and his family were staying with Jacob until they found quarters of their own.

Smiling, Nina hurried over to the front door in the foyer and, not bothering to look through the viewing port, pulled it open, thrilled that Rachel had decided against spending the night at a hotel—especially one with as dubious a reputation as the Willard. The outside lamp had been turned off, and as the door swung wide, the light from the foyer spilled onto the figure of a woman, who stood on the stoop huddled under a dark-gray coat, her face concealed in the shadows of the hood she had pulled up over her head.

"Rachel!" Nina exclaimed, beckoning her in. When the woman did not respond, Nina pulled her robe tighter against the chill night air and took a cautious step forward, her expression that of a schoolgirl who has done something wrong and is waiting to receive her punishment. "Rachel, I'm sorry about the way I spoke to you—" Her mouth dropped open as the woman pushed back her hood and looked up at her. "Phoebe!" she gasped, clutching her chest. "Y-you're . . . alive!"

The woman tilted her head in surprise and moved forward slightly, coming more fully into the light. It was not Phoebe Salomon but a woman of a similar height and age, with the same blue eyes and blond hair. This woman was somewhat more slender, however, with delicate features and thin, almost severe lips.

Realizing she had been mistaken, Nina exhaled and drew in a deep breath, then closed her eyes and slowly shook her head. "Forgive me," she apologized, looking back at the woman and forcing a smile. "You gave me a fright; I thought you were someone else."

The stranger gave a hint of a smile that softened her features. "I didn't mean to startle you," she began cautiously, her voice edged with a faint Southern lilt. "I'm Allison . . . a friend of Phoebe's. Is she at home?"

Looking at the woman more closely now, Nina saw that she wore no makeup and that her long hair had not been pinned up and was more disheveled than would be accounted for by the hood. Furthermore, her wool coat was threadbare and had several noticeable holes, as if it had been rescued from the ragman's cart.

"You're a friend of my daughter's?" she asked, her tone suspicious.

"Uh, yes," Allison repeated hesitantly.

"Then haven't you heard?"

"Heard what?"

"My daughter has passed away."

"Passed . . . ?" Allison said the word as if she did not understand the meaning.

"Phoebe is dead. She died several weeks ago."

Allison opened her mouth to speak. Her lower lip trembled, her eyes widening with shock. She gave a gasping sound as air escaped through her constricted throat, and then she threw her hand over her mouth and doubled over, sobbing loudly.

Nina raised her hand but held back, wavering between pity for the young woman and disgust at her disheveled appearance. Finally she overcame her inhibition and stepped down onto the stoop, wrapping one arm around the young woman's shoulder. "There, there," she cooed, patting Allison on the back. "It will be all right."

"D-dead?" Allison choked, grabbing the lapel of Nina's robe and looking up at her with tear-swollen eyes. "Phoebe's dead?"

Nina nodded sadly. Stepping beside the young woman and taking hold of her arm, she added, "Come inside until you calm down. You've had quite a fright."

Entering the house and closing the front door, Nina led Allison through the foyer and across the parlor to a green-velvet sofa near the fireplace. She turned on a light and started to signal Allison to sit, then remembered how dirty her coat was. Rather than offer to take the woman's coat and thus invite an extended visit, Nina steered her past the sofa to a hard wooden bench along one of the walls.

Allison paid little attention as Nina helped her onto the bench. But the moment Nina let go of her arm and started to stand away, she reached up almost in desperation, clutched the older woman's hand, and urged Nina down onto the bench beside her. "I . . . I d-didn't know," she stammered as she looked down and shook her head while wringing Nina's hand between her own. "I hoped she m-might have escaped and . . . and c-come home."

"Escaped?" Nina asked, not understanding the remark. Looking down at the huddled woman beside her, she saw in the light of the electrolier that Allison's blond hair was not only disheveled but matted with grime and dust, giving it a dull, ashen appearance. Though she was obviously destitute and looked quite haggard, she could be no more than a few years older than nineteen-year-old Phoebe had been. "You're certain you knew my daughter? What did you say your name is?"

Sniffling, the young woman replied, "Allison Grant."

"I'm sorry, but Phoebe never mentioned you."

"I don't suppose she remembered me," Allison admitted. "I spent only a short time with her, and of course she wasn't well."

Seeing Allison wipe her tear-stained face on the dirty coat sleeve, Nina winced slightly. "I'm afraid this really doesn't make any sense," she proclaimed. "You say you knew my daughter, yet I don't see how. Certainly a woman of your station could not have afforded to go to the private school that Phoebe—"

"No, you don't understand. We met at the Presidio."

"But Phoebe didn't attend the Presidio Finishing School for Young—" The words died on her lips as she drew in a startled breath and stared into the woman's cold blue eyes. Her hands clenched into fists, and her jaw set so tightly that the air hissed audibly through her teeth when she exhaled. "The P-Presidio? . . . You're from the asylum?"

"Please don't tell them!" Allison begged, reaching over and gripping the lapels of Nina's robe.

Nina grabbed Allison's wrists and tried to pull her hands away, but the young woman clutched the robe so desperately that Nina would have had to rip the material to free herself. Gaping at Allison in horrified shock, she sputtered, "Y-you kn-know? How do you know?"

Allison slowly released the robe, and her hands dropped to her lap. Closing her eyes, she began to cry again and managed to say in a halting whimper, "I w-was there . . . an inmate . . . when they brought her in. They left her in my cell and called her Mary something. She couldn't speak—never even moved. But then in the middle of the night, she seemed better."

"Phoebe was better?" Nina demanded. This time it was she who clutched the other woman's lapels.

"She wasn't fully awake," Allison clarified. "But she spoke a bit. Enough for me to learn her real name and where she lived."

"Did she . . . did she say anything? About her family? About me?"

Allison shook her head. "And when I woke up the next day, she was the same as when they brought her in."

"She never got better?"

"I don't know. They took her away, and I . . ." Allison paused and looked up at Nina, then added solemnly, "I never saw her again."

Nina began to cry softly now, and she lowered her head and turned away on the bench.

Allison reached over and gingerly touched her shoulder. "I'm sorry," she whispered. "I thought maybe she escaped during the fire, like I did, and came home. That's why I came here. I . . . I had nowhere else to go." She broke down sobbing and buried her face in her hands.

The young woman's weeping helped Nina regain her composure. She looked over at Allison and was reminded of the time Phoebe had broken down in tears and confided that she was pregnant. Yet there was something different about this woman—something far less fragile.

"What were you doing there, child?" Nina asked in a surprisingly gentle tone. "You're not like Phoebe . . . you don't seem ill at all. Whatever were you doing in an asylum?"

Allison choked back her tears and again wiped her eyes on the coat sleeve. "I wasn't always like this." She held up her hands, indicating the disreputable state of her clothing. "My stepfather's family had a plantation in Louisiana but had to leave after the Civil War. They were able to keep much of their money, and my stepfather inherited a sizable estate in Los Angeles. Nothing like this—" she quickly added, glancing around the lavishly appointed room. "But enough to live comfortably. But my stepfather . . . he—" She began to cry again.

"It's all right," Nina soothed, taking the young woman's hand and patting it.

"He—he was a cruel man," Allison continued, her voice growing steadier as she drew strength from Nina's touch. "You can't imagine how cruel. He did things to me . . . things a man shouldn't do to a young girl."

"I understand," Nina assured her, still patting her hand.

"When I finally told my mother what was happening, she confronted him about it, but he denied everything—said it was all my imagination. At first she didn't believe him, but she was so afraid of him—we both were. Before she met him, she was so very poor. He threatened to cut her off—to throw her back out on the streets. I don't know if he really convinced her or if he just wore her down." She closed her eyes. "Mother was always so weak."

"What happened?" Nina pressed.

"He convinced her that I was the crazy one—that I was the one always trying to seduce him . . . when really it was he . . ." She had to pause a moment to calm herself, and then she continued, "He also made it look as though I was stealing money from his business and jewelry and things from the house, then convinced Mother I was lying about everything. He wanted to get me out of the way, so he took me to a doctor and paid him to say I was a pathological liar and a thief. They sent me away to the Presidio—way up here in San Francisco—so there would be no scandal. That was six years ago, when I was sixteen.''

"But you got better."

"I was never sick," Allison abruptly asserted.

"I'm sorry. I didn't mean . . ." She hesitated, then went on, "I was just hoping my daughter might have gotten better—if she had lived."

"No one gets better at the Presidio," Allison said bitterly.

Nina let go of Allison's hand and stood, her mind a rush of confused thoughts about her daughter and about this stranger who seemed able to evoke the most disconcerting feelings in her. Walking a few feet from the bench, she bowed her head and sighed. "It no longer matters. Phoebe's gone now. That fire put an end to her suffering."

"The fire?" Allison asked, sounding confused.

"Yes. She died in last night's fire."

"But I don't understand. Outside, you said she died a few weeks ago. I assumed you meant soon after she was admitted."

Nina turned around quickly, her expression betraying her worry. "I . . . I wasn't totally honest. You see, Phoebe's illness came on suddenly. It was such a shock to her father and me, and we didn't want our other children to suffer, knowing their sister was sitting helpless in an asylum with no hope for a cure. Charles convinced me it would be best if everyone thought she had died. At least that way she would keep her good name." Seeing Allison's look of disappointment, she blurted, "You understand, don't you? It was for Phoebe's own good. It wasn't like what your stepfather did to you; Phoebe was beyond hope." Even as she said the words, Nina wondered why this woman's approval mattered to her. It was as if Nina were actually beseeching forgiveness from her lost daughter.

"I understand, Mrs. Salomon." Standing, she approached

and took the older woman's hands. "I'm sure Phoebe would have understood, as well."

"You won't tell anyone, will you?" Nina implored, her eyes widening. "It would shatter the family. They've already done their grieving, and to have to relive . . ."

"I won't tell," Allison promised. "You and your husband needn't worry."

"My husband died shortly after Phoebe," Nina stated in a subdued tone. "He never recovered from the shock."

"I'm sorry," Allison told her. "This has been such a tragedy for you. I'll not bother you any longer." She started from the room.

"Where will you go?" Nina called, and the young woman halted at the foyer entrance and looked back at her. "The asylum burned down; you can't return there."

Allison shook her head emphatically. "I'll never return to that place or to any place like it. They'll have to kill me first."

"What will you do?"

"I don't know." Allison shrugged. "They're searching for missing patients, so I'll have to get out of the city or find a place to hide. Maybe they'll think I perished in the blaze." She smiled. "I'll be all right, Mrs. Salomon. And your secret will be safe with me, as I'm sure mine will be with you." Nodding, she turned and walked briskly to the front door.

"Just a minute!" Nina cried out, hurrying across the foyer to where Allison was standing by the open door. "You can't go out there like that." She waved a hand in front of Allison's threadbare coat. "It looks as if you begged it off a ragman."

"I lifted it from a refuse heap," she sheepishly admitted. "I couldn't very well walk around like this." She pulled aside the flaps of the coat to reveal a coarse muslin skirt and blouse of the type worn by asylum patients.

"Someone will surely find you—and then who knows what will happen?"

"I'll be careful."

"But you don't have to go," Nina proclaimed. "You can stay right here."

"Here?" Allison said dubiously, looking around the foyer. "But your children . . ."

"My son Maurice and his wife are staying with my oldest son, Jacob, at his town house. Only my daughter Rachel lives at home, and she's away for a few days. I'm all alone, save for the help."

"But I couldn't—"

"I insist." Nina reached past her and closed the door.

"I really don't know if this is a good—"

"At least for the night," Nina cut in. "It's late, and you've nowhere to go. Tomorrow we can decide what you should do."

"If you're certain . . ."

"Then it's decided," Nina declared. She smiled warmly as she took Allison's arm and led her across the room toward the wide marble staircase that led upstairs. "First we'll get you a warm bath, and then we'll find you some more suitable clothing."

"You're too kind," Allison said, shaking her head and smiling up at the taller woman.

"But you're Phoebe's friend; I'm only doing what she would expect of her mother."

"You must miss her very much," Allison commented as they started side-by-side up the stairway.

"Yes," Nina murmured, her thoughts momentarily drifting to the recent past. She glanced at the young blond-haired woman holding on to her arm and sighed contentedly. She almost spoke Phoebe's name and had to remind herself that this lost, blue-eyed creature was some other mother's daughter. "Yes. I miss her so very much," she whispered as she led Allison upstairs, to Phoebe's room.

Phoebe Salomon felt herself becoming lighter, until she was floating upward through some dark, oppressive abyss. She did not know where she had been, nor where she was going, but suddenly the air that had been so heavy and suffocating became fluid, and she eagerly drank it in.

She heard faint sobbing in the distance and turned toward the sound, allowing herself to be pulled to it. As the crying drew closer, it also grew more gentle, until it was but a hushed sigh that escaped from her own lips.

In front of her the blackness parted, revealing a strong but flickering flame of light. The background lightened with an amber glow, which slowly took material form. Phoebe recognized the cool luster of polished silver, the sleek curves of lacquered wood, the sighing folds of silk cloth rustling gently overhead in some unfelt breeze.

Suddenly she realized that her eyes were open and she was looking up at the canopy of a bed in a room lit only by a single candle. She had no idea where she was, nor where she had been, only that she had been asleep or unconscious and had awakened in an unfamiliar room.

Phoebe felt a rush of panic. This was not her bedroom, yet it was somehow peaceful and secure. She also realized it was not the cold, barren cell she had occupied—and with that thought came the sudden remembrance of her incarceration in the Presidio Asylum for Incurables.

"Where am I?" she blurted weakly, trying to rise but discovering that her body was drained of all strength.

"Please . . . you rest," a soft, urgent voice called in a curious, high-pitched drone. Phoebe heard the shuffling of slippered feet approaching across a wooden floor, and then a small, round face appeared overhead, the complexion almond, the skin around the dark eyes stretched at the corners.

"Wh—who are you?" Phoebe asked, squinting up at the young woman, who she now realized was Chinese.

"You rest now," the woman whispered in a thick Oriental accent. "I get help."

The woman started to pull back, but Phoebe reached out and grabbed the sleeve of the woman's black robe. Looking down at her own right hand clenching the material, Phoebe thought it strange that her crippled arm had effortlessly responded when the rest of her body was unable to move.

"Where am I?" she repeated, her voice gaining strength.

"Please—you wait. I get help."

Phoebe was unable to resist as the Chinese woman pried her fingers from the sleeve and then disappeared across the room. She heard a door open and close and the sound of footsteps receding into the distance.

Again Phoebe tried to rise, but now even her right arm was too weak to react. She could turn her head, however, and was able to make out her surroundings. She was in what appeared to be a large bedroom, though the light cast by the single candle on the stand beside the bed was too faint to determine its size. Beside the candle was a porcelain Oriental vase, and just beyond it was some sort of writing desk, with several round-tipped brushes standing in a cloisonné cup.

As she glanced around the room, Phoebe realized that all the furnishings were Chinese, including the white silk canopy over the black lacquer bed. Then with a start she saw that she was wearing a blue robe, embroidered in gold with an Oriental floral motif. Her blond hair had been painstakingly brushed out, as soft as the finest silk and smelling as fresh as a spray of wildflowers.

Just then the door reopened and a rotund, bald-headed man with a braided queue entered, dressed in a long purple robe. She recognized at once that he was the Chinese man who had come to her rescue at the pier. *But when?* she asked herself as the man approached and lit a lantern on a carved lacquer dresser to the right of the bed, then blew out the candle. *And why?*

"Are you feeling better?" the man asked in flawless English, his thick lips crooking into a smile as he came closer and leaned down over her. Clasping his hands together, he drummed his stubby fingers and arched his eyebrows while awaiting her reply. When she did not answer, he continued, "You slept all day and into the night. You gave us quite a worry last night."

"I . . . I don't remember," she said weakly. She looked beyond him and saw that the young woman in the black robe had returned and was standing just inside the doorway. Phoebe figured that she must be a servant of this man in the luxuriant purple robe.

"Do you remember last night? The men who bothered you?" he asked. When she gave a slight nod, he added, "They will bother you no more."

"Where am I?" she asked.

"In my house." He gave a low bow. "May you think of it as your own."

The man turned to the petite young woman at the doorway and spoke to her in Chinese. She bowed and walked to the far side of the room, where she stood in the shadows preparing something at a table.

"My name is Sung Chien." He bowed again. "And by what name are you called?"

"I . . ." Phoebe's voice trailed off. She looked up at the man, uncertain of whether or not to confide in him. Then she closed her eyes and turned away.

"Ah, then I shall continue to call you Liu—the Stranger. You are hungry, perhaps, little Liu?" he asked, and she shook her head. "But you are tired, of course." He circled the foot of the bed to the other side. "You were quite fevered, and the—how do you call him?—the doctor said you will need much sleep."

Sung Chien turned to the woman across the room and clapped his hands. She hurried over and placed a small porcelain cup in his outstretched palm. Again he spoke to her in Chinese, and she bowed respectfully and returned to her place by the open door.

"The doctor made this to soothe your sleep," Sung Chien said as he approached the bed and held forth the cup.

Phoebe looked skeptically at the cup, which contained several ounces of milky liquid, then up at Sung Chien.

"Don't worry," he said with a smile, lifting her head from

the pillow slightly and holding the cup to her lips. "We will not hurt you. We helped you, remember?"

Phoebe stared down at the cup again, then finally nodded and opened her mouth slightly. As he touched the cup to her lips and tilted it, she took a sip and winced at the acrid taste.

"You must drink it all," he implored, holding the cup closer as she turned her head away. She frowned but allowed him to serve her the remainder of the medicine. "Very good," he declared after she had downed the contents. "You will sleep better now, Liu, my little stranger, and in the morning we shall speak again."

Indeed, Phoebe began to feel quite drowsy, and she looked up at the man but had trouble seeing him clearly. She could tell he was smiling down at her, but then he turned to the woman at the door and said something in a singsongy babble that Phoebe could not understand. She tried to focus, but the woman separated into two, then flowed back into one and floated off into the distance.

Phoebe narrowed her eyes and concentrated on the figure above her. She saw two heads, two long braided queues spinning through the air as he turned toward her. The double image shattered into four and then eight, and then everything turned as milky white as the potion she had been forced to consume.

Phoebe struggled to speak but forgot what she was trying to say. She felt herself tumbling into the darkness, returning to the heavy, suffocating abyss. Something brushed her cheek ever so delicately, a caressing hand or perhaps the whisper of a breeze. There was a hushed sigh, a pleasured moan, and then the silent, yearning cry that welled up within her, unable to escape her lips. She gave herself over to the darkness, until even the yearning faded, and she disappeared into the abyss.

Sung Chien continued to stroke the lovely woman's cheek as she drifted into a deep, forgetful sleep. It was a sleep induced not by the medicines of the herbal healer Hsiao Ch'u but by the opiated potion prepared by the young *niu yung* at

THE DECEIT

Sung Chien's command. He sighed again at the velvety feel of her smooth, pale skin, as white as precious ivory, as delicate as a porcelain doll.

When Sung Chien saw that she was soundly asleep, he turned to confirm that the *niu yung* had closed the door upon leaving. Sitting down on the edge of the bed beside the woman, he pulled the blanket to her waist. For a few moments he watched the gentle rise and fall of her chest. Then he leaned over and untied her robe at the neck, pulling it aside just enough to reveal the swell of her breasts. He started to reach for the second tie but withdrew his hand and just sat staring with pleasure.

After a few minutes, Sung Chien rose, backed away, and halted, looking toward the foot of the bed. When he had pulled the blanket to her waist, it had left her right leg partially exposed, and his gaze locked on her well-turned calf and ankle. The blanket was still draped across her feet, and he found his eyes drawn to them.

Sung Chien moistened his dry lips as he walked toward the foot of the bed and stared at her. He reached down, hesitated, then drew in a breath and lifted the blanket from her feet. Dropping to his knees, he lovingly placed one of his palms against her left sole and cupped the top of her foot with his other hand. He whispered something in his own language as he softly caressed her foot. Leaning forward, he parted his lips and pressed them to her big toe, taking it into his mouth.

As Sung Chien kissed and tasted each of her toes, his eyes closed and his throat purred faintly. He was so enraptured that he did not hear the doorknob turn or the door open. A woman stood with her right hand leaning on the jamb, her left gripping a thin bamboo cane. This was not the *niu yung* but a woman of Sung Chien's age, her neck beginning to sag and wrinkle, her face gaunt and lined.

The woman had a curiously hollow expression as she looked into the room, apparently not comprehending the scene in front of her. But then her eyes widened and grew

101

more animated, as if touched by a young, angry fire. Her hand clenched the cane more tightly, and her formerly impassive eyes narrowed with shock and rage. Still, she remained silent, watching from behind as Sung Chien slowly rose and pulled the blanket over the Occidental woman's feet.

Sung Chien walked over to the dresser, turned down the wick of the lantern, and left it burning low. When he turned to leave the room, he stopped abruptly, struck by the apparition in the doorway. His eyes quickly adjusted to the pale lantern light, and he recognized the woman. With a sharp gasp he raised a hand to speak, then lowered it and stood looking at her with hunched shoulders and a crestfallen expression.

The woman shook her head sadly but said nothing. Instead she stared down at her own misshapen feet, which had been bound in the fashion of the upper classes when she was a child, causing the bones to break as she grew larger and leaving her feet so hideously hooflike and deformed that they now were barely larger than her ankles.

With a bitter frown, the woman switched the cane to her right hand and turned away from the room. Resting her left hand against the wall and teetering precariously between it and the cane, she hobbled down the hall.

Six

IT WAS JUST AFTER TEN AT NIGHT AS NINA SALOMON PACED the floor of her bedroom, pausing on occasion to examine her reflection in the dressing-table mirror and voice her troubled thoughts.

"You did the right thing," she said without enthusiasm. "You're helping a poor soul in trouble."

She started to nod, then shook her head and walked away. "Who am I fooling?" she asked, throwing her hands in the air and then folding them across her chest. "You just don't want her to get caught out on the streets and wind up telling the police God-knows-what about Phoebe."

She spun around and returned to the dressing table. This time she dropped down in the chair and rested her elbows on the table, her hands folded in front of her chin. "It doesn't matter why you did it," she told herself. "You had no other choice. You needed time . . . time to figure out what to do." She slammed her fists down on the table. "Damn!" she blurted, closing her eyes and lowering her head. "What if she tells someone? What if they find out?"

Flattening her palms on the table and drawing in a calming breath, she looked back in the mirror and forced a smile. "She won't tell anyone; she wouldn't," Nina proclaimed with growing conviction. "She knows I could turn her in if she ever did. I could have her sent back."

Nina's smile was more genuine now. "Yes, she'll keep her promise. I'll see to it she does. . . . But how?" Her smile was edged with concern as she rose from the seat. "If only I could be certain of what to do," she whispered, shaking her head.

"Damien . . ." she intoned, her eyes widening. "Damien will know what to do."

Nina stood there for a few minutes, debating whether to call him on the phone or visit him at his hotel—and whether to do so tonight or wait until morning.

"Damien," she breathed again, looking toward the glass doors that fronted the balcony leading to the backyard. If only he would appear right now, she told herself. He'd know the right way to deal with this Allison Grant.

Suddenly coming to a decision, she hurried across the room to her cedar wardrobe. Yanking it open, she began to pore through it, pulling out first one and then another dress and tossing them onto the bed.

A half hour later, Nina was standing just outside the carriage house, wearing a brown evening dress with a rather plunging neckline only barely concealed by black lace. A knit cape covered her puffed, half-length sleeves.

"Hurry, now, Michael," she prodded the family coachman, who ten minutes before had been awakened in the apartment at the back of the carriage house.

"Just about ready, ma'am," he promised as he frantically attached the final leather trace that hitched the pair of gray mares to the black phaeton. A few minutes later he led the team from the carriage house, then set the carriage brake and offered his hand to help his mistress aboard.

"Thank you, Michael," she said as she took her seat facing forward at the rear of the coach.

"Shall I raise the top for you?" He indicated the pair of leather canopies that could be raised from behind the facing seats and connected in the middle overhead, enclosing the passenger compartment.

"Not tonight. The fresh air will do me good."

"Yes, ma'am," he replied, climbing up to the driver's seat at the front. "Where would you like to go?"

"The Baldwin Hotel."

The young coachman snatched up the whip from the holder alongside his seat, then laced the reins through the fingers of his right hand and released the brake. Popping the whip in the air, he clucked lightly, and the horses started off at a brisk walk down the drive.

The Baldwin Hotel, at the corner of Market and Powell streets, was an impressive six-story stone building with a mansard roof, capped with a dome over the corner entrance. The hotel and neighboring Baldwin Theater, constructed by the colorful E. J. "Lucky" Baldwin, dominated the city's theater life. Lucky Baldwin spared no expense for his often famous and sometimes infamous guests. Only the finest imported furnishings were used, and many of the rooms sported private bathrooms, complete with oversized zinc bathtubs, considered the height of luxury.

When Nina Salomon's phaeton pulled up in front of the canopied corner entrance, she told the coachman to wait for her while she visited a friend. Climbing out, she hurried inside and walked briskly across the cavernous lobby, so as not to catch the eye of any patrons who might know her.

She headed directly up the stairs to the second floor. Seeking out room two hundred forty-two, she hesitated only a moment before rapping lightly on the door. There was no response, so she knocked again, this time more forcefully. After a third, even louder knock, she heard a door open and close from somewhere inside the room, and then a voice called, ''Just a moment.''

Seconds later the lock turned, the door was pulled open, and Damien Picard peered out into the hall. Upon seeing Nina, he stammered her name and said, ''What are you doing here? Is everything all right?''

He was dressed in a blue plaid robe, and Nina saw that his blond hair was mussed and wet, as if he had just stepped from the bath. ''I'm sorry,'' she apologized. ''I didn't mean to disturb you, but you said to come if there was any kind of problem at all.''

''What's wrong?'' he asked in concern, pulling the door open wider.

''Can I come in?'' She looked over his shoulder and into the room. The large bed was still made, confirming that he had been taking a bath and had not yet retired for the night.

''Why, yes, certainly,'' he said a bit tentatively as he backed from the door and ushered her into the room. He closed the door and turned to face her. ''Now, what's troubling you?''

''You were in the bath?'' she inquired, looking around the room and seeing doors on both side walls. A trail of water indicated he had come from the door on the left.

He cinched his robe tighter and smiled. ''Yes. But surely that's not why you came. What happened?''

''Something *has* happened,'' she admitted as she removed her shoulder cape and draped it over an upholstered chair beside the door. ''It's about Phoebe.''

She hesitated, and he stepped closer and took her arm. ''What is it?'' he asked. ''You can tell me.''

She nodded and continued, ''Someone came to the house tonight. Someone who knew Phoebe.''

''Yes?'' he pressed when she again hesitated.

''Oh, Damien—it was someone from . . . from the asylum,'' she exclaimed, shaking her head and choking back her tears.

"Whatever do you mean? How could someone know about Phoebe? She wasn't even admitted under her real—"

"It was another patient—a young woman Phoebe's age." Nina gripped his arms. "They were in the same room for a while, and she learned Phoebe's real name."

"But how could she? Phoebe couldn't even talk."

"She did once—in her sleep."

"Are you certain?"

"This woman found out her name, didn't she?" Nina looked down and shook her head in distress. "What if she tells someone? What if they found out what happened to my dear little Phoebe?" She finally began to sob and stammered, "Oh, Damien, what am I going to do?"

Damien took her in his arms and held her close. "It will be all right, Nina. I promise you."

As he stroked her hair and whispered soothing words, Nina clutched the damp hair at the back of his neck and cried softly on his shoulder. She was comforted in his sure, powerful grip, and slowly she felt herself growing calmer. When she finally stopped crying, she relaxed her hold around his neck and pulled back slightly, suddenly conscious of how very close they were standing.

"I . . . I'm sorry." Letting go of his neck, she rested her hands on his arms but made no effort to remove his hands from around her waist. "You've been so kind, and this is really not your concern."

"I'm concerned with anything that troubles you," he replied, fixing her with his most devastating smile. "Now, I don't want you to worry about this. Together we'll figure out a solution."

Nina returned his smile and nodded.

"Who exactly is this woman? Did she say?"

"Her name is Allison Grant. She's really very nice."

"And you say she's a patient?"

"Yes—but I don't think she deserved to be there. Her step-father sounds like an odious man. He had her committed to cover the fact that he was . . . well . . . taking advantage of her.''

''I understand. But you only have her word on this, isn't that right?''

''There's something about her . . . I trust her.''

''That's all right, Nina, but we have to go on more than just trust. Did she say anything more about herself?''

''Only that her family lives in Los Angeles. And that her stepfather made it look as though she was a liar and a thief to get her committed.''

Damien released his hold and pulled away. ''Allison Grant, you say.'' He walked to a small writing table beside the bed and picked up a pencil. As he jotted the name on a slip of paper, he continued, ''I have a few friends in Los Angeles who should be able to discreetly verify her story.'' Putting down the pencil, he walked back toward Nina and stopped a few feet away, near the foot of the bed. ''Now, where is this Allison person now?''

''At my house.''

His right eyebrow rose slightly. ''You left her there alone?''

''I didn't know what else to do,'' she declared. ''But I waited until I was sure she was asleep before coming. I had to talk to you—in person—before the morning. I had to know if I'm doing the right thing.''

''Then you've invited her to stay,'' he concluded.

''Just for the night. But I'm thinking of letting her stay longer,'' she admitted. ''I don't want to send her back if there's nothing wrong with her. And if I make her leave and she's apprehended, what's to keep her from telling what she knows?''

''You have a point,'' Damien acknowledged. ''At least under your roof you have some control over her. But can you be sure she won't tell your family about Phoebe?''

''She won't,'' Nina stated emphatically. ''She knows I could turn her in if she did.''

"That's right—which also rules out her trying to blackmail you. But how will you explain her presence?"

"Phoebe once attended a boarding school in Boston, and I thought we'd pretend they met there and that Allison came to visit without realizing Phoebe had passed away."

"Excellent. You should continue to befriend this woman, while I check her story and figure out how to make sure she never tells what she knows."

"Then it's all right? I've done the right thing?"

"You've covered every corner. You didn't really need me at all." He raised his arms and shrugged his shoulders, smiling broadly.

"That's not true," she protested, coming closer and taking hold of his hands. "I don't know how I would have handled all of this without you."

"Thank you, Nina." He squeezed her hands. "That means a lot to me."

She stared into his cool blue eyes, trying to read the unspoken words. "Why?" she finally asked. "You hardly know me, Damien."

"I know enough." Releasing her hands, he took hold of her slender waist. "And I care enough." He leaned forward and lightly kissed her cheek. They stood there in each other's arms for a moment, and then Damien raised his right hand and cupped her chin. "You'd best be running along. It must be after eleven, and I haven't even finished my bath."

She looked up at him expectantly and started to speak, then held back and lowered her eyes.

Releasing her chin, Damien patted her cheek and said, "I'll call you as soon as I learn anything about this Allison woman. Now, I want you to go home and not worry about anything. All right?"

Nina nodded, then looked up at him. She felt his right hand moving from her cheek, his left hand releasing her waist. Her lips parted, and she tried to inhale, but the breath caught in her throat. She felt something rushing through her, like a wind alternately cold and hot that made her body shiver and tingle with excitement.

When Damien started to move past her toward the door, Nina reached up and touched the side of his face, causing him to pause and look down at her. His expression was questioning and uncertain—almost boyish. And he was so exceedingly handsome.

With a sigh, she threw her arms around his neck, her fingers caressing the damp curls of his hair as she pulled him to her and kissed him full on the lips. She moaned softly as their mouths opened and their tongues met, tentatively at first, then with growing ardor.

Nina's right hand slid down along his chest and inside the robe. She rubbed and pressed his skin, feeling the muscles quiver as she touched his abdomen. Her hand slipped out momentarily and searched for the cloth belt cinched around his waist, her fingers deftly loosening and undoing the knot.

"Damien . . ." she murmured as she drew the robe over his shoulders and let it drop to the floor. She stepped toward him, pushing him backward as her mouth moved down along his neck, her teeth gently teasing and biting his skin, her hands kneading his powerful shoulders and back and then gripping his bare, firm buttocks.

Nina felt Damien's hands working their way down her back, unfastening her dress hooks and then reaching down and lifting her skirt. She continued to push him backward until they bumped into the foot of the bed. Leaning into him, she climbed on top of him as he fell back onto the mattress.

"Take me," she whispered, arching her back as he pulled the dress forward off her shoulders. He reached up and undid the four hooks at the front of her corset, pulling it away and letting it slide off her back. As he began to massage her breasts through the thin material of her chemise, she slid her hands down along his abdomen, her fingers exploring him, her body yearning to feel his desire.

"Yes . . ." she moaned as she touched him, took hold of him, felt him respond to her caress.

THE DECEIT

Shortly after Nina had driven off in the phaeton, Allison Grant had taken lantern in hand and made her way down from Phoebe's third-floor room, starting on her own exploration—this one of the empty bedrooms in the Salomon mansion on Nob Hill. Her search began in Nina's bedroom.

Allison moved quickly and expertly through the room, glancing outside every once in a while to make sure the coach had not returned as she checked the jewelry boxes and mentally noted which ones held the most valuables. Turning to the large mahogany bureau on the left-hand wall, she searched the drawers and discovered in the top center one a paperboard box that contained a considerable amount of cash. The money was stuffed in it so haphazardly that she was convinced Nina had no idea how much was there. With a smile, she decided to relieve her hostess of some of the bills, and she stuffed them into the pocket of the robe she had borrowed from Phoebe's room.

Closing the box, she returned it to its original position in the drawer, telling herself she could always return for the remaining contents, along with the jewelry, should she be forced to leave the premises. For now, however, she was enjoying the idea of staying in such a lavish mansion, where she would sleep between silk sheets and dine from the finest china and silver.

Picking up the lantern, Allison started to leave. As she glanced around the room a final time, something caught her eye—a shadow cast by the lantern along the upper left face of the mahogany bureau. The bureau had three drawers across the top and four full-length drawers stacked below them. The center top drawer, which contained the box of money, was deeper than the side ones, each of which was topped by a strip of carved molding to make up the difference. The shadow that attracted her attention was along the left-hand molding, which was recessed deeper than the drawers or the molding on the right.

Allison walked back to the bureau and placed the lantern

on top of it. She touched the strip of molding over the left drawer and pushed on it, surprised when it gave slightly and then returned to its original position. She pressed a few more times, and each time the molding slid back and forth, almost as if on a spring. The right molding reacted in the same way.

"A drawer," she breathed, smiling at the discovery that a narrow drawer was hidden behind each molding strip.

She tried to push the left molding harder, thinking there might be some kind of catch that opened the drawer. When this did not work, she opened the drawer below and felt along the underside of the wood above. Her finger struck a small metal button, which she pressed, and the hidden drawer popped open.

Moving the lantern closer, Allison pulled out the secret drawer and placed it on top of the bureau. It was less than two inches deep and was lined with purple velvet. It contained photographs taken quite a few years ago. In one of them Nina, probably in her late teens, was standing in front of a store with a pair of older men, who were pointing to an overhead sign that read *San Francisco Emporium, Isidore Salomon and Abraham Hallinger, Proprietors*. Allison recognized one of the men from a framed picture on the bureau, and she assumed he was Nina's father. The other man, a burly fellow with a bald head and graying walrus mustache, had to be Hallinger, apparently Salomon's partner at the time.

As she examined the other photos, it struck her odd that virtually every one was of this other man, sometimes alone and sometimes with Nina. One photo was especially intriguing and confirmed that the man was Abraham Hallinger. It appeared to be a family portrait, showing him with a heavyset woman and a young boy, and on the back someone had written: *Abraham and Gertrude Hallinger, and Eaton, age eight*. The curious thing was that the faces of the woman and the boy had been obliterated with black ink.

The only other items in the drawer were a manila envelope and a packet of letters tied with a ribbon. She flipped through the letters and saw that each was addressed to Rachel Salomon from a man named Timothy Price, the return address being Harvard College in Cambridge. They had been sent in the fall of 1891, almost five years before. Most curious was that only the first three had been opened and read; the remaining half dozen were still sealed.

Untying the packet and opening the first letter, she quickly scanned it and realized this Timothy Price had been a suitor of Nina's older daughter, Rachel, and that he had gone off to Harvard to complete his studies. It was a typical love letter from a smitten young man, and in it he gave Rachel his address and urged her to write back at once. The second letter professed continued love but asked why she had not written. In the third letter, he was noticeably perturbed by Rachel's lack of response. The other letters were unopened, and Allison could only guess that they also begged Rachel to reply, until finally this Timothy Price gave up hope and stopped writing to her altogether.

Allison carefully retied the packet and returned it to the back of the drawer. Then she slid out the manila envelope, on which someone had written the name Jacob Salomon—Nina's oldest son. Turning over the envelope, she undid the string closure, opened the flap, and removed some letters and a pile of official-looking documents, each dated over the course of several months in late 1868 and early 1869. Along with the documents was a newspaper clipping from March of that year, announcing the birth of a boy named Jacob to Nina Salomon and her husband of less than a year, Charles Roth Salomon. The article mentioned that Nina was the only child of mercantile magnate Isidore Salomon and that her husband, Charles Roth, had changed his name upon their marriage to ensure that the Salomon legacy be continued into the next generation.

Putting down the newspaper clipping, Allison spread out the documents and began reading them, her expression growing more animated as she pieced together a history twenty-seven years past—a history Nina Salomon had been forced to bury away in a secret bureau drawer.

* * *

Damien Picard stood in his robe at his hotel-room door, holding Nina's knit cape. She finished adjusting her skirt and came up in front of him so that he could put the wrap over her shoulders. Reaching around her from behind, he closed the buttons, then stood holding her shoulders, his lips nuzzling her neck.

"Are you upset?" he whispered.

"Not at all, Damien," she said firmly, turning to face him. "I wanted to. You saw that." She smiled up at him and gently touched his cheek.

"Yes, I did." He took her hand and touched it to his lips. "And it was wonderful."

"Do you mean that?" she asked. "You . . . you don't think less of me, now that . . ."

"How could I?" He lightly kissed her lips. "I think more of you every moment we're together. And I'll be thinking more of you every minute we're apart."

Nina blushed. "I hope that's true."

"You'll see that it is." He kissed her again, then reached over and opened the door a crack. "We'll be together soon. Trust me."

"I do, Damien. But I hate this . . . this having to sneak around."

"I know. But we mustn't act foolishly. You're recently widowed, and you have your reputation to protect. For the time being, we mustn't let anyone see us together—your children especially."

"You're right," Nina conceded with a frown. "But I hate it. I wish I were able to come to you—and that you could come to me—without worrying who might find out."

"Perhaps one day. But for now we'll have to be content with whatever stolen moments we can find." When Nina looked down sadly, he playfully squeezed her chin. "Don't be depressed. Sometimes stolen moments are the sweetest moments of all."

In response, Nina threw her arms around Damien and

hugged him to her. Choking back a tear, she whispered, "Thank you . . . for caring about me." She kissed him tenderly, then pulled away and opened the door wide. "Good night, Damien," she breathed as she slipped through the doorway and headed down the hall.

Damien stood at the door, watching as she rounded the corner and disappeared down the stairs that led to the lobby. With a grin, he closed and locked the door, then turned to survey the room. The bedding was a rumpled mass of blankets and sheets, and there were still wet footsteps leading from the closed bathroom door.

"Damn," he muttered, as if suddenly recalling something he had forgotten.

Walking briskly across the hardwood floor, he yanked open the bathroom door and stepped into the steam-filled room, lit by a pair of electric wall lamps on either side of the gilded mirror above the washstand.

"Did you have fun?" a soft, feminine voice asked.

"I'm sorry," Damien professed, turning and shrugging at the naked woman in the large zinc bathtub. "There was nothing I could—"

"Don't apologize," the woman told him as she sat up from the soapy water.

Damien saw the water running down her firm, ample breasts, watched her nipples become erect in the cooler air as she arched her back and leaned against the rim of the clawfoot tub. With a sigh, he declared, "You're incredibly beautiful, Lydia."

She grinned mischievously. "I'll wager you said the same thing to Mrs. Salomon."

Damien eyed her suspiciously. "You were listening?"

"I couldn't help but hear." Seeing his expression, she added, "Now, don't go pouting. I didn't mind at all. I found it rather exciting just imagining what was going on out there." She ran her hand down her right breast and squeezed it suggestively with her palm. "In fact, I was tempted to come out and join you—if your bedmate didn't also happen to be my employer."

Feigning a frown, he replied, "If you *had,* I'd have dragged you back in here and held you under the water."

"You're just afraid you might not have been able to handle the two of us," Lydia taunted.

"I can handle the likes of you any day—or night," he countered, taking a step toward the tub.

"If you're not all used up, that is," she mocked, nodding toward his groin.

"We'll see who's used up around here."

As Damien approached the tub, he undid the belt at his waist and pulled open his robe.

"Ah, the gentleman rises to the occasion," Lydia cooed, gazing at him admiringly.

Damien started to remove his robe, but Lydia leaned forward from the tub and grabbed both lapels, yanking him toward her. Losing his balance, he managed to spin around and tumbled rear-end first on top of her. As he sank into the soapy water, they both burst into laughter, which quickly transformed to more passionate sounds as he rolled over and she deftly peeled off his soaking robe and slid underneath him, her head barely out of the water, her calves gripping the rim on either side of the tub.

Seven

AFTER LEAVING DAMIEN PICARD'S ROOM AT THE BALDWIN Hotel, Nina Salomon hurried down the staircase and started across the lobby. Though it was nearly midnight, the large, well-appointed room was still busy with patrons, mostly male, who stood talking in small groups throughout the room or caroused in front of the entrance to the massive bar, which could serve more than one hundred revelers at a time.

Nina kept her head low as she walked briskly toward the front doors, not wanting to be seen. She bumped into one gentleman, who stepped aside and politely apologized. Glancing at the stranger and nodding perfunctorily, she hurried on, eager to be back in her carriage heading home.

"Nina?" a voice called out.

Afraid that she had just been recognized, Nina shuddered but continued walking.

"Nina Salomon!" the voice exclaimed more urgently.

Recognizing the voice, Nina came to a halt with a start. She drew in a breath, turned around, and said with a warm smile, "Jacob." She sounded quite calm, but inside she was churning with the fear that somehow her eldest son had discovered what she had been doing in Damien Picard's room.

"Whatever are you doing here?" Jacob asked as he approached.

As her mind raced in search of a reasonable answer, Nina noted that he had on the same gray vested suit he had been wearing when he visited her that afternoon, but his derby was nowhere in sight. She smelled the faint odor of whiskey and guessed that he had been in the bar with friends all the while she was upstairs with Damien.

"Why, I was looking for you, Jacob," she finally replied.

"At midnight?"

"Is it midnight already?" she asked innocently.

Jacob looked at her curiously. "How did you know I was here, anyway? I never told you I'm staying at the Baldwin until Maurice and Belle find their own place."

"Why, I'm certain that you did," she insisted. "This very afternoon—didn't you mention the Baldwin?" When he shook his head, she added, "But you must have. How else would I have known to look here? . . . Unless, of course, you mentioned it to Cameron."

"It's not important," he said, waving it off. "Why did you come looking for me?"

Stalling, Nina looked around at the crowded room. "Is there somewhere we can talk—away from everybody?"

Jacob glanced around and nodded. Taking his mother's arm, he led her to one of the private sitting rooms off the main lobby. Finding one that was empty, he showed her inside. Sitting beside her on the sofa, he asked, "Now, what's this all about?"

"I've been considering what you said this afternoon, and I've come to a decision."

"About Maurice?" he said, his tone skeptical.

"Yes, and about you and Rachel, as well." She looked down and gave a convincing frown. "I'm afraid I've acted horribly toward all of you."

"And toward Maurice's new wife," he gently prodded.

She reluctantly nodded. "I suppose I haven't been totally fair—but really, everything has been in such a turmoil since the death of your father."

"And Phoebe," he reminded her.

"Of course." She sighed. "It's a wonder I've survived any of it at all."

As if impatient with her self-pity, he asked, "So what is this decision you've come to?"

"I want things to be the way they were, Jacob." She looked up at him and smiled weakly.

"Things weren't that great before," he pointed out, as if goading her.

"But they certainly were better."

"And how do you plan to get things back to those good old days?" he inquired a bit facetiously.

"I thought I'd start by speaking with Maurice. That's why I came."

"Why didn't you just go to my town house, then?"

Nina looked at him askance. "That isn't the way these things should be done," she chided. "I want you to tell Maurice that I'll entertain a visit from him if he desires."

"What about Merribelle?"

Nina inwardly cringed at the expected comment but replied calmly, "Yes, if he insists, though I think this first meeting should be between mother and son alone. Later we can find a more appropriate time to welcome his wife into the family."

"And his son," Jacob pressed.

Nina's eyes widened, and her features pulled back into a tight grimace. "I will not have that . . . that infant under my roof. Is that clear? Maurice can come alone—or not at all."

"All right, Nina. We won't talk about it now," he replied, apparently deciding it would be better to take this first small victory and not prematurely force the issue.

"If you'd be so kind as to show me to my coach . . . ." She extended her hand and waited for her son to rise and help her from the sofa.

As she stood beside him and took his arm, Jacob politely asked, "Would you care to join me for a drink before you go?"

"No, thank you. I didn't realize how late it was. I should be getting home."

She followed Jacob out across the lobby and through the front door to the waiting coach. Michael had raised the leather top, and as Nina climbed inside, she looked through the window at Jacob and said, "Thank you for visiting this afternoon. I know I've been difficult, but I do want things to be better."

"I know you do." He leaned through the open door and impulsively kissed her hand. "And I know how difficult it's been for you since Father's death. After so many years, it can't be easy being alone, with no one there to comfort or protect you."

Feeling more than a twinge of guilt, Nina gave a slight wince but covered it by saying, "At least I have my children."

"I know we haven't been much comfort to you of late. But if you're willing to try, so am I—and I'm certain that holds true for Maurice and Rachel." He kissed her hand again, then stepped back from the coach and closed the door. "I'll tell Maurice what you said," he pledged, smiling and signaling the coachman to proceed.

As the phaeton pulled away, Nina huddled into the corner of the seat and folded her arms in front of her, suddenly very cold. She took a few deep breaths and let out a sigh, then closed her eyes and leaned against the padded leather backrest.

What have I done? she asked herself, uncertain of whether she was referring to her assignation with Damien Picard or her pledge to smooth things over with Maurice and eventually accept Merribelle into the family.

But not Phoebe's bastard child! she vowed. *Not Eaton Hallinger's little bastard get!*

* * *

THE DECEIT

Phoebe Salomon bolted upright in bed and found herself panting breathlessly in the middle of a dimly lit room. She could not discern her surroundings and at first thought she was in her cell at the Presidio Asylum for Incurables. But the mattress was far too soft, and across the room there was a lamp burning, though faintly. She wondered if she could be back at home, but then her eyes continued to adjust to the light, and she realized she was in the same room where she had awakened earlier.

Leaning back against the pillows, she tried to focus her thoughts. Slowly it all came back to her—the escape from the asylum, the altercation on the pier, the rescue by a Chinese man and his servants, the ride to his home somewhere in Chinatown, the sickness and dizziness she had been feeling ever since her arrival. The last thing she could recall was waking up and being given some sort of medicine, then falling back asleep. Everything else was blackness.

No . . . there were nightmares, she suddenly remembered as fleeting images came back to her—images that had roused her from a drug-induced sleep. She could not quite make out the images, but she felt the overwhelming sense of being violated in some way, and it made her shudder with disgust.

As she grew more used to the low light of the oil lamp, she saw someone hunched over as if asleep in an upholstered armchair several feet away from the bed. Squinting, she recognized the young servant woman who had been in the room when she awoke earlier.

Glancing at the window, Phoebe guessed that it was the middle of the night, though she had no idea if it was the same night as before. She knew that a number of hours had passed, because other than feeling a sense of gnawing hunger, she seemed surprisingly strong and rested.

Pulling aside the blankets, she dropped her legs over the side of the bed and sat up. She stayed there a moment, feeling a bit dizzy but not at all nauseated. As she became more sure of herself, she pushed against the mattress and rose to her feet, grabbing hold of the footpost to steady herself.

Looking around the room, she reached up and tossed her long blond hair over her shoulder. She did so with her lame right hand, and the movement had been both effortless and without pain. She looked at the scar on her forearm, where it had been mangled by the cable car and sewn by the doctors, then flexed the fingers. They were stiff but could be clenched and unclenched at will.

With a smile, Phoebe took her first tentative steps away from the bed. Moving as quietly as possible, she walked across the room, taking care not to awaken the young servant. She returned to the bed, then crossed the room and came back a second time. When she was satisfied that she was steady enough on her feet, she headed toward the door. She was curious about where she was and who these people were.

Coming abreast of the door, she tried the knob with her right hand. When it would not turn, she tried with her left hand, thinking that perhaps her injured arm was still too weak. But the knob would not give; the door was locked. This was curious, but perhaps the custom in Chinese homes. Still, it reminded her of her time at the asylum, and she shuddered at the memory.

Circling the room, she searched the tops of the dresser and tables but found no key. She was about to give up when she realized the young servant might have it. She walked to the chair and debated whether or not to search for a pocket in the woman's black robe. Just then she saw a glimmer of metal and noticed a large brass ring in the woman's lap, partially covered by her arm. Cautiously taking hold of the sleeve, Phoebe moved the arm out of the way. The woman stirred and rolled her head to the opposite side but did not awaken.

Breathing a relieved sigh, Phoebe lifted the ring and saw that it held a single key. She hastened to the door and fumbled with the key until she managed to insert it in the lock. The bolt slid clear, and she turned the knob and opened the door.

Leaving the key in the inside keyhole, Phoebe closed the

door behind her and found herself in the middle of a long hallway. She gazed up and down, wondering in which direction to go, uncertain of what she was looking for. Seeing a faint light to the left, she headed in that direction.

The doors on either side of the hall were open, and as she padded down the hall, she peeked into each room. Apparently the building was long and narrow, for each room had windows on its far side, and enough city light spilled through to afford a sufficient view. One room appeared to be a library of sorts, with several desks in the middle and floor-to-ceiling shelves of books on either side. Across from it was a small sitting room, and just beyond it a bath.

At the end of the hall was a staircase leading down. No corresponding stairway went up, meaning that she was on the top floor, which appeared to be unoccupied by anyone but herself and the servant. As she approached the stairs she noticed that the light was coming from a corridor to the left. Turning down it, she saw a partially open door on the left, through which the light was spilling. As she slowly pushed the door open, she saw a lamp on top of an ebony dresser.

Seeing no one inside, Phoebe opened the door wide and stepped into the small room, which was empty save for the dresser and a thin mattress on the floor. The only other furnishings were a pair of heavy drapes beside a tall window that dominated the far wall. The drape on the left was flapping slightly in the night breeze.

As she stepped farther into the room, the left-hand drape shifted and seemed to separate. Phoebe blinked and tilted her head, focusing on the movement. All at once she realized that the movement was not from a breeze but from someone dressed in material as dark as the drape who was standing against it, holding it with one hand, her back to the door. As the figure moved in front of the window, Phoebe was able to discern the silhouette. It was a woman, one hand raised to the drape, the other clutching a thin cane.

With the hand holding the cane, the woman reached up and turned a clasp on the window, then pushed it outward.

Phoebe, feeling like an intruder, stepped back into the hall and was about to close the door when the woman turned sideways and looked over her shoulder directly at Phoebe. The woman was not aged, yet the years had marked her face with sags and wrinkles. Her eyes, sunk deep in her gaunt face, were curiously devoid of expression. Even her thin smile held no hint of humor or depth.

Phoebe found herself unable to move as she stared at the older woman, who bowed her head slightly and closed her eyes. She then turned back to the window and dropped her cane, which clattered to the floor. Clutching the drapes, she painstakingly raised her right foot and placed it on the low sill. With a grunt, she pulled herself up onto the sill and stood there, hanging on to the drapes and balancing precariously.

Phoebe opened her mouth to speak, but then she noticed the woman's feet and was mesmerized into silence. It was as if the woman had no feet at all, only narrow, hooflike forms that had been jammed into tiny black slippers. Shaking her head in confusion, Phoebe looked back up and saw that the woman had twisted around slightly and was looking at her again. This time the woman's smile was warm and genuine, her expression youthful and content. Again she nodded, and then she turned back to the open window. To Phoebe's astonishment the woman took a single step forward, releasing the drapes as she sailed into the darkness.

Phoebe's body went rigid through what seemed like an interminably long silence, punctuated at last by a distant thud that caused her to jerk with shock. Suddenly chilled, she shook her head and blinked, trying to convince herself she was still dreaming. But the open window in front of her was very real, as were the drapes that hung out over the sill, flapping gently in the breeze.

"My God!" she gasped, willing herself forward. Indeed it seemed like a dream, for she did not sense herself walking but rather the window floating toward her, until the sill was at her knees and she was leaning out, her hands gripping the heavy velvet drapes, her long blond hair spilling over her shoulders and flying in the strengthening wind.

There, in an interior courtyard three stories below, illuminated by a flickering shaft of light from a ground-floor window, a body lay on its back on a concrete walkway, seemingly in peaceful repose. But then the outline of the figure started to expand, flowing out in all directions, until the light glistening across the surface revealed that it was a dark pool of blood spreading from below the head.

Growing dizzy, Phoebe clutched the drapes more tightly and began to gag. She heard the sound of something ripping, then staggered as one of the drapes tore free of the rod and fell. Losing her balance, she almost tumbled through the window, but she caught her knee on the sill and managed to drop to the floor. She knelt there, leaning out the window, gagging and choking, as the heavy drape billowed open, twisting and fluttering slowly downward into the courtyard.

"No!" she shouted, watching aghast as the velvet shroud floated toward the body below. *"No!"* She felt her throat constrict, and she took in a great, gasping breath of air, which came out in a keening shriek that reverberated against the courtyard's four surrounding walls. Again and again she screamed as she clutched the windowsill and stared down at the horrifying sight below.

Additional lamps began to go on, flooding the courtyard with light. There were a number of doors along the four walls, and two of them opened simultaneously, with several people scurrying out and looking up at the source of the commotion. As they pointed up at the window where Phoebe was kneeling, one man began to shout something in Chinese, and their attention shifted to the body lying on the ground and the heavy purple cloth that lay draped nearby over the top of a dwarf pine.

Phoebe's scream turned into a gagging sputter, and she pushed herself back from the windowsill and tried to catch her breath. But she was wheezing and struggling for air, and soon she found herself on her hands and knees, her vision clouding over, her body stiffening and jerking spasmodically.

No! she tried to cry, but her throat had closed completely, and it was all she could do to keep from passing out. The room began to spin, and her heart raced faster and louder, an incessant drumming that was pounding her into unconsciousness. She reached up toward the light of the lamp on the dresser and caught a glimpse of dark-clad figures pushing through the doorway and crowding over her. She rolled over and fell onto her back, but she never felt herself hit the floor. And as she hurtled into the blackness, she wondered if somehow she had tumbled through the window and was sailing down into the courtyard—or if this was merely that dark, familiar abyss.

Eight

"THE CLIFF HOUSE, PLEASE," RACHEL SALOMON CALLED UP to the driver of the hansom cab as she lifted her navy-blue skirt and climbed inside. As Aidan McAuliffe sat down beside her and closed the door, she clasped his hand and exclaimed, "You'll simply love the Cliff House and Sutro Baths—especially the view from Sutro Heights."

"Are you sure you want to go hiking after that breakfast feast Miss Jeffries prepared?" Aidan asked, taking the seat beside her and removing the brown fedora he had worn for the occasion.

"Don't be silly," she chided, patting his hand as the carriage lurched and started down D Street, which bordered the northern edge of Golden Gate Park. "It's only a little hill, and there's the most spectacular view of the ocean and Seal Rocks. Perhaps it will remind you of Scotland."

Aidan squeezed her hand and smiled as he gazed at the way the diffused morning light gave a soft glow to her long copper hair, which was pinned in an upsweep and tucked under a small, navy-blue turban hat, trimmed with silk and velvet flowers. Looking into her penetrating emerald eyes, he whispered, "Scotland will pale by comparison."

"I'm not so sure of that," she replied, shaking her head. "Not with all those mist-shrouded highlands and mysterious lochs."

"Without you at my side anyplace would prove a poor match indeed. Even the Lady of the Lake pales when compared with you." He raised her hand and kissed it.

"You've made me so happy," she whispered, leaning closer and resting her head on his shoulder.

"How? By falling asleep the way I did last night? You must think me a fool."

"I think you nothing of the sort," she declared. "You were exhausted." She nuzzled closer and squeezed his arm. "What I *do* think is that you're the most wonderful man in the world." She leaned up and kissed his cheek.

"Perhaps, but a foolish one, at that. Any other man would have—"

"I don't want another man. I want you . . . and I'm content to wait for you. After all, there's no rush. We've a whole lifetime to fall asleep in each other's arms."

Aidan turned and took Rachel in his arms, and they shared a soft, lingering kiss. Leaning back on the seat, he turned his head toward her and just stared for a few minutes, causing her to blush. "You really are beautiful," he proclaimed.

"I owe it all to Salomon's Emporium," she confessed, sweeping her hands to indicate her outfit.

"I applaud the company purchasing agent. That dress looks marvelous on you."

Raising an eyebrow and adopting the condescending tone of an officious clerk, she protested, "Why, Mr. McAuliffe, this isn't a dress but a Newport."

"A Newport?"

"To be precise, a navy-blue ladies' Newport suit, with double-breasted jacket, tuxedo back, full leg-o'-mutton sleeves, and kick-pleated skirt with organ piping, trimmed with double rows of folded moiré silk on the collar and cuffs, and fashioned of the finest repellent storm serge.'' As she described the outfit, she used her hands to indicate each feature, as if she were a model at one of the Salomon's fashion extravaganzas.

"I'm impressed. You certainly know your Newports."

She grinned. "I'm one of the company purchasing agents, remember?"

"But are you as knowledgeable of men's fashions?" he challenged, looking down at his own suit.

"Let's see. . . ." She rubbed her chin and looked him up and down, then glanced over at the hat on the seat beside him. "Of course that's a soft fur fedora with a wide, corded-silk band," she began. "And the outfit—a single-breasted, three-buttoned cutaway sack suit with round-cornered lapels and over-and-under pockets, made of mixed dark-brown and gray wool cheviot." She looked up at him and smiled. "How did I do?"

"I haven't the slightest idea," he confessed. "It's not even my suit. I had almost nothing when I arrived in town, and Miss Jeffries was kind enough to loan me some things left behind by a guest."

"That won't do," Rachel insisted. "We'll have to pick out a wardrobe for you at Salomon's."

"I shall place myself in your capable hands," he proclaimed. "You obviously know your fashions . . . but you were wrong about something else."

"What's that?"

"It's not the dress—I mean Newport—that makes you beautiful. It's yourself."

"You don't think me too tall and skinny?" She gave a slight pout.

"Certainly not. I'm a modern man; I say to hell with those robust Lillian Russell women with their corset-busting figures and plump necks."

"Then I *am* skinny," she grumped. "Another Sarah Bernhardt."

"And what's wrong with Miss Bernhardt? I hear that

American men throw themselves at her feet.'' He shook his head. ''But no, you're neither Bernhardt nor Russell. You're Rachel Salomon, with a figure as fashionable as an hourglass and a beauty that could light the Tivoli stage without need of a lamp.''

''If you're trying to flatter me, it's working.'' She playfully slapped his arm, and they both laughed.

As the carriage continued alongside the park to the ocean, Aidan and Rachel discussed his appointment to the staff at Pacific Hospital and the work he would be doing there. Until his London murder charge was dropped, he would not be able to obtain the medical certificates he had been forced to leave behind when he fled England. But Dr. Tadeusz Obloy still wanted him to begin work at once, though for the time being he would have to remain under the doctor's supervision and would not be allowed to perform surgery.

''I'll be starting in the morning,'' he told her. ''At least it'll give me an opportunity to gather some funds, which I'll need if I have to return to England to answer escape charges.''

''Surely they won't press charges, now that you've been proved innocent of murder.''

''I'm afraid the British authorities don't take kindly to someone's escaping the Millbank Penitentiary gallows, no matter the reason.''

''Perhaps we can fight extradition—''

''No,'' he cut in. ''If there are charges to be answered, I plan to return to England and face them.''

''Well, if it comes to that, I intend to go with you and testify on your behalf,'' she announced.

''This really isn't your battle.''

''Oh, no? Who's the one who hid you in her cabin all the way across the Atlantic? And who helped you sneak ashore in Nova Scotia?''

''That's why I don't want you to come. You could be charged as an accessory to—''

''Just let them try. Wait till the public learns how you were framed and unjustly convicted. They won't stand by and let you spend another day in prison. Why, if you hadn't escaped when you did, you'd . . ." She was unable to finish.

"I'd be dead," he stated plainly. "But I'm not. And when I finally see my name cleared and can come to you as a free man, I want you to be my wife—if you still want me."

"I'm only sorry we have to wait." She started to rest her head on his arm, then suddenly sat upright and pointed through the forward-facing window of the hansom cab. "There it is!" she exclaimed.

The cab had just turned north onto Ocean Boulevard—popularly known as the Great Highway—a long, flat thoroughfare that ran beside the ocean at the city's western shore. A few blocks ahead the road curved up steeply to what looked like a magnificent white palace, which clung precariously to the edge of a cliff, seemingly on the verge of toppling into the crashing waves below.

"The Cliff House," she intoned almost reverently.

The building resembled a multistoried French chateau, capped by a square tower that had three arched windows on each side and four needlelike spires rising up from the lower corners of its tall, peaked roof. There was a round turret at each corner of the building, and numerous other spires and gables added to the aura of posh European decadence.

As the cab headed along the Great Highway, it passed in front of several large buildings that faced the water, one a massive structure with corner towers that resembled a fortress. Aidan noticed a number of small eateries and even an amusement palace, which boasted shooting galleries and sideshow attractions. One colorfully painted handbill proclaimed *Sarkon, Sword Swallower Extraordinaire, Swallows Electric Light Bulbs, Fires A Gun Barrel While It Is Down His Throat!* Even though it was still early and there were few people walking along the water, Aidan could see that these establishments catered to the throngs that converged on the beach almost every warm, fogless day.

The carriage headed up the incline and came to a halt in front of the Cliff House. Stepping out, Rachel asked the driver to wait for them, then took Aidan's arm and led him across the street, away from the building. Together they climbed a narrow path that wound up through a small forest of imported silver-tipped Australian gum trees to Sutro Heights, the home of Adolph Sutro, who at sixty-six was in his second year as mayor of San Francisco.

"All this land belongs to Mayor Sutro, an old friend of my grandfather's," Rachel explained as they topped the crest and found themselves in front of a white picket fence that bordered the property.

Aidan stared through the fence at the impressive manor house, with its angled tower and widow's walk. The yard was landscaped with dark-green cypresses, box shrubs, and pink geraniums, around which stood numerous white plaster statues of Greek gods and goddesses.

"Back in the fifties, before Mr. Sutro got involved in mining, he and my grandfather were friendly competitors in the mercantile business," she explained, then abruptly grabbed his arm and turned him around to face the ocean. "Just look at this view," she exclaimed.

Aidan gazed down at the impressive Cliff House, then beyond it to the famous Seal Rocks, dotted with cormorants and barking seals.

"What's that over there?" he asked, pointing to a bank of glass buildings, resembling a giant greenhouse, which clung to the promontory just beyond the Cliff House.

"That's the Sutro Baths," she told him. "It contains the largest indoor swimming pool in the world. Mr. Sutro completed it just a few months ago and gave it to the city as a gift." Turning back to the building below them, she continued, "The Cliff House opened at about the same time. That's actually the third Cliff House. Mr. Sutro bought the first one and had it replaced with a somewhat larger one, which burned down on the day after Christmas a year and a half ago. It was only one story high, and he decided to rebuild it on a grander scale."

"He certainly thinks big," Aidan commented.

"He can afford to. It's reputed he owns one-twelfth of the land in San Francisco."

"I'm glad you brought me here," Aidan told her as she leaned back in his arms. "It really is beautiful."

"I love it here; the air is so brisk and salty." She breathed deeply and sighed. "And I love the Cliff House, even though some people think it a bit showy and scandalous."

"Scandalous? I thought it was a hotel and restaurant."

"Yes, it is. And during the day, a woman can sit in the dining room and enjoy a mint julep or a plate of mussels bordelaise without greatly risking her reputation. But after dark . . ." She grinned suggestively.

"Well?" he prodded. "Are you going to tell me?"

"What do you think of a restaurant that advertises private dining rooms for gentlemen and their lady friends? Convention holds that a true lady would never dine in a private room."

"And you disagree, I suppose?"

"It's been my observation that the most enjoyable things in life are also the most scandalous."

"Then we'll have to dine there soon," he proclaimed.

"Grandfather would approve of you." She laughed lightly and nodded. "Nina says he was quite a rake as a young man, though I suspect he remained one right up to the end. He and his friends liked to come at night to the old Cliff House for drinks and a game of cards. Nina claims they used to bring in dancing girls in the most daring costumes; that's why she's sworn never to set foot in that place again. She only admits to having been inside once, in her early teens, when my grandfather brought her to see a woman walk across a tightrope to one of the Seal Rocks."

"I've got it!" Aidan blurted, snapping his fingers and turning Rachel to face him. "We could get married in the Cliff House, and then your mother would be forced to break her oath!"

"Better yet, she might not show up at all."

"We could always induce her to come by arranging for a

tightrope walk to Seal Rocks as part of the festivities,'' he suggested with a grin. Then his expression grew more serious. ''Do you really think she might not come—I don't mean here to the Cliff House, but if we were married somewhere more respectable?''

''I'm not sure. I've learned never to predict what Nina will or will not do.''

''It's me, isn't it?''

''She doesn't really know you.'' Rachel took his hands in her own. ''It's just that . . .'' Her voice trailed off.

''It's just that I'm not from the same walk of life as you.'' He looked down and frowned. ''I'm only a physician, and the most I can hope for is a steady job and modest income. I can't give you . . . all this.'' He swept his arm to indicate the Sutro estate and surrounding area.

''You know I don't care about that. I only care about you.'' She smiled at him tenderly. ''Now, don't be so gloomy. Nina had no warning about Maurice's marriage. Perhaps if we give her enough time, she'll get used to the idea.''

Aidan gave a faint grin. ''I'm just getting used to the idea myself.''

''You still want to marry me, don't you?''

''Of course I do—that is, unless you start frequenting those private dining rooms down there with somebody else.''

''Good,'' she declared. ''It's bad enough if the mother of the bride isn't on hand at the wedding, but if the groom doesn't show . . .''

''Oh, you could always find another groom. It's mothers of the bride that are at a premium.''

''I'm afraid Nina's premium may be more than I'm willing to pay.'' Impulsively grabbing Aidan's coat sleeve, she exclaimed, ''Let's go,'' and pulled him toward the path that led down to the Cliff House.

''But we just ate breakfast,'' he protested, thinking she was dragging him down to dine in one of the private rooms.

''Not the Cliff House. There's somewhere else we need to go.''

"Where?"

"I said we were going to get you a new wardrobe, and I also want to stop at Jacob's and see that cute little nephew of mine. But first we're going home. It's time you were properly introduced to Nina—as my fiancé."

They scrambled down the sandy path and hurried across the street to the waiting cab. Rachel called the Nob Hill address up to the driver, and then she and Aidan climbed inside. Even before the driver popped the whip over the horse's head and the carriage started away along the hard-packed dirt surface of Cliff House Road, Aidan and Rachel were in each other's arms.

Several blocks from the Nob Hill mansion, Maurice Salomon and his wife were finishing breakfast at his brother's town house. They had only been married for two days, and their period of adjustment to married life was further complicated by the presence of a third new family member, Phoebe's infant son.

"Are you certain you don't mind my starting work today?" Maurice asked as he raised his cup and drained the last of the coffee.

"We discussed all this yesterday," Belle told him, her faint Southern accent a reminder of her childhood on a prosperous Kentucky Thoroughbred ranch. "And we're agreed this is the best course of action. You need to show your family that you're serious, and we need the income if we're going to get a place of our own."

"But I hate to leave you alone with little Charlie."

"I'm a nurse, remember? We'll be fine."

Maurice pushed back his chair and stood. As he looked across the dining room at the bentwood rocking cradle that sat near the wall, he started grinning. "Just look at that boy," he declared, approaching the cradle and staring down at the bundled infant, whose face barely showed from beneath a pile of bed quilts. "I'll be damned if he doesn't have your brown hair and green eyes," he added, running a hand through his own red hair and shaking his head in wonder.

"You can't even see," Belle protested, coming over and slipping a hand through her husband's arm. "Why, his eyes are closed, and his head is hidden under that bonnet."

"I remember from yesterday." He rocked the cradle gently with his foot, and as he smiled down at the sleeping infant, the dimples on his cheeks deepened.

"You ought to—you spent half the day looking at him."

"And the other half looking at you." He leaned over and kissed her lightly on the forehead, then placed a hand under her chin and tilted her head toward him. "I love you, Mrs. Merribelle Knowles Salomon."

"And I love you, Maurice." She raised up slightly and kissed him tenderly.

As their lips parted, he caressed her cheek and gazed into her large, expressive eyes. Her face was thin and delicate, and her high cheekbones gave her a mysterious, almost exotic air. He looked down at the simple black robe that covered her nightgown, saw the way her sleek but shapely body gave it form, and found himself reaching for the tie just above her chest.

"Damn," he muttered with pleasure as he started to pull the tie and leaned forward, giving her a second, more lingering kiss.

"But Charlie . . ." She nodded down at the cradle as she pulled away slightly and covered his hand at her breast.

"He won't mind," Maurice whispered, searching again for her lips.

"But Langdon might," she said, referring to Jacob's elderly manservant, who despite his efforts to be helpful yet stay out of the newlyweds' way, might walk in on them at any moment.

"Yes, Langdon," Maurice grumped, releasing the tie and giving a defeated frown.

"Don't go looking so mournful. You'll have me crying all over your new suit." She encouraged him to stand taller, then adjusted his silk four-in-hand tie and straightened the wings of his collar. "You look devastatingly handsome this morning. All the salesgirls at Salomon's will be flocking to your desk."

"If I have a desk."

"But Jacob promised you'd have his old office."

"He didn't say anything about a desk."

Belle playfully slapped his chest. "Go on, get going. You want to make a good impression your first day at work."

"I've worked there before," he protested.

"But never full-time. You're to be an executive, and they're supposed to be the first on the premises, the last to go home."

"That will be difficult," Maurice replied, pulling a gold watch from his pants pocket and glancing down at it. "The store opened a half hour ago."

"That's all right," she said, brushing the lapels of his brown-tweed cutaway. "Jacob said to come in at your pleasure this first day."

"He also once told me to go lie in the middle of the Golden Gate Race Course during the running of a local derby."

"But you were just children then."

"That was last year!" he exclaimed, raising his hands and shrugging.

"Shh! You'll wake up Charlie."

"And how many times did he wake us up last night?" he asked, feigning a frown and narrowing his light-brown eyes.

"Not as many times as you did."

"That was different."

"He's a baby. He was hungry."

"So was I!" Maurice swept Belle into his arms and kissed her full on the lips. They embraced for a long moment, and then he pulled away and said, "I suppose I really should be going now."

"Will I see you at lunchtime?" she asked as he walked over to a sideboard and picked up his fedora.

"Only if I'm hungry," he replied with a wink, clapping the hat on his head and turning toward the front entryway.

As Maurice reached the front door, a gaunt, gray-haired man in a black suit approached from the parlor and asked, "May I summon a coach?" He opened the door.

"Thank you, Langdon, but I think I'll walk."

"As you wish."

Maurice walked out and descended the stairs to Sacramento Street. As he headed east toward the business district, he was vaguely aware of a hackney cab pulling away from the curb across the street and starting down the road alongside him. He did not realize that the cab was intentionally pacing him until a voice inside called his name.

Maurice hesitated and cocked his head slightly, then assumed he had misheard and continued walking. But again a voice cried out, "Maurice!" and the cab came to a halt.

As Maurice turned, the passenger door opened on his side, and a man called, "Come aboard—I'll give you a ride."

Maurice could not make out the person in the shaded interior, but the voice had a familiar ring that he could not quite place. Assuming it was some acquaintance and not wanting to be rude, Maurice crossed the road and stepped up into the cab, saying, "Why, thank you. I'm just going—"

His mouth dropped open. There in the forward-facing seat was Damien Picard, his onetime comrade and partner in a series of wild escapades in New York City.

Damien was dressed in a jaunty light-brown suit and carried his usual silver-knobbed cane. His hair was longer than Maurice remembered, but his blue eyes flashed just as brightly and his grin was just as mischievous as ever.

"What are you doing here?" Maurice declared, astounded at seeing his former friend—who had broken all claims to that friendship when he had raped Rachel in Maurice's own New York hotel room.

"You invited me, remember?" Damien replied nonchalantly as Maurice sat down numbly across from him.

"I never—"

"You certainly did—many times, when we were together in New York."

"But—but that was before . . ."

"Yes, that unfortunate incident with Rachel." Damien shook his head apologetically.

"Incident? You call that an incident?" Maurice flared, his normally fair complexion reddening with anger. "Good God, man! You *raped* my sister!"

"Calm down, old chap," Damien urged. He leaned forward to pat Maurice's knee, but Maurice recoiled into the corner of the coach. Shaking his head with disappointment, Damien lifted his cane and struck it against the ceiling, and the driver released the brake and started down the road.

"You know it wasn't like that," Damien said in a calm voice as he slid along his seat until he was in front of Maurice again. Adopting a convincingly penitent expression, he continued, "We were drinking, and then we smoked all that opium. I didn't know what I was doing."

"You knew. Otherwise you wouldn't have disappeared the way you did. If you were truly sorry, you would have returned and tried to make amends."

"I was scared, Maurice. Can't you understand that? Haven't you ever been frightened—really frightened?" Seeing his friend's skeptical expression, he added, "Yes, I can get scared, too. I'm not always the cocksure fellow you seem to think I am."

"Then why risk coming here now?"

"To say I'm sorry."

"You could have written," Maurice replied with a sneer.

"I missed you," Damien confessed, settling back on the seat and shaking his head. "I missed the things we used to do together—the good times we had with women . . . with men . . . with each other."

Maurice flinched and looked away. "Those days are finished," he said flatly.

Damien threw back his head and chuckled. "So I've heard."

Maurice eyed him suspiciously. "What do you mean?"

"Simply that a husband and father has little time for wild nights and wilder women."

"How did you find out?" Maurice demanded.

"Come on, now, Maurice, give me a little credit. You don't think I just happened to come upon you on the street like this, do you? I was sitting out in the cab for over an hour waiting for you to show."

"You knew I lived there?"

"And that you've gone and gotten yourself married to the first lady who crooned 'I love you.' "

"You keep quiet about—"

"I'm sorry," Damien apologized, raising his palms. "But you have to admit it was a short courtship—and an even shorter pregnancy."

"We adopted little Charles," Maurice snapped back.

"Settle down. . . . I was only kidding. I know all about it."

"But how? . . ."

"It was rather easy. It's the talk of all the salesgirls at Salomon's Emporium. It seems you devastated a fair number of them; you were considered quite the catch."

The hackney lurched to the left as it turned onto Powell Street and headed south toward Union Square.

"Let's get to the point." Maurice leaned forward and eyed Damien closely. "What exactly do you want from me?"

"I'm not here to blackmail you, if that's what you think."

"Blackmail *me*? Why, you're the one who should be worried about blackmail, after what you did—"

"That was New York, not California," Damien cut in, his comment a subtle reminder that what he did to Rachel would carry no legal weight in San Francisco. "And after all the things we've done together, don't think I couldn't put the screws to you if I wanted, what with your having a new family and a responsible job and all." He paused a moment, allowing his veiled threat to sink in. "But that's not why I came," he said reassuringly.

"Then why?"

Damien reached into his jacket pocket and pulled out an envelope. Giving the return address an ominous tap, he said, "It's from New York—a young lady named Agnes Banker. You do remember her, don't you, Maurice? Or perhaps you remember her friend a little better—a pretty young thing named Lorraine Lanford."

Maurice looked up at him questioningly, then suddenly replied, "You mean that girl who practically attacked me in the parlor of my hotel suite?"

"Precisely—while I was in the bedroom enjoying Agnes's notable charms." He handed Maurice the envelope.

Maurice saw that the letter was addressed to Damien at the Baldwin Hotel. It had been opened carelessly, ripping off the corner with the canceled stamp. "She wrote to you in San Francisco?"

"After I last saw you, she and I spent a few more enjoyable evenings together. When I left for San Francisco, I told her where I'd probably be staying. The letter arrived yesterday afternoon." He leaned across the aisle and tapped the envelope again. "Go on. Read it."

As Maurice opened the envelope, his hands trembled slightly, as if he already knew what would be inside. He began to read and grew increasingly agitated. Damien watched his eyes, guessing what part of the letter he was up to, identifying the exact moment when he read that the woman named Lorraine was pregnant by him. The letter went on to state that Lorraine was not "that sort of girl" and that Maurice had taken advantage of her by plying her with champagne. Not only had the incident shattered her, but it had left her destitute and homeless, for her parents had thrown her out on the street when she confessed her condition. The letter concluded by explaining that Agnes was acting as an intermediary for her friend, hoping that Damien would be able to convince Maurice to do the right thing by Lorraine.

As Maurice finished the letter and lowered it, his face white with shock, Damien said, "I suppose this Lorraine is hoping you'll marry her. Of course, she has no idea you've rushed off and gotten married.''

''What am I going to do?'' Maurice muttered in anguish.

''You should have thought of that before,'' Damien chided. ''Didn't you use anything for protection?''

''I didn't have time. She was all over me—I swear.''

Damien shook his head and had to force himself not to chuckle. ''You certainly are adept at getting yourself in a pickle, old boy.''

''What can I do now?'' he repeated.

Damien pointed at the letter. ''Agnes makes it clear that her friend won't consider an abortion. The only solution I see is for you to try to pay her off.''

''Do you think she'll agree?''

''There's only one way to find out. I'll telegraph Agnes at once and see how much Lorraine will settle for.''

Maurice leaned across the aisle and clutched Damien's jacket sleeve. ''I'm a married man now. I've got a son. If anyone finds out . . .''

''Don't start worrying before you know what she wants. We may be able to settle this thing very quietly.''

''You won't tell anyone?'' Maurice declared, more a statement than a question.

Damien took the letter from Maurice's hands and stuffed it back into his pocket. ''Would I do that to a friend?'' he replied, feigning innocence, then adding on a more serious note, ''Just as I wouldn't expect a friend to do or say anything that might put me in a compromising position.''

''You mean about Rachel,'' Maurice concluded.

''Precisely.'' Adopting a genial tone, he continued, ''Look, Maurice, we've both done some stupid things in the past. I suggest we put all that behind us.'' He tapped the pocket containing the letter. ''Just as we hope to put this little indiscretion in the past.''

The hackney was rounding Union Square, approaching the entrance of Salomon's Emporium.

THE DECEIT

"I think you'll understand if I don't see you inside," Damien said with a grin as the hackney came to a halt.

"Yes. I think it's best if we keep our distance," Maurice agreed.

"My intention precisely. I know how distressed your sister would be if she knew I was in town."

"Keep away from Rachel," Maurice suddenly blurted.

"Don't worry. I have no intention of telling anyone I'm in town. I suggest you keep quiet about it, as well."

Maurice reached for the door handle. "You'll let me know what that woman wants?" he asked dejectedly.

"I'll get word to you just as soon as I hear," Damien promised.

Maurice climbed out of the cab and closed the door behind him. Looking back in, he eyed Damien suspiciously. "Just make sure you stay away from Rachel—and Salomon's Emporium, as well."

"You're such a trusting friend." Damien chuckled, then tapped his cane against the ceiling.

As Maurice stood on the sidewalk in front of Salomon's Emporium and watched the hackney drive off down the street, he felt himself getting increasingly warm, and he ran a finger behind his starched collar to wipe away the sweat. Somehow he would have to buy that woman's silence, then convince Damien to leave San Francisco—before Rachel found out he was in town, and before his wife or anyone else learned the sordid details of Maurice's wastrel past.

The third time that Phoebe Salomon awoke, it was light out. She was lying on her back, her head turned toward a window draped with a thin, gauzy curtain that did little to keep out the sun. She tried to turn her head, but she felt totally drained and could not remember whether she had been awake earlier or had been having a nightmare—whether the Oriental room and Chinese faces had been real or conjured up in her sleep.

Phoebe heard whispering voices and strained to comprehend what they were saying. She fought the weakness and slowly turned her head on the pillow until she could see a group of women huddled at the far end of the room. They were Chinese, and indeed this was the room of her dreams.

"Sung Chien," she heard one of the voices say, and she saw that the woman was nodding toward her, apparently telling the others that she had awakened. There was a flurry of Chinese, and then all but one of the women scurried through the open door, shutting it behind them.

The remaining woman approached the bed and bowed to Phoebe. "You eat soon," she said in soft, broken English, and suddenly Phoebe realized just how famished she was. She tried to speak to the woman but managed only a weak smile.

As the woman returned her smile, Phoebe remembered seeing her before. She had been in the room when Phoebe first woke, and again sleeping in the chair when Phoebe had taken her key and sneaked out into the hall . . . *when I saw the old woman at the window—*

Phoebe gasped, and the young woman placed a calming hand on her shoulder. "You all right," she said. "You better now."

"Wh-what happened?" Phoebe managed to stammer, but before the woman could reply, the bedroom door swung open and the rotund, bald-headed man with the long braided queue strode in. He wore a black robe, the sleeves pushed up to show his meaty arms crossed in front of his chest. His thick lips were pressed together in a severe frown.

Sung Chien said a few abrupt words in Chinese, and the young servant bowed and retreated toward the door, where she stood attentively awaiting further commands from her master.

"Why?" was the single word Sung Chien spoke, his eyebrows arching as he stared down at Phoebe.

Taken aback, Phoebe shook her head weakly from side to side and said, "I d-don't understand. . . ."

"My wife . . . she is dead," the big man said, his voice breaking with emotion. "Why did you do such a thing?"

"That woman . . . she was your wife?"

"Why did you push her?"

Phoebe looked at him curiously, then slowly realized what he was implying and blurted, "My God, no! I never—" She suddenly felt far stronger and lifted herself up off the pillow slightly, resting on her elbows. "That woman jumped—I saw her jump!"

"You were up in the window, looking down, screaming."

"Yes—screaming because I saw her jump! Don't you understand?"

"She jumped? By herself?" he asked skeptically.

"Of course. Why would I push her?"

"Why were you there?"

"I woke up and didn't know where I was. I was going down the hall, trying to figure out what was going on."

"And you saw her?"

"There was a light on in her room, and I walked in just as she was climbing onto the windowsill . . . just as she—" Phoebe shook her head sadly.

"But why would she jump?" Sung Chien wondered aloud, his question answered as he watched Phoebe pull aside the blankets and swing her bare feet over the side of the bed to the hardwood floor.

"I should be leaving now," Phoebe said somewhat distractedly as she rose to a seated position. "I should be getting home."

As Phoebe rose unsteadily to her feet, Sung Chien stepped in front of her to block the way. "You're not well; you must stay here. When you are better, then you will go."

Stepping past him and starting toward the door, Phoebe shook her head and replied, "No, I must go home. My family will be wondering—"

"Family?" he interjected. He walked over and lifted a jacket off the top of the trunk at the foot of the bed. Holding it up to show the insignia of the Presidio Asylum for Incurables, he added, "This is your family? You want me to call this family so they can bring you back home?"

Refusing to look back, Phoebe gave the servant a look of thanks, then grasped the doorknob and pulled open the door—only to find her way blocked by a pair of bodyguards. She tried to continue forward, but they stood shoulder-to-shoulder and would not let her pass. Again she turned to the servant, who lowered her eyes and shook her head, indicating Phoebe's action was futile.

Her shoulders slumping, Phoebe turned to face Sung Chien, who was still holding up the jacket of the Presidio night attendant.

"Ah, then you will enjoy our hospitality a bit longer?" he asked, at last lowering the jacket and dropping it onto the trunk. "You have made a wise decision." He smiled again and moved forward to take her arm, but she hurried past him and returned to the bed. "Breakfast is being sent up. Then you must rest, and you will soon feel much better."

Phoebe lay down on the bed and curled up on her side, staring at the window. As Sung Chien left the room, she closed her eyes and fought back tears, making a silent vow that somehow she would get out of this place. She only hoped that she would not be forced to use the same method Sung Chien's wife had chosen last night.

Nine

"GOOD MORNING," CAMERON GREETED RACHEL SALOMON and Aidan McAuliffe as he answered the door.

"Is Nina home?" Rachel inquired, entering the foyer.

"She's still upstairs. Shall I get her?" Cameron ushered Aidan inside and took his fedora.

"We'll wait for her in the parlor," she replied, leading Aidan into the room off the right of the foyer.

"I hope this is a good idea," Aidan commented as Rachel took a seat on the large green-velvet sofa. He walked across the room to the fireplace on the far wall. "I don't think your mother was particularly fond of me when we met."

"That was the day my father died, when you tried to move him to the hospital," she reminded him. "I'm sure she doesn't hold that against you any longer."

"We'll soon find out."

"Anyway, she'll probably be too busy yelling at me to pay you any mind. Remember, the last time I saw her, she threw my brothers and me out of the house."

"Me, too," he said gloomily. He turned and leaned against

147

the marble mantel, watching the foyer entrance for Nina to make her appearance.

When she did, it was with as much drama as Aidan had observed on his first visit. She fairly glided into the room, the fur-trimmed hem of her dressing gown trailing behind her on the floor. The gown, cut with a bold flare that hugged her waist and bosom, was fashioned of a dark-green silk that shimmered like a phosphorescent sea as she moved. Her long brunette hair was in a bun, held with a Spanish-style comb, and her brown eyes seemed to flash with yellow flecks of light as she came to the center of the room and looked first at Aidan, then at her daughter.

"You've come home," she intoned with what passed for a smile, her tone barely concealing a sense of victory.

"I've come to speak with you," Rachel clarified, standing up. "That is, if you're willing to talk."

"When haven't I been willing to talk?" the older woman protested.

"It's just that the last time I was here, you made it clear I was no longer welcome—"

"Oh, that . . ." Nina waved her hand, dismissing the incident. "We were all upset and said things we shouldn't have. Consider it forgotten."

"In that case, I'd like to introduce a dear friend of mine." She nodded at Aidan, who approached. "This is—"

"Yes," Nina interjected with a nod. "The gentleman and I have already met." Her smile looked forced as she turned to Aidan.

"But you were not properly introduced," Rachel continued. "Nina Salomon, this is Dr. Aidan McAuliffe . . ." She paused as Nina reluctantly offered her hand and allowed Aidan to raise it partway to his lips, and then she added, "My fiancé."

Nina's smile froze. She slowly withdrew her hand, her eyes widening as she stared at Aidan. Then she turned back to her daughter. "Your . . . ?"

"Aidan has asked for my hand in marriage, and I've accepted,'' she announced. Her smile grew more genuine as she turned to her husband-to-be.

"I love your daughter very much," Aidan professed somewhat nervously, "and I hope to—"

"You . . . you are en-engaged?" Nina stammered, paying no attention to Aidan. "To this . . . *person*?"

"Yes, Nina. And we are going to be married within a few months." She forced herself to smile warmly at Nina. "I wanted you to be the first to know."

Nina looked back and forth between Aidan and Rachel, trying to absorb what she was hearing.

"I know this comes as a surprise," Rachel said, stepping closer and touching her mother's arm. "But I love Aidan very much, and I want to be his wife."

Cocking her head uncertainly, Nina looked her daughter up and down. "Is there . . . some reason?" she said haltingly. "Something to make you rush into marriage?"

"I'm not rushing," Rachel snapped, bristling at her mother's veiled suggestion that she might be pregnant. "The wedding won't be for some time yet. That's why I wanted to tell you right away."

"You know, with Maurice running off and getting married like that, there's bound to be talk," Nina went on. "I wouldn't want that to happen to a daughter of mine."

"Maurice got married quickly so he and Belle would qualify to adopt Phoebe's baby," Rachel pointed out.

Nina threw a hand in front of her face. "I don't want to talk about that."

"But my situation is different." Rachel reached up and lowered Nina's hand, forcing her attention. "Aidan and I are in love, and we've decided to get married. It's as simple as that. We haven't set a date yet, but there will be plenty of time to plan a small, suitable wedding."

"Small? How can a small wedding be suitable for the eldest daughter of Charles and Nina Salomon? You are the granddaughter of Isidore Salomon, remember."

"But I thought he and Grandmother eloped."

"That was different," Nina grated. "He was penniless, and her father wouldn't let her come to San Francisco with him."

"And look how wonderfully it turned out. I just hope I don't have to run away like Grandmother did."

Nina eyed her closely, weighing her options.

"Why don't we all sit down," Rachel suggested pleasantly. Nina appeared reluctant, but she allowed her daughter to lead her to the sofa, and Aidan took a seat across from the two women.

There was a long silence, with Nina looking uncertain, Rachel expectant, and Aidan uncomfortable. Finally Nina drew in a calming breath and turned to address Aidan. "When we first met, Rachel said you had studied medicine, but I had no idea you were a physician. Is that true?"

He nodded. "I had a private practice when I . . . when I left England."

"In London he was a noted surgeon, as well," Rachel put in cheerfully.

"McAuliffe, you say?" she shook her head slightly. "I'm certain Rachel told me some other name."

Aidan shifted uncomfortably on the plush upholstered seat, recalling that he had been introduced to Nina under the alias he used during his escape from England. "That's right," he admitted. "I was traveling under the name Orcutt. It's—"

"It's his mother's name," Rachel cut in, anxious that Nina not yet learn of Aidan's legal troubles. "It was some sort of problem with his traveling papers, but all that's been resolved." Eager to change the conversation, she added, "As a matter of fact, he's already been sought out for an appointment at a prominent local hospital and—"

"Which one?"

"Pacific Hospital," Aidan told her.

Nina turned to Rachel. "Isn't that the little one up on Pacific Heights?"

"But it's considered one of the most prestigious surgical

institutes in the West,'' Rachel exaggerated. ''He's starting work tomorrow.''

Nina did not look especially impressed but smiled politely at Aidan. ''And your future plans?''

''Perhaps open my own practice after I've been here longer,'' he replied, though in truth he had not yet given it any thought.

''Then you intend to remain in San Francisco?'' she asked, her expression brightening.

''Why, yes. I love what I've seen of the city. And I have no real family in Great Britain and would never want to take Rachel from hers.''

''So you can see, Nina, that I won't be disrupting the family by moving off to England,'' Rachel interjected.

''Yes, but . . .''

''And we want you to handle all the arrangements,'' Rachel continued. ''I know how disappointed you were with Maurice's marriage, so—''

''Going to some clerk at City Hall, can you imagine? That will never do for you, Rachel. If there's to be a wedding''— she made the comment with reservation—''then it's to be an affair befitting a Salomon.''

''But not *too* extravagant,'' Rachel implored.

''You let me worry about the details. People have always said that no one knows how to throw a party like Nina Salomon.'' She stood and gave a self-important smile.

Rising quickly from his chair, Aidan started to speak but was interrupted by the appearance of a blond-haired woman in the doorway.

''Mrs. Salomon, I was having trouble finding—'' the woman said, stopping abruptly upon seeing the visitors. ''Dear me, I didn't realize you were still entertaining.''

''Allison,'' Nina declared, as though equally surprised at seeing the young woman in the parlor. Stepping toward her, she said in an undertone, ''We agreed you'd stay upstairs until—''

''I thought I heard your guests leaving,'' Allison replied

with a nonchalant flick of her wrist. Sweeping past Nina, she approached Rachel, who was standing now, and said in a slightly more pronounced Southern accent than usual, "I'm sorry to barge in like this. I'm Allison Grant." She offered Rachel her hand. "And you must be Phoebe's sister. She told me so much about you."

As they shook hands, Rachel looked questioningly at her mother.

"Allison was a friend of Phoebe's," Nina put in, forcing a smile and going over to where they were standing. "You must remember Phoebe talking about her."

"I'm sorry," Rachel said to the woman. "I don't believe Phoebe ever mentioned you to me."

"Certainly she did," Nina insisted. "Why, that year she went off to Boston. She wrote us about her friend. Surely you remember."

Rachel shook her head. "I'm sorry. . . ."

"That's all right," Allison put in. "We were together only that one year. But I did like her so very much." Her bright expression shifted effortlessly to sorrow. "It was such a tragedy about Phoebe. Mrs. Salomon was telling me all about it, and . . ." She started to sniffle and took out a handkerchief from under the wristband of her wine-colored tea gown.

"Allison arrived in town yesterday and came calling on Phoebe. She had no idea," Nina explained, placing a comforting arm around the younger woman's shoulder.

"She told me to visit if I ever came to San Francisco. And then the shock of learning . . ." Choking back her tears, she dabbed at her eyes and tucked the handkerchief back under her wristband. "I'm all right," she assured them. "I just haven't gotten used to her . . . being gone."

"I insisted Allison spend the night."

"Your mother has been so kind to me," Allison told them. She smiled at Nina, then turned to Aidan, waiting to be introduced.

"This is my fiancé, Aidan McAuliffe," Rachel told her.

"I'm delighted to meet you," Allison said, and they shook hands.

"We should be going," Rachel announced, moving beside Aidan and slipping a hand through his arm.

"I hope to see you at the dinner party tonight," Allison remarked.

"Dinner party?" Rachel asked, looking at her mother, whose mouth dropped open in surprise.

"I . . . I was—" Nina sputtered.

"Weren't you inviting your children to dinner tonight?" Allison fixed Nina with an innocent smile.

"I said I hoped to speak with Maurice today and might invite him to dinner—but I didn't say when. And I said nothing about inviting all—"

"Oh, dear me." Allison threw a hand to her mouth and looked the picture of embarrassment. "I've been so confused, I get everything turned around in my head."

"We understand," Rachel said sympathetically. She turned to her mother. "It's not a bad idea, you know. Not that it has to be tonight. But perhaps if we all sat down together, we might be able to patch up our differences and start over again."

"I suppose we *could* have dinner one night soon," Nina allowed. "That is, if Jacob and Maurice are willing."

"Don't forget Belle."

Nina frowned at her daughter. "I'd *never* do that. Of course Maurice's wife will be invited. In fact, I've asked Jacob to have Maurice call on me, and I shall ask him when he does."

"We happen to be going to the town house right now. Would you like me to invite Maurice and Belle for you?"

Nina glanced at Allison, who nodded enthusiastically. "I . . . uh, suppose so. But when shall we make it for?"

"How about tonight?" Rachel suggested.

"Tonight?" Nina said, aghast. "But there wouldn't be enough time for proper arrange—"

"Precisely," Rachel explained. "This should be a simple family dinner, not a production."

"Well, if you think so." Nina wrung her hands nervously. "But you really must go, then, because there's so much I will have to do, what with the—"

"Nina, you have an entire kitchen staff to take care of everything."

"But if I don't stand over them every minute, nothing gets done properly."

Aidan moved beside Rachel and took her arm. "Why don't we leave your mother and Allison to make the arrangements?"

"Shall we say seven?" Rachel asked.

"Yes, fine," Nina replied distractedly.

"I'll call and confirm after I speak with the others," Rachel promised.

"Don't worry," Allison put in, smiling at Rachel. "I'll help your mother; we'll be ready when you arrive."

"Thank you, Allison. It was very nice meeting you."

They said their good-byes, and Aidan and Rachel headed through the foyer to the front door, where Cameron appeared with Aidan's fedora. As Cameron opened the door, Nina suddenly exclaimed, "Goodness, Rachel!" and came rushing from the parlor, her dressing robe swirling around her.

"What's wrong?" Rachel asked in concern, seeing her mother's agitated expression.

"I . . . well, I thought you might ask Maurice if . . . if he and his wife might come alone. I mean, it's really not the right time . . . not the proper setting for a baby."

Rachel clearly wanted to protest but seemed mollified that Nina had even mentioned little Charlie. Deciding to win this war one battle at a time, she held her tongue and nodded.

Nina smiled with relief. Allison came up beside her, and Nina took hold of the younger woman's arm and gripped it for support, saying, "It will be good to have the whole family together again."

So striking was the illusion that Nina was standing with Phoebe, rather than Allison, that Rachel had to blink to clear

154

the image. Feeling strangely disquieted, Rachel muttered, "Yes, it will," then turned and left the house.

As Cameron closed the door behind Aidan and Rachel, Nina signaled him to leave the room. As soon as he was gone, she abruptly pulled away from Allison, startling her. "How could you say those things?" she demanded.

"I—I don't understand," Allison replied, looking genuinely confused.

"You know I said nothing about a dinner party. I only mentioned in passing that if things went well with Maurice, I might invite him to dinner—but I never said tonight."

"I just assumed—"

"Just as you assumed my daughter had left and then came wandering into the parlor?" She shook her head in dismay. "I thought I made myself clear this morning that you are welcome to stay a bit longer but that I don't want my children involved. What if Rachel were to suspect—?"

"Surely they'd find out I'm here from one of the staff," Allison pointed out. "Isn't it better that you tell them right from the start?"

"It seems I have no choice now."

"Believe me, Rachel did not suspect for an instant that I was anything but Phoebe's schoolmate. Neither did her fiancé." She said the last word with emphasis and noted Nina's negative reaction.

"That may be so, but you really shouldn't have taken it upon yourself to invite them to dinner like that."

"I thought I was helping you out."

"How could you possibly know what would or wouldn't be of help to me?" Nina chided.

"I know you aren't pleased at the thought of having this Aidan McAuliffe as a son-in-law," Allison responded directly, nodding and narrowing one eye.

"Why, I never!" Nina folded her arms across her chest and glowered at the young woman in front of her. "Is this a fantasy of yours?" she demanded. "Was I wrong to take you in the way I did? Perhaps there's a reason you were locked up with Phoebe at the—"

"It's no fantasy," Allison cut in. "I can see the way you react every time his name is mentioned. I'm neither insane nor blind."

"But you certainly are presumptuous. To have taken it upon yourself to invite *my* children . . . people you have never met before . . ."

"I told you. I did it to help."

"And how is that supposed to help?"

"Don't you see?" When Nina looked at her in puzzlement, Allison continued, "You have no influence over your daughter when you're not speaking to her. But when you're on closer terms and can trust each other, there's no end to the influence you can wield."

Nina shook her head and waved off the comment. "My eldest daughter stopped trusting her mother a long time ago. And as to having influence, I can always bet that whenever I suggest one thing to her, she'll try to do the opposite."

"Which is why a dinner party is such a perfect idea."

Nina cocked her head. "Just what do you mean?"

"You need to approach your daughter through someone she *does* trust—her fiancé."

"You want me to get friendly with that . . . that foreigner?"

"Befriending him isn't the only way to influence Rachel. A far better way is to show her that he's not the man she thinks him to be."

"And how do I do that?"

Allison smiled conspiratorially. "Why don't we sit down and talk about it?" she suggested, nodding toward the parlor.

Somewhat reluctantly, Nina allowed herself to be led back to the parlor sofa. Once they were seated, she turned to Allison and declared, "Now, what exactly are you talking about?"

"There's more than one way to put an end to this engagement, if that's what you really want to do."

Nina looked at her curiously, wondering what exactly Allison had in mind—and why she was taking such an interest in the family's affairs. "Well, supposing for the sake of argument that I did, what would you have me do?"

"If I were you, I'd attack on two fronts at once. First, I'd see if Aidan could be tempted away from Rachel—if not permanently, at least far enough to prove that her trust in him is misplaced."

"You certainly don't expect me to flirt like a common schoolgirl with my daughter's fiancé," Nina exclaimed. "Why, the man is no older than my son."

Allison grinned. "No, that's not what I meant, though I don't doubt you could turn his head if you set your mind to it."

"Then who?" she asked, staring questioningly at the younger woman, whose smile slowly deepened. "Do you mean to say you're offering to do it yourself?"

"How could a woman resist those dark good looks and blue eyes?" Allison replied playfully, exaggerating her Southern drawl.

"But do you think he'd respond?"

Crossing her legs and taking a seductive pose, Allison crooned, "I've yet to meet the man who won't respond to a good-looking woman, given the right circumstances." She quickly dropped the stance, leaned forward, and said eagerly, "And what better place to test the waters than at a dinner party?"

Why am I even sitting here listening to this? Nina thought as she stared at the young woman, the blood rushing from her cheeks. *Here she is, a stranger, coaching me about my family. It's outrageous!*

As if reading her thoughts, Allison went on, "Of course, you can just leave things as they are and get used to having this Dr. McAuliffe as your son-in-law."

Narrowing her eyes, Nina said cautiously, "You mentioned another line of attack."

"Through Rachel," Allison replied. "If you can't prove

Aidan isn't good enough for her, convince her someone else is better. Perhaps some eligible young man from her own social class."

"No, it wouldn't work," Nina proclaimed. "Rachel has rejected every man I ever recommended to her."

"Then how about someone she's picked out herself? Surely there's someone from her past who could reappear at an opportune moment and shake up her faith in her feelings for Aidan."

Slowly Nina's eyes widened, and she began to nod animatedly. "Why, yes, there is one person. They used to be quite serious about each other. But . . ." Her smile quickly faded, and she shook her head.

"Who is it?" Allison pressed.

"No, it would never work."

"How will you know if you don't try?"

"It was foolish even to think of him. It was a long time ago; they haven't seen each other in years."

"That's perfect. Who is he?"

"Someone named Timothy Price. But he—"

"Price . . ." Allison mused aloud. "Where have I heard that name?"

"His grandfather was Jeremiah Price."

Allison clutched Nina's forearm and whispered, "The railroad magnate?" When Nina nodded, Allison exclaimed, "Fantastic! Why, the Prices must be worth millions!"

"And one day Timothy stands to inherit all of it."

"He's perfect," Allison gushed. "You said they were serious once, and he's certainly of the right social class. What could possibly be wrong with him?"

"Nothing, as far as half the women in San Francisco are concerned. He's quite the eligible young bachelor."

"Then he's the one," Allison declared emphatically.

Nina shook her head and frowned. "It's not that simple. They were quite serious once, but there was a misunderstanding of some kind, and they broke up."

"You said it was a number of years ago. Perhaps time has healed the wounds."

Nina shook her head. "It wouldn't work. Anyway, I never approved of Timothy Price. He was far too wild and had quite a reputation with the ladies . . . not at all the sort for my daughter."

"But Aidan McAuliffe is?"

"I didn't say that."

"Perhaps this Tim Price has matured. What more do you know about him?"

"Well, his name has turned up in the paper a number of times recently. He was away from San Francisco for several years and returned just this spring from Europe. In fact, one picture showed him with one of those new automobiles, one that he bought in France."

"Did they say why he came home?"

"His father's not well, and it's reported that Timothy is going to take over the family affairs."

Allison snorted. "Doesn't sound like a man who's 'far too wild' for your daughter."

"I suppose people can change," Nina admitted. "Even Maurice has begun to settle down."

"There, see?" Allison nodded. "You ought to call this Timothy Price and invite him to dinner."

"What? I couldn't do that."

"Why not?"

"They haven't been on speaking terms—"

"Because of some youthful misunderstanding," Allison interjected. "They've probably forgotten it by now." Standing, she raised her arms and proclaimed, "I think it's your duty to reintroduce your daughter and this man."

"Duty?" Nina said incredulously.

Allison faced Nina with her hands on her hips. "Is it right for your daughter to get married without first straightening out her feelings about a man she was serious about? Would you rather have her become the wife of that doctor and discover years from now that she chose the wrong man?"

"Timothy Price *would* be a far more suitable match," Nina told herself. "I mean, this Aidan McAuliffe has neither family nor money—practically a common laborer."

"Then it's decided. You must contact him at once and invite him to dinner."

"Tonight?" Nina said in disbelief.

"What better time to reintroduce old friends?"

"But this is supposed to be a family dinner."

"Aidan and I will be there, and we're not family."

"But . . . how will I explain inviting Timothy Price?"

With a mischievous grin, Allison returned to the sofa, sat next to Nina, and patted the older woman's hand. "I'm sure if we put our minds to it, we can come up with a reason."

Phoebe Salomon spent the day locked in Sung Chien's upstairs bedroom, her only visitor the Chinese woman who had watched over her when she was unconscious. Though the young woman spoke English, Phoebe was unable to engage her in any but the most rudimentary conversation.

The next time Phoebe saw the master of the house was shortly after lunch, when the servant was removing Phoebe's tray. Sung Chien appeared at the doorway with two bodyguards and spoke curtly to the young woman in Chinese. The woman glanced back nervously at Phoebe, then departed with the tray.

While she was gone, Sung Chien entered the room and closed the door behind him, leaving the guards in the hall. He approached the bed where Phoebe was propped up against the pillows and gave a slight bow. "Do you still wish to leave my house?" he asked.

Phoebe looked at him curiously, uncertain of whether or not to reply.

"Yes, you would like to leave," he answered for her, smiling thinly.

"I . . . I'm feeling better. I really shouldn't stay any longer."

"But where will you go, my little stranger?"

THE DECEIT

"I'll be all right," she told him.

"You still won't tell me your name? Are we not friends? Have I not helped you?"

"My name is . . . Mary," she lied, using the name given her at the asylum.

"Ah, little Mary—mother of the infant Jesus." He nodded. "And have you a family name?"

"King. Mary King," she said, completing the name under which she had been committed.

"Mary King. Mother of the king of kings." He chuckled. "This is a good name for Liu, the stranger."

"Can I leave now?" she asked expectantly.

"The *tai fu* says you must rest one more night. But tomorrow, if you still want to leave, we will go for a ride in my coach, and I will take you wherever you wish." Sung Chien bowed again and started to back away from the bed.

"But I really do feel better," she protested.

"You will rest tonight. Then you may leave." With a final bow, he opened the door and disappeared down the hall, leaving the door open and the guards on duty outside.

A few minutes later the young servant returned, bearing a bowl of liquid and a cloth. Closing the door, she came to the bed, bowed, and indicated she wished to wipe Phoebe's brow. Phoebe was about to protest, but she changed her mind and nodded for the woman to sit on the edge of the bed.

As the servant pulled the cloth out of the water and wrung it out, she looked around the room furtively. Then she pressed it to Phoebe's brow and leaned close, so that Phoebe could understand her as she whispered, "You must get away from this place."

"What?" Phoebe asked, pushing the woman's hand from her forehead. "What do you mean?"

"You must gain your strength and flee."

"But why?"

"It bring Sung Chien great dishonor to keep in his house the woman who caused his wife to die."

"But I told him I didn't push her," Phoebe replied brusquely.

"It is no difference if you push her or she jump. She is dead because Sung Chien brought a non-Chinese into his household—into his bed."

Phoebe looked around uncomfortably. "You mean that this was her bedroom?" she asked, and the woman nodded.

"Sung Chien say he must send you away to return honor to his household."

"I know. He told me I can leave tomorrow. In fact, he promised to take me wherever I want."

The woman shook her head rapidly.

"Won't he keep his word?" Phoebe asked. "Won't he let me go where I want?"

"When he take you for a ride tomorrow, he bring you to the *Jade Reef*."

"The Jade . . . ?"

"His ship. But he own more than just ships."

"What do you mean?"

Again the young woman looked toward the door, her eyes darting like those of a frightened animal. "He pay to bring Chinese men and women to your country."

"Slaves?" Phoebe said in disbelief.

"Not slaves—you call them servants of indenture. I am one—but a lucky one."

"Why?"

"My fellow servants are no better off than slaves. They toil in the mines and laundries with hardly enough to eat or clothe themselves, and when they try to pay off their contracts, Sung Chien add new charges."

"Is this true of you, too?"

"Yes. But at least I get to live in Sung Chien's house, with good clothing and plenty of food."

"But what has this got to do with me?" Phoebe asked.

"China also has market for slaves—but non-Chinese slaves. In Shanghai, a young woman like you would bring much money to Sung Chien."

Phoebe just stared at her in astonishment, not knowing what to think.

"It is true," the woman continued. "Sung Chien say you run away from hospital that burn down. He say they think you dead. So when he take you for coach ride, he bring you to his ship and send you to China, never to be seen again."

Phoebe looked at her uncertainly. "Why are you telling me all this?"

"I choose to come to your country. Bad enough I must now work as little more than a slave. But it is wrong for you to be sent so far away from your home."

"I . . . I don't know what to say."

"You must regain your strength and get away."

"But how?"

"Too many guards here. You must wait until tomorrow."

"But he plans to take me riding in his coach then."

"That is when you must get away."

Phoebe reached over and took the woman's hand. "Will you help me?" she asked.

"I . . . I do what I can," she promised.

"Thank you . . ." She tried to remember the woman's name, then realized she did not know it.

"My name is Kuei Mei," the servant told her.

"I will remember what you've done for me, Kuei Mei," Phoebe vowed. "And when I get away from here, I'll find a way to help you win your freedom."

"Do not worry about Kuei Mei. Just get away before he bring you to his ship."

"I will, Kuei Mei. I promise you, I will."

Ten

AIDAN MCAULIFFE PASSED THROUGH THE DOUBLE DOORS AT
the far end of the parlor in the Salomons' Nob Hill mansion
and came to an abrupt halt. Rachel, at his side, was well
aware of the initial effect the formal living room had on visitors, and she held his arm and waited while he drank it in.

Aidan had been in few private rooms this large or lavish.
It was at least fifty feet square and decorated with a contem-
porary Oriental flair. At the center of the polished parquet
floor was an enormous Chinese rug with an intricate floral
design, each petal hand-shaved around the edges to create a
three-dimensional effect. The four large sofas and more than
a dozen chairs were upholstered in a complementary floral
pattern, as was the trim on the massive green drapes alongside the high, arched windows that afforded a spectacular
view of the city. All of the end tables and other furniture
were of dark, highly polished mahogany, fashioned in a modern style that also was reminiscent of the Orient.

It was not the furnishings that drew Aidan's attention and
admiration, however, but the ceiling. It was unusually high,

curved at the walls, and painted with colorful, minutely detailed images of angels and fairies in a setting of Greek ruins, done in the new, increasingly popular trompe l'oeil school of stylized realism.

Squeezing Aidan's arm, Rachel said, "It's a companion to the one you saw today at Salomon's Emporium, in the dome above the main floor."

"It looks more dramatic here," Aidan noted.

"It's actually smaller, but it's lower and dominates the room, while the one at the store covers only a fraction of the ceiling area."

"The colors—the blues and greens, even those white clouds—they're so vibrant."

"People love or hate it—but they always react, which is precisely what Nina intended. She actually designed the basic picture and commissioned an artist to carry it out."

"Your mother really is quite creative."

"A frustrated artist, I think. Come, let's greet the others." She pulled his arm, leading him into the room.

Jacob, Maurice, and Belle were already on hand, seated together on one of the sofas. They stood as Aidan and Rachel approached, with Jacob coming forward and extending his hand.

"It's good to see you looking so much better," he commented, shaking Aidan's hand. "How does your arm feel?"

Aidan rubbed his left upper arm. "It was little more than a scratch," he assured him.

"And you wouldn't have even got that if you hadn't been pushing me out of the path of that bullet. I owe you a debt of gratitude."

"Yes," Maurice interjected, stepping forward and pumping Aidan's hand. "And Belle tells me that congratulations are in order."

"A toast to the future bride and groom," Jacob exclaimed, filling two glasses with sherry from a decanter on a table beside the sofa. He handed them to Aidan and Rachel, then picked up his own. As soon as Maurice and Belle took their glasses, Jacob raised his high and intoned, "May your engagement be short and sweet, your marriage long and even sweeter." He tipped the glass to his lips, downing the contents in a single gulp.

As the others sipped their drinks, a voice called, "Have you started the party without me?"

The group turned to see Allison Grant coming through from the parlor, dressed in a stunning blue, ermine-trimmed gown, which perfectly hugged and shaped her slender yet well-curved form. As she approached, Rachel looked at her curiously, wondering why the dress seemed so familiar, then suddenly realizing that it had belonged to Phoebe. Rachel felt a twinge of anger—not so much toward Allison as toward Nina for having let someone wear Phoebe's things.

"You must be Merribelle," Allison declared, not waiting for an introduction as she headed straight for Belle.

"This is Allison Grant," Rachel put in as the two women shook hands.

"A pleasure to meet you," Belle said. "Rachel told me about you during her visit this morning."

"You must be from Kentucky," Allison guessed upon hearing Belle's Southern accent. "But it's faded. Have you spent much time in the North?"

"In Albany, New York. And from what part of the South are you?" she asked, noting Allison's own lilting speech.

"My family was originally from Louisiana, though I grew up in Southern California." Smiling, she turned to the two brothers. "Now, one of you must be Jacob, the other Maurice." She held her hand out to the red-haired one. "Maurice?"

"At your service," he replied, shaking her hand. "How did you know?"

"Your mother said you were a red-haired devil when you were young."

"He's hardly changed with the years," Belle commented with a grin.

"Which leaves Jacob," Allison concluded, turning to Maurice's older brother.

Jacob did not immediately take Allison's offered hand, so caught up was he with gazing into her vivacious blue eyes. When she repeated his name and he realized he was staring, he quickly smiled, raised her hand to his lips, and kissed it lightly. "At your service," he said graciously, reluctantly releasing her hand. "Would you care for a sherry?"

"Just a little." She indicated how much she wanted with her thumb and index finger.

As Jacob was pouring the drink, Nina made her usual grand entrance. She wore a gown of gold satin, trimmed at the throat, wrists, and hem with striking black lace.

"I see everyone has arrived," she announced as she glided across the floor to where they were gathered. "Jacob, if you would be so kind . . ." She waved a hand toward the decanter, and her eldest son poured her a glass, as well. As soon as he handed it to her, she raised it aloft and proclaimed, "A toast to my son Maurice and his lovely bride. May their lives be long and productive."

After everyone took a drink, Nina lowered her glass and approached Belle. Holding out her hand, she said, "I'm afraid I've been so distraught of late that I did not properly welcome you into the family before."

Belle took Nina's hand and accepted a polite kiss on the cheek.

"I must have seemed a dreadful wretch to you, when in truth I always thought you'd make a wonderful wife for my son. I've always believed a good marriage settles a young man down, and I must say that Maurice looks as if he's wearing this marriage well." Turning to him, she asked, "Is it true you're going to work at Salomon's?"

"I began today," he replied, beaming.

She reached up and kissed him lightly on the cheek. "Your father would be proud of you. Surprised perhaps, but proud. He always thought you'd have a good head for business, if you ever got it out of the clouds." She smiled, indicating her comment was meant to be taken humorously. "Dinner will be served a little after seven thirty, so let's all sit and get better acquainted."

After the women sat on the sofa, the men took seats on chairs to either side. The conversation was friendly and purposely light. Nina appeared to be in a surprisingly good mood and spent most of her time speaking with Maurice and Belle.

Allison was at the far end of the sofa, next to Rachel, with Jacob and Aidan in chairs beside them. While Allison did her best to engage Aidan in conversation about his work and his life in Great Britain, he answered politely but curtly, focusing his attention on Rachel. Jacob, on the other hand, was more than willing to answer any of Allison's questions in depth, though she directed only enough to him to be polite.

"San Francisco must be such a change from Louisiana, Miss Grant," he said to her during a lull in the conversation.

Her reply was a guarded smile and the comment, "Why, not really, Mr. Salomon. We have a city in Louisiana, as well. And actually my family moved to Los Angeles many years ago—before I was born."

Later, when he tried for the second time to get her to address him by his first name, she reluctantly complied, though several times thereafter she called him Jason by mistake. Furthermore, she failed to ask him to use her first name, leaving him no recourse but to continue calling her Miss Grant.

Allison had just asked Aidan—she said his first name correctly every time—to describe the difference between a doctor and a physician when a nearby table clock struck seven-thirty, the tone echoed a few seconds later by the big grandfather clock in the adjoining parlor. She glanced over at Nina, who abruptly rose and turned to face her visitors.

"I've an announcement to make," she declared, raising her hands like a conductor about to start a symphony. As all eyes turned to her, she continued, "You know we have gathered in honor of the marriage of my son, Maurice Salomon, to his lovely wife, Merribelle. But I have brought us together to share another event of great importance."

THE DECEIT

Rachel and Aidan shared an expectant smile, hoping Nina was about to give her formal blessing to their engagement.

Plunging ahead, Nina went on, "As my children know, the summer is always a special time for our family—and for the entire family of patrons and staff at Salomon's Emporium. It is special because of a tradition started by my father, Isidore Salomon—a tradition with an unbroken history of over twenty years: the Salomon's Emporium Summer Fashion Extravaganza. Unfortunately, this summer—our first one in our magnificent new building on Union Square—tragic events conspired to put a halt to this most noble of traditions." With a broad smile, she clasped her hands in front of her and announced, "It is my belief that your dear departed father and sister would not wish to see such a tradition fall by the wayside because of them. And so, in honor of Charles and Phoebe Salomon, I have decided to hold the most magnificent extravaganza Salomon's has ever seen."

"But Nina, we had agreed—" Maurice started to say but was stopped by his mother's raised hand.

"I have considered the issue from all angles, and I am firm in my resolve," she told him.

"Have you considered how much work it will be?" Rachel asked. "You know how tiring these events are for you."

"It is precisely what I need to get my mind off things."

"I think Nina is right," Jacob declared, standing and approaching his mother. "It will be good for her to get involved in something. And of course she'll have the full assistance of the staff."

"And perhaps you, too, Rachel?" Nina asked, turning to her daughter. "You always enjoyed helping me organize the extravaganza."

"I . . . uh, yes, I'd be delighted to help," Rachel reluctantly agreed, glancing helplessly at Aidan. "Have you considered any suitable themes?" she asked her mother.

Nina grinned with satisfaction. "The theme has been chosen—one that will capture the imagination of the entire city." She waited for their expectations to build, then exclaimed,

"This year, the Salomon's Emporium Summer Fashion Extravaganza will honor the inventive spirit of America and the world as embodied in the horseless motorcar."

"Automobiles?" Jacob said, scratching his balding pate. "But how—?"

"Just think of it," Nina enthused, raising her hand and drawing a picture in the air. "A gentleman in a jaunty tweed suit and leather cap. His lady seated beside him in a wide-brimmed hat tied below her chin with a gauzy scarf. A gleaming black automobile with polished wooden spokes and a plush leather seat. It will be the talk of San Francisco."

"But Nina, we can't feature an automobile," Rachel protested. "They're extremely hard to come by; Charley Fair had to import his motorcar from France. Why, there are less than a dozen in the entire city. Who knows how long it would take to ship one in for our show?"

"One? Who said anything about one?" Nina's smile broadened. "Along with the most beautiful fashions for an afternoon of motoring, I intend to display a whole fleet of automobiles on the main floor of Salomon's Emporium."

"Impossible," Jacob proclaimed.

"But Jason, it isn't," Allison interjected, again forgetting his name. She looked at Nina. "Please tell them," she urged.

"I've already made preliminary arrangements to hire at least half the automobiles in San Francisco."

"Hire?" Maurice asked. "Who would rent us—?"

"Every motorcar owner in San Francisco will be vying to have his vehicle included in our show. It will be a badge of honor—especially when they realize what other people are donating their cars. Why, they'll be afraid of being left out of the social event of the season."

From beyond the adjoining parlor, the doorbell sounded.

"And if you're still skeptical," Nina added, "someone has just arrived who should lay your doubts to rest."

Just then Cameron came to the entrance of the living room and said, "Madam, your visitor has arrived."

Signaling the butler to wait for one moment, Nina turned

back to the others. "I have taken it upon myself to invite a special guest to join us for dinner—a young man who not only knows everything about automobiles but whose presence on the organizing committee of our extravaganza will guarantee it is well attended by the cream of society. And by being the first to loan his new Panhard motorcar to Salomon's Emporium, he will also ensure that we have no shortage of automobiles come extravaganza night."

Turning to the doorway, she nodded to Cameron, who headed back through the parlor to the foyer, where the guest was waiting. Returning a moment later, he stepped into the living room and announced, "Madam, ladies and gentlemen, Mr. Timothy Price."

Cameron stepped back and ushered in a handsome young man in his midtwenties, dressed impeccably in a black, long-tailed dress suit with stand-up collar and silk bow tie.

As Tim Price came across the living room to where the others were all standing now, his expressive brown eyes flashed with an energy that was mirrored in his sure, confident stride. His light-brown hair was cut full and had a slightly wild streak that added to his dashing good looks. His mustache drooped slightly at the corners and quirked now into a smile.

"It's been such a long time," he said in a smooth yet forthright tone as he walked directly to Jacob and held out his hand. "It's good to see you again."

"And you, Tim." They shook hands briskly. "Just how long has it been?"

"Years. I've hardly been home since I went off to college." Turning in place, he said to Maurice, "I'll be damned if it isn't that red-haired young boy who used to follow me around the schoolyard—or was it the racetrack?" Chuckling, he grasped Maurice's hand, then pulled him closer and clapped him on the back. "You're all grown up, Maurice. You look fantastic."

"I always was grown up," Maurice protested. "It's just that you were a few years more grown up than me."

"And this must be your bride." He turned to Belle and raised her hand to his lips. "Mrs. Salomon, you are far too beautiful to be married to a drudge like this." As he released Belle's hand, Maurice cuffed him lightly on the shoulder. "And a violent drudge, at that," Tim added.

"Mr. Price," Nina interjected, coming alongside him and taking his arm. "I'd like to introduce a family friend." She turned him toward Allison. "This is Miss Allison Grant. She and Phoebe attended the same Boston school."

"We were practically neighbors," Tim commented, raising her hand to his lips. "When Phoebe was in Boston, I was attending Harvard College. Perhaps we chanced upon each other in one of Boston's fine libraries."

"I don't believe so, Mr. Price. If we had met, I'd surely have remembered." She smiled at him coquettishly. "Furthermore, my days at the library were few and far between."

"You don't appear to have suffered for it."

Nina tugged gently at his arm and said, "We have another friend of the family with us this evening. Mr. Timothy Price, I'd like you to meet Dr. Aidan McAuliffe, late of England."

As they shook hands, Aidan was surprised at the other man's grip. Though Tim Price was a few inches shorter than he, Aidan saw that he had a muscular though compact physique.

"A physician?" Tim asked. "Or are you one of those academicians like the ones I knew at college, who wielded their doctorates like swords to slay unsuspecting dragons like me?" His grin was so genuine that Aidan could not have taken offense even if he had been an Oxford don.

"I'm a surgeon. I wield mine like a scalpel—the unkindest cut of all."

"Ah, but one of the most necessary."

Aidan watched as Tim turned now to the only person he had not yet greeted. Smiling gently at her, he breathed, "Rachel . . ."

Ever since Tim Price had come into the room, Rachel had been standing stiffly. But as he fixed her with his warm expression, she seemed to relax. Smiling, she said, "Tim—it's good to see you after so many years."

She offered her hand, and as he raised it to his lips, he lingered slightly longer than propriety allowed. As soon as he released it, she reached out self-consciously and took hold of Aidan's arm.

Seeing that Rachel and Aidan were in some way connected, Tim adopted a more cautious tone. "You look as though life has been treating you well since I last saw you."

"I'm happy," she replied, squeezing Aidan's arm. Her smile would have looked more convincing were she not so noticeably disconcerted by Tim's presence. "In fact, Aidan and I are engaged to be married."

"Congratulations," Tim quickly offered, nodding at Aidan.

"Shall we withdraw to the dining room?" Nina cut in, stepping between Aidan and Tim. "Would you be so kind?" she asked Aidan, holding out her hand.

Aidan could do nothing but offer his arm to Nina, who drew him away from Rachel and started toward the formal dining room. Maurice and Belle followed, with Allison quickly taking Jacob's offered arm, as she and Nina had planned, leaving Rachel standing with Tim Price.

"May I?" he asked politely, extending his right arm.

Hesitating but not wanting to cause offense, Rachel slipped her hand through his arm and allowed him to lead her from the room.

As they followed behind the other three couples, Tim reached over and patted her hand on his arm. "It really is good to see you again," he said softly, letting his hand come to rest atop hers.

Tensing, Rachel tried to slip her hand from beneath his. But his grip was firm and strong—and not at all unpleasant. She drew in a calming breath, relaxed her hand, and kept her eyes straight ahead.

The dining room resembled a long medieval hall, with a narrow, rough-wood table down the middle and numerous flags and banners suspended from poles that angled out from the walls. The table, centuries old and imported from a Spanish monastery, was too narrow for head chairs but could easily seat two dozen. Just now it had four high-backed chairs spaced on each side, with another dozen lining the walls.

Each gold-trimmed plate bore an ornately written name, and as the guests circled the table, they found their name cards and sat down, the gentlemen assisting the ladies and then taking their own seats. To Aidan's dismay, he discovered he was at the end of the far side, nowhere near Rachel. Allison, then Jacob, and finally Nina sat to his left, and across from him was Belle, with Tim, Rachel, and Maurice to her right.

As dinner got under way, Aidan could see he would be obliged to spend most of his time conversing across the table with Belle, for beside her, Tim had shifted his chair toward Rachel and was describing his travels abroad, leaving Maurice's wife unattended. Though Rachel glanced at Aidan several times and gave him a reassuring smile, he sensed she was enjoying Tim's recitation of how he had conquered Europe and come home to take over the family railroading empire, one day to conquer the coming age of the horseless carriage.

Aidan was also concerned about the attention the pretty young blonde on his left was giving him. He could see that Jacob was smitten with Allison, so he did his best to keep his conversations with her brief. Instead he spent the duration of the meal discussing newborn infants, feeding schedules, and childhood illnesses with Belle, who as a nurse and new mother was especially pleased at the prospect of having a doctor in the family.

Aidan responded to all of her comments and questions politely and with as much enthusiasm as he could muster—given that he was secretly using his steak knife as a scalpel and his fork as a retractor and probe, slowly peeling back Tim Price's epidermis and dermis, slicing through the rectus abdominis and peritoneum, until he bared the entire length of the intestines, which he proceeded to slowly and ever so surgically disembowel.

Later that night, as Rachel and Aidan were being driven back to the Hotel Willard in the family's two-horse phaeton, Rachel noted that he was uncharacteristically quiet. When she asked him about it, he said he was merely tired; after all, it had been a long day, and he still had not fully recovered from spending a whole night and day treating the victims of the asylum fire.

For a while they rode in silence, Rachel holding on to his hand and resting her head on his shoulder. He seemed cold and stiff, and she knew it was more than mere fatigue. "It's Tim Price, isn't it?" she finally blurted, sitting upright on the plush leather seat. "Well, isn't it?" she asked, leaning up and turning his face toward her.

"No," he said a bit testily, turning toward her. "Why would you say something like that?"

Rachel had never heard him use this tone with her and was somewhat taken aback. "I saw the way you were looking at us," she told him. "It wasn't my fault that he was seated next to me. I was just being friendly."

"He was the one being friendly—a bit too friendly, I'd say."

"You're not jealous, are you?" she asked incredulously. "Whatever for?"

"Why shouldn't I be?" The anger seemed to well up in Aidan. "He's handsome, glib—and oh, yes, he's filthy rich."

Rachel nearly laughed. "He's just a child."

"He looks full grown to me."

"Well, he isn't. Trust me; I should know." She fell silent now, a bemused smile lighting her expression. Aidan's jealousy was making her feel especially desirable, and she was rather enjoying it.

"What exactly was there between you two?" Aidan finally asked, turning on the seat and taking her hands in his own.

"It was nothing, really."

"Tell me about it."

"We . . . well, we just dated. That's all."

"It seems to have been more than that."

"Not really. He had just started college, and I was working for my father."

"Was it serious?" Aidan pressed.

"I suppose so. But we were much younger then, and Nina was set against the relationship." She laughed lightly. "I don't know what surprised me more tonight—Tim's presence or that Nina invited him. She saw Tim as a real carouser and was always warning me about ruining my reputation if I continued to see him."

"Which probably made you want to see him all the more."

She laughed again. "Yes, I suppose so. And Maurice was so enamored of him. Jacob was already quite the young businessman in those days, but Maurice had a wild streak in him—like Nina, from what I've heard of her youth."

"You're joking. Nina?" Aidan slipped his arm around Rachel, who snuggled up to him.

"Perhaps that's why she's the way she is now—fighting in us the very things she hates in herself."

"What about Tim?" Aidan asked, bringing the conversation back to the point.

"Maurice was crazy about him and did everything he could to promote our relationship. I think Tim was like the older brother Maurice always wanted—someone to take him to the racetrack and sneak him into risqué stage shows."

"But it didn't work out, obviously."

"I know." Rachel shook her head questioningly. "And I never figured out why."

"What do you mean?"

"Tim transferred to Harvard in his sophomore year. Things appeared to be all right between us, and when he went away, he promised to write and send me his address. I never heard from him again."

"Not in all these years?" he asked.

She nodded. "I suppose that happens sometimes when a

young man goes off to college in a faraway city. I just didn't expect it to end like that.''

"Did you try to write to him? Through his family, perhaps?''

"I was going to, but Nina convinced me it wasn't proper to chase after a man. I think she was thrilled to see it come to an end.'' She drew in a breath and let it out slowly. "It was a long time ago. It's all over with now.''

"Are you sure?''

Rachel looked up into his questioning eyes. Frowning slightly, she said stiffly, "I told you it was.'' She looked away, falling into silence.

A few minutes later the phaeton pulled up in front of the Hotel Willard. As Aidan reached for the door handle, Rachel grabbed his arm.

"I'm sorry,'' she whispered, her eyes welling with tears.

"You don't need to apologize. I shouldn't have interrogated you like that. We're not even married.''

"Do you still want to marry me?'' she asked quickly, as though she had seen a look of doubt in his eyes.

"Of course I do. But . . .''

"But what?''

"It's nothing. I'm just very tired tonight.'' Again he started to open the door.

"I don't have to go home tonight.'' Rachel smiled gently at him. "I could stay here another night.''

Aidan turned and looked back at her. He realized what she was offering him, yet something inside of him hesitated, not ready to take that final step. "You told your mother you'd return home tonight,'' he said a bit feebly.

"I've told my mother a lot of things and then done exactly the opposite.''

"I . . . I don't know.'' He shook his head.

Rachel felt a lump form in her chest, and a sense of dread washed through her. "I don't want to force you, but—''

"Look, Rachel . . .'' He leaned back toward her and took hold of her hands. "We've taken quite a big step in getting engaged. I think perhaps we should wait a little, make sure we're doing the right thing, before we do anything that would make it impossible to turn back.''

"You mean you're not sure you want to marry me?'' she asked, the dread solidifying.

"I'm sure. But I want us to be more than sure.'' He looked into her eyes for a long moment, then cupped her chin in his hand. "I never want to do anything to hurt you, Rachel. I love you.''

She looked down, sniffling back her tears.

"I do, Rachel. That's why I want us to wait for a while. If our love is as real as we believe it to be, it will survive a few days—even a few months. And then we'll have a lifetime together, sure in the knowledge that it truly was love that brought us together.''

She nodded, forcing a smile.

As Aidan stepped from the carriage, he looked back in and asked, "Shall I bring your things down from the room?''

Rachel shook her head and in a faltering voice stammered, "I . . . I'll send someone for them . . . tomorrow.''

"Can I take you to dinner tomorrow night?'' he asked, and again she nodded. "Good night, Rachel,'' he whispered with a reassuring smile as he closed the door and stepped back onto the curb.

The tears in Rachel's eyes spilled over as the matching gray mares started forward and the black phaeton rode off into the gathering fog.

Eleven

EARLY THE NEXT MORNING, AIDAN MCAULIFFE MADE A DE-
tour downtown on the way to his first day of work at Pacific
Hospital. Having requested that the hackney cab wait for him,
he entered the hospital where his shoulder had been treated
after he had received the gunshot wound several days earlier.

Walking through the lobby, he approached the front desk
and told the nurse on duty, "My name is Dr. Aidan McAuliffe. I received a message that one of your patients requested
to see me. His name is Jeremy Mayhew."

The nurse looked down at a logbook on her desk and
scanned the entries. "Yes. Mr. Mayhew asked us to contact
you, and our records listed the name of your hotel. Mr. Mayhew is in room fourteen. Just go down that corridor and turn
left at the end." She pointed out the direction.

As Aidan started down the hall, he recalled the incident at
the restaurant Il Calderone. During dinner, Jacob had been
shot at by a crazed gunman but had been pushed out of the
way by Aidan, who sustained a flesh wound to his upper left
arm. When the gunman found himself confronted by a police

officer, he shot the officer and turned the gun on himself, committing suicide. The gunman, who was enraged at Jacob for having him arrested for embezzling, was Eaton Hallinger—the father of Phoebe's baby.

The murdered policeman, it turned out, had entered the restaurant on an entirely different mission: to arrest Aidan McAuliffe so he could be extradited to England and face the gallows. Accompanying the policeman was Jeremy Mayhew, whose family had framed Aidan for murder and who had hunted Aidan from London to Nova Scotia and finally San Francisco. During the shoot-out with Eaton Hallinger, Jeremy sustained a life-threatening gunshot wound to the chest, and Aidan had operated on him right there on the floor of the restaurant, using kitchen implements as surgical tools.

Aidan had managed to save Jeremy Mayhew's life, even though he knew Jeremy could turn him over to the police. However, when Jeremy regained consciousness and realized what Aidan had done, he at last believed that Aidan was not responsible for his sister's death. To Aidan's surprise and delight, he promised to have Aidan's name cleared in England.

Aidan hesitated in front of room fourteen. He realized that Jeremy Mayhew might have changed his mind, now that he was recovering from his wound, and that several police officers could be waiting in the room, ready to take Aidan into custody. But he shook off the thought, telling himself that Jeremy could as easily have sent the police to arrest Aidan at his hotel, rather than giving him an opportunity to escape again. Furthermore, Aidan had vowed not to run any longer; if the police were waiting, he would return to England and put his fate in God's hands.

He pushed the door open and peered inside, breathing with relief upon seeing that the room was occupied by only a single person, a man who sat in a chair near the window with his back to the door. Entering, Aidan called quietly, "Mr. Mayhew?"

The man in the chair turned to see who had addressed him.

He was a few years older than Aidan and had curly black hair and a mustache, which suddenly lifted at the corners as he smiled with recognition.

"Dr. McAuliffe," he declared, his voice sounding a bit scratchy. "Please, come in . . . and close the door."

Shutting the door, Aidan approached. As he came around the chair, he saw that Jeremy was not wearing a shirt and had a wide bandage around his chest and over one shoulder.

"Won't you sit down?" Jeremy said, indicating that Aidan should get a chair from across the room.

Aidan retrieved the chair and placed it a few feet from Jeremy's, angling it toward him. "I received your message this morning," he told him. "Are they treating you well?" He nodded toward the bandage around Jeremy's chest.

"As well as can be expected for a man brought back from the dead." He grinned. "They told me that you used a kitchen knife as a scalpel, a pair of tongs as a retractor, and a skewer as a probe to find and remove the bullet."

Aidan returned a cautious smile. "It was the best I could come up with."

"I'm just glad you weren't at a blacksmith's shop at the time. I'd rather get carved and dressed like a turkey than cauterized with a flaming brand."

Aidan laughed pleasantly and commented, "You appear to be recovering well."

"Thanks to you. They say you saved my life."

"I'm a surgeon. It's my job."

"You could have let me die." He fixed his dark eyes on Aidan. "No one would have found out who you are or why I was there."

Aidan shook his head. "I couldn't have done that. I've taken an oath."

"I know about all that," he said, dismissing it with a wave of his hand. "Still, I might've disregarded my oath if I'd have been in your shoes. I can tell you, I was terrified when I looked up and realized it was you who was about to operate on me. Thank God I passed out."

Aidan smiled warmly. "I'm just glad I was there to help you."

Jeremy chuckled. "That's ironic, because if I hadn't been pursuing you, none of this would have happened in the first place. It's all the fault of my family's misplaced conviction that you were responsible for my sister's death, when in reality you were trying to save her life after she was—" His throat caught, and then his already raspy voice cracked further as he continued, "After she was carved up by some back-alley abortionist."

The thought of the unconscious woman, pale as chalk, lying on his examining table made Aidan blanch. She had been a pathetic sight, bleeding profusely from a punctured uterus, and he cursed the butcher who was responsible. "I wish I could have saved her."

"I believe you." Jeremy leaned forward in his chair. "That's why I sent for you. If you remember, when I regained consciousness I told you I'd contact my father and see about having the charges against you dropped." He reached beside him and withdrew a folded piece of paper that he had tucked under his leg. "I received this last night."

Aidan unfolded the paper. It was a telegram from Jeremy's father, Gordon Mayhew, which read:

HAVE REVIEWED INFORMATION YOU SENT RE DOCTOR AIDAN MCAULIFFE. PRIVATE INVESTIGATION FURTHER REVEALS THAT PROSECUTION WITNESSES LIED AT TRIAL. OUR LAWYERS HAVE TURNED OVER EVIDENCE TO PROSECUTOR AND CONVINCED HIM TO TAKE IMMEDIATE ACTION. JUDGE HAS AGREED TO OVERTURN CONVICTION BASED ON NEW EVIDENCE. CHARGES OF ESCAPE AND UNLAWFUL FLIGHT ALSO BEING DROPPED. CONFIRMATION WIRED TO AMERICAN AUTHORITIES. FINAL PAPERS TO BE SENT TO DOCTOR MCAULIFFE IN SAN FRANCISCO.

As Aidan reread the message, Jeremy said, "That talk of a private investigation is just to protect my father. What the telegram doesn't let on is that his own agents were the ones who paid those people to lie at your trial. I knew about it but did nothing. I . . . I don't know what to say, other than I'm sorry.'' He lowered his head and shook it.

"Your father was convinced that I was guilty. He thought he was seeing justice done."

"We made a tragic mistake—one I'll have to live with for the rest of my life."

Shaking the telegram in his hand, Aidan looked up at him and smiled. "Well, you've begun to put things right."

"That doesn't excuse—"

"There's no point in dwelling on the past; it can't be changed. And perhaps some good has come out of all this."

"What do you mean?"

"If you and that officer hadn't entered the restaurant when you did, who knows how many people that gunman might have killed? And more personally, if I hadn't been forced to flee England, I'd never have met my future wife."

"You're going to be married?" Jeremy asked eagerly. "To that woman who was with you?" When Aidan nodded, Jacob added, "I'm delighted."

Aidan held up the telegram. "And this means we don't have to wait for months. We can begin preparations at once." He stood and held out his hand. "Thank you for what you've done," he said, shaking Jeremy's hand.

Jeremy slowly shook his head. "All the thanks go to you, Dr. McAuliffe. When you get back to London, I'd be honored to buy you a drink."

Aidan smiled. "If I return, it will be only to visit." Folding the telegram and placing it in his pocket, he turned and started from the room. Pausing at the door, he looked back and smiled. "It seems I'm to become a San Franciscan now."

"You look distracted," Nina Salomon observed as she poured a cup of tea for her daughter, who sat beside her on the sofa. "We really must concentrate if we're to have any hope of putting our summer spectacular together in barely a month's time.''

''I'm sorry,'' Rachel said, shaking her head as if to clear it. ''I was thinking, that's all.''

''Would you care to share it with your mother?'' Nina probed, handing her the cup.

''Really, it was nothing.''

''Apparently nothing about the extravaganza,'' Nina chided. ''You really must pay more attention; there's so much to do.''

''I will, Nina. I will,'' Rachel promised. She took a sip of the tea, then leaned over to the small table in front of them and picked up her mother's list of the items to purchase or rent for the fashion show, tentatively scheduled for late in July. ''Where were we?'' she asked, scanning the chart. ''Yes, the floral arrangements . . .''

''What is it, Cameron?'' Nina interjected, seeing the butler come into the parlor.

''A telephone call for you, madam. The gentleman did not say—''

''Yes, Cameron,'' she cut him off abruptly. She turned to Rachel. ''Will you excuse me, dear?''

As Nina started from the parlor, Allison Grant came down the stairs, wearing another of Phoebe's outfits, this one a simple brown serge skirt topped with a tan shirtwaist.

''Allison,'' Nina said, striding past her. ''We've been discussing the extravaganza. Perhaps you could share ideas with Rachel.''

''Of course,'' Allison replied, heading toward the sofa and greeting Rachel.

Leaving the two women, Nina hurried through the foyer to the pantry just off the kitchen. Her heart raced as she picked up the receiver, gave her name into the mouthpiece, and heard Damien Picard say in his lilting French-Creole accent, ''It's been a day and a half, and I've thought of nothing but you.''

''I was hoping you'd call,'' she replied somewhat cautiously.

"Did you think I wouldn't? I was only afraid that you might be having second thoughts and—"

"No," Nina blurted, feeling a bit breathless. "Never."

"Then I must see you again."

"I . . . I'm not . . ."

"Don't you want to see me again?" he pressed.

"Yes, but—"

"Then come to my hotel room."

"Now?" she asked incredulously. Her heart was pounding.

"In two hours—at noon. I've arranged for the hotel to send up a lavish lunch, and we can dine together on fine china and linen . . . and on silk," he added suggestively.

"But Allison and my daughter are here. How will I explain—?"

"Rachel is there?" he asked in surprise.

"Yes. She returned home last night."

There was a long pause, and then she heard him say, "And Maurice . . . have you made amends with him yet?"

"All the children were here for dinner last night."

"Wonderful. You can tell me all about it at noon." Then he added, "You do want to see me again, don't you?"

"You know I do. It's just—"

"Then say you'll come. I promise you won't regret it."

"I'd like to . . . very much."

"Then come. Tell them you have to go shopping or something. You can think of an excuse."

"I suppose I could. . . ." She hesitated, then said more eagerly, "Yes, I will."

"I'll have lunch delivered a few minutes before you arrive so we will not be disturbed."

"I'll be there at noon."

"Wonderful," he exclaimed. "And bring along a healthy appetite; I promise you'll leave satiated."

There was the click of the other phone being hung up, and then Nina returned her receiver to the cradle. She gripped the phone for a few moments, breathing heavily and wondering if she was doing the right thing. He was so much younger, and she was only recently widowed. But before Damien, it had been years since she had been really touched by a man—long before her husband's repeated heart attacks turned him into an old man at fifty-five.

"I'll be there," she whispered, closing her eyes and shaking away any thought of propriety or guilt. "I must."

She returned to the foyer, still feeling a bit dizzy with the thought of illicit passion, and was thrust back to the present situation by Allison, who swept toward her and gushed, "Look who's here, Mrs. Salomon."

Nina glanced beyond the young woman and saw that Timothy Price had arrived while she was on the telephone. He was dressed in a brown tweed suit and held a pair of soft leather gloves in his left hand.

"Good morning, Mrs. Salomon," he said, stepping forward and taking her hand. "I stopped by to thank you for a splendid evening last night . . . and to show you my Panhard. If the automobile is to be the theme of your extravaganza, you should begin by examining one firsthand."

"You brought your motorcar?" Nina asked, her voice edged with excitement.

"It's right outside. Would you care for a spin around the park?"

"Why, I really don't . . ." She could feel the color return to her cheeks at the thought of her coming assignation with Damien.

"Go on, Nina, it will be fun," Rachel prodded, sidling over and taking her mother's arm.

"I really don't think I'm ready for such derring-do."

"It's perfectly safe," Tim assured her.

"I know, but I . . ." She hesitated, intrigued by the idea. But her other commitment was far more impelling. "No, really, I'd rather not. Perhaps some other time, after I've grown accustomed to the idea."

"At least come out and look at it," Tim insisted.

"Why, of course. Let's all go."

"And then perhaps these young ladies would like to climb aboard for a ride."

"Yes, that's a wonderful idea," Nina said quickly, turning to Rachel. "Wouldn't you like to go for a drive?"

"I . . . I suppose it would be fun," she said hesitantly.

"Fun? It will be thrilling," Tim declared. He turned to Allison. "And how about you? The seat is modest, but it should hold the three of us without discomfort."

Allison was beaming with anticipation, but Nina sent the young woman a cautionary glance and saw her expression shift as she realized this was the perfect opportunity for Tim and Rachel to be alone together.

"I'd be delighted," Allison said, and as Nina's smile hardened, she quickly added, "but perhaps another time. I'm feeling a bit under the weather today."

"Some other time, then," Tim replied with a smile. Turning to Rachel, he noted her attire, a brown wool skirt and white shirtwaist, and said, "The fog hasn't fully lifted. Might I suggest a cape of some kind?"

"I'll go upstairs and get my jacket, then meet you out front," she said.

Nina noticed with pleasure that Rachel was blushing slightly. "And don't hurry home," she told her daughter. "I have some errands to run; I may not return until this afternoon."

As Rachel headed into the foyer and up the stairs, Tim Price pointed toward the front door and declared, "Ladies, shall we go outside and take a closer look at the future?"

"Hold on to your hat," Tim warned Rachel as he shifted the gear lever to the first forward position and pushed a lever to release the brake and engage the clutch of the open-bodied automobile. The large, rubber-rimmed rear wheels jerked into motion, propelling the vehicle down the paved drive.

Grabbing the side of her seat, Rachel hazarded a glance at her mother and Allison, who were standing on the stoop, waving and laughing with delight.

"Dear me," she murmured as the engine sputtered, gasped, and then popped with a series of tiny backfires.

"Jessah will settle down in a moment," Tim said cheerfully as he moved the long-handled steering tiller to the left, directing the vehicle around the curve and down to the open gate. He stepped lightly on the foot brake, then turned out onto the street, heading west toward Golden Gate Park.

"I thought this was a Panhard," Rachel called above the puttering din of the engine.

"It is—specifically a Panhard-Levassor, imported from Paris."

"Then why did you call it Jessah?"

"Every car deserves a name, and this sprightly little terror reminds me of my first sheepdog, Jessah."

Rachel smiled as the automobile jostled them together. "Yes, I remember her. She nipped Maurice on the calf when we all went bicycling one Sunday."

"No, Jessah had passed away by then. That was Joshua."

"Does your family name everything with a *J*?"

"Ever since my grandfather Jeremiah and his brother Jebediah made their first fortune with the J & J Freight Company, everyone in our family has been named with a *J* for good luck."

"Then how did you become Timothy?"

"I'll let you in on a secret if you promise never to divulge it," he replied with a note of mystery as he steered around a parked cabriolet and waved at a young boy who was tugging at his mother's arm and pointing at the car.

"I'll never tell," she pledged.

"Timothy is my middle name. My full name is James Timothy Price Jr. They say that when I was barely into knee pants, I informed the family I hated being a junior and would only respond to the name Timothy. Old man Jeremiah was practically senile by then, so my parents decided to indulge me, and the name James was dropped forever."

"I prefer Timothy," she told him. "You don't look like a James."

"And what does a James look like?" he asked, eyebrows rising.

"Someone far more staid and . . ." She rubbed her chin, trying to think of the right description.

"And responsible," he put in. "Someone like your brother, Jacob—another *J* person."

"I didn't say that."

"Ah, but that's what you always thought."

"I never wanted you to be more responsible—or staid," she protested.

"But your mother did."

Rachel was uncomfortable with the direction their conversation was taking, especially in light of Aidan's comments the night before. She felt somehow disloyal to her fiancé, riding alone in an automobile with a man about whom she had once felt something close to love. In a somewhat subdued tone, she replied, "Nina appears to like you well enough now."

"I noticed that." Tim nodded ruefully. "And it makes me more than a little suspicious."

"I know the feeling," Rachel agreed. "I think she's championing your cause because she doesn't approve of my engagement."

"But she made no secret of not approving of our relationship back when we were going out."

"That was before she met Aidan."

"And what's wrong with Dr. McAuliffe? He seems like a nice enough fellow."

"It's not Aidan, it's—"

"Don't tell me," Tim cut in, raising his right hand. "He was born in the Scottish highlands, but his hill wasn't Nobby enough for her," he punned.

"Precisely."

"And what do you think?"

"About Aidan? . . . I think he's the most wonderful man I've ever known."

"Yes, but do you love him?" Tim said boldly.

"I should think that would be none of your concern," Rachel said stiffly, clasping her hands on her lap.

"Better hold on," Tim said, nodding toward the intersection ahead. "We're going around the corner."

Rachel grabbed hold of the seat just in time, for Tim jerked the steering tiller to the right, and as the little vehicle rounded the corner, it caused a nearby dray horse to rear up.

As the driver of the wagon fought the reins and flung a stream of oaths at his animal and the passing motorist, Tim laughed and exclaimed, "Someday everyone's carriage will be horseless; either it will be fitted with an internal-combustion engine or its horse will have died of fright."

"You're incorrigible," Rachel declared.

"That's what you used to like about me," he replied, laughing again as he slipped his arm around her shoulder and gave her a hug.

Though she was clearly uncomfortable, Rachel said nothing about the gesture but quickly sat upright on the narrow seat. It would have been rather difficult to fit Allison on board as well, she realized, though Rachel would have welcomed the company at this point.

For a while they rode in silence, and then Tim began to explain the operation of his automobile, one of the first to mount the engine in the front and use a chain drive to power the rear wheels. Comparing European gas-driven vehicles such as the Panhard to the steam-powered cars that were more common in the United States, he pointed out that the engines were simpler, far less dangerous, and could propel the vehicle three times as far on the same amount of fuel.

Rachel listened attentively to his discourse, though in reality she was less interested in how a Panhard worked than in its obvious and immediate effect on passersby. She delighted in the reaction of pedestrians, who gathered on the sidewalks or rushed into the street to admire the unusual vehicle. Children were especially captivated and seemed totally fearless, running out in front of the car or chasing behind it to the point of exhaustion.

THE DECEIT

Upon reaching the Stanyan Street entrance to Golden Gate Park, Rachel said, "I thought there's an ordinance against driving automobiles in there."

"That's only on weekends," he replied, pointing the vehicle into the park.

Rachel knew that the ordinance was not limited to weekends and that Tim had decided to risk being cited, but he certainly could afford the fine, so she decided to say nothing. In any case, few people were in the park this Thursday morning, and it was unlikely they would encounter any policemen.

The Panhard puttered west along the main thoroughfare past the elegant white-glass Conservatory, a Victorian botanical greenhouse patterned after the one at Kew Gardens near London. As it continued alongside the music concourse and Japanese tea garden, the remaining evidence of the successful California Midwinter Fair held in the park two years earlier in 1894, Tim looked over at Rachel and said, "Your mother told us to take our time. Why don't we ride to the Cliff House?"

"I'm not sure about that," she said, noticeably uncomfortable at the suggestion.

"You always loved it out there, and now they've got that monstrous new palace of iniquity hanging off the edge of the cliff. We can climb up Sutro Heights and pretend we're pushing it into the sea."

"It wouldn't be right," she muttered, shaking her head.

"Because we used to go there before—when we were seeing each other? But that was ages ago; we were both young then. Let's not spoil the present by dwelling on the past."

She turned to him and smiled. "I didn't mean to spoil things. I know it was a long time ago, and I'm certain you've changed. I know I have."

"All for the better, from what I can see," he complimented, then frowned slightly and added, "Well, not quite all. There's that little matter of your engagement."

"I'm very happy," she said emphatically.

"I wonder if you'd have been so happy with me?" he

mused. "It looks as if we'll never know—and after I've gone to all the trouble of becoming staid and responsible enough to win your mother's approval." He shook his head with dismay, then grinned. "Oh, well, I suppose we can't turn back the clock to a time before we drifted apart."

Rachel glanced up at him and was struck with how much he resembled that exuberant young man for whom she had once cared so much. In a cautious voice, she said, "We can go out to Sutro Heights, if you still want to."

"Wonderful. And if you get hungry, I'll have one of those beach vendors serve us up the biggest bowl of steamers this side of Boston. Or if you'd prefer, we can dine in the Cliff House on champagne and terrapin bordelaise and watch the seals leap through the whitecaps below."

"I'm afraid the Cliff House isn't the sort of place for an engaged woman to be dining."

"Ah, but if you were engaged to the right man . . ."

Rachel looked at him as he gave an exaggerated pout. She could not help but smile.

Aidan McAuliffe had been kept busy all morning at Pacific Hospital, touring the facility with Dr. Tadeusz Obloy and meeting the other members of the staff. He was genuinely excited at the prospect of working again and was doubly pleased at having received word that criminal charges against him had been dropped in England. Yet now, as he went for a long lunch-hour stroll through the city streets, he was strangely discomfited and uncertain about what the future might hold.

He had begun to feel uneasy during the dinner party the previous night, when Rachel was reintroduced to her former boyfriend. It had grown worse when he returned to the Hotel Willard and watched her drive off for home. And now, just when everything appeared to be going so well for him, he was troubled by the haunting fear that their engagement might be a tragic mistake.

The fear had first flooded over him when he read the telegram and commented that he and Rachel need no longer wait to get married, and it had not yet abated. *We can plunge headlong into matrimony and perhaps live to regret it for the rest of our lives,* he thought as he crossed the broad expanse of Van Ness Street, the dividing point between downtown San Francisco and the outlying district where the hospital was located.

Aidan was certain he loved Rachel, yet suddenly he feared that his love was not fully reciprocated. Was it just his imagination? Or was it the reappearance of Timothy Price?

Aidan shook his head and frowned. It was both of those things, and more. It was also the dawning realization that he and Rachel had met under extraordinary circumstances and fallen in love during the excitement of his escape from England. In the following weeks, their love had been forged by the deaths of loved ones and the birth of a new child, then tested under the fire of a deranged killer's gun and in the flames of an asylum blaze. But would that love stand the test of year upon year of peaceful, routine existence? Could the daughter of one of the wealthiest families in San Francisco be content with the son of a common Edinburgh laborer, a man who could offer her little but modest security and his love?

Aidan had wandered deeper into the downtown area, heading into the North Beach district with its quaint eateries and immigrant shops. The streets were filling with people as offices and businesses closed for the lunch hour, and numerous strangers bid him a pleasant good day as they walked by. Aidan noted that in this district few people wore the well-tailored suits and fancy dresses favored by their more prosperous brethren a few blocks away.

As Aidan headed southeast through the district along the main thoroughfare, Montgomery Avenue—which would be renamed Columbus Avenue after the great earthquake of 1906—he noticed an occasional Oriental man or woman. The environment altered dramatically when he crossed Stockton Street and turned right onto Dupont. Whereas the two- and three-story unpainted brick buildings of North Beach appeared somewhat somber, the bricks here were painted a brilliant red, with glossy orange or blue lintels. Lanterns hung from the windows over the sidewalk, and the stoops and wrought-iron window balconies were covered with porcelain flowerpots.

As Aidan walked through this foreign world, beneath banners emblazoned with incomprehensible yet visually poetic Chinese words, he recalled his first visit to this district with Rachel, when their fortunes had been told by a strange little man named Hsiao Ch'u, who ran an herbal medicine shop at the corner of Jackson Street. The man's predictions had come startlingly true, and remembering his gift to Aidan of a three-inch-diameter sphere of rutilated quartz in a carved-lacquer box and his invitation to return at any time, Aidan decided to pay him a visit. Perhaps Hsiao Ch'u would offer some insight into Aidan's troubling situation.

Aidan found the little shop on the corner two blocks down Dupont Street. He glanced at the window display of a half-dozen flasks of different-colored liquids, each containing the preserved carcasses of snakes, toads, sea horses, or other animals considered medicinal.

He opened the door and walked in. From floor to ceiling were rows of tiny, unmarked drawers and narrow shelves, lined with unlabeled bottles of powders and liquids. Seeing no sign of the proprietor, he took out his pocket watch and noted that his lunch hour was almost half over. If he waited, he would have to return to the hospital by cab.

Just as he was about to leave, a high-pitched voice called, "Hsiao Ch'u happy his American friend Aidan McAuliffe come back." With that, the little white-haired man emerged from the curtained doorway that led to the back room, where he once had cast Aidan's fortune.

"Hello, Hsiao Ch'u," Aidan replied, bowing respectfully. "I was out for a walk and decided—"

"Hsiao Ch'u knows why you come. Shall we?" He waved an arm toward the back room.

THE DECEIT

"If you don't mind. . . . I'll be glad to pay—"

"You pay Hsiao Ch'u by your presence." He pulled aside the curtain and motioned for Aidan to enter.

Stooping down slightly at the low doorway, Aidan passed into the little room beyond. Only a straw mat, several embroidered silk cushions, and a wooden chest against the left-hand wall adorned the room. Remembering the procedure from before, Aidan removed his shoes and sat cross-legged on the cushion nearest the door.

Hsiao Ch'u sat down facing him on the mat. "Last time *I Ching* foretell *Ting,* the Caldron."

"Yes," Aidan replied. "And it was remarkable how almost everything you said came true and—"

Hsiao Ch'u stopped him with a raised hand. "Message was for you. It is enough that you received guidance you sought."

He opened the chest and removed the objects he used to cast the *I Ching,* a Chinese form of divination based on Taoist philosophy. Unrolling a small straw mat, he removed a bundle of fifty smooth, polished yarrow stalks. After removing one stick, he placed the pile in front of Aidan and said, "You must think of question or concern. You need not tell me. But when it is clear in your mind, you will divide stalks."

Aidan visualized Rachel's gleaming copper hair and thought of their times together. As he asked himself whether or not they were doing the right thing by getting married, he divided the bundle in two. Hsiao Ch'u quickly placed one stick from the right-hand pile between the little finger and ring finger of his left hand, then began counting off the left-hand pile in groups of four. The entire procedure was long and meticulous, with Aidan having to redivide the bundle a number of times and Hsiao Ch'u counting them off again and placing various numbers of sticks between the fingers of his left hand. But eventually the process was complete, revealing a hexagram formed of six solid or broken lines, stacked one above the other.

After writing the hexagram on a piece of paper with a

small calligraphy brush, Hsiao Ch'u pointed at it and intoned, "*Ming I*. In your language, Darkening of the Light." He frowned slightly as he lifted a hand-sewn book and turned the pages until he found one with the same hexagram at the top.

"Light sinking into the earth," he began, translating the oracle for Aidan. "Superior man must be cautious, reserved. Yet must persevere and not despair, for once darkness has climbed to heavens, it will plunge back to earth." He looked up at Aidan and smiled.

"I'm not sure what that has to do with my question," Aidan admitted.

"First hexagram tells of your situation now. Difficult times are ahead. Darkness is ascending. But just when you think all is lost and darkness has overcome light, it perish of its own darkness, for it needs light to survive!"

Aidan shook his head. "But I asked about getting married. I don't understand—"

"Ah, this is beginning of your answer. See here?" He pointed to the top pair of lines, each of which was a broken one with a small *X* in the middle. "These are changing lines," he explained. "In your language, *I Ching* means Book of Changes. In time these two will change to their opposites." Beside the hexagram, he drew a matching one, but with the top lines solid instead of broken. "Here is your future." He tapped on it and smiled. "It is *Chia Jên*, the Family." He flipped some pages in the book until he found the corresponding oracle. "The Family speaks of persevering woman who is foundation of the home."

"Then it is right for Rachel and me to be married?"

Hsiao Ch'u tapped the book and closed his eyes. "I see darkness all around this woman and her family. Someone wishes them harm—from outside and within. Darkness shall undermine the light by trying to crush it and by planting within it a false light. But if you and woman persevere, if you have faith, darkness will destroy itself at very moment it attempts final destruction of light. And when it dies of its own hand, that is when two of you should wed." Abruptly he stood and said, "There is visitor. I will return."

Aidan had not heard anyone enter the shop, but as the little man padded around the mat into the main room, he left the curtain open, and indeed a young Chinese woman was waiting patiently at the counter. She was petite, and though she was not overly attractive, she had a pleasant smile.

As the woman began to converse in her language with Hsiao Ch'u, her smile changed to a look of concern, and Aidan wondered what illness might have brought her to the shop and whether the old man's herbal remedies would be as efficacious as the chemical-based pills a Western physician would prescribe.

The conversation continued for several minutes, and then Hsiao Ch'u went behind the counter and stepped onto a raised platform. Taking down several bottles from the shelves at his back, he measured various amounts of liquid into a beaker of sorts and poured the mixture into a vial, which he stoppered with a cork. He spoke to her in a low, serious tone as he handed over the vial, and then each bowed. The woman exited to the street.

Returning to the back room, Hsiao Ch'u said, "I am sorry, but woman's mistress in need of medication."

"I understand," Aidan assured him as he put on his shoes and stood up.

"One more thing," Hsiao Ch'u said, touching Aidan's forearm. "I spoke of darkness that is destroyed in trying to consume light. But in death, darkness plants a seed that one day must grow into darkness or light. Cultivated with acceptance and love, seed will join light that nourishes it. Cultivated with hatred and fear, seed will again become darkness from which it sprang." Seeing Aidan's confused expression, he smiled and shrugged his shoulders. "I am sorry if I confuse you. I do not understand myself half the time." He giggled.

Hsiao Ch'u led the way back into the shop and over to the front door. As they stopped to say good-bye, Aidan removed a billfold from his inner jacket pocket and said, "I really would feel better if you'd let me pay you for—"

"Medicines can be purchased," Hsiao Ch'u declared, holding up his hand. "Truth—and confusion—cannot."

Smiling, Aidan returned the billfold to his pocket. "I am in your debt," he told the old man, extending his hand. As they shook hands, he added, "If ever I can be of service to you, don't hesitate to contact me. I'm on the staff at Pacific Hospital and can be reached there any weekday." •

Opening the door, Hsiao Ch'u bowed and invited Aidan to return whenever he wished. The two men said good-bye, and Aidan strode out to the street and hailed a cab, all thought of the Chinese man's strange words temporarily erased as he realized how soon he was expected back at the hospital.

Twelve

As Maurice Salomon made his way through the lobby of the Baldwin Hotel, he slipped a gold watch from his pants pocket and noted that it was almost ten past one—ten minutes after the time indicated in the message he had received at Salomon's Emporium. He shrugged it off; he did not look forward to this meeting and did not particularly care if Damien Picard was left waiting for a while. But he knew the only way to resolve his unfortunate situation was to face it head-on, so he climbed up the wide staircase and searched the second-floor hall until he found the room number his assistant had written down when taking the telephone message just before noon. He paused a moment, drew in a steadying breath, and rapped loudly on the door.

"Yes?" Damien called in reply. "Come in."

Maurice pushed open the door and entered room two forty-two. The draperies were drawn, and it took a moment for his eyes to adjust to the dim light and see Damien lying on the bed, lounging on top of the disheveled blankets in a dressing robe, apparently wearing no pajamas underneath.

"It's right over there," Damien said, hardly glancing at Maurice as he waved an arm toward a rolling cart covered with platters of half-eaten food and an ice bucket holding an open bottle of champagne. "You can take it away."

"It's me," Maurice declared, closing the door behind him and approaching the bed. "Aren't you even dressed?" He waved a hand toward the robe.

"Maurice?" Damien asked in surprise, bolting upright on the bed.

"Yes, Damien. Who did you think it was?"

"Why, someone returning for the lunch cart." He swung his feet over the side of the bed and stood, cinching his robe tighter. "Whatever are you doing here?" he asked, running a hand through his mussed blond hair.

"Come on, Damien. I got your message and—"

"Message? But I said to come tomorrow at one."

Shaking his head, Maurice pulled out the message slip and said, "Mr. Gelde wrote it down right here: one o'clock Thursday, June 25. That's today."

Coming around the bed, Damien took Maurice's arm and started to lead him back to the door, saying, "He got it all wrong." His tone was increasingly agitated.

"Look, Damien, I'm already here. If you've got something you want to tell me—"

"You'll have to come back tomorrow," Damien blurted, steering him toward the door.

Maurice eyed his friend suspiciously. Looking around the room, he saw a light spilling from beneath a closed door and thought he heard the sound of running water. Glancing at the double setting on the cart, he realized his friend had a guest. With a mock frown he said, "You'll never change, will you?"

Damien smiled sheepishly. "You know what they say about old dogs. . . ."

"Well, I can see it's an inopportune time, so I'll go back to the store and berate Mr. Gelde for getting your message wrong."

"I'll see you tomorrow, Maurice." Damien clapped his friend on the shoulder.

"How about noon? It's hard to get away at one."

"Sure thing," he replied, reaching for the doorknob.

Maurice nodded toward the bed and grinned. "Don't do anything I wouldn't."

"That leaves just about everything, doesn't it, old pal?"

As Damien started to turn the knob, the bathroom door swung open, and a tall, attractive, older woman emerged. "Can you help with these hooks?" she asked, looking downward as she reached behind her head and tried to close the hooks at the neck of her brown, floor-length dress.

Stunned into silence, Maurice stood motionless at the door, gaping at his mother.

"Damien," Nina Salomon went on, moving forward a few more steps and then looking up. Seeing the man standing beside Damien, she cocked her head slightly, as if in confusion. Suddenly she gasped, threw a hand to her mouth, and stammered, "M-M-Maurice!"

"What's going on?" Maurice demanded, looking from Nina to Damien, who stood frozen in place, the picture of incredulity.

"It . . . it's not what you—" The words caught in Nina's throat.

"How could you?" her son asked softly in disbelief, shaking his head.

"I didn't . . . I was just—"

"Don't try to invent some story," Maurice blurted, taking a step toward her. "It's perfectly obvious what's going on here." He turned to leave, then stopped short in front of Damien. Grasping the lapels of Damien's robe with his left hand and twisting, he said bitterly, "You're a real bastard." He raised his right fist as if to strike him but then held himself in check.

"It's not his fault," Nina exclaimed.

"It isn't, is it? Then how do you explain . . . ?" He released the robe with a jerk. "It's too disgusting to even talk about."

"It isn't!" Nina exclaimed, moving forward and trying to take Maurice's arm; he shook her away. "I'm a woman. I have a right to some happiness." When Maurice turned away, she pulled at his sleeve and demanded, "Look at me! I'm only human—I'm no saint."

Maurice gave an ironic laugh and muttered, "The understatement of the century."

"You're not being fair—"

"I'll tell you who's not being fair," he cut in loudly. "*You're* not being fair—to the memory of my father! Hell, he's only been gone a few weeks."

"Your father died years ago," she said bitterly. "At least that part of him which was a man."

"Shut up!" Maurice snapped. "He was a saint! Anyone who could have lived with you—"

She slapped him full across the cheek, then buried her face in her hands and began to sob.

Holding his stinging cheek, Maurice hissed, "I'm getting out of here." He glowered at each of them. "I can't take the smell."

He started toward the door to the hall, but Damien pushed it closed and stepped in front of it. "You're not being fair to your mother," he told Maurice.

"And I suppose you are? You're fair, all right—a fair-haired ponce, trading your charms to lonely older women for whatever you can get!"

"It's not like that!" Nina flared, choking back her tears.

"Oh, it isn't?"

"He hasn't taken anything from me."

"You just haven't gotten the bill yet," Maurice railed.

"Come on, Maurice, be reasonable," Damien tried to say, but Maurice cut him off with a shake of his fist.

"I know you," he grated. "I know how you operate." He turned toward his mother. "How exactly did he get to you? How did he worm his way in?"

"It wasn't like that," she protested.

"I came looking for you," Damien interjected. "It was the night you got married. Your mother didn't know where you were, and she let me spend the night in the guest room."

"The guest room?" Maurice said disbelievingly. "Hah!"

"It's true!" Nina insisted. "He never touched me—really. I . . . I wanted him to, but he didn't." She lowered her head in shame.

"That's a new one," Maurice remarked, eyeing Damien skeptically.

"I take full responsibility," Damien professed.

"It was my decision," Nina cut in, again taking her son's arm. This time he did not pull it free. "I'm the one who came here. I wanted it to happen."

"But why?" he implored, gripping her arms as if to shake her. "Why did you do it?"

Nina looked down and shook her head. "You wouldn't understand. You're young, and your love is young. But I'm forty-five."

"You're still a youthful woman," he told her. "In time a suitable man—"

"Suitable? Your father was *suitable*." Silent tears coursed down her cheeks as she looked up at him and said with quiet forcefulness, "Perhaps just this once I wanted something that wasn't so damn suitable. Is that such a crime?"

Maurice drew in a breath and let it out in a long sigh. Dropping his hands to his sides, he shook his head. "I'm sorry," he finally whispered. "I'm the last one to be judging you, Nina."

"Don't hate me," she begged, reaching toward him but then pulling back her hand.

"I don't hate you, Nina. I'm just so confused about everything that's been going on."

"I know you don't believe this, Maurice—" she clenched her hands into fists "—but I . . . I love you."

"I know you do," he said weakly, taking her hands in his own. He could feel her trembling and was struck by how much she looked like a hurt child, rather than his strong-minded mother. "It's all right. We'll pretend I never walked in here."

Her eyes brightened with hope. "You mean . . . ?"

"I won't tell anyone. I promise."

Nina pulled his hands to her cheeks and smiled up at him. "Thank you," she breathed.

As she released his hands, he backed away, looking a bit uncomfortable. "I really must be going now," he muttered, reaching for the doorknob.

"I'll see you tomorrow?" Damien asked as Maurice opened the door.

Maurice nodded numbly, then turned and strode away down the hall.

Slowly Damien closed the door, then turned to Nina, who looked to be on the verge of bursting into more tears. "It's all right," he whispered, moving closer and taking her in his arms.

"I . . . I'm so m-mortified," she stammered, sobbing on his shoulder.

"Maurice is a good son; he'll keep his promise."

"But it's so embarrassing. My own son, walking in like that . . ."

"It's all over," he soothed, kissing her cheek lightly and noting how she stiffened at his touch.

Pushing against his chest, she said, "I should be going."

"I'll only let you leave if you smile for me." He playfully shook her chin. "Just a little one." When she grinned in spite of herself, he said, "That's better. You'll see—things will work out for the best."

"I don't see how."

"They will if you want them to—and if you work for it. You should start by doing what you can to promote Maurice's position at Salomon's Emporium—especially to Jacob. I think Maurice is a little unsure of his management ability, and a few kind words from you might be just what he needs. It would also go a long way toward ensuring that he keeps his promise.''

"I'll try," Nina agreed, "but Jacob rarely listens to what I say where the business is involved. He'd prefer it if I stuck to organizing the fashion shows and kept out of everything else.''

"Yes, from what Maurice has told me, Jacob can be a difficult sort.''

"He's headstrong, all right.''

"Not at all easy to manage," Damien added, and Nina nodded. "Maurice would never be like that, I'd wager. So anything you can do in his behalf would only serve to help you in the long run.''

Fingering the lapels of his robe, she said, "Yes—I always felt closer to Maurice.''

"Then let him know that. There's nothing weak about showing someone that you care.''

"You're right," she said, her smile more genuine now. Reaching up, she kissed his cheek. "You've been so considerate. I'm sorry for those things Maurice said to you.''

Damien gave a wave of the hand. "He was just upset. I admire him for standing up for his mother." He grinned. "Don't worry about Maurice and me—we'll soon be sharing a drink again and laughing over old times.''

He walked to the wardrobe, took out Nina's wool cape, and brought it over to her. Stepping around behind her, he closed the remaining hooks at the back of her dress, then slipped the cape over her shoulders.

When he escorted Nina to the door, he stopped short and said, "I'd almost forgotten. It's about that young woman— Allison Grant. I wired a well-connected friend in Los Angeles yesterday, and he checked out her story. Not only is it true, but it turns out that her stepfather is quite the scoundrel. He lives well enough, but his money is largely ill-gotten. And regarding his claims that she stole money and jewels from the family, it's common knowledge he regularly squandered it himself and then blamed her in order to hold off his creditors."

"Then why didn't someone—a relative or family friend—do something to get her out of that awful place?"

"That's the tragedy of it all. Apparently no one knew where she was. The story he put out was that she ran off with a young sharpie and hadn't been heard from since."

"What do you think I should do?" Nina asked.

"I see nothing wrong with letting her stay for a while, if that's what you want to do. In fact, I'm having my friend in Los Angeles draw up a letter for her stepfather to sign, rescinding the order to have her committed. We can use the letter to ensure that she never tells anyone what she knows about Phoebe."

"Do you think he'll sign it?" she asked.

Damien nodded. "If he doesn't, we'll threaten to expose him for the wretch that he is. He'll sign just to keep things quiet."

"You're a dear!" she exclaimed, kissing him again.

"Now, run along—before I refuse to let you go." He gave her a hug, then opened the door. They said good-bye, and she started briskly down the hall.

As Damien closed the door and leaned against it, his face broke into a wide grin. *Perfect,* he thought. *Everything went perfectly.*

Indeed, there had been no mistake about the message he had left for Maurice. From the start it had been his intention for Maurice to walk in on Nina and him. And it could not have worked better. Nina now found herself inextricably bound to Maurice—bound by the fear that he might reveal her indiscretions with Damien. This gave Maurice more power than he realized, and with Damien's help, he would soon begin to wield that power, not against Nina but against Jacob.

Damien was convinced the eldest Salomon child was the key to this whole affair. From all he had heard, Jacob was too strong-willed and independent to be controlled easily. But with Jacob out of the way and Maurice at the helm of Salomon's Emporium, there was no telling how far Damien would be able to go—how much power, influence, and wealth he would wield.

"All I have to do is remove Jacob from the scene and secure my grip on Maurice," he breathed aloud. "And after tomorrow, my hold on Maurice will be assured."

Less than a dozen blocks away, Phoebe Salomon was being led into the inner courtyard of Sung Chien's multistoried Chinatown home. Sung Chien was already waiting there for her, seated inside his ornate landau coach. As a pair of bodyguards took her to the coach, she glanced around quickly but knew there was no way to escape. There were doors on each of the four walls surrounding the courtyard, and beside them stood bodyguards. In one wall were double doors, large enough for the coach to pass through. They were closed and barred, and guards waited on either side for the command to open them.

Phoebe was ushered into the coach and was settled in the backward-facing seat directly opposite the corpulent merchant in his flowing purple robe. As his thick lips pulled into what passed for a smile, he leaned forward and patted her knee. She shrank back into the seat to distance herself from him, suddenly feeling quite uncomfortable in the Oriental robe and embroidered silk jacket she had been given.

Peering through the window, she saw a door open along one of the walls, and then Kuei Mei appeared and started across the courtyard, with one of the bodyguards at her side. Not having seen the young servant for the past few hours, Phoebe had feared that her sole ally had abandoned her, and now she felt a rush of relief and a tinge of hope.

Kuei Mei and the bodyguard came to a halt at the coach door and bowed. At Sung Chien's nod, they stepped up into the coach and closed the door behind them, the bodyguard sitting beside Sung Chien and Kuei Mei beside Phoebe. Then Sung Chien reached through his open window and waved, and the men at the double doors removed the heavy wooden bar and pulled both sides open.

A moment later the coach, drawn by a matched pair of white horses, started through the doors and down an alley that led to the street. It was immediately joined by a pair of smaller carriages, one at the front and one at the rear, each bearing a contingent of Sung Chien's bodyguards.

As the coaches left the alley and pulled out onto the street, Phoebe tried to get her bearings, a task made difficult because she was facing backward. She guessed they were on Pacific Avenue but was surprised to see that they were heading west, away from the pier where the *Jade Reef* was docked.

"Where are you taking me?" she asked, her voice thin and strained.

"Then you do not wish to stay with us any longer, my little stranger?" Sung Chien asked.

"You said I could leave today."

"And so you shall. I thought you would like to see the city, and then we will take you where you wish."

Phoebe glanced at Kuei Mei, who averted her eyes but seemed to shake her head slightly, as if signaling Phoebe to remain silent. Not knowing what to say anyway, Phoebe sat back in the seat and looked out the window at the passing buildings as the coach slowly headed up into Pacific Heights toward the Presidio.

It was several minutes later that Phoebe realized with a sickening dread that they were heading directly for the Presidio Asylum for Incurables. She knew there had been a fire, but as yet she had no idea as to the extent of damage.

Her heart raced as they neared the Presidio, and she considered leaping from the moving coach and trying to make her escape. Casually she moved her hand toward the door handle, waiting for an opportunity. It came a moment later, when the coach stopped briefly at the corner of Broderick Street, two blocks from the edge of the Presidio. Suddenly she yanked on the handle—only to discover it was locked from the outside and would not move.

THE DECEIT

Sung Chien did not react, either oblivious to her action or pretending he had not seen it. Defeated, Phoebe slumped against the back of the seat, closing her eyes as the coach started forward, not even noticing as they drew abreast of the site of the asylum.

"A tragedy," Sung Chien said as the coach came to a halt. "A terrible tragedy."

Phoebe forced open her eyes and looked out the window, gasping at the sight of the leveled building. The remaining walls had been demolished, leaving only piles of charred beams and bricks, with crewmen carting off the rubble in wagons that lined the circular drive.

"There are still patients on the loose, I am told," Sung Chien said in a mischievous tone, leaning through the open window and surveying the devastation. "We can only hope they are apprehended soon so the public need not be at risk by a bunch of lunatics running free." Seeing the tears that had begun to course down Phoebe's cheeks, he asked, "Is it upsetting to you?"

Phoebe looked down and closed her eyes but did not reply, cringing as Sung Chien leaned across the aisle and again patted her knee.

Sung Chien called out a command, and the coaches started up again. Phoebe jerked slightly as something touched her forehead but opened her eyes to see that it was Kuei Mei, wiping her brow with a cloth. "You not look well," Kuei Mei said in an undertone.

"I'm all right," she replied, but Kuei Mei shook her head and repeated her observation.

Removing the cloth, Kuei Mei spoke softly to Sung Chien in Chinese. The big man peered at her questioningly, then finally nodded and turned to address Phoebe. "The *niu yung* says you are feverish, Liu. Would you like some of the *tai fu*'s medicine?"

Phoebe did not reply but merely turned away and closed her eyes. Indeed moisture had formed on her brow, though it was not due to fever but to the wet cloth Kuei Mei had carried in the folds of her robe and used on her.

Sung Chien signaled Kuei Mei to proceed, and the young woman took out a small vial from beneath her robe. Removing the cork stopper, she placed it to Phoebe's lips and said, "You drink this."

Phoebe hesitated but finally took a small sip. Grimacing at the acrid taste, she pushed the vial away and said, "I've had enough, thank you."

Kuei Mei held the vial closer and said softly but firmly, "You must drink it all; it is good for you."

Seeing the determined look in the young woman's eyes, Phoebe allowed her to raise the vial, and she downed the entire contents, fighting the urge to gag at the bitter taste.

As the coach turned into the Presidio and headed down the winding, forested roads to the northern waterfront, Sung Chien spoke pleasantly of the beauty of San Francisco. He urged Phoebe to look out across the mile-wide Golden Gate to the hills of Marin. Then as they rounded a bend and the downtown area came in sight, he pointed to the skyscrapers that dotted the Market Street business district and marveled at the great brick-and-steel wonders that were rising all over the city—"buildings that will stand for a hundred years as a testament to the spirit of your people."

As he continued to look out the window and describe the passing scenery, Phoebe stared at his face and realized how very repugnant he was, his features bloated and exaggerated, his complexion pasty. A dull nausea began to form in her stomach, and she did not know whether it was from this feeling of revulsion or the bitter medicine she had consumed.

The three coaches emerged from the Presidio and started along the waterfront, passing beside Fort Mason. Phoebe knew now that they were finally heading toward the *Jade Reef*, and she realized that their outing past the asylum and through the Presidio had been both a warning about the power Sung Chien wielded over her and a final sightseeing tour before she was spirited aboard his ship and carried off to the Orient, never to be heard from again.

The sense of nausea and revulsion increased as the coach came to a halt at the foot of Lombard Pier. The big steamer was still docked beside the pier, and crewmen were scurrying around the deck, taking up lines and preparing the vessel to sail.

The bodyguards filed out of the accompanying coaches, and two of them came over and opened the door of Sung Chien's coach.

Sung Chien stepped out first and turned to help Phoebe down. When she pulled away from him, he smiled and said, "I would like to show you my flagship steamer, and then you will be free to go where you wish." Seeing her hesitate, he slipped a hand into a hidden pocket of his robe and withdrew the two ten-dollar bills that had been in the pocket of the coat Phoebe took from the asylum. "I almost forgot—this is yours," he said, handing her the money. "So you can see we have no desire to hurt or upset you. If you will just accompany me for a few moments, I will see that you are taken wherever you wish."

Phoebe glanced across the coach and saw that several bodyguards were standing beyond the closed door, while two more had come up beside Sung Chien. There was no possibility of escape, and she turned to Kuei Mei, her eyes betraying her fear.

"It is all right," Kuei Mei reassured her, smiling gently and patting her hand. "You do what is asked, and everything will be fine."

Reluctantly Phoebe turned to Sung Chien and allowed him to escort her from the coach, but she suddenly felt very weak, as if her legs and arms had turned to rubber. Shaking off the feeling, she stepped down to the ground. Kuei Mei climbed out beside her, taking hold of her arm to steady her. Sung Chien started toward the ship, signaling the women to follow. They had no choice, for the bodyguards had come up on both sides and behind the women.

At Kuei Mei's side, Phoebe wobbled toward the gangplank that led up to the deck of the ship. The dizziness had overwhelmed her, and she had to lean against the smaller Chinese woman for support. The nausea returned, and with it a true fever, leaving her woozy and disoriented.

Phoebe remembered the other times she had gone into convulsions and worried that the same thing was about to happen. But this feeling was different, centering in her belly, as if she had eaten something spoiled and was about to vomit.

Letting go of Kuei Mei, Phoebe clutched her stomach and doubled over. Her knees were giving way when two of the bodyguards saw what was happening and grabbed hold of her arms. Kuei Mei rushed up to her master and spoke excitedly in Chinese, but he shook his hand and waved her off, then blurted a command to the guards, who lifted Phoebe in their arms and carried her up the gangplank, with Sung Chien and Kuei Mei following close behind.

The moment the guards laid Phoebe on the deck, she began to gag and retch. She rolled onto her side, gripping her stomach and vomiting. Quickly kneeling beside her, Kuei Mei positioned Phoebe so that she would not choke and suffocate, cradling Phoebe on her lap and speaking soothing words of comfort as the vomiting subsided.

Slowly Phoebe relaxed, though her body continued to shiver. She felt something cold on her face and realized that Kuei Mei was using the moist cloth to wipe her mouth, and then she heard the young woman whisper that everything would be all right. Suddenly Phoebe's body began to jerk spasmodically, and then she seemed to float away into that strange inner darkness.

Kuei Mei saw Phoebe's eyes roll back in her head and began to panic. Thinking fast, she stuffed the cloth between Phoebe's teeth just as her jaw tightened, clamping down on it rigidly. The blond woman's face went white, and her body stiffened and shook wildly.

Terrified, Kuei Mei shouted at Sung Chien, who could see that the woman was having a seizure far more violent than the one she had experienced before at his house. Sung Chien started to shake his head at Kuei Mei, then seemed to change his mind and nodded. He turned to one of his bodyguards and fired off a command. The man bowed, raced down the gangplank and over to the front escort carriage, and shouted something to the driver as he climbed inside. A moment later it raced off down the street.

Hours seemed to pass as Kuei Mei held Phoebe on her lap, stroking her arms and face and waiting for the seizure to pass. In reality it was only minutes, and by the time the carriage came barreling back down the street and onto the pier to the gangplank, the convulsions had eased, though Phoebe was still unconscious and her body continued to jerk slightly with spasms.

The carriage door opened, and a little man with a long white braid hopped out and scrambled up the gangplank. It was Hsiao Ch'u, summoned at Kuei Mei's request and Sung Chien's reluctant command.

Nodding at Sung Chien, Hsiao Ch'u knelt beside the blond woman and quickly examined her, pulling back her eyelids and inspecting her fixed, dilated pupils. He spoke briefly to Kuei Mei in Chinese, then approached Sung Chien, who stood with arms folded in front of him, towering over the little man.

"This woman must be brought to my shop at once," he said in Chinese.

"But that is impossible," Sung Chien declared, also in his native tongue.

"Why?" Hsiao Ch'u looked around the deck and saw the activity of the crewmen, then turned back to Sung Chien and glared at him accusingly. "Perhaps because you are sending this woman away on your ship?"

"What are you—?"

"This ship is being prepared to sail, and you intend to send this poor creature off to China aboard it."

Sung Chien glowered down at him and began to sputter a denial, but Hsiao Ch'u raised a fist and jabbed it at him.

"I do not care what you are up to here," the little man went on, "but I tell you this woman will not live to see Shanghai. Indeed, she may not live to see the morning rise in San Francisco."

"She's just ill. You can give her something—"

"She needs more than I can give her here! She needs careful attention and many days of rest. If you try to send her off on this ship, she will surely die."

"I cannot take care of her any longer," Sung Chien declared. "She has already stayed too long in my house."

"You must let me treat her at my shop," Hsiao Ch'u said flatly, nodding with portent.

"Your shop?"

"You will have her brought there at once, or else I will inform the authorities that you have kept her a prisoner since that asylum burned down." He paused dramatically, then added, "I saw her clothing when I first treated her. Do not deny where she is from."

The muscles of Sung Chien's jaw tensed, and he grated, "I have an investment here—" He stopped abruptly, shot a glance at the woman lying unconscious on the deck, and said bitterly, "I've had enough of her. Take her away." He pointed a stiff finger at Hsiao Ch'u. "But I never want to see her again. She is your responsibility now."

Hsiao Ch'u nodded, then turned to a pair of bodyguards and directed them to carry the woman to the carriage. The men looked over at Sung Chien, who signaled them to comply.

As Phoebe was carried down the gangplank, Hsiao Ch'u bowed to Sung Chien, then said, "I will need the *niu yung* to come along."

"Why?" Sung Chien asked suspiciously.

"I need her help if I am to save this woman's life."

Sung Chien stared at Kuei Mei, then back at the old man. "She may go. But she must return to my house tonight, or my men will come and take her and the woman."

Hsiao Ch'u bowed. Turning, he motioned for Kuei Mei to

follow, and together they descended the gangplank and climbed into the carriage, where Phoebe was lying on one of the seats.

Standing at the rail of the ship, Sung Chien muttered an oath. With a bitter sigh, he raised his arm and waved for the coachman to proceed, and the carriage clattered away down the pier.

Thirteen

JACOB SALOMON GLANCED AT THE WALL CLOCK IN HIS OFFICE and noted that it was just past two o'clock. He had asked Maurice to examine the purchasing orders and compare them to the bills of lading—an onerous task that he himself had performed before Charles Salomon's death and was now to become Maurice's responsibility. He had promised to meet with Maurice and review the procedure before the end of the day. *I'll just finish these papers first,* he decided, returning to the letters that had been prepared for him to sign.

A light rapping on the half-open door interrupted him, and he looked up and called, "Yes?"

The door opened slightly and an elderly, white-haired man leaned in. "You've a visitor, Jacob," he said.

"Show him in, David." Jacob noted that the older man seemed uncomfortable using first names. David Gelde had been a longtime assistant to Jacob's father and was having to adjust to Jacob's more modern business style. When Charles had occupied this office, Nina had insisted that the staff use a more formal form of address.

A bit hesitantly, Gelde raised a hand and said, "It's not a he, sir, but a young lady. Miss Allison Grant."

Jacob's expression brightened. "By all means, show her in." He stood and straightened the lapels of his jacket.

The door opened wide, and Gelde backed to the side and said, "Miss Allison Grant."

Allison swept into the room and turned in a circle, taking in the plush furnishings. "A magnificent office—and so spacious," she said admiringly. "Well befitting the head of Salomon's Emporium." She approached the desk and with a smile held out her hand. "Good afternoon, Jacob."

Coming around the desk, Jacob gave her hand a polite kiss. "To what do I owe this pleasure?"

"I've never been in Salomon's, so I asked Cameron to fetch me a cab. And here I am."

"I'm delighted you are. Would you like a tour?"

"I was hoping you'd ask. That's why I came up here first." She looked over at the papers on the desk. "I don't want to take you from your work, though."

"It can wait," he said, dismissing the papers with a wave of his hand. "Would you care to leave your wrap here?"

"Yes, thanks." She unbuttoned her shoulder cape, and he stepped behind her and removed it, carefully folding it over the back of a chair.

"That's a lovely gown," he remarked, admiring the way she filled her blue dress, styled in a French fashion that was only beginning to catch on in America. Though it had the traditional leg-o'-mutton sleeves, they were cut daringly low at the collar, leaving her neck and much of her shoulders exposed. He did not recognize it as the very dress he had given his youngest sister, Phoebe, for her last birthday.

"And you look so distinguished—like Prince Albert himself with that trim beard and jacket." She slipped her hand through his arm and declared with a smile, "I'm ready to see your kingdom."

"Princedom, I'm afraid."

"Not forever, I'd daresay," she replied.

As Jacob led Allison through the outer office, he told David Gelde that he would return in a while. Then he escorted her along the hall to the elevator and down to the first floor.

"We moved into this building last fall," he explained as he led her onto the main floor and over to the head of the nearest aisle.

"It's magnificent," she declared, coming to a halt and peering down the aisle to the pavilion at the center of the mammoth room, which was two stories high and half a city block in each direction.

"We decided to expand when we learned there were plans to open the Emporium on Market Street."

"Nina mentioned another Emporium."

"There was a time when practically every store in the city called itself one kind of emporium or other. But this new store is called just the Emporium; they opened last month in a seven-story building on Market Street, and they're proving to be quite a competitor. At least it keeps us on our feet."

"Can they get away with calling themselves that?"

"We considered taking them to court, but Nina would not hear of it. She thinks they sound like a common five-and-dime and would prefer to see us simply called Salomon's; she believes it's more suited to a place that caters to a finer clientele."

"I agree."

"Then Salomon's it shall be," he said, grinning. "Shall we?" he asked, pointing down the aisle.

Jacob led her past neatly arrayed displays of ladies' apparel and accessories. One counter held an assortment of gloves, from simple knit Jerseys with silk-embroidered backs to the fashionable elbow-length, suede mousquetaires. Nearby, a display tree was hung with chatelaine purses of seal- or lizard-grained calfskin, with short chain or leather hook straps to attach them to a belt.

They continued down the aisle past counters that contained hairbrushes of every style and type, from engraved silver and fancy-backed celluloid to simpler ones with wood or hard-rubber handles.

"Look at those," Allison declared, pulling Jacob over to a display of ladies' and gentlemen's hair goods. "How would I look in that?" she asked, pointing to a stand that held a full black wig. A card in front of the stand read: *La Tosca Puff Bang, In The Latest Style, Light And Fluffy, Made Of Naturally Curly Hair On A Ventilated Foundation, For Ladies Who Do Not Require A Heavy Front*.

"May I assist you, ma'am?" a saleswoman asked, coming up behind the counter. Suddenly she recognized Jacob and said, "Excuse me, Mr. Salomon. I didn't see you."

"Good afternoon, Emma," he said jovially. "Miss Grant and I were just admiring your display."

"There's one for you!" Allison exclaimed, stooping down and pointing into a glass case at her waist. On the shelf was a full mustache and beard of dark-brown human hair, and beside it a small goatee. "How about trying the big one on?" she asked playfully.

"One beard is enough," he replied, stroking his own trim beard and then taking her arm and steering her away from the counter. "Good day, Emma," he called behind him as they wandered down the aisle.

Jacob led Allison to the pavilion at the center of the floor. It was an open-topped, eight-sided platform with a free-standing Corinthian column at each corner. Steps led down from between the columns to the eight golden walkways, which radiated across the floor like a sunburst, dividing the floor into eight wedges.

"On special occasions we hold concerts here, with chairs going around in a complete circle." He pointed to the open, wide area between the pavilion and the beginning of the aisles.

"It must look magnificent at night, with the electroliers lit." She gazed up at the electric chandeliers that ringed the recessed dome, which matched the trompe l'oeil ceiling in the living room of the Salomon mansion.

"It really is splendid. Perhaps you'd like to come back some night, and I could turn them on for you to see."

Allison squeezed his arm and smiled up at him. Suddenly she glanced beyond him and said, "Oh, look—here comes Rachel."

Jacob turned to see his sister approaching on the arm of Timothy Price.

"Hello, Jacob," she called, nearing the pavilion. "Allison, I didn't expect to see you here."

"I got tired of sitting at the house by myself."

"Nina's still out?"

"She left a little before noon and was still gone when I went out."

Rachel looked at her brother. "Tim was kind enough to take me for a ride in his Panhard. It was quite thrilling."

"Rachel thought I should see where the extravaganza will take place," Tim put in, circling in place and looking around at the pavilion and surrounding area.

"Nina suggested we put the cars around the perimeter, with one right on the pavilion," Rachel told him.

"My Panhard, of course." He nodded. "Yes, I think it will work fine. The only problem will be getting the cars through the front door."

"There's a bigger door at the back for deliveries," Jacob informed him.

"Tim was just about to drive me home," Rachel explained to Allison. "Would you care for a ride?"

Allison glanced up at Jacob with a questioning look. Turning back to Rachel, she replied, "Thank you, but no. I'd like to spend some more time here and perhaps do a little shopping." She paused, then added, "And after that, I believe I have a dinner date. Isn't that true, Jacob?"

Startled, Jacob looked down at Allison. Seeing her coy smile, he grinned and said, "It certainly is . . . that is, if you'd care to dine with me this evening."

"I'd be delighted. And perhaps Rachel and Tim would care to join us," she suggested.

"That's a wonderful idea," Tim replied. "Would you like to, Rachel?"

"I . . . I'm afraid not. Aidan and I already have made plans."

"Perhaps some other time, then." He gave a gracious smile.

"Perhaps," she replied a touch nervously. "I really should be leaving for home now."

"Of course. Good day, then," Tim said, bowing to Jacob and Allison. Rachel said good-bye, as well, and they headed back down the aisle toward the front door.

"I hope I wasn't too bold," Allison said once she and Jacob were alone again.

"Just bold enough," he declared, offering his arm. "And where would you like to dine?"

"Why, right here on the pavilion—after the store closes—with the electroliers lit and a string orchestra playing at our side." She gave a playful chuckle.

"I suppose I could have my man Langdon fetch us covered dinners from the Palace dining room. And for an orchestra, we could bring over one of those new graphophones from aisle seven, and if we put our ears very close to the amplifying horn and are very quiet, we just might hear some faltering tenor belting out a wavering rendition of 'Buffalo Gals.'"

"That would be heaven," she exclaimed with a laugh.

As Jacob continued the guided tour, Allison noted not only the wealth of goods all around her but also the deference with which the employees treated him. She was pleased, now, that Aidan McAuliffe had shown no interest in her during Nina's dinner party. Though she had not been particularly attracted to Jacob when they first met, she found herself growing increasingly intrigued, if not by Jacob himself then by the power and respect he commanded.

Her thoughts were interrupted by Jacob's asking if she wanted to see their new display of photographic equipment. "If you'd like," she replied. "But I'd so much like to examine the new Paris dresses. I'm afraid that being around your family has made me feel terribly out of fashion.''

"Then we'll have to do something about that," Jacob declared as he led her toward the women's department.

Let Tim Price be the one to separate Rachel and Aidan, she mused as she squeezed his arm and imagined how easy it was going to be to get Jacob to purchase her a new outfit. *It will be much more fun figuring out ways to separate Jacob from some of his money.*

In the apartment above his shop on Dupont Street, Hsiao Ch'u knelt beside a mattress on the floor, delicately holding Phoebe Salomon's forearm to determine the rate and character of her pulse at several energy points. She was lying very still, unconscious but no longer shaking.

After a couple of minutes, Hsiao Ch'u lowered her arm and looked over at Kuei Mei, who was crouched at the other side of the mattress. "You speak English, yes?" he asked in Chinese. When she nodded, he continued, "We will speak in this woman's language so as not to frighten her."

"But she is not awake," Kuei Mei replied in English.

"Her body sleeps, but she is aware of what is happening. When she awakens, she will not remember. But it best to keep patient calm and relaxed so she can assist from within." He stood. "I bring some things up from my shop." With a bow, he left the small, simply furnished room, one of two in which he lived above the shop.

Kuei Mei looked around as she sat holding Phoebe's hand. The room contained this straw-filled tick mattress, several chests along one wall, a child-size table with two rough wooden chairs, a set of book-lined shelves, and a counter with assorted cooking utensils. The room was austere, even by Chinatown standards, and she wondered if the *tai fu* was really so poor or simply chose to live in this fashion.

A few minutes later Hsiao Ch'u returned, bearing a tray laden with small piles of herbs and a few metal utensils. Taking up a thick piece of ginger, he used a sharp knife to cut a quarter-inch slice, then poked a number of holes in it with a metal pick. Pinching together some packed, stringy leaves and molding them into the shape of a small cone, he placed the cone on top of the ginger, which he then carefully positioned on Phoebe's forehead. After lighting a kitchen match, he touched it to the tip of the cone until a thin curl of acrid smoke spiraled upward.

Blowing out the match, he watched the tobaccolike herb as it smoldered on top of the ginger. Occasionally using a pair of tweezers, he moved the ginger to a different spot on Phoebe's forehead so the radiant heat would not burn her skin.

"This called moxabustion," he explained, as much for Phoebe's understanding as for Kuei Mei's. "We burn moxa made of mugwort"—he pointed to the cone of pressed leaves—"to alter flow of *chi* energy and drive out excess wind and cold *chi*." He smiled at Kuei Mei. "Powder of Three Miraculous that you prepared for her did much to improve flow of damp *chi*, and now I treat wind and cold *chi* obstruction."

When the cone of herbs had burned nearly to the bottom, he removed the ginger and set it on the tray, the mugwort still smoldering. Next he mixed various herbs into a pile on the tray and transferred the mixture to a small metal pot, which he carried to the counter and filled with water from a pitcher. Lighting another match, he pulled forward a small double-burner oil stove, raised the wick on one of the burners, and lit it. Placing the pot on the burner, he returned to the floor mattress and said, "Water must boil down and be refilled two times. Third time we only warm water, not boil. Then she drink it."

"And if she does not awaken?" Kuei Mei asked anxiously.

He narrowed one eye and nodded. "She awake soon."

They waited in silence as the water warmed and broke into a boil. The pot was quite small, containing little more than a cup, so it did not take long for the water level to lower. After a while, Hsiao Ch'u checked the pot and saw that most of the water had evaporated, leaving a thick, murky sludge. He refilled the small pot and repeated the procedure.

"Come quickly," Kuei Mei called softly but urgently in Chinese, forgetting to speak in English.

Hsiao Ch'u turned to see that the blond-haired woman was stirring as she regained consciousness. "You are all right," he said soothingly as he knelt down and stroked her arm. "You are with friends."

Phoebe's eyes fluttered open, then closed again. She gave a weak moan and tried to rise.

"You must rest," Hsiao Ch'u urged, grasping her shoulders and easing her back against the mattress.

"Wh-where . . . ?"

"You are with Kuei Mei at house of friend," Hsiao Ch'u told her as she opened her eyes and tried to focus. "Kuei Mei helped you escape."

Slowly Phoebe was able to focus on the two people who hovered over her. Recognizing Kuei Mei, she said, "What happened? The . . . the ship . . ."

"We take you away from there," Kuei Mei told her, smiling excitedly. "You are safe now."

"You must rest," Hsiao Ch'u urged. "Soon you feel better, and then we talk."

Half an hour later, Phoebe was sitting up on the mattress, sipping from a cup filled with the mixture Hsiao Ch'u had prepared.

"This is horrible," she said with a grimace. "Do I have to?"

She looked up at Hsiao Ch'u, who stood over her. He smiled and nodded, motioning for her to finish the liquid. She forced herself to take another sip, and though the brew was the most bitter, awful drink she had ever tasted, she had to admit that it settled her still-queasy stomach.

"You feel ill from medicine Kuei Mei gave you."

"I am sorry," Kuei Mei said, kneeling beside Phoebe. "It was the only way."

"What do you mean?"

Hsiao Ch'u pulled over one of the small chairs and dropped down onto it. Resting his hands on his knees, he leaned toward Phoebe and smiled. "Earlier today, Kuei Mei came to my shop. She told me Sung Chien was about to take you to his ship and that he wanted medicine for your journey. I prepared liquid to make you fevered, sick in stomach. During ride to ship, Kuei Mei pretended you were ill and served it to you."

"I would have told you, but when I returned, you were already gone from your room, and I did not see you again until we were in the coach," Kuei Mei explained.

Hsiao Ch'u laughed, slapping his knees with his hands. "We fooled Sung Chien good with our plan! When you got sick, Kuei Mei was to send for me so I could convince Sung Chien you too ill to travel. But liquid worked more strongly than expected. You should only have gotten ill; instead you had what your doctors call seizure."

Phoebe nodded. "At least it convinced Sung Chien to let me go," she said, draining the last of the liquid and handing the cup to Kuei Mei.

"This not your first seizure," Hsiao Ch'u noted. "How long have you had them?"

"Not very. The first was . . . it was after an operation." She closed her eyes and shook her head at the memory of what had happened to her unborn baby. "I think it was the worst seizure, because when I finally came to, I was in that asylum." She looked up at Hsiao Ch'u, her eyes betraying a glimmer of hope. "Do you know what's wrong with me?" she asked expectantly.

"I believe you suffer what doctors call epilepsy."

"Can I be helped?"

"Your doctors have not much success with this illness."

Phoebe's shoulders sagged. "Then there's no hope," she muttered.

"Do not give up hope," Kuei Mei implored. "Our Chinese doctors treat this imbalance. Is that not so, *tai fu*?"

"We have some success treating this imbalance. It cannot always be cured but can be controlled."

"Controlled? How do you mean?"

"You can learn to feel changes that come before a seizure, also ways to reduce its strength. And some preparations lessen power of seizure; these I can make you."

"Will you teach me?" she asked eagerly.

Hsiao Ch'u shook his head uncertainly. "Our ways are very different from those of your doctors."

"I can learn," she insisted. "If you'll teach me."

"Chinese healing based on different principles than your medicine. It could take much time and study. . . ."

"I have plenty of time," Phoebe told him. "In fact, I have nowhere to go."

"Surely there is somewhere you can go."

"My mother was the one who sent me to that asylum. I won't risk going home and being sent back again."

"But when she sees that you are better . . ."

Phoebe raised her hand and shook her head firmly. "I'm not going back there . . . not yet." Looking up at him anxiously, she implored, "Won't you help me? Won't you let me stay here for a while?"

Hsiao Ch'u stared back and forth between the young American woman and Kuei Mei, then swept his hand in an arc to indicate his modest lodgings. "This not comfortable place for woman such as you."

Phoebe chuckled and shook her head. "You should have seen my cell at the asylum."

Hsiao Ch'u closed his eyes and breathed in deeply. Slowly exhaling, he looked back at her and said, "You may stay here until you feel ready to leave."

"Thank you," Phoebe exclaimed, beaming as she reached over and gripped Kuei Mei's hand.

"But you may stay only if you agree to be student, not patient." Seeing her questioning expression, he added, "A student is one who participates, while a patient wants only to lie back and let doctor do work."

"I understand," she said, nodding.

"You will soon discover I am very lazy doctor indeed." He laughed lightly, and the women joined in.

Kuei Mei stood and looked at each of them. "I must leave now. If I do not return soon, Sung Chien will send his men to get me."

"Does she have to go back there?" Phoebe asked Hsiao Ch'u, her voice edged with distress.

"It is as we agreed," he said, nodding.

Kuei Mei bowed to Hsiao Ch'u, then turned to Phoebe and said, "Sung Chien called you Liu, the Stranger. I do not know your name."

The young blond-haired woman hesitated, then firmly replied, "My name is Phoebe. Phoebe Salomon."

"I hope to see you again one day, Miss Phoebe Salomon." Kuei Mei bowed respectfully, then turned quickly and hurried from the room, her eyes welling with tears.

When Aidan McAuliffe arrived at the Salomon mansion on Nob Hill after finishing his first day of work at Pacific Hospital, he was greeted at the door by Nina, who acted somewhat surprised to see him.

"Rachel and I have plans to dine together this evening," he explained.

"Ah," she breathed, nodding thoughtfully, then added pointedly, "She never mentioned it when she returned from her drive with Tim Price. I'll go up and see if she's ready yet." She moved from the door, then almost as an afterthought asked, "Won't you come in?"

Aidan stepped into the foyer, where he stood crushing his fedora between his hands, feeling awkward and annoyed. He watched as Nina swept upstairs, her overly long evening dress trailing behind her on the wide marble steps. What she had said about Rachel's being with Tim Price undeniably perturbed him, but he reminded himself that it was Nina who had said it, and he resolved to hear Rachel's version before letting his jealousy erupt.

He only had to wait a few minutes, and then Rachel came down, looking stunning in a green gown with black lace trim. Over her arm she had a brown, fur-trimmed cape, which she handed to Aidan to help her put on.

"I hope you weren't waiting long," she said, buttoning the cape and turning to kiss his cheek.

"Shall we go?" he asked a bit abruptly, opening the door and leading her out.

Taking his arm, Rachel accompanied him down the stairs and over to the waiting gurney cab. "Where shall we dine?" she asked. "We haven't been to the Palace yet, and on Kearny Street there's a new French restaurant that's becoming the rage."

"Actually, I went for a walk at noon and found a little restaurant I'd like to go to, if you don't mind."

"Of course not," she declared, taking his hand and stepping up into the cab.

A moment later they were riding down Nob Hill toward North Beach, eventually coming to a stop in front of a small building just off Mason Street. Hand-painted letters on the window read *Rigoletto's*, and a small red-and-green awning hung over the single, unassuming door.

"Is this it?" Rachel asked, a bit surprised at not having heard of the establishment before.

Aidan paid the cabbie, then turned to lead her inside. "It's a bit modest, but people in the area claim it serves the best Italian food in San Francisco."

"Let's see for ourselves," she said eagerly as he opened the door and ushered her inside.

Rachel found herself in a crowded, noisy little restaurant that at best would be called modest. The walls were light blue and bereft of decoration, with unadorned navy drapes over the three windows that lined the outside wall. The square tables were covered with simple white linen, the china and crystal of the most common sort, and there were easily twice as many tables as at the restaurants Rachel usually frequented, so that the patrons were packed almost one on top of another. And they were a lively bunch, the men in plain frock suits that either had seen better days or had no better days in them, the women in coarse-fabric dresses that tended toward gray and brown.

At first Rachel seemed taken aback that Aidan had brought her here, but as he led her to an empty table at the rear, she grew genuinely intrigued by the air of good cheer around her. "I think it's delightful," she declared as Aidan took her cape and she sat down.

"You do?" he asked with a bemused smile, draping the cape over one of the empty chairs and taking a seat to Rachel's right. "I didn't realize it would be so crowded."

"It's refreshing—and not as stuffy as the places my family usually goes." Leaning toward him, she took his right hand. "Tell me, was there a reason you wanted to come to this place specifically?"

Aidan shrugged. "I suppose I've been feeling a little uncomfortable with all the fine meals and fancy service I've had since arriving in San Francisco." He glanced around. "This is really more similar to the places I was used to in Edinburgh and London."

"You're homesick, aren't you?"

"A little. But no, that's not really the problem."

"Then there *is* a problem."

Placing his left hand over hers, he smiled thinly and said, "There's something I want to discuss."

"About us, right?"

Aidan nodded, his smile fading. "All day I've been considering our engagement, and I'm no longer certain it's the best course of action."

"A course of action? That's what you consider it?" she said a bit testily, withdrawing her hand.

"No, Rachel. It's just that I've had time to think about things, and—"

"And you want to back out." She gave a pout, then said in a hush, "Is it that you don't love me?"

"I *do* love you," he declared, then realized he had made

229

the comment loud enough for the nearest tables to hear. Lowering his voice and leaning toward her, he waved a hand to indicate the surroundings and continued, "This is my kind of place—somewhere I can feel comfortable. But you come from a completely different world. I worry that our backgrounds are too dissimilar—that eventually one of us will be unhappy. I don't want to take you from the kind of life you're accustomed to. And I don't think I could ever get used to living in a house that has more bathrooms than family members."

Rachel started to grin, then chuckled aloud. Taking his hand again, she said, "Whatever has gotten into you, Aidan McAuliffe? I thought that by now you knew me well enough to realize that mansions and fancy restaurants are of little importance to me. I'd be glad to settle for weekend picnics at the park and an occasional dinner at a restaurant just like this—provided it's with you."

"Being the wife of a physician is far from easy," he pointed out. "I could be called away at any time of day or night."

"When you return, I'll be waiting there with a hot cup of tea and a smile."

"And if I open my own practice, I'll as likely be paid with a homemade pie as with hard cash."

"We'll serve it with the tea or take it on those picnics in the park—provided it isn't rhubarb." She gave a distasteful grimace.

"I'm afraid any outings in the park will have to be taken in a beat-up old buggy; it will be a long time, if ever, before I can afford one of those newfangled automobiles like your friend Tim Price drives."

Rachel eyed him closely, then nodded knowingly. "That's what this is all about, isn't it?"

"What do you mean?"

"Tim Price. His money and his motorcar." When Aidan looked down uncomfortably, she squeezed his hand and continued, "I feel nothing but friendship for Tim. Anything we had was a long time ago. Certainly he's handsome—but not as handsome as you. And while he may be considered a good catch in this town, I'm already holding on to the only man I ever want to catch.''

''Do you really mean that?'' he asked.

''Yes, I do. And furthermore, I'm a pretty good catch myself. You'd better act quickly, or I just might slip away,'' she challenged.

Aidan began to smile. ''I think you really do love me.''

''That's what I've been trying to tell you.''

''Then marry me.''

''Just tell me when and where,'' she proclaimed.

''As soon as possible.'' He reached into his jacket pocket and produced the telegram he had been given that morning by Jeremy Mayhew. ''I received this today,'' he said, handing it to her.

Rachel read it quickly, her face breaking out in a broad grin. ''This is wonderful!'' she exclaimed. ''Why didn't you tell me before?''

''I didn't want you to feel obligated to marry me, now that I'm a free man.''

''You foolish boy,'' she said playfully, pressing the telegram back into his hands and holding them. ''Do you think I'd let a man like you remain free for even a minute?''

''Then when shall we get married?''

Rachel thought for a moment, then nodded. ''Three weeks from Saturday. That will give Nina just enough time to make plans but not enough to let them get too far out of hand.''

''I love you, Rachel Salomon,'' he whispered.

''And I love you, Dr. Aidan McAuliffe,'' she replied, pulling him toward her. Oblivious to their surroundings or to the waiter, who had just approached with their menus, they leaned close and shared a soft, lingering kiss.

''*Bravo!*'' a voice called from a nearby table.

''*Bellisimo!*'' the waiter echoed, tucking the menus under his arm and applauding.

As the other patrons joined in, clapping and cheering, Rachel abruptly pulled away from Aidan, her cheeks flushed with embarrassment. But as she saw the genuinely warm, approving expressions of the people all around her and heard their encouraging response, she began to smile, well aware that such a bold display of affection at any of the restaurants she usually frequented would have been met with frozen stares and muttered imprecations.

Beside her, Aidan pushed back his chair and stood, raising a hand to acknowledge the applause. Then, with a mischievous grin, he impulsively bent down and kissed Rachel full on the lips, to the clamorous cheers of the crowd.

Fourteen

ALLISON GRANT WAS OUT TAKING A WALK THE NEXT MORN-
ing when Rachel Salomon and her mother again sat down to
discuss plans for the coming fashion extravaganza. Rachel
tried several times to bring up the topic of her wedding, which
was tentatively set for Saturday, July 18, three weeks from
the following day. However, every time she mentioned the
subject, Nina sidestepped the issue and shifted the conversation back to the fashion show.

Shortly before noon the doorbell rang, and the butler
opened the door to find a young boy staggering under the
burden of two dozen cut roses. Accepting the flowers, Cameron carried the bouquet into the parlor and announced,
"Miss Rachel, these have arrived for you."

Thunderstruck, Rachel leaped up from the sofa and rushed
to Cameron. Seeing an envelope stuck in the bouquet, she
carefully withdrew it.

"Shall I have them put in a vase?" Cameron asked.

"Yes, of course," Nina said, moving up beside Rachel.

As Cameron and the bouquet departed, Rachel turned the

envelope around in her hand and saw that it bore merely her first name.

"Well, open it," Nina prodded.

"Aidan is such a dear," Rachel commented as she tore open the envelope and pulled out the card. It read: *Had a wonderful time yesterday. Let's do it again soon. Tim.*

"Tim?" she said incredulously.

"Isn't he the perfect gentleman," Nina proclaimed, taking the card from her daughter's hand and reading it.

A moment later Cameron returned with the vase, filled with flowers.

"Aren't they magnificent?" Nina gushed as Cameron placed them on one of the tables.

"They *are* beautiful," Rachel admitted, going over and inhaling the distinctive aroma.

"There must be two dozen at least. Can you imagine? And to hire someone to bring them out to the house. That certainly was thoughtful of him."

"Yes, Nina," Rachel said with a hint of annoyance, though she, too, was touched—and a bit unsettled—by the gesture.

"I once thought Mr. Price a bit on the wild side, but I must admit he's become quite the responsible young man."

"One day he'll make some woman a wonderful husband," Rachel commented, smiling as she carefully pulled one of the stems from the vase and held it to her nose.

"He used to be quite taken with you, Rachel. And from what I've seen the past few days, I'd say he still is."

"He's just a friend."

"Does a friend send two dozen roses?" Nina clucked her tongue lightly. "Mark my words, the man is smitten with you. You should consider yourself lucky and—"

"Nina!" Rachel blurted, lowering the rose and glowering at her mother. "I'm engaged to be married. If Tim is still infatuated with me, he'll just have to get over it."

"But you used to care about him, as well. And I saw the way you two were looking at each other the other night—and yesterday when you came back from that drive."

THE DECEIT

"I told you—Aidan and I are engaged to be married," Rachel said testily.

"It's not too late—"

"I simply will not discuss this with you!" Rachel cut her off, raising her hand and turning away.

"But have you considered what you're doing? Truly considered?" Nina moved in front of her daughter. "I'm certain this Dr. McAuliffe is a likable enough fellow, but what can he really offer you?"

"Love," Rachel snapped. "You've heard of that, haven't you?"

"But Tim Price could offer you love—and so much more." She grasped Rachel's arms. "Why, soon he'll control one of the biggest fortunes in all San Fran—"

"Is that the only thing you care about? Money?" Rachel roughly pushed her mother away from her and stalked across the room. "I'm sick of hearing you talk about money—as if it were a . . . a god!"

"It's not such a bad thing," Nina shot back, following her out into the foyer. "If you want to know what's bad, consider what it would be like to be penniless. Imagine how long your love would last then."

"You're impossible!" Rachel railed, storming into the cloakroom just off the foyer. She reappeared carrying a heavy shawl and barreled past her mother. "Excuse me, but I need a change of scenery and some fresh air!"

Rachel stormed to the front door and yanked it open—only to find herself face to face with Tim Price, who was raising his hand to press the bell push.

"Uh, hello," he said, looking surprised. Glancing down, he saw that Rachel was holding a rose in her hand. "I see you received my present," he added, smiling expectantly.

"Thank you," she replied a bit abruptly, tears coming to her eyes. "But I'm afraid I cannot accept it."

She pressed the flower against his chest, and as he reached up to take it, he pricked himself on one of the thorns and gave a slight gasp.

"And I'm afraid I won't be able to work on the fashion show with you—or see you again." She choked back a tear. "I . . . I'm engaged to be married," she stammered, pushing by him and tossing her shawl over her shoulders as she hurried down the drive.

Tim Price just stood there, sucking his bleeding finger and staring in bewilderment at the crushed rose in his hand.

Shortly after noon, Damien Picard left his second-floor room at the Baldwin Hotel and went downstairs to the lobby, cane and derby hat in his left hand. It took only a moment to find Maurice Salomon, who was standing by himself near the front desk.

"How are you?" Damien asked jovially as he approached. When Maurice reluctantly shook his offered hand but did not reply, he went on, "You could've come upstairs, you know."

"I thought it better to wait here and send someone up, in case you weren't alone."

Damien chuckled. "No worry of that today, old boy." He clapped Maurice on the shoulder. "How about some lunch?"

"I'm not very hungry."

"Come on—you've got to eat something."

Maurice glanced around, checking to make sure no one he knew was there who might see him with Damien. "I suppose just a little . . ."

"That's the spirit." Seeing that Maurice was looking toward the hotel dining room, he added, "But not here. Let's take a little walk."

Damien put on his hat and shifted the silver-knobbed cane to his right hand, then led the way across the lobby to the front door. Maurice donned his own fedora, and the two men headed out onto Market Street, turning left toward the distant Ferry Building at the foot of the street.

At the corner of Ellis Street, they passed the Peerless, a tavern popular along the famous "cocktail route," a circuit of some twenty high-class taverns along Market, Kearny, Sutter, and Powell streets. Here every evening at five, top-hatted men in expensive Prince Albert coats, with lavishly brocaded vests and silk cravats, would travel the route, traditionally in a clockwise direction starting at the corner of Sutter and Kearny. Proceeding from one tavern to the next, they would drink cocktails with names such as Bonanza and Stone Wall and enjoy a free hot buffet, served every night at five and again at midnight. These lavish meals were known as free lunches and consisted of everything from Virginia ham cooked in champagne to platters of sausage and smoked salmon to terrapin baked in the shell with a cream and sherry sauce.

The two men continued down the street. At the corner of O'Farrell, Damien pulled up short and looked across the wide thoroughfare to the building called the Midway Plaisance, where men could pay ten cents to see exotic dancers from the Orient swirl about in gauzy, daringly revealing outfits. He grinned at Maurice and commented, ''I suppose now that you're married you've no interest in entertainment such as that.'' He laughed aloud.

''Come on,'' Maurice muttered, continuing down the road.

At the next corner Damien said, ''I know the perfect place for lunch. It's right up here.''

Maurice allowed himself to be led up Kearny Street two blocks to the corner of Sutter, where they halted in front of the Reception Saloon.

''Shall we?'' Damien asked, pushing through the swinging doors without awaiting a reply.

Damien led the way past the long mahogany bar, set beneath a bank of crystal chandeliers and backed by an enormous beveled mirror, to a table off to one side of the dining area. Many of the tables were occupied with patrons enjoying a light midday meal, with several women among the number. After five, however, the Reception Saloon, along with almost all the establishments on the cocktail route, would be closed to women, not by rule but by virtually unbroken tradition.

Almost immediately upon sitting down, they were approached by a bartender in a white jacket, who inquired if they would like to dine. Damien ordered a platter of cold cuts served with pickles, rye bread, and pumpernickel, along with a Black Velvet, a cheerful drink made of champagne with a float of stout. Maurice chose only a bowl of onion soup and a glass of Sazarac, a Gold Rush-era drink made of rye, bitters, absinthe, and anisette, supposedly the first cocktail ever served in San Francisco.

As they waited for their drinks to be served, Maurice asked somewhat nervously, "Have you had word from New York?"

"I've been giving a lot of thought to your current position," Damien responded enigmatically.

"My position? Do you mean regarding that woman?"

Damien leaned forward across the table and said with a tone of great portent, "I'm referring to your position at Salomon's Emporium."

"Damien, whatever are you talking about?"

Damien started to reply, then paused as the waiter returned with their drinks. Damien thanked the man, waited until he withdrew, and continued, "You're a bright, ambitious fellow. Hell, we both are. That's why I know what I'm talking about when I say you should be wielding more influence in the family business."

"For God's sake, I just started work this week."

"You've been working on and off for the past few years. You told me as much in New York." Damien sipped at his drink.

"But never in an executive role. I just worked summers during school to pick up some extra spending money."

"Still, your future could be a bleak one, given the current situation."

"What situation?" Maurice asked suspiciously.

"Your older brother and your mother." Seeing that Maurice was about to interrupt again, Damien raised his hand and said, "Just hear me out for a moment." He put down the glass and clasped his hands in front of him. "Salomon's Emporium is like a carriage with two drivers: Nina and Jacob. Right now, your father's death has left Jacob at the reins.

But from what I know of your mother, she won't sit back for long and let someone else make the decisions. And you and I both know that your mother and your brother are like oil and water together.''

"That's true of Nina and any of us.''

"But even more so with Jacob.''

"How do you know all this? You've never even met Jacob. . . .'' Maurice hesitated. "Or have you?''

"No,'' Damien assured him. "But Nina has said enough—''

"You've obviously spent more time with Nina than I would have guessed,'' Maurice cut him off. He paused, then added, "Why don't you get to the point.''

"The point is that Salomon's needs someone firmly at the reins. And that person could be you. Believe it or not, your mother trusts you—a lot more than she'll ever trust Jacob. And another thing—after that incident in my room yesterday, you have her where she won't want to oppose you for fear you might reveal what you saw.''

"What about Jacob?''

"There can only be one driver. Either you start planning to be that person, or you'll spend the rest of your life as your older brother's toady.''

"This is preposterous,'' Maurice declared, shaking his head and starting to rise from his seat.

Grabbing the sleeve of Maurice's cutaway suit, Damien pulled him back onto his chair. "Just a minute, now,'' he flared, frowning at Maurice. "I deserve to be heard through. After all, I've been looking out for your interests all along.''

"If you're referring to that letter from Agnes—''

"More than that. For instance, arranging to have you walk in on Nina and me. You don't really think that was an accident, do you?''

"You've got incredible nerve,'' Maurice exclaimed, shaking his head in wonder. "You get caught with your pants down yesterday, and now you not only try to make it sound as if it was a good thing but that you planned it all along.''

"What matters isn't whether or not it was accidental but that you've now got something you can hold over your mother—an edge that may come in very handy one day."

Just then the waiter returned with their orders. As soon as he was gone, Maurice whispered harshly, "If you made me come all the way over here just so that you could—"

"Relax, Maurice. I said I was watching out for you, and I am." He smiled smugly. "I telegraphed Agnes Banker like I promised and suggested a cash settlement. Yesterday morning she wired back that Lorraine is willing to go along, provided the funds are ample enough and come on an ongoing basis so that her child will be properly provided for."

"What will it take?" Maurice pressed.

"A thousand dollars up front, and five hundred a month until the child reaches its majority," Damien said flatly.

Maurice swallowed hard. "I have some savings, but I used most of it paying the first year's lease on a small house Belle and I are moving into next week. There's no way I can pay that kind of money regularly without someone finding out. Nina doles out my allowance, and Jacob controls my salary at Salomon's."

"Damn, Maurice . . . I'd have thought someone like you would be flooded with money."

"That's not the way things work in my family. Nina has made sure everything is in her name, and she pretty much controls what we each receive."

"Jacob, too?"

"He gets a substantial salary. But the bottom line is that Nina owns Salomon's Emporium and will continue to until the day she dies. Her father founded it, remember. Charles was little more than a caretaker."

"But if you were in charge there, rather than Jacob, you could pay yourself whatever you want, and no one would be the wiser," Damien pointed out.

"No," Maurice blurted, waving off his friend's comment. "I have to do something about this matter now, Damien—

right now," he said desperately. "I've got a wife—a new son. If word were to get out . . ."

"You said you have savings. Can you come up with the initial payment?"

"Yes, and perhaps the first two or three months."

"Good. Then let's take this one month at a time. A few months from now we may have figured out some other way to come up with the money."

Maurice reached across the table and gripped his friend's forearm. "You've got to help me, Damien. I'll pay the woman whatever she wants. Just figure out a way to keep her quiet." He released Damien's arm and slumped back in his chair, looking drained and defeated.

"I suggest you and the woman have no direct contact," Damien told him, sampling one of the cold cuts on his plate. "It will only lead back to you." When Maurice nodded, he went on, "Can you make out a draft for the initial payment? I'll be the go-between for now, and I'll get her to sign something guaranteeing she never reveals the source of the funds or the father of her child."

Numbly, Maurice said, "I'll draw it up at the office and send it over to your hotel."

"You'd better not make it out to Lorraine Lanford—that would leave a trail of evidence that eventually could get you in trouble. Just make it out to me, and I'll issue one in the same amount to the woman."

Maurice nodded, then slowly rose from his seat. He glanced down at his uneaten bowl of soup. "I'm sorry, but I'm not hungry," he said, shaking his head.

"Don't worry, Maurice. We'll work this thing out."

Turning, Maurice walked past the bar to the front door. Without looking back, he pushed through the swinging doors and walked out.

Watching him go, Damien picked up the small fork from the platter of cold cuts, speared a gherkin, and popped it into his mouth, grinning as the swinging doors settled back into place.

At the far end of the room, a woman rose from where she was sitting alone in the shadows and crossed the room, coming up behind Damien. "May I join you?" she asked, placing a gentle hand on his shoulder.

"But of course," he said without looking behind him. He waved a hand at Maurice's empty chair.

The woman circled the table and sat down. Placing her large leather shopping purse on her lap, she lifted Maurice's drink and looked at Damien questioningly.

"He never touched it."

"There's no point in letting it go to waste," she replied, raising the glass in front of her. Damien raised his, as well, and as they clinked glasses, the woman intoned, "To my brilliant big brother, Damien Picard."

"Half-brother," he corrected her with a playful shrug. "And to my resourceful half-sister, Allison Picard."

"Allison Grant," she reminded him with a knowing smile.

"I stand corrected—Allison Grant," he replied, his eyes sparkling with delight as he looked at his younger half-sister—the very woman he had planted in the Salomon household.

After taking a sip, Allison set Maurice's glass down and asked, "Did everything go as planned?"

"Exactly," he declared, beaming. "The letter you wrote fooled him completely. We'll be getting a thousand dollars for starters, then five hundred a month."

"What I've brought could prove far more lucrative."

Allison reached into her shopping purse and withdrew a manila envelope, which she placed on the table in front of Damien. He noted Jacob Salomon's name on the front, then opened it and removed the contents. As he examined the papers inside, his smile broadened.

"If you want to drive a final wedge between Jacob and Nina, those papers I found should prove the trick," Allison said.

"But does he trust you enough to listen?"

"He trusts me," she replied with a confident smile. "He'll

listen to whatever I tell him—and do whatever I say." She started to lift the glass and take another drink, then asked, "What about Maurice? Are you as sure of him?"

"Don't worry, Allison. By the time Jacob is out of the picture and Maurice takes over Salomon's Emporium, it will be your brother who is calling the shots."

"Half-brother," she corrected, clinking her glass against his.

Grinning at her, Damien tipped the Black Velvet to his lips and downed the remaining contents in a single swallow.

Fifteen

"HERE I COME!" RACHEL SALOMON CALLED INTO THE PAR-
lor as she raced down the stairs, across the foyer, and over
to the cloakroom. Snatching up one of her shawls, she hurried back toward the parlor, where Aidan McAuliffe was
waiting. "I'm sorry I took so long," she apologized, rushing
over and giving him a kiss.

"That's all right," Aidan said without enthusiasm.

"Why the frown?" she asked. "Aren't you excited? It's
the Fourth of July—the one hundred twentieth anniversary of
our Republic—and we're going to spend the evening listening
to the bands and watching the fireworks in the park. And best
of all, we're to be married two weeks from today. What more
could you ask for?"

Looking dejected, he replied, "I could ask not to have to
say what I came to tell you."

"But I thought you came to take me to the park."

"I'm afraid I can't go."

"You can't? But Aidan, we made plans."

He put his hands on her shoulders. "The hospital called

me at the hotel. One of the surgeons is ill, and they need me to come in.''

"Oh, no, Aidan. But it's the Fourth, and—''

"That's precisely why I have to go. This is one of the worst nights for hospitals, what with all those penny firecrackers being tossed around. We're certain to lose several fingers and an eye or two.''

Rachel shuddered. "That's terrible.''

"Apparently it's the American way of having a good time.'' He shrugged.

"Isn't there anyone else? You've only been there a week and a half.''

"Which is precisely why Dr. Obloy called me. You don't think one of the senior staff would want to give up their Fourth, do you? Furthermore, I'm Scottish, so the holiday isn't supposed to mean anything to me.''

Rachel frowned, then stepped into his arms and embraced him. "I understand,'' she whispered. "I told you I'd make a good physician's wife, and I'm not going to start complaining even before we get married.'' She kissed his cheek. "You just go to that hospital of yours and patch up all us foolish Americans who don't know how to have a good time without blowing ourselves up.''

Giving her an appreciative smile, he told her, "You don't have to stay home, you know. Perhaps Maurice and Belle would like to go to the park with you.''

She shook her head. "They just moved into their new house today. I'd rather not bother them.'' She smiled up at him. "Please don't worry about me. It wasn't the band and fireworks that intrigued me but the idea of spending an evening with you.''

"I'll make up for it tomorrow,'' he promised, drawing her closer. "What do you say to a picnic at the beach?''

"I'd love it,'' she declared. Taking his arm, she led him toward the front door. "Now, let's get you on your way. There are probably two or three fingers already waiting to be examined.''

Rachel opened the door and accompanied him to his waiting hackney cab. Kissing him good-bye, she held the door for him, then closed it and stepped back, waving as the cab headed down the drive and turned onto the street.

For a long while she just stood there, her arms folded across her chest, listening to the distant popping of firecrackers. She imagined the small boys who had sneaked into Chinatown to spend their pennies at the colorful Oriental butcher shops, which specialized not only in meat and fish but in assorted housewares and—most importantly to the boys—fireworks of every size and description.

There was a sudden flurry of little explosions, and Rachel involuntarily flinched, shaking her head and smiling. She looked down toward the road, waiting to see a boy or two running along the sidewalk, tossing firecrackers as they went. Indeed the booming resumed, but there were no wild-eyed youths accompanying it. Instead, Timothy Price's Panhard came backfiring around the corner, its oil head lamps blazing.

The vehicle turned up the drive, and Tim waved as he pulled to a halt in front of Rachel. Switching off the engine, he called, "A happy Fourth of July to you, Rachel!"

"Good evening, Tim," she answered, her tone somewhat reserved.

"I know what you said last time I was here, but it's been a whole week, and I thought perhaps you might've cooled down a trifle."

Rachel grinned and approached the car. "I was pretty dreadful, wasn't I?"

"Yes, if you call crushing a rose dreadful—and damn near putting me in the hospital at the same time!"

"Hospital?" she said in surprise.

With a grin, Tim held up his right hand. The finger that had been pricked by the rose thorn was enveloped in a bandage so huge that it made the finger look the size of a baseball.

"That thorn really did hurt," he said with an exaggerated

pout. As he turned his hand over, the mock bandage slid off and fell into his lap. Quickly picking it up, he blushed and shrugged. "Well, maybe not *that* much." He tossed the bandage over the rear of the car.

Unable to keep herself from laughing, Rachel came up to the side of the car and leaned against it. "I'm sorry about the way I acted. It wasn't your fault. I was angry at my mother, not you."

"Rachel, I'm the one who should be apologizing to you, and that's exactly why I stopped by. It was wrong of me to presume on your kindness. You told me you were engaged, and I had no right to behave the way I did."

"It's all right; I didn't mind. It was flattering, actually."

"I guess I was hoping it would be more." He grinned, then stroked his drooping brown mustache. "Ah, well, I'll just have to see whom else I can woo with my charming little antics."

"There's always Sue Ellen Lange," Rachel suggested with a hint of humor. "She had quite a crush on you in school, if I remember correctly."

"You ought to," he declared. "I seem to remember you two getting into a hair-pulling fight over me."

"We did not," Rachel protested.

"That's what it looked like to me."

"Oh, you thought all the girls were fighting over you."

"Weren't they?" he asked with mock innocence.

"Yes—over who would get stuck going out with you."

"You cut me to the quick," he groaned, clutching his heart. "Crushing roses, then egos. Were you always this cruel?"

"Am I that horrible?"

"I'm afraid so," he teased. "But I'm doing my best to overlook it." Noticing her evening shawl, he asked, "Were you leaving? If there's somewhere I can drop you off . . ."

"No, thanks. I was just going in."

"But there's a wonderful concert and fireworks at the park tonight. Perhaps you and Aidan would like to join me."

Rachel gave a loud sigh. "I'm afraid Aidan was called to the hospital tonight. Thank you anyway."

"But aren't you going? Half of San Francisco will be there."

"I . . . I think not." She backed away from the car.

"Look, Rachel, if it's because of what happened before, I promise I'll be the perfect gentleman. No roses—not even a dandelion. But it's simply unconscionable that you should stay home and miss the event of the summer."

"Well, it's true I had wanted to go, but—"

"Then come with me . . . as friends." He smiled up at her so genuinely that she could not help but smile in return. "I promise I won't bite," he pledged, then patted the steering tiller and added, "And neither will Jessah."

"I suppose there would be no harm. . . ."

"Then come on. It's the Fourth of July!"

Rachel's grin widened. "Yes, I think I'd like to," she declared as Tim hopped out of the vehicle and hurried around to give her a hand aboard. Returning to the driver's side, he reached into the motorcar, set the controls, then went to the front and gave the starting crank a few turns. The warm engine came to life immediately, and Tim leaped into his seat, shifted into gear, and released the brake. With a sputtering backfire, the Panhard jolted forward and jounced its way down the long, circular drive.

"It certainly is a delight to be home!" Jacob declared as he stood in front of the gold-framed, full-length mirror in his dressing room.

Almost two weeks had passed since he had taken a room at the Baldwin Hotel and his brother's family had taken over his town house, but finally they had found a suitable house to lease and had just moved into it. Now Jacob was in the mood to celebrate—not only his return home but the enjoyable week he had spent since the previous Thursday, when Allison Grant had been so bold as to invite him to dine at the pavilion in Salomon's Emporium—a week in which he had seen her twice for lunch and once during the weekend for a drive in the park.

Buttoning the bottom tab of his starched white dress shirt to his black pants, he smoothed the plaits and examined himself in the mirror. "Perhaps I gained too much weight since returning from the Orient," he said with a frown, turning for a side view of his stocky physique.

"You look the picture of health," his gaunt, gray-haired manservant declared, carrying over Jacob's collar and black silk tie.

"Thank you, Langdon. But I'm not so sure. . . . Women these days like a well-put-together man. Perhaps if I stand straighter." He tried various poses, alternately pulling in his stomach and arching his back. "Would you bring me those new suspenders from on top of the bureau?"

"These, sir?" Langdon asked, putting down the collar and tie and picking up a set of unusual-looking black suspenders with a heavy webbed plate across the back.

"Yes."

As Langdon brought it over, he read the label on the back. "Dr. Gray's Back Supporting Suspender. . . ." He raised an eyebrow dubiously. "Do you think this necessary?"

"It came on good recommendation from Thomas Clingman of our men's department. It's quite popular these days."

Langdon shook his head in dismay as he handed his employer the suspenders. Jacob quickly slipped his arms through the new pair, then buttoned it in place. From the front it almost looked like an ordinary pair, except for the elastic bands attached at the bottom and chest that circled to the webbed brace at back.

"Just pull those there," Jacob said, indicating the buckles at the back, which when tightened added additional pressure and forced the wearer into an upright position.

Langdon did as instructed, while Jacob stood straight and drew back his shoulders. When the brace felt sufficiently tight, he said, "That will do, Langdon," then turned in front of the mirror, examining his posture from every angle. He nodded approvingly. "My tie and Belmont, please."

Langdon handed Jacob the Belmont, a two-inch-high, stiff collar with forward-protruding, gently curved wings. Jacob positioned the collar, struggling a little with the small button at the front but finally managing to close it. He wrapped the black tie around his neck and quickly fashioned the bow, but it came out crooked. Undoing it, he tried again, fumbling through the procedure. Finally he shrugged his shoulders, sighed with frustration, and grumped, "I'm useless tonight. Can you help?"

Langdon undid the tie, then expertly knotted it and adjusted the bow. "There, sir," he said, stepping back so Jacob could see how he looked.

"Excellent," Jacob beamed, patting his stomach and turning again to the side. Seeing some lint on his pants, he plucked it off, then bent over to brush his knee. Groaning slightly against the pressure of the brace, he stood back up and frowned.

"Allow me, sir," Langdon said, retrieving a small clothes brush from the bureau and wiping the pants legs.

"I feel like a trussed-up turkey," Jacob complained, shaking his head.

"If you don't mind my saying so, sir, I think you look better in your regular suspenders—far more natural and at ease."

Jacob nodded. "I certainly don't want to look uncomfortable tonight." Coming to a decision, he declared, "Take this godawful contraption off me, Langdon."

"With pleasure," the older man replied, undoing the buttons at the back as Jacob released the ones at front. A moment later they had the support suspenders off and his usual black dress ones in its place.

"Much more civilized," Jacob said with a smile.

"You will make quite the impression, sir," Langdon complimented, helping Jacob into his waistcoat, a three-button vest with elaborate silk-brocading on the front. Finally he brought over the full-dress evening jacket, cut straight across at the waist and with tails that reached nearly to his knees. Langdon smoothed and adjusted the satin lapels, making sure they hung straight and the gap at the waist was even, so the waistcoat would be properly visible.

Jacob stroked his beard and nodded, pleased with the trim he had received from the barber at the Baldwin Hotel just before moving back to his town house that afternoon. "It's good to be home," he exclaimed once again.

"And good to have you back with us," Langdon replied, speaking for himself and the cook, Beatrice, who comprised the household staff.

"I hope it wasn't too much of an imposition on you and Beatrice having my brother and his family here."

"Not at all," Langdon assured him. "They were delightful, and the baby was the perfect gentleman."

Jacob smirked. "But I'm sure they feel better moving into their own place, even if it's only a lease."

"Mrs. Salomon sounded quite enthusiastic about the house and asked me to extend an invitation for you to visit as soon as possible."

"Perhaps tomorrow." Jacob took a last look in the mirror. "I'm as ready as I'll ever be. What time is it?"

Langdon removed a plain, serviceable pocket watch. "Six-fifty, sir. Your guest will arrive at seven."

"Then we'd better get down there."

Jacob led the way downstairs, and Langdon withdrew to the kitchen to check on the progress of dinner. For the evening, Jacob had hired Lydia, the kitchen helper at his mother's house, to assist Beatrice with the preparations.

Jacob entered the modest but well-furnished parlor to the left of the front door and spent the next ten minutes pacing back and forth between the red plush sofa and the fireplace, pausing every once in a while in front of the window to see if the coach he had hired for the occasion had arrived. It did so at precisely seven, and Jacob hurried down the hall and called for Langdon, then retreated again into the parlor.

When the bell rang, Langdon was on hand to open the door. "Good evening, Miss Grant," he said pleasantly, nodding to dismiss the coachman, who had escorted Allison up the stairs. In the distance, the Fourth of July fireworks could be heard going off throughout the city.

"Langdon, isn't it?" Allison smiled at him as she stepped into the entryway and he closed the door behind her.

"Your wrap?" he asked, and she unbuttoned her black evening cape and handed it to him, along with her evening bag. "Mr. Salomon is in the parlor," he added, indicating the room to the left.

As Allison swept into the room, Jacob held out his hands and declared, "I'm so glad you came." Taking her hands, he raised one and kissed it, then held her away from him as he admired her pale-blue satin gown, with its tight-fitting waist and flared skirt, trimmed with ivory lace at the throat and hem. "It looks delightful on you," he remarked, nodding approvingly.

"Thanks to you for buying it for me," she replied with a coy blush.

"Yes, but you picked it out."

"I know, but you were far too generous to offer."

"To insist," he corrected her.

"And I truly appreciate it."

"What good is running a mercantile establishment if I don't get to give away some of the merchandise on occasion?"

Impulsively, she leaned up and kissed his cheek. "You are a good man, Jacob Salomon," she whispered, looking down demurely.

He touched his cheek. "And now a happy one." Smiling, he held out his arm and said, "I believe dinner is about to be served. Shall we?"

She took his arm and accompanied him down the hall to the dining room. The table, which normally sat six but could be opened for larger gatherings, was laid out in the finest silk-embroidered linen, with Excelsior ruby crystal, French Haviland china, and fine Waverly silverware.

Jacob showed Allison to her seat just to his right, then sat down at the head of the table. He unstoppered the wine decanter and filled their glasses, raising his in a toast. "To your good health—and to the health of our Republic on this Fourth of July," he declared.

"And to homecomings," she added.

As they sipped the sauterne, Langdon brought out the first of a series of covered silver dishes and tureens, beginning with terrapin soup, then quickly advancing to oysters on the half-shell and frog's legs au sec, finally reaching the main course: a roast of lamb, served with a variety of vegetables in various cream and wine sauces.

Jacob and Allison conversed, laughed, and ate their way through the seemingly endless meal, which concluded with a platter of hand-painted chocolate and fondant bonbons surrounded by two dozen tiny frosted cakes and cookies.

Throughout dinner, Allison was completely attentive to Jacob, intent on every word he said and encouraging his ideas and dreams for the future. Jacob could not have been more delighted with the way the evening was proceeding, and on one occasion he shared a private knowing smile with Langdon, who was well aware of his employer's interest in this particular woman and who now was convinced she returned his affection.

At the conclusion of the meal, Jacob escorted Allison to the parlor, where she excused herself to freshen up. She asked Langdon to retrieve her evening bag, then followed him to a dressing room on the ground floor.

As soon as she was alone in the room, Allison plopped down onto a small chair in front of the vanity and gave a protracted sigh. Staring at herself in the oval mirror, she frowned and sighed again. "He can be such a boor," she breathed. Shaking her fist at her own image, she hissed, "If I hear one more story about Salomon's Emporium, I think I'll throttle him." Breathing deeply, she settled down and began to grin. *At least the food was good,* she thought with a satisfied pat to her stomach. *If only he weren't so bearish— and more of his hair were on top of his head than his chin.*

She opened her evening bag and rummaged inside until she found her face powder, which she opened and applied sparingly to her cheeks and nose. Replacing the tin, she stood and straightened her dress, then picked up her bag.

"Well, let's go get this thing finished with," she told herself, turning and exiting the room.

As Allison entered the parlor, Jacob met her with a pair of brandy glasses in hand. Allison placed her evening bag on a table beside the sofa and took one of the glasses. "Shall we sit?" she suggested, indicating the sofa.

As they sat down, Jacob noted Allison's more subdued expression and asked, "Is something the matter? Wasn't dinner to your liking?"

"Oh, yes, it was indeed," she assured him, placing a hand on his forearm. "It's not that."

Growing concerned now, Jacob took her hand and said, "Is there some way I can be of help?"

"I'm afraid I find myself in a bit of a dilemma." She held his gaze for a long moment, until he began to look unsettled. Then she went on, "It has to do with some information that has come to light—information that affects someone who has become very dear to me."

Taking the bait, Jacob patted her hand and said, "I hope you know that you can be completely frank with me."

"I know, Jacob. But this has to do with your family. With Nina, and with . . ." Her voice trailed off, and she lowered her eyes.

"You can speak openly here. I promise to keep everything in the strictest confidence."

"But you don't understand," she blurted, looking back up at him and shaking her head in anguish. "You see, your mother has begun to confide in me—almost as if I were the daughter she lost."

Jacob sighed and nodded slightly. "That's only natural.

After all, you were a friend of Phoebe's, and you bear a certain resemblance—''

"It's gone beyond that. She's told me things she wouldn't even tell a child for fear they would never forgive her." Again she looked away, and this time a tear rolled down her cheek, which she quickly wiped away.

"Please tell me," he pressed. "Let me help you."

"I don't know what to do." She started to cry softly, muttering through her tears, "I . . . I don't want to hurt you, Jacob."

He moved closer and took her in his arms, pulling her head against his shoulder. "There, now . . . it can't be that bad. Nothing you say could hurt me. Not if you speak plainly. Not if you tell me the truth."

Allison choked back her tears and stammered, "It—it's about your . . . f-father."

"Charles?"

"No . . . your real father."

Jacob's body went rigid, and then he pulled back stiffly and looked down at her. "What do you mean?" he asked woodenly.

"I didn't think you knew," she said, wiping the remaining tears from her cheek.

"What do you mean—real father?"

"That's what I was afraid to tell you, Jacob—that Charles Salomon was not your father."

"What are you talking about?" he asked incredulously.

"Nina told me all about it. I know I shouldn't break her confidence, but now that I've gotten to know you, I don't see how I can remain silent." She paused, then asked, "Do you remember your grandfather's former partner?"

"Abraham Hallinger? Of course. Why?" Seeing her hesitant expression, he shook his head in disbelief and said, "Hallinger? Are you saying . . . ?"

"I'm afraid so."

"But that's impossible. My mother hates that man with all

her—'' He stopped abruptly, realizing the import of what he had just said.

Allison took his hand. ''Do you want me to go on?'' she asked cautiously, and when he nodded numbly, she said, ''Your mother was only seventeen; Hallinger was more than twenty years her senior. I don't know how it began, but they had a passionate affair. When Nina found out she was pregnant, she confronted him, but he was married and had no intention of leaving his wife. Nina was too mortified to tell her father, so she did the only thing she thought possible.''

''She married Charles?''

''More than that. He was ten years older and was a clerk of some kind at the store. Nina knew he idolized her, so she seduced him and let him think the pregnancy was his fault. It was a simple matter to convince him to marry her. Not long after, Nina forced Hallinger to dissolve the partnership and sell his interest to Charles. Your grandfather never even knew the real reason.''

Jacob slowly shook his head. ''I can't believe it. My mother has done a lot of strange things—but Abraham Hallinger? It's preposterous.''

''I know. I found the story hard to believe, and I don't even know Hallinger. I told her as much, and that's when she showed me this.'' Allison reached to the side table for her purse. Opening it, she withdrew the manila envelope that bore Jacob's name. ''It's all in there,'' she told him. ''Letters between your mother and Hallinger about what happened; legal papers, dissolving the partnership.''

Jacob opened the envelope and perused the contents, his face growing paler as he read. ''My God!'' he suddenly blurted, dropping the papers into his lap. ''Hallinger's wife was pregnant at the time! Of course, she had to have been. Eaton was only a few months older than me.''

''I think that's why he refused to leave his wife.''

''But that means . . .'' He turned toward her, his face a mask of anguish. ''Eaton—he was my half-brother.''

''Why, yes, he would be, wouldn't he?''

"But he's dead." Jacob's shoulders slumped, and he lowered his head into his hands.

"What is it?" she asked, pulling his hands from his face. "What's wrong?"

"God forgive me," he muttered, closing his eyes and trying to look away.

Allison raised his chin, forcing him to look at her. "You have to tell me what's wrong."

"I . . . I killed him."

"You what?" she said in disbelief.

"Not directly, but I discovered he was embezzling from the bank where he worked. I turned him in. He was arrested, and when he got out on bail, he committed suicide."

"That wasn't your fault."

"It wouldn't have happened if I hadn't gone after him for what he did to Phoebe."

"Phoebe?"

"Didn't you know? He was the one who got her pregnant." A look of awareness came over him. "Now I understand why Nina was so violently opposed to their relationship—and to Phoebe's baby."

"Oh, I see," Allison said. "It's as if Nina's own sins came back to haunt her through her daughter, Phoebe."

"It doesn't make any sense. Why should Phoebe have to suffer for Nina's mistakes?"

"And her own, don't forget," Allison pointed out. "Nina didn't force her to get pregnant."

"It still seems cruelly unfair. And on top of all that, I end up causing the death of my own half-brother."

"Nina had more to do with that than you did," Allison said. "It was her lies and deceptions that created this entire situation. If she had been honest with you about your real father, none of this would have happened."

Jacob stood abruptly, clutching the papers in his hand. "Well, there have been enough lies," he declared, his voice steady and sure.

"What do you mean?" Allison asked, standing beside him and placing a calming hand on his arm.

"I intend to confront Nina about this and have it out once and for all," he stated firmly.

"But I . . . but . . . oh, dear," Allison stammered.

"What is it?"

"Your mother . . . I broke her confidence telling you all this. I would be mortified if she—"

"I won't let her know it was you," he assured her.

"But how will you explain having found out?"

"There are these letters and things."

"That's right." She nodded in agreement. "I can put them back where I found them, and you can figure out a way to accidentally discover them." Her expression brightened. "Would you do that?"

"Of course, Allison. Where does she keep them?"

Allison described the hidden drawer in Nina's bureau, where she had first discovered the papers and later removed them to show Damien and then Jacob.

"I'll do exactly as you suggested," he told her, returning the papers to the envelope and handing it back to her. "And just to be sure, I won't confront her tomorrow but will wait until Monday, so that she has no reason to suspect you told me anything tonight."

"You're a dear," Allison said, taking his hand.

"No. You're the dear one—for caring enough to tell me the truth. It's something my own mother was never willing to do."

"She's a fool."

Jacob stared into Allison's blue eyes, as cool and pure as a mountain lake. With a slight shake of the head, he whispered, "And I'd be a fool if I didn't do this." He took her face in his hands and kissed her tenderly on the lips.

Allison leaned into him, slipping her arms around his back and pulling him closer. She had to admit that this first real kiss was far more pleasant than she had expected, and as he started to pull away, she drew him closer and kissed him again.

Perhaps Jacob Salomon was more attractive than she had thought, Allison mused as they continued to kiss. His power and wealth certainly were attractive and would be even more so if he did not have to share it with the rest of the Salomon family. But Damien was working to remove Jacob from the picture entirely, she reminded herself as their lips parted and she rested her head on his chest. Suddenly she found herself wondering if that was the wisest course of action. Though Damien insisted he could get anything he wanted out of Maurice, wasn't Allison proving she could just as easily control Maurice's older brother?

Half-brother, she reminded herself. *Just like Damien*. She and Damien knew they had the same mother—a colorful New Orleans madam who had raised them on the premises of her French Quarter bordello. But their fathers could have been any of a hundred different men.

Allison smiled ruefully as she pulled away from Jacob and looked up at him. She had thought there was nothing she and this balding bear of a man had in common. Yet now they shared the pain of having a father they never knew. They also had half-brothers, though Allison had not killed hers—at least not yet.

Allison laughed lightly, causing Jacob to look down at her curiously. "I think I like you, Jacob Salomon," she exclaimed, her tone genuinely playful as she gave a toss of her long blond hair and caressed his trim brown beard.

Sixteen

THE WEEKEND OF THE FOURTH WAS OVER, AND THE WORK-
week began as usual Monday morning, with the employees
of Salomon's Emporium in high spirits, sharing stories of
their celebrations. Jacob Salomon was less attentive to their
greetings than usual, but he had something important on his
mind, and he was marking time until he could act upon it.

Shortly after noon, Jacob went to the family home on Nob
Hill and greeted his mother rather brusquely in the foyer. "I
was in the area, and Maurice asked if I could pick up a few
things he left behind when he moved out," Jacob told Nina,
pulling out a small list and waving it perfunctorily in front
of her.

"Why, yes, of course," she said, noting his cool, abrupt
behavior. "Can I help you with something?"

"That's not necessary," Jacob replied, walking toward the
marble stairway. "Everything should be up in his room; I'll
just run up and be right down."

"Can I have the kitchen prepare you some lunch?"

Jacob shook his head. "I'll be stopping at home before

returning to Salomon's, and Beatrice will have something for me.''

Turning away, he dashed up the stairs, struggling to contain his anger. He went directly to Maurice's old room on the third floor, where he rummaged around as if searching for the requested items, which he had pretended his brother asked him to retrieve. Snatching up a couple of ties from a box on top of the bureau and a shirtfront from one of the drawers, he headed down to the second floor.

At the top of the stairs that led to the foyer, Jacob called, ''Nina, I couldn't find his handkerchiefs; I'll check Father's room.'' As he turned away, he caught a glimpse of his mother entering the foyer from the parlor and glancing up at him.

Jacob proceeded into the guest room that formerly had been his father's bedroom and pretended to be looking around. After a couple of minutes he stepped back out into the hall, walked quietly to Nina's door, and rapped lightly. When there was no response, he opened the door and slipped inside, going directly to the bureau, opening the left-hand drawer, and pressing the catch that released the hidden drawer above. There, just as Allison had promised, he found the manila envelope, along with a number of photographs and a packet of letters.

First Jacob scanned the photos and noted that most of them were of Abraham Hallinger. The image of the man he now knew was his real father stirred a variety of emotions in him, from anger to curiosity to sorrow. Realizing he would have plenty of time for reflection later, he put them on top of the bureau and picked up the packet of letters. They were from Tim Price to Rachel, and most had not even been opened. Had Rachel ever received them? he wondered. Deciding he would show some of them to her at a later date, he slipped several from the packet and put them in his jacket pocket. The rest of the packet he returned to the drawer, so they would not be missed. Finally, he pulled out the familiar manila envelope and checked inside to make sure the papers regarding his birth were still there.

Before confronting his mother downstairs with the envelope, Jacob decided to check the hidden drawer on the right to see what other secrets they might reveal. He placed the envelope on top of the bureau and reached for the drawer when suddenly a voice barked, "What do you think you're doing?"

He was startled into silence as he spun around to see his mother standing in the doorway.

"How dare you come in here and—!"

"How dare *me*?" he asked incredulously. "What about this?" He snatched up the manila envelope and waved it in front of him.

Nina gasped, throwing a hand to her mouth as she realized the gravity of what had happened. Retaining her indignation, she forced her hand down and glared at him as she snapped, "You had no right to look in there!"

"I was looking for Maurice's handkerchiefs; I had no idea I'd trip open your clever little hiding place and discover I'm a bastard, just like Phoebe's little Charlie!"

Striding toward him, Nina lashed out and slapped her son full across the face, then recoiled in horror at what she had done.

Grabbing his cheek, Jacob narrowed his eyes, looking like a bull about to charge. But then he shook his head and began to grin wickedly. "Whom were you hitting? Me—or my real father?" he challenged. "Or maybe it was yourself."

"You can be unspeakably cruel."

He gave a short, mocking laugh. "If I am, I came by it honestly, at the knee of a master—or mistress, to be more accurate." Tearing open the envelope, he yanked out some of the papers and shook them in front of her face, almost crushing them in his fist. "You whored yourself for him!" he raged. "No wonder you've turned into such a bitter woman—you threw away your self-respect for . . . for what?"

"It . . . it wasn't like that," she stammered.

"No? It's all in here—don't try to deny it. You knew he was married. You knew he'd never leave his wife. Yet when his wife was pregnant and put him out of her bed, you eagerly took him into yours. Why?"

"I . . . I don't know . . . but it wasn't . . ." Her voice trailed off, her face growing twisted with a mixture of anger and shame.

"It was Grandfather, wasn't it? You were trying to get at him, weren't you?"

"Th-that's ridiculous," she blurted. "Why would I—?"

"Because you hated him!" When she started to object, he held up his hand and went on, "You know it's true. Now that he's dead, you talk about him as if he's a saint—just like you do with Father. But I remember how you acted toward him—toward both of them—when they were alive. You always feared and hated Grandfather, and you seduced his partner so you could destroy the only things he cared about: his business and his pride."

"But he never knew. He never found out."

"Because when you got pregnant, you knew he'd throw you out and you'd have nothing—not money, not power, not even Abraham Hallinger. So you swallowed your pride and settled for Charles."

"You have no idea what it was like living with your grandfather!" she flared, storming past him and banging her fists against the top of the bureau.

"And you don't know what it's like living with you!" he retorted.

"You bastard!" she snarled, spinning around. Realizing she had raised her fist to strike him again, she dropped her arms at her sides and began to sob.

"Yes, a bastard. That's exactly what I am," he replied bitterly. Coming closer to her, he gripped her shoulder with his free hand. "Damn it, Nina, I had a right to know."

"You had no such right!" she raged, pulling her arm free and glowering at him. "It's been buried for almost thirty years! You should have left well enough alone!"

"I didn't ask to find this," he said, holding up the papers.

"Am I the only one who knows?" he added. "Did Father ever find out?"

"Charles never knew—but your real father did. And he knew I'd make his life a living hell if he ever told anyone." She started to nod. "Yes, I let him into my bed, as you so generously put it. But actually it was his wife's bed, whenever she went off to the country for her health. I was barely sixteen when it started, and when I turned seventeen and found out I was with child, I threatened to tell my father and Abraham's wife if he didn't find a way to make it right. But decent people don't get divorced, so I got my revenge by marrying that poor excuse of a man you knew as your father and making Abraham sell us his share of the business for twenty cents on the dollar." She laughed. "I've been making money for this family ever since! Not your grandfather. *Me!*" she blared. "I'm the one who built his two-bit storefront into the grandest mercantile establishment west of the Rockies! And I'll be damned if I let any man ever take it away from me! Not Abraham Hallinger—not even you!"

"Nobody's trying to take away—"

"Don't think he hasn't tried," she cut him off. "He's never forgiven me for taking Salomon's Emporium from him. He's tried to buy me out; he's even tried to run me out."

"He's just a banker."

"Who do you think is one of the major investors of that new Emporium on Market Street? Why do you think I insisted we enlarge our own building?"

"But that made good business sense."

"I don't give a damn about that. All I care about is this family—and seeing that bastard in hell!"

Jacob shook his head and sneered. "You don't really care about this family—only yourself."

"Everything I've done has been for you and your brother and sisters!" she railed.

"For Phoebe? Were you thinking of her when you forced her to have that abortion? When you killed her?"

Nina gasped. "How dare you—!"

"You're a damn hypocrite! It was all right for you to make a mistake, but let Phoebe do something that might sully the good Salomon name . . ." He paused, his eyebrows rising, and he began to nod. "That's really all you care about, isn't it? The family name. That's why you made Father change his from Roth to Salomon."

"We had a business to think about—a reputation that was built on the name Salomon. My father had no sons—only me. It was his legacy, and I protected it for you and your brother."

"But *I'm* not really a Salomon," he proclaimed. "My name should have been Jacob Hallinger."

"You've got your grandfather's blood running through you!" she hissed, glaring at him with blazing, angry eyes. "You're a Salomon, and you will be until the day you die!"

"You may have given me your name, but you won't turn me into . . . into you!"

Calmly and firmly, Nina said, "You *are* a bastard. You were from the moment you were born. You were always the most difficult, the most headstrong—the most unforgiving."

"I'm *your* son, remember? Yours and Hallinger's. At least Rachel and the others were tempered by Charles. But me? I've just got you—and one of San Francisco's most cutthroat financiers." He laughed bitterly. "Quite a heritage. I should be proud." He turned and started from the room, inserting the papers back into the envelope.

"Where are you going with that?" she asked anxiously.

"This?" he asked, turning and holding up the envelope. "It's mine now, Nina. It's your legacy to me."

"What are you going to—?"

"Don't worry, *Mother*." He used the term purposefully, knowing she had always hated being called that, as if she were far too young to be anyone's mother. "I have no intention of telling the world about your little indiscretion. Not for your sake, but for Father's. He deserved more in life than what he ended up getting." He turned and walked from the room, never looking back.

* * *

Maurice Salomon was examining purchase orders at the desk in his small office on the top floor of Salomon's Emporium when he was interrupted by a knock on the open door and a cheerful voice calling out, "So this is why you gave up your wastrel ways."

"Damien, what are you doing here?" Maurice blurted, looking up and seeing Damien Picard standing in the doorway, hat and cane in hand.

As Damien walked in, he turned in a circle, examining the somewhat cramped quarters, which contained little more than an oak desk and a pair of chairs. "I should think they'd have provided you something a bit more lavish."

"It was good enough for my brother all the years my father was alive," Maurice said a bit testily as he rose, crossed to the door, and shut it.

"Ah, so Jacob has your father's office now—an impressive suite, I'd wager."

"It's important that he create a good image when business associates visit."

"Yes, I can see he wouldn't want to entertain them in here." He ran a hand across the back of one of the chairs that faced the desk, then examined his fingers as if looking for dust.

"What are you doing here, anyway? I told you never to come here. What if Jacob were to see—?"

"Relax, friend." Damien sat down in one of the chairs and waited until Maurice had resumed his seat. "I waited outside until I saw him drive off in a carriage at noon."

Maurice eyed him suspiciously. "You don't even know who he is."

"True, but your mother showed me his picture in the parlor. Quite an imposing fellow; looks the part of a successful businessman." He lifted his cane and waved the knob toward Maurice's suit. "You ought to get rid of those cutaways and put on something with a double breast."

"Look, let's get to the point, Damien," Maurice said flatly.

"Tell me why you risked coming here—and then get out of here."

"Temper," Damien warned, grinning facetiously. Lowering his voice, he said, "It's about that New York situation. I've been in touch with Agnes Banker by telegraph, and all the arrangements have been made. Every month you'll deposit the agreed-upon funds in a local bank account I'll set up under my name, and then I'll transfer them to Lorraine Lanford. In return, she'll sign a letter promising never to contact you or make any future claims on you regarding the child. Furthermore, the child will never be told the true identity of his father." He grinned smugly. "I said I'd watch out for you, old friend."

Maurice slumped in his chair and nodded in thanks, obviously drained by the entire experience.

"Have you given any more thought to where you'll get the money?"

"What?" Maurice muttered, looking distracted.

"The money each month. How are you going to get it without anyone noticing?"

"Something will work out; it always does."

"How about what I said about Salomon's Emporium? You certainly don't want to sit in this hole of an office the rest of your life, reviewing bills and ledgers." He waved a hand over the papers that covered the desk.

"If you're talking about moving in on Jacob, then no, I haven't given it any serious thought."

"You ought to," Damien told him as he rose.

"I'd never do anything to jeopardize my brother's position in this company," Maurice declared, standing also.

"Fine—don't make any concerted effort. Just promise me you won't pass up any opportunities that might happen your way." His eyes twinkled mischievously, as if he knew an opportunity of some sort was on the verge of presenting itself.

"You'd really better be going." Maurice walked over to

the door. "Jacob was only going out for a while; he could return at any moment."

"Consider me gone," Damien intoned as he walked over to the door. Stepping up beside Maurice, he lifted his cane and rested it directly under Maurice's chin. "If married life ever gets a little boring, just give your good friend Damien a call. I'm certain I can come up with something to help you pass the time."

Maurice pushed the cane away, nodding absently as Damien walked from the office and headed down the hall.

Leaving his door open, Maurice sat back at his desk and tried to resume work, but he was distracted by thoughts of his past—by regrets for things he had done that now were coming back to haunt him. Worst of all was the feeling he had failed the people he loved—Rachel in particular. She would be devastated to know that Damien Picard was in town and that both Maurice and Nina had been in regular contact with him. He knew he should do something—either force Damien to leave town or else tell Rachel what was happening. But he felt powerless. Not only did Damien know about the seamy things Maurice had done in the past, but he also was aware of Maurice's difficulties with that woman in New York. Why had he been so stupid? he wondered. Had that single night of passion been worth all of this?

Maurice envisioned his beautiful wife and knew he would be crushed if anything came between them. But would his fathering an illegitimate child before he met Belle be sufficient to destroy the love they had discovered? Maurice doubted it, yet he was unwilling to put it to the test.

He shook off the thoughts and picked up one of the bills of lading from a pile on his desk. He was just comparing it to the original order when Jacob came storming into the office and began to pace in front of the desk. Fearing that somehow Jacob had run into Damien on his way in and figured out what was going on, Maurice asked cautiously, "Is something the matter, Jacob?"

"Yes, something's the matter," his older brother replied,

coming to a halt behind one of the chairs and banging on it with a fist. "I can't stand her, Maurice. I simply cannot put up with her any longer."

"Nina?" he asked, recognizing Jacob's expression.

"Of course Nina. This time I've had enough."

"What are you talking about?"

"Oh, the usual." Jacob waved a hand in the air, then circled the seat and dropped down into it. "I was just over at the house, and we had words."

"What about?"

"It doesn't matter. It just seems as if my whole life has been one big disagreement with that woman."

"I know what you mean," Maurice agreed.

"Not really. She's always favored you, Maurice. Even when you were your wildest, she made excuses for you. If *I* had ever tried some of the stunts you pulled, she'd have nailed me to the wall."

"Well, at least you're grown now. There isn't—"

"Am I?" Jacob cut in. "I don't feel grown up—even when it comes to this store. She always finds a way to remind me that she owns this place and that any decision I make must be done at her pleasure. Well, I've had enough."

"What do you mean?"

"I've decided to leave."

"But you have your own town house and—" Maurice stopped abruptly, realizing his older brother was not referring to his living arrangements. "You're not really thinking of quitting, are you?"

"I'm afraid so."

"But whatever for?"

"For myself. Everything I have here was handed to me. I think it's time I found out how I would do on my own."

"What will you do?" Maurice asked, flabbergasted.

Jacob shrugged. "Take a job. Go into business for myself. I'll figure out something."

Maurice shook his head, then began to grin. "You're just kidding, aren't you? You'd never leave Salomon's."

"I would, Maurice," he replied, his voice firm with conviction. "And I am."

"But what will we do without you?"

"You're here now, Maurice, and Rachel knows this business inside and out." He smiled ruefully and added, "And there's always Nina."

"I don't know," Maurice said cautiously. "Aren't you overreacting a little?"

"Maybe," Jacob admitted. "But actually I've been thinking about it for a long time—since before Charles died. I never would have left while he was alive; it would have hurt him too deeply. But now that he's gone and you've come on board, I think it's time. This latest row with Nina is just another reason to take the step." He clasped his hands in front of him on the desk. "I want you to tell me the truth, Maurice. Do you think I'm being foolish?"

Maurice rubbed his forehead as he considered the situation. He saw his brother's expectant expression and wondered whether he wanted support for his decision or someone to talk him out of it. "It's not for me to say," he began. "I'm sure you can make a success of yourself no matter what you try—and I suppose there would be more satisfaction creating something out of nothing. Then again, Salomon's Emporium is also a challenge; there's plenty of room for growth and expansion."

"I just don't feel as if the decisions are really mine. This is Nina's company—and Charles's—and one day it will belong to their children."

"But you're one of the children."

"I know, but . . ." He hesitated, not wanting to say what he had discovered about his real father. "Look, I'm twenty-seven, and I don't really know if I've got what it takes to make it on my own in the world. I want to make my own mark. Can you understand that?"

"Yes, I do. And if you feel so strongly about it, I think you should give it a try. Don't worry about Salomon's—it practically runs itself."

"Are you sure?" Jacob asked, sounding a bit uncertain.

"I am. You do what you have to, and let us worry about things here."

Jacob rose to leave. "I plan to get started at once. Don't worry, I won't leave you in the lurch, but I think it would be best if I moved out of the office. I'll give you as much help as you need, and you'll always be able to call on me."

Maurice stared at him numbly. "You're really going through with this?" he asked in disbelief.

Jacob smiled at his younger brother. "I have faith in you, Maurice," he told him. "I've been wanting to do this for a long time, and your coming into the firm has finally given me the opportunity. I owe you a debt of thanks, and I want you to know that whatever happens between Nina and me, I'll always be there if you need me."

Jacob strode from the room, leaving his younger brother sitting at the desk. Maurice started to smile, though not with pleasure for his unexpected good fortune but with sheer amazement at how Jacob's audacious decision had turned everything around so dramatically.

The next evening, Jacob Salomon was ushered into the enormous library of one of the stateliest mansions on Rincon Hill. He proceeded directly to the plush leather chair in front of an ornate walnut desk and sat down, nodding at the burly, bald-headed man who sat behind it gazing at him over the top of a pair of reading glasses. As the man removed the glasses, he raised his bushy gray eyebrows, enlarging his already big brown eyes. He did not smile but carefully stroked the edges of his enormous white walrus mustache.

"I was surprised to receive your calling card," the man began in a gruff, humorless voice. "I was going to turn you away, given the recent events regarding my son, but I was curious why you would come here. If it's to apologize for your role in that affair—"

"I'm not here to discuss Eaton," Jacob cut him off. "At least not directly." As he stared at Abraham Hallinger, he noted for the first time the striking similarities between the man and himself.

"Why exactly did you come?" Hallinger asked, opening an engraved silver box on the desk and removing a Havana cigar. He did not offer one to Jacob.

"I always wondered why I was so much stockier than the rest of my family—and why I alone am losing my hair." He nodded knowingly. "I never would have guessed, and now it seems so obvious."

Hallinger squinted at Jacob as he lit a match and touched it to the tip of the cigar, drawing in slowly. As he let out the smoke, he said, "What did Nina tell you?"

Jacob shook his head. "Nothing—not until I found letters and papers she had kept since I was born. And then she was forced to admit the truth."

"Which truth?"

Jacob looked at him suspiciously, then finally said, "That you're my father. That when you got her pregnant and refused to leave your wife, she married Charles and forced you out of the business—"

Hallinger cut him off with an abrupt laugh. "*Her* truth, I see."

"And yours is different?"

"It's unimportant," he replied, waving off the matter. "You have the facts sufficiently correct."

"Then you *are* my father? You don't deny it?"

"Why should I?" Hallinger took another pull on the cigar, then opened the case and presented it to Jacob, who shook his head. "So why have you come? Surely not to tell me something I already know."

"But why did you do it? Why didn't you ever tell me?"

"Nina and I agreed even before you were born that her husband and my wife would never know the truth—not even her father, Isidore, though at first she threatened to tell him. I was the one who talked her out of it."

"By selling out your share of the business?"

"Partially. And by convincing her it would only end up

working against her. In the end she saw the wisdom of what I said.''

''Why did you care?''

''This may come as a surprise to you, but I didn't want her to be hurt any more than she already was. And I cared about Isidore.''

''I thought you hated him. Nina always told us that you two never—''

''Again, that's her truth. To me, your grandfather was one of the great men of this city. Sure we fought and argued, but it was that spark between us that made the business dynamic.'' He raised the cigar and examined the burning tip. ''You know, I've been watching you from a distance over the years, and I see some of that same fire that burned so brightly in Isidore—and burns so dangerously in Nina. Charles never had it, I'm afraid.''

''But you did?''

Hallinger grinned. ''Your mother and I would have made quite a combination, but it just wasn't to be. I really did care about her, you know.'' He took another puff, leaning his head back and exhaling the smoke slowly over his head. Narrowing one eye at Jacob, he said, ''And why exactly have you come? Do you intend to blackmail me or something like that? Because it won't work. My wife is dead, and I don't much care what people think anymore.''

''No—I don't want you to give me anything.''

''Then what? I can't believe you just wanted a chat with your father—not after you saw to it that I lost my firstborn son.''

''When I went after Eaton, I had no idea he was my half-brother. I only wanted to make him pay for what he did to Phoebe.'

''And that you did. I have to admit I found myself admiring the way you engineered his arrest. It was a maneuver worthy of a Hallinger—even an unacknowledged one.''

''But what I did directly caused the death—''

''The boy was a disappointment to me—always was. He

273

had no fire in his belly—only in his groin. He could have beat those embezzling charges if he hadn't gone off half-cocked and put a tragic end to everything.''

''Then you don't blame me?'' Jacob said incredulously.

''Who has time for blame? Darwin said it best. I'm just pleased that this time the fittest one also turned out to be of my flesh.'' Hallinger paused, then added, ''You still haven't told me why you've come.''

''I'm thinking of leaving the family business,'' Jacob said flatly.

''Salomon's Emporium? But you're the head of the family now. The business community sees you as the heir apparent.''

''Nina will be the true head of Salomon's Emporium as long as she lives—no matter how little she has to do with the day-to-day operations. And I want as little to do with her as possible. I want to strike out on my own and see what I'm made of.''

''Go into business for yourself?''

''Precisely.''

''Perhaps with a little help from your real father?'' Hallinger asked pointedly, then nodded and smiled. ''It wouldn't be proper to give you a place at my bank, but perhaps I can contact one of the other banks and—''

''I'm not a banker. And I didn't come here looking for a handout—rather, an investor. I've decided to go up against my mother head-to-head. I plan to open a competing store.''

Hallinger gave a bemused grin. ''And you thought I might want to contribute to this direct assault on Salomon's Emporium?''

''Haven't you wanted to do precisely that for a long time? Isn't that why you're backing the new Emporium on Market Street?''

''Who told you that?''

''Nina. She also said you tried to buy her out several times.''

Hallinger chuckled and shook his head. ''It's true I once

privately offered to purchase Salomon's, but that was a number of years ago when the company was on hard times. It was a straight business proposal, and I mistakenly thought your mother and Charles would profit by it. Instead it redoubled Nina's efforts to succeed, and the company has been expanding ever since. So I suppose I indirectly contributed to Salomon's current success. And as for the Emporium, my bank is one of half a dozen such institutions that have given the company financial backing. But it has nothing to do with trying to destroy Salomon's. Hell, just check your own records and you'll see we gave Charles a half-million-dollar line of credit last year.''

"Then consider my proposal a simple business proposition, also," Jacob said.

"And what do you intend to use for collateral?"

"Myself—my years of experience."

"Do you think that's enough?"

"It was for you and my grandfather years ago. And it will be for me."

Hallinger tapped the cigar against an ashtray and grinned. "You do your grandfather proud—and me, as well." He started to nod. "Yes, I'll back this new venture of yours—on one condition."

"Which is?"

"I will be an equal—though silent—partner. In return, I'll provide whatever funds you'll require to open a store that will rival both Salomon's and the new Emporium. But we won't be doing it to destroy Nina, rather to create the finest mercantile establishment in all San Francisco."

Jacob sat looking at his father, gauging his character and the true depth of his commitment. Finally he rose, held out his hand, and said simply, "Agreed."

Hallinger shook Jacob's hand. "I'll have my lawyer draw up the necessary papers, and at my bank tomorrow I'll set up a business account with an open line of credit in your name."

"For now, I'd prefer to keep this between the two of us," Jacob told him.

Hallinger nodded. "Don't worry," he assured him. "I'm a master at that."

He picked up his cigar and inhaled deeply as he watched his son turn and walk from the room.

Seventeen

As Phoebe Salomon bent down to the low counter and lifted the iron teapot with her injured right hand, she extended it in front of her, concentrating on keeping the muscles of her arm firm and steady, as Hsiao Ch'u had shown her during the two weeks she had spent in the two-room apartment over his herb shop. The arm was nearly equal in strength to her left one now, and she had sufficiently mastered the use of her fingers to be able to write legibly.

Pleased with the progress she had been making, she bent her elbow and lowered the pot. She noted with satisfaction that there was very little soreness in the forearm and hand as she raised the sleeve of her Chinese robe and poured the boiling water into a smaller porcelain teapot filled with black tea leaves.

After returning the iron pot to the stove and lowering the wick, Phoebe carried the teapot and a small cup into the next room and sat in the only full-sized chair in the apartment. She looked down at the letter she had begun, which Hsiao Ch'u had been encouraging her to send to her mother. She had written the date—Wednesday, July 8, 1896—and had started the salutation with the word *Dear*. She had been unable to get beyond the first letter of her mother's name, and after staring down at the crooked *N* for the third or fourth time, she abruptly snatched up the paper and crumpled it into a ball.

Swirling the teapot gently, Phoebe poured some of the amber liquid into the cup and wrapped her right hand around it, feeling the warmth spread through her fingers. She closed her eyes and focused on the sense of warmth, trying to empty her thoughts as Hsiao Ch'u had been teaching her to do in order to control the seizures she had been experiencing since losing her baby. She did not force the thoughts from her mind but allowed them to drift through without attaching to any particular one.

After a few minutes, Phoebe found herself visualizing her mother, so she opened her eyes and took a sip of the tea, dispelling the image. Increasingly of late she had thought of Nina with a mixture of yearning and loathing.

"A fire both needs and consumes wood that gives it life," Hsiao Ch'u had told her when they were discussing her relationship with her mother. "Such is your mother's love for you; it needs and desires object of its affection, yet threatens to devour it with its dark intensity."

"But what can I do?" she had asked him. "Will I ever be able to see her again and not be consumed?"

"You must become like mountain lake, fed by secret spring that never runs dry. Fire of your mother's love cannot feed upon lake, yet she may come to you and be refreshed, and you will be replenished from within."

Phoebe did not feel at all like a mountain lake, nor had she been particularly successful at learning to empty her thoughts. Still, her two weeks in the home of Hsiao Ch'u had proved to be among the most tranquil and relaxing of her life and had afforded her the opportunity to examine herself for the first time. She had experienced no further seizures, though she had felt on the verge of one a couple of times. She credited this to the peacefulness of her surroundings and the methods and herbal medications Hsiao Ch'u had provided.

Though she knew the time was coming when she would have to confront her mother, Phoebe did not yet feel strong or confident enough to face that ordeal. In fact, it was whenever she considered going to see Nina that she felt the curious flushed sensation that preceded a seizure. She had been learning to overcome the response through meditation and visualization but was convinced she was not yet ready for the final test.

At least she could take heart from the likelihood that her sister and brothers had returned from their respective trips to England, New York, and the Orient, making it less likely Nina would try to send Phoebe back to an asylum, especially after seeing how fully she had recovered. A wave of longing for Rachel's company passed through Phoebe, bringing tears to her eyes. She wondered what Nina had told Rachel and her brothers about her absence; whatever it was, she was sure it was not the truth.

Her thoughts were interrupted by a knock at the door in the next room, which opened onto the narrow staircase that led to the back of the herb shop. Since Hsiao Ch'u always knocked so as not to walk in on Phoebe unannounced, she assumed he had come up for an afternoon cup of tea.

She headed into the main room, where Hsiao Ch'u had been sleeping on a floor mattress during her stay, and pulled open the door. She was surprised to discover the young servant from Sung Chien's household. "Kuei Mei," she said, smiling. "Please, come in."

With a slight bow, Kuei Mei entered. "My master sent me for medicine for his headaches," she explained, "and the *tai fu* said I may come up to see you."

"I'm so glad you did. Would you care for some tea?"

Kuei Mei shook her head. "I must be back soon, or Sung Chien will become suspicious."

Phoebe eyed her curiously. "Suspicious of what?"

Kuei Mei lowered her eyes. "That I will try to run away."

"But why? You've had opportunities before but have never taken them."

"This is different," she said in a barely audible voice.

Seeing how distressed her friend was, Phoebe took Kuei Mei's arm and led her into the room she was using as a bedroom. "You must tell me what happened," Phoebe said as she directed Kuei Mei to sit in her chair.

"It is not your concern," Kuei Mei replied. "I not wish to cause you worry."

"I'll be more worried if you don't tell me what's going on," Phoebe insisted. "Is Sung Chien going to send you off to Shanghai, like he tried to do to me?"

"Not that," Kuei Mei said abruptly, trying to put Phoebe's mind at ease. "But the time has come for me to leave his household."

"You're going to leave Sung Chien's house? That's good, isn't it?" Her question was answered by a look of despair. "What's wrong? Please tell me," Phoebe pleaded as she knelt in front of Kuei Mei and took her hand. "We're friends, aren't we?" When the Chinese woman nodded, Phoebe went on, "Then there should be no secrets between us."

A single tear rolled down Kuei Mei's cheek. "I always knew Sung Chien would make me leave his household one day to do work that bring him more money. That is why he has not touched me—so I be worth more to first buyer."

Phoebe stared incredulously at her. "You mean he is going to force you to . . . ?" Her voice trailed off as Kuei Mei nodded.

"I am being sent to one of the places he runs, perhaps tonight. First, one of his wealthy friends will purchase right to take my maidenhood. Then I will be put to work."

"Kuei Mei! How dreadful!" Phoebe declared. "We cannot allow such a thing."

"There is nothing to be done. Sung Chien holds my papers of indenture. Until I work them off, there is nothing I can say."

"But how can he force you to break the law? Surely if we tell the authorities—"

"Your police do not enforce law in Chinatown. We have our own system, and there is no one who will help a lowly servant of Sung Chien." She looked up and gave a faint smile. "You must not worry about me. I know for a long time what awaits me, and I am prepared to carry out the wishes of my master." She stood and wiped away a tear. "Thank you for your friendship and concern. I must go now." Moving quickly past Phoebe, she glided through the main room and over to the door.

Hurrying to Kuei Mei, Phoebe reached out and took her hands. "You must have faith," she told her friend. "Somehow you will be delivered from this fate."

Kuei Mei forced a smile, then started down the stairs.

Alone again, Phoebe was distraught with worry and anger. She remembered what Hsiao Ch'u had taught her about controlling her emotions, but nothing could calm the rage she felt toward Sung Chien. Yet she did not have any of the frightening symptoms that preceded a seizure, and she wondered if it was because she felt no personal fear and was convinced her anger was righteous.

A few minutes later, Hsiao Ch'u came upstairs to ask if Phoebe knew why Kuei Mei had looked so upset when she returned to the shop. When Phoebe told him of the fate that awaited the young woman, Hsiao Ch'u nodded thoughtfully and stepped over to the low counter, where he began to prepare a fresh pot of tea.

"Isn't there anything we can do?" Phoebe implored.

"We discuss Kuei Mei before," Hsiao Ch'u replied, lighting one of the gas burners. "For her to win freedom, she must work off cost of her papers, as well as what Sung Chien has spent on her behalf since coming to San Francisco."

"But that could take years."

"I am afraid so. Sometimes new expenses are added more quickly than old ones are worked off, so person is never able to win freedom."

"But that isn't right."

"It is the way that it is," he said simply. "It not help Kuei Mei for us to complain about system that binds her."

"Then what will help her?" she asked.

"We must purchase her papers. Perhaps after you return home, you arrange for someone to go to Sung Chien with enough money—"

"But we don't have time for that," Phoebe protested. "She said she expects to be taken there tonight."

Hsiao Ch'u shook his head sadly as he removed a pinch of tea leaves and dropped them into the porcelain pot. "I would purchase her contract myself," he told her. "I have enough money saved, but Sung Chien would never agree—not after way I spoke against him on your behalf. He would decide he could earn more money by working her in brothel than by letting me buy her papers for their current worth."

"Perhaps if I were to go to him with the money," Phoebe suggested.

"Sung Chien never sell to woman—especially woman he believes caused dishonor to his household."

"Then how can we ever hope to make him sell?"

"Perhaps there is one way," Hsiao Ch'u declared as he turned off the stove and poured the boiling water into the pot. "He might sell if he believes purchaser is someone worth currying favor—perhaps an Occidental with some influence in city." He began to nod. "I know of man who might be willing to help."

"Who is it?" she asked eagerly.

"He is surgeon at Pacific Hospital." Hsiao Ch'u turned and narrowed his eyes at Phoebe. "Are you willing to seek out this man and bring him message from me?"

"Of course," she declared.

"His hospital is near asylum that burned down. You would be at some risk of being recognized and captured."

"I'll take that chance," she said flatly. Glancing down at her Oriental robe, she added, "However, if there is any way to obtain a more suitable dress . . ."

"I know of shop just outside Chinatown where I can purchase something more appropriate."

"Wonderful." She grinned enthusiastically. "When shall we start?"

"First we must steel ourselves, like warriors preparing for battle."

"How?" she asked.

Hsiao Ch'u turned to her and smiled. "By sharing cup of tea, of course."

Two hours later, a cab carrying Phoebe Salomon pulled up in front of Pacific Hospital. She had on a plain brown frock dress of the most ordinary and unflattering style, over which she wore a simple black shawl. Her blond hair was pulled into a severe bun and had been powdered somewhat to remove the luster. During the past weeks she had been indoors so much that her skin had a pale, unhealthy pallor, which she did not cover with makeup so as to further conceal her identity.

Entering the hospital, Phoebe asked to meet with Dr. Aidan McAuliffe and was ushered to a small office near the surgical ward.

"Please wait in here while I summon him," the nurse said pleasantly, pointing to one of the seats and leaving.

As Phoebe sat down, she glanced around the office, which appeared to have been recently occupied. The room contained little more than the chair she was sitting on and a desk that was bare save for a framed picture that faced away from her. There was a window that looked out onto an air shaft, and a small stand behind the desk chair that held a number of folders in an open vertical file.

Phoebe was reaching to examine the framed picture when the door opened, and she turned to see a handsome, clean-shaven man in his late twenties, with brown hair and pale-blue eyes. He wore the white jacket of a surgeon, and as he smiled and began to speak, she was immediately put at ease by his pleasant manner and his faint Scottish lilt.

"Good afternoon," he began, holding out his hand as she rose from the chair. "I'm Dr. Aidan McAuliffe. The nurse said you wish to speak with me?"

"It's a pleasure to meet you, Dr. McAuliffe." She shook his hand and sat down again as he circled the desk and took his own seat. "I've heard so much about you from a mutual friend."

"Indeed? And who could that be?"

"A Chinese gentleman named Hsiao Ch'u."

Aidan's eyebrows rose in surprise. "I'm afraid I'm at a disadvantage. The last time I saw him, he didn't mention a woman friend."

"We only recently met. My name is Fiona," she introduced herself, not wanting to use her own name or the one given her at the asylum.

"And how may I help you, Fiona?" he asked, folding his hands in front of him on the desk.

"Hsiao Ch'u sent me to make an unusual request of you." She leaned forward in the chair. "Hsiao Ch'u and I have a young friend named Kuei Mei, who is indentured to a Chinatown businessman named Sung Chien. The man has decided to put her to work in a house of prostitution, and Hsiao Ch'u and I are trying to free her. The only way to do this is to purchase her contract."

"How does this involve me?"

"As a woman, I can't buy the contract. And though Hsiao Ch'u has enough money, Sung Chien won't sell to him either, since he can earn more money working her in the brothel than giving her up for the price of the contract. However, Sung Chien's business depends upon his maintaining good relationships outside of Chinatown. If someone like you requested to purchase the contract, he might be cautious about turning you down."

"That's all you want?" Aidan asked. "I'd be glad to buy this woman's freedom. However, I'm afraid I don't have a great deal of money at my disposal right now, though I might be able to arrange with a friend—"

"We will supply any needed funds," she assured him.

"Then I'll be glad to do what I can. Just let me know when Hsiao Ch'u needs me."

"I'm afraid we must act at once if we're to free Kuei Mei," Phoebe told him. "We learned this afternoon that Sung Chien plans to turn her over to the brothel tonight." She looked up at him expectantly. "Would it be possible for you to return to Chinatown with me right now? Hsiao Ch'u is waiting at his shop, and the two of you can visit Sung Chien and try to make the transaction."

"Well . . . I suppose so, if I can make arrangements with our chief surgeon. But I can only be gone a couple of hours, since I'm on duty later tonight."

"Thank you so much," she declared. As Aidan started to rise, she looked at him sheepishly and said, "I'm afraid there is one more thing I haven't told you yet."

"What's that?" he asked, sitting back down.

"To follow the plan devised by Hsiao Ch'u, you'll have to pretend you wish to marry Kuei Mei. It's only to win her freedom," she quickly assured him. "You won't be expected to follow through."

Aidan grinned. "That's good, since I don't think my fiancée would appreciate finding out I already got married."

"You're engaged?" she asked, her voice betraying a slight disappointment. She liked this kind man and sensed in him qualities she felt she could trust.

"To a remarkable woman," he exclaimed. He picked up the framed picture and turned it toward her, saying, "Rachel Salomon and I are to be married a week from Saturday."

Phoebe's already pale features went white as she gaped at the photograph of her sister. She looked up at Aidan, but he was gazing down admiringly at the picture, unaware of her reaction.

"Isn't she beautiful?" he asked, shaking his head in wonder. Turning it away from Phoebe, he sighed and stood up. "I'll just be a moment, and then we can leave." He barely glanced at her as he circled the desk and disappeared out into the hall.

Phoebe was hardly able to move as she stared at the back of the frame. Slowly coming to her senses, she reached forward, picked it up, and turned it around. Rachel's features blurred as tears welled in Phoebe's eyes. A moment later they were running down her cheek, and she reached up and wiped them with the back of her hand.

"Rachel," she whispered, touching the photograph in the frame. Her sister's image was smiling up at her, and she knew at last that it was time to go home.

Across the city, Jacob Saloman found Rachel waiting at his town house when he returned from work. As soon as Langdon took his hat and coat at the front door and announced that she was in the parlor, he strode into the room and said, "Rachel, I'm glad you came. As a matter of fact, I was going to call on you this evening and—"

"Is it true?" she cut in, rising from the sofa. "I just left Belle, who wanted to talk to me about Maurice. She said he's been preoccupied with work and acting strangely, and she was worried that he was dissatisfied at home. But then this morning she forced an admission out of him . . . about you." She approached where he was standing. "Is it true?" she repeated.

At first Jacob thought she was referring to Abraham Hallinger's being his father, but then he realized she meant his decision to leave Salomon's Emporium. He drew in a breath and nodded. "Yes, it is. I only decided yesterday and was going to tell you this evening."

"How can you leave the business?" she demanded. "And without consulting anyone but Maurice. What happened? Did you two have a disagreement or something?"

"No, nothing like that," he insisted, walking past her and coming to a halt behind the sofa. Placing his hands on the back of it, he slowly shook his head. "It has nothing to do with Maurice. It was my decision alone."

"But if you've only just decided, why does Belle say that Maurice has been acting strangely for the past couple of weeks?"

"I've no idea. I suppose he's still adjusting to things at work—and to married life."

"And so you're going to leave him in the lurch? That makes no sense."

"It does to me," Jacob replied, turning away and falling silent. He had resolved to keep the truth about his parentage from Rachel and Maurice, but he had not anticipated the cost of such a secret. For it to create misunderstanding and discord between Rachel and him would only compound the effect of Nina's deception.

She came around the sofa, walked up to him, and gripped his left arm. "Tell me what's wrong, Jacob. You and I could always talk; don't shut me out now."

"It's . . . personal."

"What's wrong? Belle says you told Maurice you wanted to go it alone. Surely there's more to it than that." When he did not reply, she added, "What has Nina done?"

Jacob looked down and shook his head.

"This must be worse than the usual problems we have with her. I want you to tell me what it is."

Jacob looked up into her sympathetic eyes. Slowly he nodded. "If I tell you, I want you to promise not to try to talk me out of my decision."

"If you're set on leaving, I won't try to stop you."

"All right." He walked across the room to a small writing desk. Opening the bottom drawer, he took out the manila envelope with his name on it and brought it over to Rachel. "I found this hidden in Nina's bureau." He handed it to her. "Go ahead—read it."

Rachel took the envelope and sat down. Opening it, she pulled out the contents and placed them on her lap. Methodically she read through the papers and letters, slowly shaking her head in amazement. When she had read enough to understand the full impact of what had happened twenty-seven years ago, she looked up at him and asked, "How long have you known about this?"

"A few days."

"And Nina knows you found out?"

Jacob nodded. "We had words, to say the least."

"Which ended with your decision to quit the business."

"More or less, though I didn't decide until yesterday. And it wasn't really out of the blue. I've been considering it for a long time; this was merely the catalyst."

Rachel returned the papers to the envelope. Rising from the chair, she walked over to her brother and handed him the envelope. As their fingers touched, she clenched his hands and looked up at him with tears in her eyes. "I'm so sorry," she whispered.

"There's really nothing to be sorry about. I'm still the same person, only now I know the truth of my past."

"But to find out in such a way . . ." Reaching up, she wrapped her arms around his neck and kissed his cheek. "I love you, Jacob."

"And I love you, too," he replied, pulling away from her and smiling. "Really, don't feel bad about this. I confess I was pretty shattered at first, but in the past day I've been feeling stronger than ever in my life. It's as if I've finally gained my independence."

"But at what cost? Losing your job, your livelihood—"

"I chose that myself."

"But what will you do?"

"I'm going to open my own store."

She looked at him incredulously. "Where? When?"

"Right here in San Francisco, as soon as I can arrange the financing."

"Competing with Salomon's Emporium? Nina will be beside herself. She'll cut you off without a penny."

"Don't worry about me," he assured her. "I've some money saved, and I expect to have investors."

"Nina will never stand for it," Rachel declared.

"She can do what she wants. San Francisco is a big, growing city, and I, for one, don't see competition as a threat but as an opportunity to expand the market.''

"Are you certain you're doing the right thing?'' she asked, and when he nodded, she forced a smile. "Then I wish you the greatest of success." Again she kissed him on the cheek, then turned toward the front door. "I'd better be going now. Nina's expecting me for dinner."

"I'd rather nothing were said as yet about my business plans."

"I'll let you make the announcement when you feel ready," she promised. "Good-bye, Jacob."

"Rachel . . .'' Jacob hesitantly called after her, causing her to turn around and look at him questioningly. "I don't want to interfere, but there's something else I think you should know."

As Rachel watched, he crossed back to the writing desk, where he returned the manila envelope to the open drawer and removed several letters. "I found these in the same place as those papers." He held them out to her.

She approached cautiously, as though sensing the dramatic effect those letters would have on her life.

When Rachel stormed into the dining room of the family home on Nob Hill, waving the letters from Timothy Price, her mother was inspecting the dinner settings. "How could you be so heartless?'' Rachel raged, tossing them onto the plate in front of Nina. "Who the hell gave you the right?''

Nina was stunned into silence as she stared down at the incriminating envelopes. When she finally opened her mouth to speak, Rachel cut her off with a wave of the hand.

"I don't want to hear your excuses—your lies! I know what you did, and there's no forgiving it."

"You . . . you don't understand," Nina stammered, raising a hand beseechingly toward her daughter.

"I don't, do I? It's obvious you hid Tim's letters in order to break us up—and now you're trying to get us back together in order to destroy my relationship with Aidan.''

"It's not that simple. Those letters were a long time ago. Tim was so wild then; you were young and innocent."

"I was never so innocent that I couldn't watch ut for myself."

"But a young, respectable woman and a man with Tim's reputation. Who knows what might have—?"

"You mean I might have gotten pregnant—like you did!" Seeing Nina's shocked expression, she added, "Yes, Jacob told me—just as you should have told him years ago, instead of poisoning him with lies about his real father."

Nina's expression turned to raw anger. "Why, that little bastard! He promised not to tell—"

"He's my brother, for heaven's sake! And if he's a bastard, it's thanks to you!"

Repressing her anger, Nina snatched up the letters and shook them in her fist. "Why do you think I kept these all this time? I always meant to tell you one day—when the time was right."

"And when was that going to be? The night before my wedding?" She grabbed the letters from her mother's hand and started for the door to the living room.

Stomping up behind her, Nina railed, "Why do you think I invited Tim to that dinner party? Did you ever consider that I might have been trying to correct what happened years ago— that perhaps I was giving you the chance to find out whether or not you really love Tim before rushing into marriage with that foreigner?"

Rachel gave a harsh, abrupt laugh and faced her mother. "Are you trying to tell me you're sorry? Nina Salomon has never been sorry for anything in her life."

"You think you're so perfect? Well, you're not," Nina flared. "Of course I hid those letters. Any mother in her right mind would have done the same. Or have you forgotten you almost ran off with Tim when he went to Boston?"

"I wasn't looking to run off with him but away from you!"

"You little slut!" Nina hissed, narrowing her eyes.

Rachel grinned wickedly. "You should be proud of yourself, Nina. You raised a bastard and a slut—a pair of sluts, actually; we mustn't forget Phoebe's little indiscretion with Jacob's half-brother. Tell me . . . what exactly does that make you?''

"Shut your mouth, young lady!"

"Not until I'm damn good and ready."

"If you're so sure of your feelings for that Scotsman, you wouldn't care about ancient history like those letters!" Nina shot back, raising an accusing finger at her daughter.

Rachel glared at her mother, unable to speak because of the rage within her.

As though sensing that she had hit a nerve, Nina continued, "If something's come between you and your fiancé, my dear, it's not because of my actions but because of Timothy Price."

"You're way off the mark," Rachel declared, though she could hear her voice falter a bit.

"Am I? Then what were you doing riding off with Tim on the Fourth of July? Don't think I didn't see you."

"We're just friends," Rachel protested. "Aidan had to work, and Tim offered to take me to the Fourth of July concert in the park."

"Did you tell your future husband?" Nina challenged.

"Well, no, but . . . it really wasn't important."

"Don't tell *me* that—tell your fiancé. And then go look Tim Price in the eye and tell him you no longer care about him."

Rachel stared down at the letters, then up at her mother, her eyes narrowing with contempt. "I see no point in staying for dinner," she said, turning away.

"Where are you going?" Nina demanded. "When will you be home?"

"Wherever I want . . . and whenever I want," Rachel answered, starting from the room. Pausing at the door, she looked back and added, "From now on, just keep your nose out of my affairs. And as for my marrying Aidan—that foreigner, as you call him—you can forget about coming to the ceremony. It would feel more like a funeral than a wedding!'' Spinning around, she strode from the room.

When Rachel reached the front door, she was out of breath and a bit dizzy from anger. Cameron, the butler, was already standing there, her cape in his hand. Apparently he had been able to hear the entire argument and knew she was not staying for dinner.

"I'm sorry, Cameron," Rachel told him.

He nodded and held the cape open for her. "Shall I have Michael bring around the carriage?" he asked.

"Thank you, but I'm just going for a walk. I'll be back later." She buttoned the cape and waited for him to open the door.

"Miss Rachel," Cameron said cautiously as he turned the doorknob. "May I speak with you?"

"But of course. What is it?" She saw the butler glance around nervously and, noting his discomfort, suggested, "Perhaps we could step outside."

Cameron smiled with relief and opened the door. As soon as they were on the landing with the door closed, he said, "I've been here many years—since you were a child—and you know how I've always vowed not to speak out of turn about anyone else's activities."

"We've always appreciated your discretion, Cameron," she reassured him.

"I'm afraid recent events compel me to break that vow. I feel it my duty to confide in you, Miss Rachel, if I may."

"You know you can speak openly with me. What is it?"

"It has come to my attention that one of the newer members of our staff has been sneaking off to meet with a gentleman at his hotel. Normally I would not interfere in such matters of the heart, but in this case I must. It turns out this gentleman is someone she met when he was a houseguest of your mother's. I'm afraid it is quite a breach of ethics."

"Can you tell me who this woman is?"

Cameron looked somewhat more uncomfortable but replied, "It's Lydia, from our kitchen staff."

292

Rachel nodded, then asked, "What would you like me to do?"

"Frankly, I'm not sure. Normally I'd recommend terminating her employment, but this situation is more . . . complicated."

"How do you mean?"

"Well, I'm uncertain of the repercussions, and I don't feel at liberty to discuss the matter with Mrs. Salomon."

"Why not? Nina is in charge of the household staff, and you did say the man is a friend of hers. If a decision must be made regarding Lydia, surely she should make it."

Cameron seemed even more disconcerted. "I'm afraid I'm not being entirely clear. But it's so difficult—"

"Please be open with me, Cameron. I won't break your confidence."

The butler drew in a deep breath and let it out in a sigh. "The problem is that your mother is seeing this same gentleman."

Rachel cocked her head in confusion. "You don't mean to say that Nina . . . and this man . . ."

"I believe so. She put him up in the guest room one night a few weeks ago, then spirited him out in the morning without anyone's knowing. Lydia stumbled upon him, however, which is how they met."

Rachel felt her anger toward Nina begin to blossom anew. "How do you know all this?"

"I confess I was aware the gentleman was upstairs at the time, but I knew it was not my place to comment. However, Lydia later bragged to someone else on the staff about coming upon him in the bedroom, and later about . . ." His voice trailed off.

"Go on," she urged him.

Cameron took another deep breath and plunged ahead. "It seems that Lydia took up the gentleman's offer to visit his hotel room. She was sharing his bathtub when he was called away to the door. She ended up trapped in the tub the entire time your mother and this man were . . . well, in the bedroom . . .''

Shaking her head in dismay, Rachel murmured, ''I understand.''

''You can see my quandary. If I fire Lydia, she may make public what she knows about Mrs. Salomon. Yet she's betrayed our trust and cannot be allowed to remain on the staff.''

For a few moments Rachel did not move, pondering the consequences of the various courses of action. Then she shifted her stance and asked, ''Do you know who the man is, Cameron?''

''Only that he's far younger than Mrs. Salomon and is staying at the Baldwin Hotel—and that his first name is Damien.''

Rachel gasped. ''Damien Picard . . .'' she uttered, gripping the sleeve of Cameron's jacket as her legs seemed to weaken.

''Lydia definitely said Damien. I don't know the gentleman's surname.''

''The Baldwin Hotel?'' she asked, her voice steadier.

''That's right. I don't know the room number, however.''

Releasing his sleeve, she said with resolve, ''Have Michael bring around the carriage at once.''

''Yes, Miss Rachel.''

''And Cameron, don't tell anyone what we spoke about.''

''As you wish, miss.''

As Cameron reentered the house, Rachel walked to the edge of the drive and waited for the carriage, her arms folded against the sudden chill that swept through her body.

Eighteen

IT WAS EARLY EVENING WHEN HSIAO CH'U AND AIDAN McAuliffe were ushered into the parlor of Sung Chien's spacious Chinatown home and were shown to a pair of plush chairs upholstered in Oriental silk. A matching footstool was brought for Hsiao Ch'u, since his short legs did not reach the floor. While they waited for their host to make his appearance, they were served tea by two women dressed in traditional black robes.

When they were briefly alone, Aidan whispered to Hsiao Ch'u, "Is one of them the woman Fiona told me about?" Hsiao Ch'u shook his head, and Aidan added, "I hope we're not too late."

The two men sipped their tea and nodded politely to the servingwomen, who padded in and out with trays of little Chinese pastries, which they served to the men and then placed on small tables beside their chairs. After about ten minutes, a male servant appeared at the hallway door to announce his master, and the visitors rose.

As Sung Chien swept into the room, both Aidan and Hsiao

Ch'u were taken aback by his elegant attire. He was dressed in the finest double-breasted Prince Albert dress suit, the knee-length jacket protruding over his enormous belly. The stiff, high-winged collar he wore barely contained his bulging neck, and the silk ribbon bow tie looked far too small for his massive head.

Though Aidan thought Sung Chien's appearance almost comical, the large-bellied man seemed unaware of it as he smiled and approached, disregarding the respectful bow given by Hsiao Ch'u and holding out his hand American-style to his other guest. "I am Sung Chien," he said in flawless English as he shook Aidan's hand. "Welcome to my home." Giving Hsiao Ch'u a perfunctory nod, he suggested, "Shall we sit?" and indicated the chairs.

Aidan and Hsiao Ch'u resumed their seats, while Sung Chien took a chair facing them. When he signaled toward a rear doorway, one of the servingwomen immediately poured him a cup of tea.

"And to what do I owe the pleasure of a visit from the honorable *tai fu* and his esteemed guest?" Sung Chien asked with uncharacteristic deference as he sipped the tea and turned to Hsiao Ch'u.

"I bring good friend, Dr. Aidan McAuliffe, to ask great kindness of Sung Chien, for which you will be recompensed liberally."

Sung Chien's eyes widened with interest as he turned to Aidan. "Your calling card said you are a physician?" he asked.

"Dr. McAuliffe is noted physician and surgeon in England and United States and currently heads surgical staff at Pacific Hospital," Hsiao Ch'u exaggerated.

Sung Chien smiled. "And how may I be of service to you, Dr. McAuliffe?" he asked.

Aidan glanced at Hsiao Ch'u, then looked back at Sung Chien. "I have come looking for a wife," he stated plainly.

"And you come to me?" Sung Chien said with surprise, cocking his enormous head and looking curiously at Aidan.

"I am afraid I find American women far too independent and strong-willed," Aidan explained. "I require a woman who understands the challenge of being the wife of a physician and will place her husband first in all things."

Sung Chien nodded with understanding. "You desire a Chinese wife."

"That is why I consulted my colleague, Hsiao Ch'u."

The little man leaned forward in his chair and nodded sagely. "Such arrangements quite sensitive, and I thought good friend Sung Chien might know young woman without family in America who might be suitable for doctor. Of course he wishes woman who is virtuous, respectful, and innocent."

Aidan patted his breast pocket, where he kept his billfold. "I'm prepared to pay whatever fee you feel appropriate for your time and trouble and to reimburse you for any loss you may incur by such an arrangement."

Sung Chien waved his hand, as if dismissing the offer. "I am certain the good *tai fu* and I can make whatever arrangements are necessary," he assured Aidan. "First we must find a suitable wife."

"I am indeed in your debt," Aidan told him, "and I will rely upon the good judgment of yourself and Hsiao Ch'u. After all, it was Hsiao Ch'u who encouraged me to proceed in seeking such a marital arrangement."

"Not me but *I Ching*," Hsiao Ch'u corrected. When Sung Chien nodded respectfully at the mention of the ancient system of divination, Hsiao Ch'u turned to him and said, "When Dr. McAuliffe sought my advice, I consulted oracles, which indicated fifty-fourth hexagram, *Kuei Mei*. In his language this means Marrying Maiden. This told us that signs for such a union were auspicious."

Sung Chien's eyes widened at the pronouncement, and he declared, "There is a young woman in my employ who was given the name Kuei Mei at the orphanage in China where she was raised. In fact, she is the *niu yung* who recently spent an afternoon at your shop, assisting you with a patient."

"The *niu yung* is named Kuei Mei?" Hsiao Ch'u asked, feigning ignorance. "Surely this is not coincidence but great portent of blessings to come for both you and my good friend Dr. McAuliffe should you bring matter to successful conclusion." He nodded silently as he sipped his tea, waiting for Sung Chien to make the obvious suggestion.

It took but a moment for the big man to take the bait and say, "Perhaps Dr. McAuliffe would care to meet the woman named Kuei Mei. She is young and virtuous, and she has no family that might object to such a union."

"Wonderful idea," Hsiao Ch'u put in. "Furthermore, I have seen her to be especially skilled as a nurse; she would be most understanding of your position, Dr. McAuliffe."

Aidan grinned and declared, "I would very much like to meet this Kuei Mei."

With a broad smile, Sung Chien clapped his hands, and one of the male servants appeared at the door. Sung Chien spoke to him in rapid Chinese, and the man bowed and headed down the hall. A moment later he returned with Kuei Mei.

The young Chinese woman was dressed in a black robe as she padded into the room. From her expression, Aidan guessed that she suspected something was afoot when she saw Hsiao Ch'u and himself, an Occidental stranger, but she contained any surprise or excitement and bowed politely to Sung Chien and the visitors.

"You will note that she is clean and well-trained," Sung Chien said, speaking of her almost as if she were not in the room. "And she speaks English, as well." Turning to the woman, he said something in Chinese.

Kuei Mei faced Aidan and gave a soft smile. "It is a pleasure to meet you, Doctor," she said in English.

"And I'm delighted to meet you, Kuei Mei," he replied.

"You must call her *niu yung*," Hsiao Ch'u corrected with a raised hand, and Aidan nodded that he understood.

"Does the *niu yung* meet with your pleasure?" Sung Chien

asked. "I assure you that she is virtuous in every way and has never known a man."

"She seems delightful," Aidan replied. "May I question her?" When Sung Chien signaled for him to proceed, he turned back to Kuei Mei and said, "Tell me, *niu yung*. Do you wish to have me for a husband?"

Kuei Mei looked at him in surprise, then glanced at the two Chinese men. Finally she lowered her eyes and replied, "It is my wish to do whatever my master desires."

The wealthy merchant signaled Kuei Mei to withdraw. As soon as she left the room, he turned to Aidan. "You see that she will do whatever her master requires, whether that master be Sung Chien or Dr. Aidan McAuliffe." He grinned. "You will surely be satisfied with a wife such as this."

"I'd like to marry this *niu yung*," Aidan announced. "Just tell me what is necessary."

Sung Chien nodded, then turned to Hsiao Ch'u and began to speak in Chinese. The two men conversed pleasantly for several minutes, after which Hsiao Ch'u turned to Aidan and smiled. "Matter is settled; *niu yung* is free to leave with you at once."

Startled, Aidan began to ask, "But how much—?"

He was cut off by Hsiao Ch'u, who raised a cautioning hand and said, "My most esteemed friend Sung Chien honored to have been able to serve you in this matter by making gift of *niu yung*."

"Thank you for your assistance and generosity," Aidan said as the three men stood.

"It has been my pleasure," Sung Chien replied, again shaking Aidan's hand. "If you will excuse me, I will arrange for the *niu yung* to gather her things." He bowed to Hsiao Ch'u, then turned and headed from the room.

"What happened?" Aidan asked as soon as they were alone.

Hsiao Ch'u smiled broadly. "This transaction will cost no money. Instead I agreed to provide medical services free for Sung Chien's household and others in his employ. This allows Sung Chien to do great service for noted Occidental physician. As a man who has many dealings with local authorities, Sung Chien has learned that such favors often provide benefits to him in the future.''

A moment later Kuei Mei was ushered back into the room, carrying a small carpetbag that contained the few items she possessed that were not the property of Sung Chien. Aidan began to reach for the bag, but Hsiao Ch'u signaled him to let her carry it. Kuei Mei spoke a few words in Chinese to Sung Chien, and by their tone Aidan guessed they were words of thanks for his many kindnesses. Then she walked over to where Aidan was standing and took a position a few steps behind him.

Aidan and Hsiao Ch'u took their leave of Sung Chien, thanking him for his generous assistance. At the merchant's signal, one of his men opened the door, and the two men and Kuei Mei headed out into the night.

The trio did not stop until they had gone two blocks and rounded the corner, where they came upon Phoebe Salomon standing on the sidewalk waiting for them. Kuei Mei's eyes lit with excitement as Phoebe rushed over and embraced her.

Composing herself, Kuei Mei turned toward Aidan and announced to Phoebe, ''This is to be my husband.''

Phoebe began to laugh, and the two men joined in. When Kuei Mei looked at them in confusion, Phoebe said to her, ''Dr. McAuliffe is already engaged to be married.''

''But I do not understand. . . .''

Phoebe wrapped her arm around her friend's shoulder. ''Like the medicine you used to help me escape, Hsiao Ch'u used his friend to win your freedom.''

Realizing the entire story was a ruse, Kuei Mei turned to Aidan and smiled. ''I am forever in your debt.''

''It is I who am indebted to you—to all of you,'' Aidan insisted. ''I know what it's like to be imprisoned, and you've done me a great service by allowing me to help.'' He pulled out a pocket watch and glanced at the time. ''But now I must be going. I'm on duty at the hospital tonight.''

"Thank you for all you've done," Phoebe said, offering her hand.

"It has been a pleasure, Fiona," he replied, raising her hand to his lips.

"I . . ." She hesitated, as if debating whether or not to divulge her true identity. Finally she said, "I want to congratulate you on your upcoming marriage. I hope you find great happiness with your future wife . . . with Rachel Salomon."

Hsiao Ch'u noted the intensity of feeling with which Phoebe said the woman's name. Though he knew at once that Aidan's fiancée was Phoebe's own sister, he remained silent.

"Please don't hesitate to call if I can be of any further assistance," Aidan told Hsiao Ch'u and Phoebe. Then he said good-bye to Kuei Mei and turned up Dupont Street toward Montgomery Avenue, where he would be able to find a cab to take him back to Pacific Hospital.

As Phoebe stood, watching Aidan depart, her eyes welled with tears. She felt someone take her hand, and she turned to see Kuei Mei beside her, smiling.

With a grin, Phoebe wrapped her arm around her friend's shoulder and said, "Let's go. We certainly have something to celebrate tonight." The two women, with Hsiao Ch'u at their side, started down the street toward the herb shop.

Rachel Salomon asked Michael, the family coachman, to accompany her into the Baldwin Hotel, and as they entered the busy lobby, she indicated he should wait inconspicuously at the back of the cavernous room.

Walking over to the front desk, she gave the night clerk a demure smile. When the portly fellow asked how he could be of service, she said, "I'm looking for Mr. Damien Picard. Can you tell me what room he's in?"

The clerk smiled apologetically. "I'm sorry, but we don't give out room numbers. I can send someone up to his room with a message, though, if you'd like."

Pouting prettily, Rachel said, "But I so wanted to surprise him. You can't even tell his own sister?"

"Oh, Mr. Picard is your brother?" The clerk glanced around to make sure no one in authority was in the vicinity. Quickly he looked down at the guest list, then said, "I really can't tell you—even if you were to ask two hundred forty-two times." He emphasized the number and raised one eyebrow suggestively.

Rachel looked at him curiously and was about to ask what he meant when she realized what he was doing. "Was that two hundred forty-two times?"

He nodded. "I'm sorry, but that's the rule."

"I understand. Thank you," she told him.

Turning, she headed over to where Michael was standing near the staircase that led to the second floor. She glanced back to make sure the night clerk was no longer watching her, then said to Michael, "Room two forty-two." He nodded, and she started up the stairs, confident that if she did not return in ten minutes, he would come up after her, as she had instructed him during the ride to the hotel.

Reaching the second floor, she followed the numbers toward Damien Picard's room. She had no desire to see him; in fact, the thought of him sickened her. But with the knowledge of his meddling with her family, she felt compelled to take action to stop him, and the only way she knew to start was to confront him. At least Michael was nearby, giving her some measure of safety.

Reaching room two hundred forty-two, she drew in a deep breath and steeled herself, then raised her hand and rapped on the door. She waited a few moments, then knocked again. Still no one answered, so she tried a third time, placing her ear close to the door to see if she could hear anything from within. No sound was coming from the room.

Her heart pounding, Rachel tried the knob, but it was locked. She stared in frustration at the door, wishing she could get inside to search his things for any evidence that she might be able to use against him. Just then the clerk appeared in the hallway, a ring of keys in his hand. Walking up to her, he said, "I noticed your brother's gone out and left his keys at the desk. I thought since you were here to surprise him . . ." Grinning, he nodded toward the door and jangled the keys.

"Would you?" she asked coyly.

As the portly man chose the proper key and inserted it in the lock, Rachel found herself wondering if he really believed she was Damien's sister. Most likely not, she decided, but the man obviously thought Damien Picard would not mind finding a beautiful woman in his room and perhaps would reward the clerk nicely. As he pushed the door open and ushered her inside, she guessed she was not the first woman he had seen go into Damien's room at night.

"Thank you so much," she told him, watching as he lit a gas lamp on the writing desk and then politely bowed and left the room, shutting the door behind him.

Once she was alone, Rachel took a deep breath and quickly surveyed the bedroom and then the bathroom, in which Lydia supposedly had been trapped during Nina's visit. Returning to the bedroom, she began riffling through the dresser drawers, uncertain of what she was looking for but convinced there would be something worthwhile. She found it when she came to the writing desk and discovered the letter from Agnes Banker. Quickly reading it, she deduced that her younger brother was being blackmailed by some woman named Lorraine, whom he supposedly got pregnant during his recent stay in New York City.

Realizing this would account for Maurice's strange behavior, which had troubled Belle, she stuffed the letter back into the envelope and opened her cape to slip it into an inner pocket. Just then she heard the sound of metal rasping against metal, and her body went rigid as her pulse raced. She spun around to see the door burst open and Damien Picard enter. He was smiling and started to greet her, as if he had been forewarned by the clerk. But then he realized who she was, and his features went cold and hard.

"Mr. Damien Picard," she said with a calm strength that surprised even her. "We meet again."

Damien narrowed one eye. "What are you doing here?" he demanded, his tone angry and suspicious.

"Shouldn't I be asking you that?" Though Rachel's heart was pounding with revulsion for this man—and fear of him— she was surprised at how confident her anger was making her.

Damien closed the door and circled to the side, eyeing her closely. "This is my room. You have no right—"

"You speak to me of rights?" she blurted, her anger bubbling through. "After all you've done?" Suddenly she gave an abrupt laugh. "The audacity of you . . . to show your face in San Francisco after what you did to me. I could have you thrown in prison for—"

"That was New York," he said coolly. "Your testimony means nothing here."

"You'd be surprised how much weight the Salomon name holds in San Francisco."

It was Damien's turn to chuckle. "The days of the vigilance committees have been over for forty years. What happened in New York holds no water in San Francisco."

"Perhaps we should put it to the test," she challenged.

"Look, there's no need for us to fight," he said, adopting a more congenial tone. "I admit my actions were terribly wrong—just as I told your brother. But I was drunk that night; I didn't know what I was doing. And ever since, I've had to live with the shame of what happened."

"I might have believed you if you hadn't disappeared the way you did. If you hadn't come to San Francisco and—"

"I came to help your brother."

"Because of this?" she demanded, sneering as she held up the letter from Agnes Banker. "You and she probably set up the whole thing together—including the meeting between my brother and this Lorraine." Remembering how her father had been tricked into thinking Jacob was his son, she added,

"Why, if the woman is indeed pregnant, I wouldn't be surprised if *you* are the real father and not Maurice."

"You don't know what you're talking about," Damien snapped, taking a step toward her. "That letter is none of your business—and neither are your brother's affairs." He started to reach for the letter, then pulled back his hand. "Did Maurice put you up to this?" he asked.

"He has no idea I'm here."

"Then how did you know where to find me?"

"You leave an impressive trail, *Mr. Picard*." She said the name facetiously, with no pretense of respect. "One need only follow the likes of our scullery maid. And if that proves too challenging, there's always the grand lady of the house herself. I'll bet you treated them more gently than you did me. Or do they like it rough?"

Damien was stunned into silence. His face tightened with anger, and finally he snarled, "You little bitch. I should've finished you—"

"Come on!" she prodded, waving him closer. "The clerk who let me in here will make a wonderful witness at your trial if you have the guts to touch me again. So will my coachman, Michael, who's been instructed to come up if I haven't returned in ten minutes."

Damien's hands were clenched into fists, and he seemed to be making a supreme effort of will to keep from leaping at Rachel and killing her. "Get the hell out of here!" he hissed, shaking his head with rage.

"Not until I tell you why I came," she said in a calm, steady voice. She gave him a moment to wonder what she was going to say, then went on, "I'm giving you until tomorrow night to leave San Francisco. If I find out you haven't left, or if you ever return, I intend to reveal everything I know—what you did to me in New York, how you're conspiring to blackmail Maurice, even your affair with my mother—and I'll reveal it not only to my family but to the police. We may have no vigilantes in San Francisco anymore, but by the time our lawyers and their investigators get through with you, we should be able to come up with enough evidence to satisfy the most demanding of juries.''

''You're bluffing,'' he retorted. ''You'd never subject your own family to the scandal—''

''Try me,'' she cut him off with a confident smile. ''I suggest you leave town while you're able, Mr. Picard . . . that is, unless you're convinced that your activities, present and past, will stand up under scrutiny.'' She tucked the letter from Agnes Banker into the inner pocket of her cape. ''Don't bother to show me out,'' she said, starting from the room.

Bolting forward, Damien grabbed hold of her arm just as she was reaching for the doorknob. ''You're playing way out of your league,'' he warned, twisting her toward him.

Holding herself steady and fixing him with an unwavering gaze, she replied, ''If you're as smart as you think you are, you'll take my advice and get out of town while you have the chance. If not, I intend to unmask you for the snake that you are.'' She jerked her arm free and yanked open the door, leaving him gaping openmouthed as she strode away down the hall.

Nineteen

"HELLO? IS THIS JOSEPHINE JEFFRIES?" RACHEL SALOMON spoke into the mouthpiece of the telephone in the pantry of her Nob Hill home. "I'm sorry to bother you so early in the morning, but I'm trying to reach Aidan McAuliffe. This is his friend—"

"Rachel Salomon?" the voice on the other end asked.

"Yes," she replied. "Can you tell me if he's there?"

"I'm afraid not. I believe he stayed at the hospital last night." There was a slight pause, and then Josephine asked, "Is something wrong?"

"Not really." Rachel's tone was far from convincing. "But if he comes back, will you ask him to contact me at once?"

"Of course. If there's anything I can do . . ."

"No, thank you, Miss Jeffries."

After saying good-bye, Rachel clicked the cradle and immediately had the operator put her through to Pacific Hospital. When she asked to speak with Aidan, the woman who answered said, "I'm sorry, but Dr. McAuliffe is in the operating theater and cannot come to the phone."

"I thought he worked last night," Rachel said.

"That's right. Yesterday and last night. But a couple of our doctors have taken ill, and he was asked to cover again this morning."

"I see," Rachel replied, realizing Aidan probably had stayed at the hospital so he could catch a few hours of sleep between shifts. "Is it possible to leave a message?"

"Of course, but we cannot pass it along until he comes out of surgery."

"Just ask him to contact Rachel Salomon when he can."

"I will, Miss Salomon."

"Thank you." She said good-bye, then hung up the phone and stared at it a few moments. She had so wanted to discuss with Aidan the events of the previous night, but she supposed it could wait a few hours longer. Instead she would first resolve the other situation that was troubling her. Ringing through to the operator, she asked, "Could you connect me with Mr. Timothy Price at the James Price household?"

"Just one moment, ma'am."

Rachel listened to the clicks as the connection was made and heard the phone ringing. When it was answered, the operator said, "I have a call for Mr. Timothy Price." The man at the other end said he would summon Mr. Price, and then the operator told Rachel, "Your call has been put through, ma'am." She disconnected her headset from the line, leaving Rachel to continue the conversation.

After a minute or so, a man came on the line and said, "Hello? This is Tim Price."

"Tim, this is Rachel."

"Rachel!" he declared with enthusiasm. "I'm so glad you called. Ever since the fireworks display last Saturday, I've been wanting to call and apologize, but frankly—"

"There's nothing to apologize for."

"But it was so presumptuous of me to kiss you like that. There was really no excuse for me—"

"Tim, I need to speak with you," she interrupted. "Can we meet somewhere?"

"Now?" he asked in surprise.

"Yes, if it's not too early."

"No, not at all. Would you like me to come by? We could go for a drive."

"That would be fine."

"I'll be right over," he told her, his tone expectant, yet cautious.

"Thank you, Tim."

Hanging up the phone, Rachel went to the cloakroom for her cape. Donning it, she chose a wide-brimmed straw hat, knotted the silk-scarf ties under her chin, and walked quietly through the foyer; she had not seen her mother yet that morning and had no desire to, given their angry words the evening before. She asked Cameron to tell Aidan, if he called while she was gone, that she would contact him when she got back. Then she took a seat next to a window and waited for Tim.

Twenty minutes later he came riding up in the Panhard named Jessah. He looked dashing in a light brown suit that matched the color of his hair and mustache. After stopping the car, he hopped down from the seat and held his arm out for Rachel.

Except for a brief hello, they did not try to speak over the noise of the engine as they took their seats. Tim set the transmission lever to forward, then released the brake, automatically engaging the clutch. With a jarring clash of gears, the vehicle lurched forward, belched out a few weak backfires, then settled down and sputtered up the street, clearing a path through the carriages and buggies by alternately spooking the horses and their drivers.

"I thought we'd drive by the ocean," Tim called above the racket of the engine, and Rachel nodded.

They rode in relative silence, Tim waiting for Rachel to say what was on her mind, Rachel uncertain how to begin. It was not until they were almost at the beach, with the traffic thinning to but a few carriages heading in both directions, that she hesitantly began, "Tim, I don't want you to get the wrong idea. . . ."

"I have no idea other than being pleased that you wanted to go for a ride—and that we've met again after so long a time." He glanced over at her and smiled, then shifted the car to its fourth and fastest speed, so that they were racing out alongside Golden Gate Park at a brisk eighteen miles per hour.

"That's what I want to speak with you about," she said awkwardly. "I mean, about before, when we used to see each other. I wanted to apologize."

"There's no need. We were much younger then."

"Yes, but things happened that I didn't understand at the time."

"How do you mean?"

"I was quite hurt when you went away to college."

Tim looked over at her curiously. "But you know I had to go. It was only going to be for a few years, and we could have seen each other on holidays."

"That's not what I'm talking about. It was . . ." She fell silent as she gazed at the ocean, which had come into view over the sandy hills ahead. "Can we pull up at the beach?" she asked.

Tim shifted down through the gears, slowing the vehicle as they approached the end of D Street. He turned right onto Ocean Boulevard and drove slowly until he found a wide shoulder on the opposite side along the beach. Pulling the automobile to a halt facing the water and shutting off the engine, Tim turned to Rachel and took her hand. "You have my full attention, Miss Salomon," he declared with a beguiling smile.

"Please, let me say this without interruptions," she asked.

Tim cocked his head, as if considering whether or not to make a flippant remark. Realizing she was serious, he released her hand. "All right, Rachel. What do you want to tell me?"

She took a deep breath and plunged ahead. "I said I was really hurt when you left—not because you went away but because you promised to write and I never heard from you."

"But I—" he started to object, but she looked up at him and raised her hand.

"Please, let me finish." She paused, then went on, "When I didn't receive a letter from you, I assumed you no longer cared about me or perhaps had met someone else at Harvard. I might have written, but I didn't have your address, and as I said, I was quite crushed. Now I realize that you must have been feeling the same way. You see . . . until last night I didn't know that you actually did write to me. I never received the letters." She reached into her cape pocket and produced the letters Jacob had given her.

"But how can that be?" he asked, looking dumbfounded as he took the letters and turned them over in his hands.

"Nina," she replied flatly. "My mother intercepted your letters and kept them from me. She actually thought I'd thank her one day."

Tim shook his head ruefully. "I might've known. She made no secret of her disapproval of me." He looked up at her questioningly. "Then why has she been championing my cause these past few weeks?"

"Isn't it obvious? She's decided that you're a more appropriate match for me than Aidan McAuliffe."

Tim grinned humorlessly. "I suppose that about seals my fate."

"What do you mean?"

"What daughter would go for the man championed by her mother?"

"You're not being fair to yourself, Tim." Rachel took his hand. "Any woman would be proud to have you care about her. *I'm* proud, and I always will be."

"But not in love? . . ." It was as much a statement as a question.

Leaning toward him, Rachel lightly kissed his cheek. "I know now that our relationship didn't have to end—that it was all a misunderstanding engineered by my mother. And I know I cared deeply about you then and still do now. If things hadn't gotten so badly confused, we might be married today, and I'm sure I'd be very happy. But—''

In Rachel's eyes, Tim could read the words she was having difficulty saying. ''But fate dealt us a different hand,'' he responded for her.

''Yes. And the truth remains that I am in love with Aidan McAuliffe. I can't change my feelings, even though a part of me says I owe it to you to try.''

Tim touched his forefinger to her lips. ''You needn't say any more. It's enough to know that you still care about me . . . that you didn't reject me back then.'' He smiled faintly. ''Aidan McAuliffe is a lucky man indeed. And from what I've seen of him, he'll make you a worthy husband.'' He chuckled. ''And what better recommendation can he have than being at the bottom of your mother's list?''

Rachel laughed at his remark, and when he joined in, the humor was infectious, and several moments passed before they could contain their mirth. The laughter having served to release some of the tension, Rachel leaned back against the seat and sighed. ''Aidan and I are going to be married a week from Saturday, Tim. I'd be honored if you'd be our guest.''

Tim shook his head. ''I wish you the greatest happiness, but I think it would be better for all of us if I weren't there.''

''I'm sorry,'' she whispered.

He reached over and pressed the letters into her hand, then patted it. ''You needn't be,'' he told her, smiling warmly. ''Now, let's get going, before I get accused of shanghaiing the bride.''

Tim hopped out of the car and cranked the engine, then climbed back in and started north along Ocean Boulevard, turning right onto A Street and heading east toward the downtown area. As they made their way through the avenues, from Forty-ninth toward First, Tim suggested they turn north and drive through the Presidio on their way back to Nob Hill. As it was a lovely July day, with a cloudless sky and no sign of fog, Rachel readily agreed, so Tim turned left onto Fourteenth Street and headed toward the public square that bordered the Presidio along Lake Street.

The buggy and carriage traffic increased as they neared the square, and as they circled it, Tim had to keep the Panhard in first gear to avoid upsetting the horses. He turned the vehicle into the Presidio and started along one of the winding dirt roads that led down toward the waterfront. Working the hand and foot brake simultaneously, he expertly steered the vehicle around the sharp curves.

Rachel was enjoying the view of the hills across the Golden Gate and the touch of the slightly cool breeze against her face. Feeling exhilarated and finally at peace, she moved closer to Tim and slipped a hand around his arm, smiling at him as he worked the tiller. "I'll always care about you," she said. "I just hope you have no regrets."

"None at all," he reassured her as the motorcar veered around a curve and approached a crossroad on the right just ahead. There was a rather precipitous drop to the left, and he edged the car away from it, pulling back on the brake as the road dipped sharply.

Rachel was grabbing the rail beside her when she heard a fierce stomping and clattering and an almost unearthly shriek. Jerking her head to the right, she saw a buggy racing toward them along the crossroad, the horse almost barreling into the front of the Panhard. The animal veered wildly, just missing the car, which was forced to the left.

Rachel caught a glimpse of the driver of the buggy, and her eyes widened with horror and shock. She saw the horse rear up, its fierce neighing more like a death scream. And then she felt the front wheel of the Panhard drop over the lip of the road as the car skidded across the dirt. Tim fought the tiller, but he had lost control of the vehicle, and a second later the other front wheel went off the road and the car went bounding down the steep embankment.

Rachel tried to hang on, but she was bounced from the seat. She heard a horrifying crash as the car struck a tree, and then she felt herself being propelled through the air. After that, everything abruptly went black.

"Whoa, there!" the driver of the buggy shouted as he struggled with the reins and fought to calm the horse. When at last it settled down, he set the brake and leaped from the buggy. Pausing only briefly to pat the horse, he dashed to the side of the road and stared down at the crushed remains of the automobile, which had careened through the underbrush and smashed into a tall eucalyptus tree.

Damien Picard could hardly contain his gleeful excitement. "Yes!" he hissed as he started scrambling down the embankment toward the vehicle below. It was a prize well earned, he told himself as he thought of how difficult it had been to follow the motorcar all the way from the Salomon mansion, where he had been waiting for Rachel to emerge.

The car had left him far behind on its way out along Golden Gate Park, but he had caught up with it at the beach and again later at the public square beside the Presidio. When he realized the driver would be heading onto the winding Presidio roads, he had whipped his horse to a gallop, taking a side road that met the main one at this intersection. He had waited until he saw the car approaching, then had driven the buggy in front of it, forcing the automobile from the road.

Damien saw Rachel lying on her back without movement amid the underbrush some twenty feet farther down the embankment from the car. The driver—the one Damien's half-sister had described as Timothy Price—had not been ejected from the car but was sprawled facedown over the engine box, either unconscious or dead.

Stumbling the last of the way through the underbrush, Damien grabbed hold of the seat back to steady himself as he caught his breath. He was just starting around the vehicle, heading toward Rachel, when the driver began to moan.

Quickly Damien worked his way forward around the shattered rear wheel and pulled himself up onto the seat, bracing his feet against the front wall so he would not fall forward in the steeply angled car. Tim Price was stirring now, his head moving from side to side. Grasping Tim's suit jacket at the shoulders, Damien pulled him away from the engine box and back into the seat. Holding him in place with one hand, he grabbed hold of his hair and pulled his head back. Tim's nose looked broken, and his face was covered with blood. His eyes were still closed, but he began to moan louder as he slowly regained consciousness.

Cursing under his breath, Damien eased his grip on the jacket, allowing Tim to slide forward as he grabbed hold of his hair with both hands. Standing up, he eased Tim back over the smashed engine box, returning him to the position in which he had found him. Damien cursed again, then yanked Tim's head back and rammed it forward against the twisted metal. Closing his own eyes in distaste, he smashed Tim's face again and again into the metal, until the moaning was replaced by the sickly crunch of bone breaking.

When Damien was certain that the man was dead, he let go of the hair, and the head lolled lifelessly to one side. Glancing only briefly at what remained of the face, Damien turned away in disgust and climbed from the compartment.

Drawing in a deep, steadying breath, he turned to where Rachel was lying in the brush. As he started toward her, he slipped and went sliding down the embankment on his rear, stopping himself just as he came alongside of her. Pulling himself to his hands and knees, he brushed himself off. He could see that she was breathing, her chest rising and falling shallowly, and he looked around for a suitable object with which to finish the job. Nearby was a good-sized rock that had been dislodged by the accident and had come rolling down the embankment. Crawling over to it, he hefted it in his hands and nodded.

He moved back beside Rachel. Holding the rock in front of him on the ground, he whispered, "I warned you that you were out of your league."

He was just lifting the rock in both hands when a loud voice shouted, "You all right?"

Lowering the rock, Damien spun around and looked up the embankment to see a pair of men standing at the edge of the road. Behind them was the cabriolet in which they had been riding when they came upon the scene of the accident.

Damien cursed as the two men began sliding down the slope toward him.

"What happened?" the bigger of the men asked as he reached what remained of the car.

"They must've run off the road," Damien called back, standing beside Rachel. "That one's dead," he added, waving a hand toward the body sprawled across the front of the car.

The two men glanced at Tim Price and turned away in horror at the sight of his smashed face. While the smaller man remained at the side of the car, steadying himself, his partner continued down to where Damien was standing. "She alive?" he asked, nodding at the woman.

"I was just checking," Damien replied, stepping aside so the man could examine the body.

"Yep," the fellow declared, kneeling beside Rachel and placing his cheek close to her mouth. "She's breathin', but maybe not for long."

Just then Rachel let out a dreadful moan and started to lift herself upright.

"Easy, there," the man said, pushing down on her shoulders. "You're hurt bad."

Rachel's eyes opened, and she looked directly at Damien, who stood nervously a few feet away. "D-D-Damien," she stammered, her eyes widening as she stared up at him. Her eyelids slowly lowered, but she forced them open and repeated the name.

"It's all right," the big man told her. "You're gonna be all right."

It was apparent that Rachel was struggling to remain conscious, but slowly she lost the battle, and her eyes fluttered closed.

"We better get her out of here," the big man declared, standing and looking at the other two.

"What about him?" his partner said, jerking a thumb behind him toward Tim Price's body.

"He must be that Damien fellow," the man replied. With a shrug, he added, "Forget him. They can pull him out later."

"We'd better not move her," Damien advised. "Why don't you two go summon an ambulance while I stay here with her?"

"Smitty can go," the big man said, indicating his partner. "I'll wait here with you."

Realizing they were not going to leave him alone and give him the chance to end Rachel's life, Damien quickly waved at Smitty and said, "I'd better go. My buggy is a lot faster than that big cabriolet."

Smitty shrugged, but he and his friend made no objection as Damien started up the embankment.

Climbing onto the roadway, Damien looked down at the men and shouted, "I'll be back with an ambulance!" Then he turned and raced over to his buggy.

Hopping aboard, Damien took up the reins and released the brake. "Sure I'll be back," he muttered with a sneer as he slapped the reins against the horse's back and took off at a gallop down the winding dirt road.

Twenty

MAURICE SALOMON BURST THROUGH THE FRONT DOOR OF Pacific Hospital and hurried over to the nurse's station. "Is Dr. McAuliffe here?" he asked, glancing agitatedly down the hall.

"Mr. Salomon?" she inquired, and he nodded. "Dr. McAuliffe is expecting you. Just go down the corridor and turn right; the nurse there will show you to his office."

Crushing the fedora in his hand, Maurice strode down the hall and turned right, practically barreling into Aidan.

"How is she?" he blurted, looking beyond him toward the rooms that lined the halls.

"Relax, Maurice," Aidan urged, clapping him on the shoulders. "Everything's going to be all right."

"Then she's alive?"

"Yes."

"Thank God!" His body sagged, as if drained with relief. "How is she?"

"Come over here," Aidan replied, leading Maurice by the arm to a bench along the wall. As they sat down, Aidan faced

Maurice and said, "Rachel sustained quite a blow to the head. I'm afraid she's still unconscious."

"You mean she might not . . . ?" His voice trailed off with fear.

"In these situations, there's no way of knowing. But her vital signs are strong, and we've every reason to believe she'll come out of it all right."

"What about . . . her friend?" He stumbled over the word.

Aidan shook his head. "Tim Price died on impact."

Maurice groaned and looked down. "How did it happen?" he mumbled, shaking his head.

"They went off the road and struck a tree not far from here in the Presidio. A couple of men found them and brought her in." He sighed. "It's too bad they didn't get her here sooner. Apparently she was conscious for a time—which is a good sign," he quickly added. "But someone else was at the scene first and went to summon an ambulance. When he hadn't returned a half hour later, the two men gave up waiting and brought her here themselves."

"Can I see her?"

Aidan stared at the floor for a moment, then said, "Let's wait for Jacob to arrive."

"You've sent for him?"

"Yes. He should be here soon."

"What about Nina?"

Aidan shook his head. "She doesn't know yet. I thought it best to let Jacob call her after he gets here." He paused, then asked, "Tell me, Maurice, what do you know about a fellow named Damien Picard?"

Maurice's face blanched. "Damien? Why?"

Aidan reached into his coat pocket and held out an envelope, which Maurice instantly recognized as containing the incriminating letter from Agnes Banker.

"H-how did you get this?" Maurice stammered, taking the letter.

"I found it in Rachel's cape."

"Rachel?" he said incredulously. "How could she have gotten it?"

"There's more," Aidan went on, his tone growing even more serious. "Apparently Rachel said the name Damien a few times when she briefly regained consciousness. She was looking up at the fellow who was first on the scene, but the other two men assumed she was referring to the driver, who of course turned out to be Tim Price."

"Damien? Are you sure?"

"Yes. Do you think he could have been the man who left the scene?"

"It couldn't be." Maurice shook his head in disbelief. "She must have gotten this letter from him somehow and in her daze was thinking about it."

"They said the fellow at the scene acted strangely, and one of them noticed blood on his jacket, though it could have been Tim Price's."

"Did they say anything else about him?" Maurice asked.

"Just that he was tall and slender and had blond hair."

"Damien . . ." Maurice muttered, lowering his head into his hands.

Aidan gripped the younger man's forearm. "I want you to tell me who this Damien is and what he has to do with Rachel."

Maurice started to nod but did not look up at Aidan as he said, "Damien Picard. I befriended him in New York this last trip. He and I . . . well, we shared some wild times."

"Involving this woman and her friend?" Aidan pressed, pointing at the letter in Maurice's hand.

"Yes. And one night, shortly after Rachel arrived, Damien . . ." He shook his head, clutching the letter in his fists.

"Tell me, Maurice."

Looking up at Aidan, his eyes beseeching forgiveness, Maurice said, "Damien and I were drinking—and smoking opium. I . . . I passed out. And when I came to, he had just finished attacking Rachel."

"He what?" Aidan gasped.

"He . . . he raped her, Aidan." Maurice began to sob. "I'm s-sorry," he choked, wiping away tears. Steadying his voice, he continued, "Rachel decided against having him arrested—I think for my sake. Shortly after that I met Merribelle, and Rachel and I agreed we'd never tell anyone what happened."

"So what is he doing in San Francisco?"

"You read the letter. I got that woman pregnant, and Damien arranged for me to pay her off. I tried to get him to leave town, but he threatened to expose what I'd done."

Aidan looked at Maurice as if seeing him for the first time. "Listen, Maurice, I don't particularly care about the things you've done in the past. But didn't you consider that he might try to do something to Rachel again?"

"He promised to keep away from her, and she didn't know he was in town." Maurice hesitated, narrowing his eyes in thought. "Unless she found out from Nina."

"Nina? What does she have to do with it?"

Maurice's shoulders sagged. "She met Damien the night of my wedding—when he arrived in town and went to the house looking for me. I'm afraid they've become lovers."

Aidan shook his head in utter disbelief. Rachel's family was so riddled with deceitfulness and uncontrolled appetites that he marveled at her forthright, honest nature. Standing, he paced down the hall, then turned and came back. "Maurice," he said, stopping in front of him. "I don't like any of this. Rachel had this letter—and you say she had to have gotten it from Damien. Perhaps she found out he was in town and confronted him. If he knew she had the letter, or if she threatened to expose him—for this or the rape or maybe even his affair with Nina—he just might have been desperate enough to come after her."

"What do you mean?" Maurice asked cautiously.

"Rachel called here this morning and left a message for me to contact her. By the time I did, she already had left with Tim Price. Maybe she wanted to tell me something about

Damien or this letter. I don't know. I just have the feeling that the man at the scene of the accident was Damien Picard.''

''And that he engineered it?'' Maurice asked. When Aidan nodded, Maurice lowered his head in shame.

''Do you know where he might be?'' Aidan sat back down beside Maurice. ''For God's sake, if you know, tell me.''

Maurice seemed to steel himself. He looked up at Aidan with new determination in his eyes and said, ''He's staying at the Baldwin Hotel—room two forty-two.''

''Thanks,'' Aidan told him, rising as if to leave.

''Where are you going?''

''After him, of course. If he knows Rachel recognized him, he may try to leave town.''

''I'm going with you,'' Maurice declared, also standing.

''You should be here in case Rachel awakens.''

''I'm going, Aidan.'' He grasped Aidan's arm and started down the hall. ''Come on—we're losing time.''

Hurrying outside, Aidan convinced one of the ambulance drivers to take them at full speed to the Baldwin Hotel. As they rode, Maurice told Aidan about discovering Nina in Damien's room and of his suspicions about Damien's motives. Aidan did not find it too difficult to imagine that a woman as vain as Nina could be taken in by a younger man, especially one as smooth and attractive as Damien Picard seemed to be.

Less than fifteen minutes later they were running into the hotel lobby, with Maurice rushing directly to the room while Aidan questioned the desk clerk. By the time Maurice returned to report that the room was unlocked and empty, Aidan had already learned that Damien had paid his bill and left less than half an hour before.

Heading back outside, the two men considered their options. ''The Ferry Building!'' Maurice exclaimed, snapping his fingers. ''If he's leaving town, he's got to go either to the Ferry Building to catch the eastbound trains in Oakland or to the Southern Pacific depot at Townsend and Fourth streets for a train to the south.''

"You take the ambulance to the Ferry Building," Aidan told him. "I'll take a cab to the depot."

"Fine," Maurice replied, hurrying over to the ambulance and climbing into the front seat.

Aidan followed him, adding, "Whatever you do, Maurice, don't let him leave town—even if you have to restrain him by force."

"If he's there, I'll get him," Maurice assured him.

"Good. And if I don't find him at the depot, I'll go to the main police station and make a report. Perhaps they can drag him in and hold him until Rachel recovers enough to tell us what happened."

Shaking Maurice's hand, Aidan told the driver to drop Maurice off at the Ferry Building and then return to the hospital. A moment later the wagon was bounding off down Market Street.

Running over to one of the hansom cabs parked alongside the hotel, Aidan asked the driver to take him to the Southern Pacific depot, then climbed inside and pulled the door shut. As the cab started from the curb, Aidan recalled what Maurice had told him about Damien's affair with Nina. If Damien *had* seduced Nina to bilk her out of money, he just might chance going there to get some traveling funds. After all, he had no reason to suspect that anyone would be onto him so quickly, and he might risk the visit if it would provide him with additional cash.

The cab had made a wide U-turn around Market Street and was just about to turn right onto Fourth Street when Aidan opened the door and leaned out. "Forget the depot!" he called up to the driver in the raised perch at the rear. "Do you know the Salomon house on Nob Hill?"

"Sure thing," the cabbie called down to him, reining the horse to a halt.

"Take me there—and make it as quick as you can!"

The driver bobbed his hat and snatched up the whip. As

Aidan slammed the door shut, the man popped the whip over the horse's head and tugged at the reins, expertly turning the hansom cab left onto Stockton Street and heading at a trot toward Nob Hill.

Damien Picard stepped out of the hackney cab a block from the Salomon mansion. Paying the driver double the fare, he said, "Wait here. I'll be back shortly, and then I want you to drive me to the Southern Pacific depot."

Leaving his bags in the cab, Damien turned and ran up the street toward the rear of the mansion. Slipping through the rear gate, he stealthily crossed the grounds and circled the stable to the outer staircase, which led up to Nina's second-floor balcony.

Racing upstairs, he tested the balcony doors and was pleased to find them unlocked—and even more delighted that the room was empty. Contrary to Aidan's theory, Damien had no intention of confronting Nina about money or anything else, for that matter. He had an entirely different purpose in risking a visit, and he set about it at once.

Closing the glass doors, Damien hurried across the room and opened the door a crack, checking to make sure no one was outside. Slipping into the hall, he made his way to the stairway that led up to the third floor. It was still fairly early, and he prayed that Allison would be in Phoebe's room as he headed down the hall and knocked lightly on the door she had described to him.

"Who is it?" his sister asked, and with a sigh of relief, Damien turned the knob and stepped inside. "What are you doing here?" she blurted, rising from the dressing table, where she had been doing her hair.

"Shhh!" Damien whispered as he shut the door and approached. "Where's Nina?"

"Downstairs, I guess. Why?"

"Have you heard anything?" he asked. Seeing her confusion, he added, "About Rachel."

"Nothing. What is it? What's going on?"

"Somehow Rachel found out I was at the Baldwin, and she came there last night and threatened to have me arrested if I didn't leave town."

"Did you believe her?"

"Yes," he said flatly. "And trust me, she could've made things difficult for us."

"Could have?" Allison said suspiciously. "What have you done?"

Damien allowed himself a slight grin. "I followed her and that Timothy Price fellow on their morning drive. In the Presidio, I ran them off the road."

Allison just gaped at him in amazement.

"Price is dead. I tried to finish off Rachel, but some bastards came on the scene before I had a chance." He shrugged. "I'm afraid she saw me."

"She knows it was you?"

He nodded. "That's why I came here. It's murder now; we've got to get away before she tells what happened."

"This is ridiculous, Damien," she told him, shaking her head. "What in God's name were you thinking of when—?"

"Look, there's no time for debate. There's a cab down the street waiting to take us to the train station."

"You can go if you want to," Allison declared. "I'm staying here."

"Don't be crazy. We've got to hurry and—"

"I've worked damn hard to earn Nina's trust—and Jacob's affections," she cut him off. "And it's been working better than we expected. In fact, you may have been off the mark when you decided to get Jacob to leave the business; he's far easier to control than Maurice or Nina will ever be. Why, I bet one day he'll be richer than both of them combined."

"That's all well and good. But we won't be able to spend his money behind bars."

"I had nothing to do with what happened to Rachel," Allison pointed out, walking away from the dressing table. "I'll be damned if I give up everything I've been working for because of your stupidity."

"Listen, *little sister,* I was the one who planned this whole thing, and I'll be the one who decides when it's going to end. Now, they're onto me, and it won't take long for them to connect the two of us. Then where will you be?"

"I can take care of myself."

"You're being ridiculous," he bellowed, losing his temper. "We're getting out of here now—while we have the chance." He grabbed hold of her arm and pulled her toward the door.

For a moment Allison held back, staring into his cold blue eyes. Finally she shrugged and muttered, "Let me at least get my things."

"Be quick about it," he replied, releasing her arm.

As she reluctantly began gathering a few of the possessions she had accumulated during her stay at the Salomon home, she was interrupted by the sound of hooves clattering outside on the drive.

"What's that?" Damien snapped, rushing to the window and looking out. "Someone just pulled up in a cab."

Coming up beside him, Allison peered down at the hansom cab and saw a man climb out and run toward the front door. "That's Rachel's fiancé—Aidan McAuliffe," she said as the front doorbell rang.

"Damn it!" Damien raged, striking his fist against the sill. "They must know!" He turned to Allison. "Forget your things—we're getting out of here!"

Not awaiting a reply, he grabbed his sister's arm and pulled her toward the door. Opening it and glancing up and down the hall, he led her to the staircase and down to the second floor. As they headed to Nina's room, they could hear the downstairs front door open and the butler greet Aidan McAuliffe. They quickly slipped into Nina's room and shut the door.

Letting go of Allison's arm, Damien dashed over to the glass doors and opened them. "Come on!" he whispered, turning and waving her toward the balcony.

"I'm not coming," Allison declared as she stood with her back against the writing desk beside Nina's bed.

"Damn it, Allison, there's no time for this. They're going to find out about us and then you'll—"

"Not if you don't tell them," she replied, her voice steady and calm.

"You're not being reasonable," he said, forcing a smile as he started toward her. But he pulled up short, and his smile vanished as he stared at the sharp, long-bladed letter opener she had snatched from the desk and now held pointed ominously at his midsection.

"This is insane," he said, stepping closer and reaching for the letter opener.

"I'm sorry," was all Allison said as her hand darted forward and plunged the blade deep into his belly. Jerking the blade free, she stabbed him a second time, then a final time to the chest.

Damien stared wide-eyed at the blood spurting from around the letter opener that was sticking out of his chest. His mouth opened, and he reached his bloody hand toward Allison as he sagged to his knees. With a gurgling moan, he fell backward onto the floor and lay there gasping, his eyes slowly closing, his body jerking spasmodically several times and then relaxing into death.

Staring down at the body of her dead half-brother, Allison tightened her jaw and felt her facial muscles twitch. She glanced down at her bloody hands, then at the letter opener, engraved with Nina's initials, still protruding from Damien's chest.

Dropping to her knees, she drew in a deep breath, closed her eyes, and began to scream.

Downstairs, Aidan was just asking Cameron if anyone matching Damien Picard's description had come to the house, when suddenly he was cut off by a wailing scream from above. Running toward the stairs, he took them two at a time, the butler close on his heels.

When he reached Nina's door, he yanked it open and dashed inside, halting abruptly upon seeing Allison Grant kneeling beside the body of a blond-haired man who could only be Damien Picard.

Allison was crying hysterically, and Aidan hurried to her and pulled her away from the bloody body. Helping her to her feet, he took her in his arms and urged her to be quiet, but she stammered, "I was p-passing the room and . . . and heard n-noises. I came in and—and I found this man breaking in from the balcony. He . . . he grabbed hold of me and said he wanted to see Nina. I lied. I said she was gone. He . . . he started to hit me. Somehow I grabbed that—" She waved a hand behind her toward the letter opener in Damien's chest. "I must've stabbed him." Her sobbing grew louder.

"It's all right," Aidan soothed. "He was a murderer; he would've killed you rather than be captured."

As Aidan held her close against him, he heard footsteps and turned to see Nina Salomon come striding in, drawn from downstairs by the screaming. She pulled up short and stared at the body on the floor. It took a moment for her to realize what she was seeing, and then she gasped and let out a piercing shriek that sent a cold chill down Aidan's back.

"Damien!" she sobbed, staggering toward the lifeless body on her bedroom floor.

Cameron rushed over to her and tried to pull her back, but Nina pushed him away roughly and dropped beside Damien, calling his name over and over as she wrapped her arms around his neck and laid her head on his shoulder.

Aidan, still holding Allison, shook his head sadly as Nina's face and hair turned red with her lover's blood.

Twenty-one

IT WAS JUST AFTER DAWN ON FRIDAY, JULY 10, WHEN RA-
chel Salomon regained consciousness, nearly twenty-four
hours after the accident in the Presidio. Aidan McAuliffe was
alone in the room with her, the rest of the family having gone
home late the night before. Roused from sleep by the faint
sound of moaning, he bolted upright in the chair he had
placed beside the bed and took her hand.

"Rest easy, Rachel," he told her as he caressed her cheek.

"Wh-what . . . ?" she stammered, her eyes opening partway and trying to focus on him.

"You've been in an accident. You were quite bruised and
suffered a concussion, but there were no broken bones. You
should be up and around in a few days."

Rachel seemed to remember what had happened, for her
eyes opened wide with fear, and she gasped, "Damien!" She
tried to say more, but Aidan pressed a finger to her lips.

"Please lie still, Rachel," he urged. "We know all about
Damien Picard."

"But he—"

"Damien is dead," Aidan said flatly, and all the breath went out of her in surprise. "After the accident, you spoke of him, and Maurice helped us find him," Aidan explained. "But when he tried to escape, he was killed."

"Were you the one . . . who killed—?"

"No, Rachel. He went to your house—to get money, we think. Allison found him, and when he attacked her, she managed to stab him. She was very lucky."

Rachel sighed with relief. Then suddenly the fear returned to her eyes, and she said, "Tim? What about Tim?"

"I'm afraid he wasn't so lucky. He died in the accident." Aidan did not add that an autopsy had shown that he had been killed by Damien after the car struck the tree.

As Rachel's eyes filled with tears, Aidan leaned over her and took her in his arms.

"I'm so sorry," she whimpered. "I've made such a mess of things."

"You did nothing of the kind," he whispered.

"Nothing would have happened to him if I hadn't—"

"Damien was responsible for what happened, not you."

Looking up at him in anguish, Rachel asked, "How will you ever forgive me? I said I wouldn't see Tim again, and then I went and—"

"Rachel, I know about the letters from Tim," Aidan told her. "A few were in your pocket, and Jacob told me how your mother hid them from you. I understand that you had to see him. I can also understand if you've discovered that it really wasn't me you were in love with but—"

"Not in love with you?" Rachel declared, her voice more forceful. "You foolish man—of course I love you."

"But Tim . . ."

"I went for that drive to apologize for what happened and to tell him I'm in love with you."

"You did?"

"Yes. And he understood and wished us happiness."

"Oh, Rachel, I *do* love you," Aidan exclaimed, kissing her delicately on the lips.

THE DECEIT

They sat in silence, with Aidan holding Rachel's hand as she continued to regain her strength. After a few minutes, she looked up at him somewhat anxiously and asked, "Do you still want to marry me?"

"Our wedding is set for next week—provided you feel strong enough to walk down the aisle."

"I don't need to walk, Aidan. I'll be floating." She pulled him closer and kissed him again.

Aidan sat back in the chair, still gripping her hand, as he said, "One thing about the wedding, though. Would you mind if we changed our plans and didn't marry in a church? After all, you're family is actually Jewish, and—"

"Nina would be mortified if we married in a synagogue. She's been trying to cover up our heritage for years."

"I wasn't talking about a synagogue."

"What, then? City Hall?"

"I'd rather leave it a surprise, if you don't mind."

"Whatever you want is all right with me," she assured him. With a mischievous grin, she added, "Especially if it means upsetting Nina's wedding plans."

Aidan smiled and nodded. "She has taken to her room; I doubt she'll come out in time for the wedding."

"Good."

"Just leave everything to me—and Merribelle and your brothers. They're helping with the arrangements." Aidan glanced over and saw a nurse standing in the doorway. "Yes?" he asked her.

"Someone is waiting in your office for you—a family friend, I believe."

"I'll be right there," he told her, and the nurse departed. Turning back to Rachel, he said, "You rest now; I'll be right back." He kissed her forehead and stood, then paused and added, "There's one other thing you should know."

Rachel looked up at him questioningly.

"Among your things we found the letter about Maurice and that woman in New York."

"I want to tell you about that . . . about everything."

"Not now. There'll be plenty of time to talk about it when you're feeling better."

"But you should know what happened to me—"

"I know what Damien did to you in New York. It doesn't change the way I feel about you." He squeezed her hand lovingly. "But you ought to know about what he tried to do to Maurice."

"Tried to do?"

"That letter from New York was phony. Maurice and I tracked down that woman named Agnes Banker by telegraph yesterday and found her at a different address than the one on the envelope. The woman knew nothing about the letter and insists that Lorraine isn't pregnant. Apparently the letter was a forgery Damien sent to himself so he could bilk Maurice out of some money."

"What a relief," Rachel breathed. "Does Belle know?"

"That's up to Maurice, though I think he intends to tell her everything and make a fresh start of things."

"I'm glad," she said with a smile.

Aidan gently kissed her lips, then left the room. As he walked along the hall toward his office, a swell of emotion rose up within him. So much had happened in the past day, and now he was flooded with relief that Rachel was alive, with anger that Damien Picard had harmed her, and with astonishment at the actions of Nina and Maurice. But mostly he felt grateful that the woman he loved was well and indeed loved him in return.

When he reached his small office, he opened the door and was surprised to see the blond-haired woman named Fiona, whose Chinese friend he had helped to rescue the night before last.

"Dr. Aidan McAuliffe," she said, rising from the seat and holding out her hand. "It's so good to see you again."

"How is your friend Kuei Mei?" he asked, shaking her hand politely.

"Wonderful. For the time being she has moved into the

apartment with Hsiao Ch'u. They'll have a lot more room now that I'm moving out."

"Oh? Where are you going?"

"I've decided it's time to go home. That's what I wanted to speak with you about."

"Me?" Aidan asked curiously.

"Yes. You see, my name isn't Fiona." She drew in a deep breath. "It's Phoebe . . . Phoebe Salomon."

A week later, Rachel Salomon stood in the parlor of her Nob Hill home, being assisted by Allison Grant in making final adjustments to her wedding gown. It was Saturday morning, July 18, 1896—her wedding day—and she still had no idea what the arrangements were for the ceremony and reception. Though she had been home from the hospital for two days and had pleaded with and cajoled her family, everyone had conspired to keep her unaware of the plans, saying only that the day was to be a surprise.

At noon, Rachel was ready, her copper hair pulled into a sweep, her emerald eyes highlighted with a hint of mascara, which had only recently come into fashion and was still considered a touch risqué by the self-appointed arbiters of social morality. She was dressed in an ivory, embroidered-silk gown with ruffled white lace at the throat and cuffs and a train that trailed several feet behind her. The sleeves were puffed slightly at the shoulders, and the flared bodice highlighted her sleek, curvaceous figure.

As Rachel headed into the living room and turned in place in front of one of the huge mirrors that lined one wall, the doorbell rang, and the butler admitted Jacob, dressed to the hilt in a formal black suit with tails. Handing Cameron his top hat, Jacob made his way through the parlor and approached the two women in the living room.

"You look magnificent!" he exclaimed. "You do, too, Rachel," he playfully jested, coming over to his sister and kissing her cheek.

"You'll muss her rouge," Allison cautioned.

"Why, my little sister will be blushing so hard that the rouge will pale by comparison." He turned to Allison and tenderly kissed her hand. "You do look wonderful," he told her, gazing down at her stunning silver gown. "You'll be the belle of the ball—next to the bride, of course."

As Allison smiled with pleasure, Rachel came up beside her brother and took his arm. "And you'll catch the eye of every woman there when you walk me down the aisle," she declared. "I'll be so proud to have you give me away. I only wish Father . . ."

"I know." Jacob raised her hand and kissed it, as well.

"Jacob," she said softly, turning his face toward her. "Is there any chance you'll reconsider your decision to leave Salomon's? After all that's happened, I hoped—"

"I'm sorry, Rachel, but I'm firm in my decision."

"But you've always known what Nina's like. Perhaps you two could discuss things and resolve your differences."

"I'm not really angry at her anymore. But I've considered the situation carefully, and I think my decision is the best— for everyone. I want this chance to strike out on my own. And I also believe that Maurice, as Charles's only natural son, deserves to see what he can make of himself and his father's business."

"There's no convincing you otherwise?" she asked, and he shook his head. "Then I wish you the best of luck." She leaned up and kissed his cheek. "I'm certain San Francisco is big enough for two Salomon enterprises."

"Thank you, Rachel." Offering his arms to the two women, he said, "Shall we go? The coach is waiting outside." As they took his arms, he hesitated and asked, "Is it just the three of us?" He nodded upward, indicating Nina, who had barely left her room during the past week.

"I'm afraid so," Rachel told him. "I know she and I had some harsh words, but I was hoping we could put the past— both Tim and Damien—behind us and try to be a family again. But she insists she's too ill to attend. I suppose she's too embarrassed by her relationship with Damien. And I'm sure she'd find it a bitter pill to attend a wedding she so strenuously opposed.''

"It's more than that," Jacob told her as he led them through the parlor to the foyer, where Cameron was waiting with Jacob's top hat in hand. "We didn't want to tell you until you had recovered from the accident—and then we agreed it might be best to wait until today."

"What do you mean?" Rachel asked as Cameron gave Jacob his hat and opened the door. In the driveway beyond was an ornate gilded coach with a team of four matching grays. A narrow red carpet had been laid between the door and the coach to protect the train of Rachel's gown.

Clapping his hat on his head, Jacob replied, "This week it came to light that Nina treated Phoebe far more shamefully than we ever imagined, which is why she's afraid to show her face in public. Come—I'll show you."

Again offering the women his arms, he escorted them down the stairs. As they approached the waiting coach, the door opened, and a woman emerged from inside, dressed in a lovely blue gown that matched her eyes and complemented her lustrous blond hair.

"Phoebe?" Rachel mumbled, shaking her head in disbelief. "My God, it's Phoebe!" she exclaimed, rushing forward into her sister's waiting arms.

As the two women embraced and cried, Jacob explained how Nina had committed Phoebe to the Presidio Asylum for Incurables and how Allison actually met her there, not at the boarding school. Phoebe could not recall their meeting, however, probably because of the state she was in when she was admitted.

"There'll be plenty of time to discuss all this later," Jacob concluded, ushering the women over to the coach. "If we keep the groom waiting any longer, he might leave."

As Rachel climbed inside, she saw that Belle was seated with little Charlie on her lap. Suddenly she realized that Phoebe's return could be a devastating blow to Belle and Maurice, who had grown so attached to Phoebe's baby.

As if reading her thoughts, Phoebe sat down beside Belle and stroked the baby's cheek. "Isn't my little nephew beautiful?" she said with a warm smile, turning to Rachel, who sat across the aisle beside Allison and Jacob. "I'm so grateful to Belle and Maurice for providing such a good home for Charlie. I know he'll be happy—and in more suitable circumstances—living with them."

Phoebe's smile had a bittersweet edge, and Rachel knew she must have gone through a tremendous struggle after learning her baby had survived the abortion and been adopted by Maurice. Rachel gave her younger sister a great deal of credit for apparently deciding that Charlie would be better off in a stable household, with a mother and father and without the stigma of being considered illegitimate.

Looking around, Rachel realized that her other brother was not on hand. "Where's Maurice?" she asked.

"He's still at Salomon's Emporium," Belle explained. "It's Saturday—the store's open—and he had some work to take care of before joining us."

"We'll pick him up on the way," Jacob put in, reaching through the window and knocking on the side of the coach. At his signal, the coachman took up the reins and started the horse down the drive.

High above the front yard, standing unseen in a shaded third-floor window, Nina Salomon looked down at the departing coach, tears streaming down her cheeks. The hint of a smile played across her features as she reached toward her children. Her hand began to shake ever so slightly, and the smile faded as her lips silently fashioned the words she had never been able to say: *I'm sorry.*

Her hand dropped limply at her side. Choking back her tears, she turned from the window and walked away.

As the coach headed toward Salomon's Emporium, Rachel touched up her makeup, which had been streaked by her tearful reunion with Phoebe. Jacob, meanwhile, opened a picnic basket on the floor and took out a bottle of champagne, wrapped in a white cloth. Leaning through the open window, he popped the cork and waited as the foam overflowed into the street. Next he produced five glasses from the basket, filled each one, and served them to the women, keeping the last for himself.

Raising his glass, he declared, "I'd like to offer a prewedding toast." He smiled at each of them. "Today is a day of renewal and love. It is a day in which we will be welcoming a new person into our family as well as celebrating the return of a loved one we thought had been lost." He tipped his glass toward Phoebe. "Let us drink to renewal and love!" Jacob thundered.

After everyone had taken a sip, Jacob raised his glass again. "I have a second toast to make—this one to another person I hope has come into our lives to stay." Turning to Allison, he proclaimed, "I offer a toast to the woman who has made me the happiest man in the world by agreeing this very morning to become my wife—Miss Allison Grant!"

Allison beamed as the surprised women congratulated her and raised their glasses.

A few minutes later they arrived at the front entrance of Salomon's Emporium on Union Square. Jacob hopped out of the coach and consulted with the liveried doorman, an elderly black man named Powell who had been with Salomon's for the past twenty years and had become a fixture on the streets of the city. Stepping back to the coach, Jacob leaned in and said, "Maurice hasn't come down yet. Why don't we wait for him inside?"

"Inside?" Rachel said incredulously. "I can't go in there like this." She stared down at her wedding gown.

Jacob cleared his throat. "I shouldn't tell you this, but it seems the workers on the floor have planned a little ceremony to wish you well. They're all lining up just inside even as we speak." He motioned out the window, and Rachel noticed that a gold carpet had been rolled out onto the sidewalk for her entrance.

"Come on," Belle declared. "It will be fun." Cradling little Charlie in her arms, she moved to the door and with Jacob's assistance stepped down to the street.

"Well, I suppose so," Rachel said uncertainly as the other women climbed out.

Rachel was the last to emerge. She stood for a moment as Allison adjusted the train of the wedding gown, and then she took Jacob's arm and approached the front door, following behind the other three women.

"Good day, Powell," she said with a smile as she entered the store.

"And a good day to you, Miss Rachel," Powell called after her as she disappeared inside.

Rachel looked disoriented as she walked out onto the main floor. Salomon's Emporium had undergone a transformation. The counters and display cases had been removed from the main aisle, which led from the front door to the central pavilion, and had been replaced with two sections of seats, filled with people dressed in formal attire. The aisle between the seats had been polished a brilliant gold, and the pavilion at the end of it was bedecked with orchids and roses. The entire store looked like the setting for a lavish ball, complete with a small orchestra seated on the pavilion.

Rachel looked beyond the pavilion and saw that another aisle had been cleared on the opposite side of the floor and that linen-covered tables had been set out, laden with platters of food and chafing dishes filled with every imaginable delicacy.

"Aidan suggested we change the theme of the summer fashion extravaganza from motorcars to weddings," Jacob whispered to Rachel with a smile. "And your wedding and reception shall inaugurate the event. Shall we?" He held out his hand and nodded down the aisle.

Just then the orchestra began the wedding processional from Wagner's *Lohengrin*. Her eyes filling with tears, Rachel saw Aidan McAuliffe walk in front of the pavilion, where an altar of sorts had been created. Behind it, ready to perform the ceremony, was the mayor of San Francisco, Adolph Sutro, looking resplendent behind his enormous white sideburns, which came so close to connecting at his chin that they could rightly be considered a beard.

Rachel floated down the aisle, only vaguely aware of the beaming faces all around. Her attention was fixed completely on the most handsome man she had ever seen. Her heart raced, and she felt as if her knees would give way as Aidan took her hands and smiled with pride and delight at his bride-to-be.

Rachel heard little of the brief ceremony and later would barely be able to recall having said the words *I do*. But say them she did—and with enthusiasm. And as Aidan swept her into his arms and they shared a tender, lingering kiss, the orchestra began to play a sprightly air, and the audience burst into applause.

Rachel gazed up into Aidan's piercing blue eyes, and he pulled her close and whispered, "I love you, Rachel Salomon McAuliffe." She replied with a kiss filled with passion and the promise of more.

ABOUT THE AUTHOR

After growing up in Glen Cove, New York, Paul Block pursued a degree in creative writing at the State University of New York, first in Binghamton and then at Empire State College, during which he spent a year writing poetry in Great Britain and motorcycling through Spain. In 1973, he journeyed to San Francisco, where he created several unsold teleplays and novels, a collection of poetry, and two children. Following a series of odd jobs and several years in the newspaper business, first in Los Angeles and then in Albany, New York, he became an editor for Book Creations, Inc., which has produced such bestselling series as WAGONS WEST, THE AUSTRALIANS, and THE KENT FAMILY CHRONICLES.

Though Paul has written five westerns published under various pseudonyms, the SAN FRANCISCO novels are the first to appear under his own name. He currently serves as Creative Director of Book Creations, Inc., and lives with his family in Delmar, New York.

*Watch for the next book in
the* SAN FRANCISCO *series
coming to you soon from Lynx Books!*